Under the Chinese Dragon
A Tale of Mongolia

by

F. S. Brereton

Under the Chinese Dragon
A Tale of Mongolia
by F. S. Brereton

ISBN: 978-93-68092-42-1

Published by

DOUBLE 9 BOOKS

2/13-B, Ansari Road
Daryaganj, New Delhi – 110002
info@double9books.com
www.double9books.com
Tel. 011-40042856

ABOUT THE AUTHOR

Frederick Sadleir Brereton was a British author known for his adventure stories, particularly those set in exotic locations. He wrote numerous novels, many focusing on themes of exploration, bravery, and the challenges faced by characters in foreign lands. Among his most notable works are "Under the Chinese Dragon," which showcases his talent for weaving thrilling narratives with historical and cultural details.

Brereton often drew from his experiences and knowledge of various cultures, creating vivid portrayals of life in places like China and Mongolia. His writing reflects a deep interest in the spirit of adventure and the complexities of human relationships amidst challenging circumstances.

Brereton's books remain popular among readers who enjoy action-packed tales filled with adventure and intrigue. His legacy continues in the realm of children's and young adult literature, where his stories inspire a sense of wonder and exploration of the world.

CONTENTS

Chapter I
Ebenezer speaks his Mind

Mr. Ebenezer Clayhill was a man who impressed his personality upon one, so that those who had once obtained but a passing glimpse of him could not fail but recognise him, however long afterwards.

'Fust it's his nose what strikes yer,' had declared old Isaac Webster, when ensconced with his bosom friends of an evening down in the snug parlour of the 'Three Pigeons.' 'It's just the most almighty one as ever I seed, and I've seed a power of noses, I have, Mr. Jarney.'

He sniffed and looked across at that individual, as if he challenged him to disprove the statement, or even to doubt it; for Jarney was a cross-grained fellow, an old weather-beaten boatman, into whose composition quite a considerable quantity of salt seemed to have been absorbed. The man was short in stature and in manner. There was an acidity about his voice which made him the reverse of popular, though when he held forth in the cosy parlour of the public-house there were few who failed to listen; for Jarney had travelled. Unlike Isaac Webster, he had not been a stay-at-home all his days, but had seen things and people which were strange for the most part to the old cronies who gathered together of an evening. No one dare dispute Jarney's statements, for to do so was to lay oneself open to a course of scathing, biting sarcasm, in which Jarney excelled.

Isaac coughed, finding that Jarney had failed to answer. 'I've seed a power of noses, I have, Mr. Jarney,' he repeated in his most solemn tones.

The boatman, comfortably quartered in a huge arm-chair in the centre of the circle about the blazing fire, twisted his eyes round till they were fixed on the speaker. He pulled the short clay which he was smoking out of his mouth with a hand bearing many a tar stain, and contemplated it with much interest. His lips curled back in what was meant to be a derisive smile, then back went the pipe between his toothless gums.

'You've seed a sight of noses, you have, Mr. Webster,' he growled. 'Well, so has we all. There's noses all round us most of the day. I could yarn to yer about a nigger man 'way out in the Caroline Islands who'd a nose that you couldn't pass in a day's walk, it war that big and attractive. But you was talkin' of this here Ebenezer Clayhill.'

'Him as ain't long come to these parts,' interposed another of the men gathered about the fire. 'Him as you're acting gardener to, Mr. Webster.'

'Or rather, him as has gone and married the lady as you've been gardener to this three years past,' ventured a third. 'Mrs. Harbor that was; now Mrs. Ebenezer Clayhill.'

Webster nodded at the circle. It was true enough that he was gardener at 'The Haven,' the house occupied by Mrs. Clayhill, and it was also true enough that that lady had recently married; for but a few months before she had been known as Mrs. Harbor. The folks at Effington, a little fishing hamlet along the Hampshire coast, were sufficiently acquainted with the lady already; for in a small place there is not much news, and what there is quickly becomes common property. But Mr. Clayhill was a recent importation, of whom the villagers were as yet almost ignorant, so that Isaac Webster, who, naturally enough, had better opportunities of knowing him than the others at Effington, had been called upon to give his opinion on his new master.

'Well, as I was sayin', when I was interrupted,' Isaac began again, glaring across at the old salt lounging in his chair, 'I was sayin' that the fust thing you notice is his nose, it's that big and red. I'd swear to it in a court of law without a quiver. Then there's his eyes; ain't they sharp, just! For the rest of him, I don't know as there's much to say. He seems a pleasant-spoken gentleman, though I ain't so sure as he don't want already to cut down wages.'

The announcement, short as it was, provided food for conversation for the rest of that evening, and we may be sure that Mr. Ebenezer was as frankly and as completely discussed in the parlour of the 'Three Pigeons' as he had ever been in his life before. But we were saying that he was a man who impressed his personality upon every one, and Isaac was not by any means wrong when he stated that Ebenezer's nose was the chief characteristic. It arrested one's attention at the first instant, till one realised that further scrutiny would be a rudeness, and promptly fixed one's gaze on some other part of his person. Elsewhere there was not much that was favourable; for the gentleman who had so recently married Mrs. Harbor was some fifty years of age, and had a decidedly shifty air. His eyes were placed closer together than is customary, while his jowly cheeks, his pendulous eyelids, and the lines and seams about his face seemed all to accentuate the immediate impression of distrust which he inspired. For the rest, he was moderately tall, stout and broad-shouldered, and very bald.

Three months after his marriage, when he had settled down at 'The Haven,' Mr. Ebenezer Clayhill was engaged one day within his study. The morning post had brought him a number of bulky documents, and these lay spread out before him. One in particular seemed to occupy his attention, for he perused its contents for the third time at least, and sat regarding the lines thoughtfully. Slowly, as he took in the meaning of the document, his fat hands came together and he rubbed them over one another, as if he were particularly pleased. His small pig-like eyes lit up ever so little, while the lines across forehead and face smoothed themselves out a trifle.

'We have pleasure in informing you that this matter is now satisfactorily concluded,' he read, again beginning to go through the document. 'As we have advised you from time to time the question of Mr. Harbor's fate was one for the courts to deal with, and delay was inevitable. But we are now able to report that the Judge in chambers gave us leave to presume Mr. Harbor's death, on the evidence provided, and which, we may say, seemed to us to be absolutely conclusive. This being so, there is now no reason why Mrs. Harbor, as the executrix of the will of the late Mr. Harbor, should not at once proceed to obtain probate on it. For this purpose we shall hold ourselves at your disposal, and beg to remain.—Faithfully yours,

Jones & Jones,
Solicitors.

P.S.—We are in error in saying that Mrs. Harbor as executrix, etc. Of course, it should have been Mrs. Ebenezer Clayhill. We beg to apologise.'

The reader may wonder why such a short and apparently unimportant letter should occupy Mr. Ebenezer so greatly, and we hasten at once to supply that necessary information which will enable him to understand matters completely. After all, with every fact before him, the reader can hardly fail to comprehend Ebenezer's pleasure, for the letter before him practically relieved him of all further worry as to the wants of this life. A needy fellow till three months ago, Ebenezer, with that communication before him, felt that he had no longer any need to scheme, no cause to lay crafty plans and carry them out with much guile and cunning; for his wife would benefit under the will mentioned, and with her, as a natural consequence, Ebenezer himself.

But still Mr. Clayhill was not quite satisfied in his own mind as to this fortune upon which he could now almost put his hand; and for some three hours he paced his study, occupying himself sometimes in a listless, harassed manner with the documents on the table, while he awaited the coming of a member of the firm of solicitors who had written to him.

'Shan't feel quite sure till I've had a talk with this fellow,' he told himself, screwing his eyes up, while a deep line grooved his brow, which added not at all to his attractiveness. Indeed, at such moments Ebenezer looked more like a malefactor than a peaceful country gentleman. 'Shan't feel comfortable or safe till I've had a chat, and not then till the money is in the bank. Ah, there's David. A hulking big lout to be sure! Seems to me the time has arrived when he should do something for his living.'

The ugly frown was accentuated as Mr. Ebenezer looked out of his window. The latter faced the wide, gravelled drive of 'The Haven,' and gave an uninterrupted view down it as far as the gate, and beyond to the edge of the village. And following his gaze one saw a lad mounted on a fine horse, riding towards the house. He was some fifty yards distant, so that a clear view of him was to be obtained, and though Ebenezer had ventured to term the youth hulking, there were few who would have agreed with him; for David Harbor was slim, if anything, and, as well as it is possible to judge of a youth when mounted, of a good height. One thing was very certain; he sat his horse splendidly, as if accustomed to the saddle, and though the animal was without doubt spirited, as he proved now that he was on the gravelled drive by curvetting and prancing, David managed him with hand and knee and voice as only an accomplished horseman can do. For the rest, the youth seemed to be some eighteen years of age, was decidedly fair, and by no means ill-looking. Even as Ebenezer regarded him with a scowl David wore a sunny smile, unconscious of the unfriendly eyes that were scrutinising him. But a second later he caught a view of Mr. Ebenezer, and at once the young face became serious and thoughtful, while David returned the scrutiny with an honest glance that caused the other to turn hastily away.

'A hulking lout is what I call him, and Sarah agrees,' muttered Ebenezer. 'That is a comfort. When I married her I had fears that this stepson of hers might create trouble between us. But I was wrong; Sarah thinks as little of him as I do. We'll soon send him about his business; then there'll be no riding of fine horses, or idling the hours away if I know it. David shall work for his living, as I had to. He shall learn what it is to be pinched, and then, if he does not behave himself, he'll be thrown completely on his own resources. What luck that old Harbor left things as he did!'

'Looks as if he'd like to eat me,' was the remark David made to himself as he rode round to the stables. 'I've seen a row coming these past two weeks since he and mother came back home. He doesn't like me any better than—but there, I'll not say it. Only I've a feeling that I'm not wanted here. I'm in the way; I'm expensive. My living costs money; that's what I'm being rapidly made to feel.'

He slid from his saddle, unbuckled the girths, and having placed it on a wooden horse outside the harness room, led the beast into the stable. Within five minutes of his disappearance there a cab drove up to the door, and Mr. Edwin Jones, the solicitor, was announced. At once he was ushered into Mr. Ebenezer's room, and was presently seated in an arm-chair. From that point of vantage he surreptitiously scrutinised Mr. Ebenezer.

'Queer old boy,' he told himself. 'Lor', what a nose! And I don't like his looks altogether. But then, he's a client; that's sufficient for me. Ahem!'

Mr. Ebenezer picked up the letter which had attracted so much of his attention.

'I wanted to ask some questions,' he said. 'There is now, I presume, no further doubt as to this matter. Mrs. Clayhill is entitled to proceed with the will left in your possession by Mr. Harbor?'

'Ahem! that is so,' admitted the solicitor. 'As mentioned in our letter, and carrying out your instructions, we applied to the courts, and the judge before whom the matter came has gone into the evidence fully, and has given leave to presume Mr. Harbor's death. That being so, the way is clear to prove the will and obtain probate. There can be no hitch, unless, of course, ahem!—unless another later will is forthcoming.'

'Quite so, quite so,' exclaimed Mr. Ebenezer, hurriedly, 'But there is no other will. Mr. Harbor left England three years ago for China. You are aware that he was fond of unearthing old matters dealing with buildings and *objets d'art*. He was attacked by Boxers and killed. He executed this will two years previously, on his marriage to Mrs. Clayhill, and, undoubtedly, he saw no reason to alter it.'

'Of course not, of course not,' came from the solicitor. 'Only, there is the son. This will leaves a small sum for his maintenance and schooling up to the age of twenty-one. Afterwards he comes in for two thousand pounds. Not much, Mr. Clayhill, for an only child, when the estate is so large, roughly eighty thousand pounds.'

The gentleman who was seated in the arm-chair coughed deprecatingly, and glanced swiftly across at Mr. Ebenezer. He did not like the ugly frown which showed on his client's face, as he surveyed him.

'Glad I'm not David,' he told himself. 'And from what I have learned I can't help feeling that Mr. Harbor must have executed a later will. But there you are; it is not to be found. We have no information about it, while our late client is undoubtedly dead, killed out in China. It's bad luck for David; I like the boy.'

'Perhaps,' he said, a moment later, 'you will obtain Mrs. Clayhill's signatures to these documents, when we can at once set about proving the will. As I am nominated as co-executor with Mrs. Clayhill, I can complete them when I return to the office. I shall of course leave the payment of David's allowance to Mrs. Clayhill.'

Mr. Ebenezer beamed when at length his visitor had gone. He rubbed his hands together craftily, and then blew his enormous nose violently.

'Well, Sarah, what do you think of that?' he asked, looking across at Mrs. Clayhill, who had joined him in his room. 'The matter is practically finished. The will is to be proved in the course of a few weeks, and then we can settle down. There will be no questions to ask, and none to answer.'

'And so far as I am concerned, no answers forthcoming,' replied his wife. 'After all, it is true that Edward wrote to me from China just before his death, saying that he was settling his affairs again, in other words that he was making a new will. But what is the good of mentioning that? If he did as he intimated, no new will has been found. Besides, I have reason to know that any alteration would not have been to my benefit. Edward had of late been a worry to me.'

At the back of her mind Mrs. Clayhill remembered how she had come to marry Edward Harbor. He was then forty years of age, and possessed of one boy, David. His wife had died some years before, and there was no doubt that Edward in selecting his second wife had chosen one whom he imagined would willingly travel with him. But, after a year or more of life in England, Mrs. Clayhill had resolutely refused to stir a foot out of the country. Edward, to his great sorrow, had to go alone, leaving David in his wife's charge. Moreover, there was little doubt but that once her husband was out of sight, Mrs. Clayhill had endeavoured to forget him, and that with some success, so that Edward received only the most fragmentary letters, with long intervals between. Taking all the circumstances into consideration, it was but natural that Edward Harbor, smarting under the treatment meeted out to him by a wife, to whom at the time of their marriage he had willed almost all his possessions, should have made drastic alterations. Let us say at once that he had made a new will, only the latter, owing to his untimely death, had never reached the hands of his solicitors. Nor was there any record of it in China. Mrs. Clayhill, it seemed, was the only one who knew that a change had been made, and she had craftily not uttered a word on the subject. So it happened that David was to be robbed of his father's possessions, while his stepmother, who had disliked the lad from the beginning, with Mr. Clayhill, the husband she had acquired after the death of Mr. Harbor, were to come in for all the money, knowing all the while that, though such a step was legal, it did not represent Edward Harbor's wishes.

'And the boy—what of him?' asked Mrs. Clayhill tartly.

Ebenezer grinned; matters were going splendidly for him. 'Oh, David,' he said. 'He's got to learn what it is to work; I'll send him up to a city firm. No more idling or riding blood horses for him, my dear.'

It was a heartless arrangement, and one is bound to admit, from the acquaintance we have already of Mr. Ebenezer, it was to be expected of him. As for Mrs. Clayhill, though boasting some attractions, she was not, as the reader will have guessed, a fascinating woman. Where David was concerned she could be a dragon, and we are stating but the truth when we say that, for the past three years, the lad had been glad to return to school to escape from a home which was that only in name to him.

'Ah, there he is,' suddenly exclaimed Mr. Ebenezer, as a heavy foot was heard in the hall, while, within a second, the door of the room was flung unceremoniously open, and David entered.

'Helloo!' he cried, cheerily. 'I'm after a book. Disturbed you, eh? Sorry.'

He turned on his heel, and prepared to leave, for he could see that the two who were now responsible for him were discussing some matter. 'Having another jaw,' he told himself. 'That's what they're always after now-a-days. Something to do with money, I suppose. Or it's me; shouldn't wonder. They ain't over fond of David Harbor.'

It was not his fault that he did not speak or think more respectfully of his parents. After all, though only related to him by the accident of marriage, they were his lawful guardians, and had they been kind, David would have been only too glad to behave as a son to them. Goodness knew, the lad sometimes ached for a happy home.

'David!' The word came in peremptory tones from Ebenezer. He perched himself in the centre of the hearth rug and blew his nose violently. Mrs. Clayhill sank languidly back in her chair, and regarded her stepson as if he bored her greatly. 'Come back, David.'

'Well? What is it?' David swung into the room again, and stood holding to the handle of the door.

'Shut the door. Now, I want to speak to you. You're eighteen?'

'No, seventeen and five months. They tell me I look eighteen.'

'Humph! In any case you're old enough to understand. You realise, of course, that I cannot be responsible for your upkeep.'

David staggered. He knew very little of monetary matters, but had always understood that his father was a rich man and had made ample provision for his family. 'I don't understand,' he replied.

'Let me put it plainly. Your father is dead; he has left a small sum with which to defray your expenses. That must be sufficient; you must now fend for yourself.'

'But,' gasped David, hardly able to gather the drift of the conversation, 'he has left a great deal more than that for the upkeep of the family. I am one of the family.'

'True,' admitted Ebenezer, ruefully, 'you are one of the family, but that does not give you leave to enjoy yourself and be idle. Your father specified only a sum for your expenses. The remainder of his possessions are left to your stepmother to do with as she likes. She does not intend that you should stay here longer and have a good time. You are to work for your living. You are to go to an office in London, where your success will depend on yourself entirely.'

'But—.' David was thunderstruck. He had no intention of idling. As a matter of fact he hoped soon to enter an engineering school, where there would be plenty of work for a keen young fellow. What staggered him most was Ebenezer's iciness and his statements with regard to the possessions left by Edward Harbor. 'But,' he gasped again, 'there is surely some error. I don't count on money left me by father. I will work for my living, and show that I can earn it the same as others. But he made a will in China. He wrote to me about it. Everything was left to me, with a handsome allowance to mother.'

The words came as a shock to the two conspiring to do our hero out of his patrimony. Till that moment Mrs. Clayhill had imagined that she was the only person to whom Edward Harbor had written. But she forgot David, or put him out of her calculations because of his youth; whereas, as a matter of fact, Edward had been more than open with his son.

'It is no use mincing matters, boy,' he had written. 'Money is more or less useless to me, for I love the wilds, the parts forsaken by man these many centuries. Still, I have, by the chance of birth, large possessions to dispose of, and in the ordinary course they would go, in great part, to your stepmother. But you are old enough to understand matters. We cannot agree. She will not bear exile even for a few months, for my sake, and, to make short work of an unpleasant matter, I fear I must admit that I was mistaken in marrying her. As it is, I have reconsidered my affairs, and have recently remade my will. At the first opportunity I shall hand it into safe keeping. But here it must rest till I go down country. Needless to say, I have arranged that my property shall descend to you, with certain payments for your stepmother.'

'But—gracious me! Hear him!' cried Mrs. Clayhill, in a high falsetto.

'That is a lie,' declared Ebenezer, flatly, his eyes narrow, his brow furrowed, a particularly unpleasant look on his face. David flushed to the roots of his hair. He had never been called a liar, save once, by a boy bigger than himself, and him he had soundly thrashed. He stepped forward a pace, while his eyes flashed. Then he pulled himself together, and closed his lips firmly. A second later he was holding to the handle of the door again.

'It is the truth,' he said, firmly. 'I have the letter to prove it. He wrote telling me that he was sending the same information to my stepmother.'

This was a bomb in the heart of the enemy's camp with a vengeance. Mrs. Clayhill's face flushed furiously; she appeared to be on the verge of an attack of violent hysteria. Ebenezer, on the contrary, became as white as his own handkerchief. He glowered on David, and stuttered as he attempted to speak. It was, in fact, a very sordid affair altogether.

'David! How can you?' came from Mrs. Clayhill. 'I never had a letter. Your father made no change in his depositions.'

'In fact,' declared Ebenezer, bringing his hands together, and endeavouring to display an air of placidity, 'he left but one will, and that in favour of your stepmother. His death has been presumed by the courts, and now the will I speak of shall be administered. You are a pauper, more or less. You are dependent on a small allowance, payable by us, and on your own wits. You will employ the latter from this moment. I have accepted a post for you in a shipping office. You will live in rooms in London, and your hours of work will extend from eight-thirty in the morning to six at night. You begin immediately.'

To say that David was flabbergasted was to express his condition mildly. It had been his intention from an early age to become an engineer, and his father had encouraged his ambition. Suddenly he suspected that this work in London was only a plot to get him out of the way, and that his stepmother had received the letter of which he had spoken. It angered him to have his future ordered by a man almost a stranger to him, and one, moreover, who had taken no pains to hide his ill-feeling. Besides, David was proud and quick-tempered.

'I'll do nothing of the sort,' he exclaimed quickly.

'You disobey me, then?' demanded Ebenezer angrily.

'I decline to go into an office.'

'Then you leave the house to-morrow. Your allowance shall be paid to you regularly. You can fend for yourself.'

For a moment the two conspirators glared at David, while the latter held to the door. Even now he was loth to think evil of his stepmother, though there had never been any affection between them; for Mrs. Clayhill was essentially a worldly woman. Had she not been so she could not have sat there and seen this youth cheated of rights which she knew were his. She could not have allowed her second husband to proceed with the proving of a will which she knew thoroughly well did not represent her late husband's wishes. But she was a grasping woman, and had long since determined to oust David. Also she had in Ebenezer a cold-hearted scoundrel who backed her up completely.

'You will do as you are ordered or forfeit everything,' she cried, in shrill tones, that were a little frightened.

'Which means that you are not wanted very particularly here, and had better go,' added Ebenezer sourly. 'Take this post or leave it. It makes little difference to me; but idle and enjoy yourself here any longer, you shall not.'

David took in a deep breath; the situation was only beginning to dawn upon him. It was the climax that he had more than half expected, but which, boy-like, he had put out of mind. But here it was, naked and extremely sordid. He was not wanted; these people had no interest in Edward Harbor or in his son. In fact, that son stood in their way. Money was the cause of all the trouble. The two before him were conspiring to rob him, David, of the possessions intended for him by his father. Straightway David formed a resolution.

'You wish me to leave,' he said, as quietly as he could. 'I will go at once. You tell me that I am a pauper. Very well, I will work for myself; but I give you notice. I will search this matter out; it is not yet absolutely proved that father was killed. He might have been made a prisoner; his death has only been presumed. But I will make sure of it one way or the other. I will hunt for that will of which he wrote to me and to my stepmother. And when I find him or it I will return; till then, remember that I ask no help from either of you. I will fend for myself.'

He turned on his heel, closing the door noiselessly after him. Promptly he went to his room, packed his few valuables and a spare suit in a valise, not forgetting underclothing. Then he crossed to the stables and emerged a few moments later with his bicycle. A somewhat scared couple of conspirators watched him, as he pedalled down the drive and out through the gate.

'Pooh! Let him go. A good riddance!' blustered Ebenezer, blowing his nose.

'I'm afraid of him; he was always like that,' exclaimed Mrs. Clayhill tearfully. 'David is a most determined boy; he will search this matter to the bottom.'

'Which happens to be particularly deep,' ventured her husband. 'Come, Sarah, threatened people live long. Before he is anywhere near China we shall have the will proved, and the money will be ours. We can afford to laugh at the young idiot.'

They saw David swing out into the road and disappear past the village. From that moment for many a week, he was a dead letter to them. But distance did not help them. The fact that they were committing a wrong preyed on the newly wedded couple. In the course of a little while the memory of David had become to Ebenezer and his wife even more trying than his actual presence. The proving of the will, the free use of the money could not end the matter. Conscience spoke sternly and unceasingly to Mr. and Mrs. Clayhill.

Chapter II
The Road to London

It was approaching evening as David Harbor swung out of the drive gates of 'The Haven,' and turned his back upon the inhospitable house and the stepmother who had behaved so disgracefully to him. His head high, a queer sinking at the heart, but his courage undaunted for all that, he pedalled swiftly through the village of Effington, nodded to the sour old salt Jarney, who, by the way, always had a smile for David, sped past the 'Three Pigeons' public-house, where the local tittle-tattle of the place was dispensed, together with ale, and was soon out in the open country.

'Time to sit down and think a little,' he said to himself, resting on his pedals and allowing his machine to glide along down the incline till it came of its own accord to a rest. 'Now, we'll sit down here and think things out, and have a look into this affair. I must consider ways and means.'

He was a practical young fellow, was David Harbor, and already the seriousness of the move he had made was weighing upon him. Not that he was inclined to hesitate or to go back, not that at all, only the future was so clouded. His movements were so uncertain; the absence of some definite plan or course of procedure was so embarrassing.

'Three pounds, thirteen shillings and fourpence halfpenny,' he said, emptying his purse, and counting out the money as he sat on a roadside boulder. 'Riches a month ago when I was at school, poverty under these circumstances, unless—unless I can get some work and so earn money. That's what I said I'd do and do it I will. Where? Ah, London!'

Like many before him, his eyes and thoughts at once swept in the direction of the huge metropolis, at once the golden magnet which attracts men of ambition and resource, and the haven wherein all who have met with dire misfortune, all who are worthless and have no longer ambition, can hide themselves and become lost to the world.

'Yes, London's the place,' said David, emphatically, pocketing his money. 'I'll ride as far to-night as I can, eat something at a pastrycook's, and sleep under a hay-stack. To-morrow I'll finish the journey. Once in the city I'll find a job, even if it's only stevedoring down at the docks.'

For a little while he sat on the boulder letting his mind run over past events; for he was still somewhat bewildered. It must be remembered that such serious matters as wills and bequests had not troubled his head till that day. Boy-like, he had had faith in those whose natural position should have prompted them to support the young fellow placed in their care. He had had no suspicions of an intrigue, whereby his stepmother wished to oust him from a fortune which his father's letter had distinctly said was to become his. He had imagined that things would go on as they were till he had finished with his engineering studies; then it would be early enough to discuss financial matters. His recent interview had been a great shock to him.

'I begin to see it all now,' he said. 'And I can understand now what Mr. Jones, the solicitor, meant when last I saw him. He wanted to warn me against Mr. Ebenezer, but did not dare to make any open statement. I'll go to him: I'll take that letter.'

He had taken care to carry away with him everything he prized most, and his father's correspondence was at that moment securely placed in an inside pocket. David laid his fingers on the letters, and then read the one in which Edward Harbor had referred to the disposal of his fortune.

'Yes, I'll take this to Mr. Jones,' repeated David, with decision. 'I've always liked him, and father trusted him implicitly. But I'll ask for no help; I mean to get along by myself, if only to show Mr. Ebenezer that I can be as good as my word. There; off we go again. No use in sitting still and moping.'

It was wonderful what a difference a plan made to him: David felt ever so much happier. The future, instead of appearing as a huge dark cloud before him, dwindled away till it was but a speck; his old, sunny looks came back to a face somewhat harassed a little while before, and thereafter David pedalled at a fine pace, placing the miles behind him swiftly, and sending the colour to his cheeks. It was getting so dark that in a few minutes he would have to light his lamp when he detected a figure walking along the road in front of him, and as he came level with the man the latter hailed him.

'Helloo there,' came in cherry tones, 'how many miles do you make it to London?'

'Sixty-four,' answered David promptly. 'You're walking there?'

'Every inch of it,' came the hearty answer. 'I've done it before, and will do it again. Railways are too expensive for the likes of me to waste money on 'em. You off there too?'

David jumped from his saddle, and walked his machine beside the stranger, who was obviously a sailor. His baggy breeches told that tale distinctly, while the breeziness of the man, and his many nautical expressions would, even without the assistance of a distinctive dress, have made his profession more than probable.

'Got a week's shore leave, and mean to walk up to see the old people,' said the stranger. 'Stoker Andus I am, from the *Indefatigable*. Who are you? By the cut of your gib you'll be a gent same as our orfficers. Ain't that got it?'

David laughed at the man's breeziness and straight way of asking questions.

'I'm looking for a job,' he said promptly, 'though I believe I am what you have described. But I've had a row at home, and now I'm off to find work.'

The stoker, a man of some thirty years of age, came to an abrupt halt, and swung round to have a close look at David. 'Run away, has yer,' he exclaimed. 'Then, bust me, if you ain't a silly kid. I did the same once when I was about your age. Ran from a home as wanted me, ran from parents that knew what was best for me. I can see that I was a fool now that I'm older. Jest send her astern, mister, and let's get in and talk it over. Now, what's the rumpus? Done something you was expressly ordered not to, eh? Got into debt, perhaps. Been smokin' and takin' the governor's bacca? It's one of them, ain't it? And here are you a makin' your mother that wretched—'

'Heave to for a bit,' cried David, laughing in spite of himself, and unconsciously employing one of the stranger's nautical expressions. 'You think I'm a fool, eh? Think I'm treating some one badly?'

From the very first he had taken a fancy to the handsome, clean-shaven tar tramping his way to London, and he realised in a flash that the honest fellow, with experience of his own behind him to help, was endeavouring to give advice, and encourage what he considered to be a truant to return home. Brusquely and in true sailor fashion Andus answered him.

'If I'm aboard the right ship, and you've cleared off from a good home, then you are a fool, a precious big 'un, too,' he cried. 'And there ain't a doubt as you're treatin' some one badly; mostlike it's your mother. P'raps it's your father. Anyways, let's drop anchor hereabouts and put on a smoke. I can yarn when I'm smokin', and since it's dark now, there's no need for more hurry.'

He led the way to a gate, sat himself on the top rail, and having produced a cake of tobacco, a knife and a pipe, shredded some of the weed into the latter.

'Well,' he began again, when he had got the weed burning, and huge billows of smoke issuing from his lips. 'You've had a few seconds to think it over. Andus ain't a fool, mind you, youngster, and he ain't tryin' to give lessons to one as has heaps more eddication. But I've seed one as was sorry for running away from home. That's me. I know one as has never ceased to feel that he did wrong, and has suffered in consequence. That's me again, all the time. And I ain't a goin' to fall in alongside of another and keep me mouth shut when I know as he's headin' straight up for the same rocks and shoals, and is in danger of breakin' hisself to pieces. There you are. Take that from one who knows what he's talking about.'

He lapsed into silence for a while, puffing smoke from his lips, and occasionally looking down at David, who stood within a few feet of him. As for the latter, the more the sailor talked, the more he liked the man. There was an honest ring about his breezy tones, a direct manner about the words he used that captivated our hero. Not for one moment was he fearful that he himself would change his plans, whatever was said. No, David had now considered his movements very thoroughly. He told himself that it was not he who had behaved badly. It was his stepmother and her husband. But, in case of error, he would put the facts before this open-minded sailor.

'Supposin' you was to stop here to-night, and then ride back to-morrow,' suggested Andus, cooly, as if he were saying the most commonplace thing. 'This home of yours ain't far, and you'd be there by breakfast time. They'd be so glad to see you that the row would be forgotten. You'd start in fresh again, with new paint above and below, and everything ship-shape. What do you say to that, youngster?'

'That your intention is a good one, and your advice the same under usual conditions,' declared David, warmly. 'But this isn't an ordinary running away. I'll tell you how I came to leave home.'

He sat down on the rail of the gate and told Andus quietly how his parents had treated him, and how he was sure that the two were conspiring to oust him out of property meant for him by his dead father. 'In any case,' he ended, 'I was not wanted. I was to leave the house and go into an office, though it was well known that I hoped to go to an engineering college. I refused the office, and was told to clear out. Now, tell me frankly what you think.'

The sailor dug the blade of his knife deep into the bowl of his pipe, and stirred the contents thoroughly before he ventured to reply. There was a deep line across his forehead, while his eyes were half closed. David could tell that easily, for the moon was up now, and the night was unusually bright. Then Andus struck flint and steel, and sucked flames into his pipe till our hero thought he would never cease.

'Tell me about this solicitor,' he suddenly demanded. 'He was a friend of your father's?'

'And of mine,' answered David. 'I like him. I am sure that he tried to warn me against the man who married my stepmother.'

'Then jest listen here, youngster,' cried Andus, breezily. 'I take back all the words I was flingin' at you. You ain't such a fool as I took you for. What's more, I'm precious nigh certain that it's you that's bein' done harm to, and not these here parents of yours. A precious fine couple to be sure! Heavin' overboard on a dirty night wouldn't be too much for 'em. Seems to me that they has the best of the argument at this moment. From what I've heard they has the handlin' of the money and the arrangement of things. They know everything, while you ain't got a one to help you. But if you was to see this solicitor you'd be better off. You get right off to him and ax fer his advice. Andus may be all very well for guiding a chap back to his home when he's makin' a fool of hisself, same as Andus did when he was young, but bust me if he's fit to advise here. Get right off to London.'

'I will; meanwhile we'll spend the night together. What were you going to do?' asked David, feeling better already for his chat with the sailor.

'Why, sling me hammock under one of these here straw stacks,' cried Andus. 'It'll be warm in there, and a chap can sleep better than in a strange bed. To-morrow I'll be up at the first streak of light, and headin' for the nearest village. I'll be able to eat a bit by then, and afterwards I'll leg it for London.'

'Then I propose that we leg it now for the nearest village, have a meal and then find a suitable stack under which to sleep. I'm real hungry; I've had little since breakfast.'

Andus fell in with the arrangement willingly, and together they tramped along the high road till they came to a village. There they obtained a meal of bread and meat, washed down with cocoa, for Andus was one of many, a rapidly increasing band in the Royal Navy, who are sworn teetotallers.

'And now for another smoke and a doss under a stack,' cried the sailor, as they left the village. 'The moon's that bright we might jest as well push on for a while till we get sleepy. Then we'll get into a harbour o' some sort, and lay to for the night. To-morrow afternoon you'll be in London, and with a bit of luck I'll be there by nightfall. I often get a carter or some such chap to give me a lift. Once a gent on a motor ran me clean through; but that was unusual luck.'

'I'll send you up by train,' declared David generously. 'I haven't much, but can spare enough for your ticket.'

'Then you jest won't,' came warmly from the sailor. 'I tell yer, sir, I don't forget those days when I was a fool and ran from home. Bust me! I hadn't too much cash, and well remember there wasn't a halfpenny to spare. You ain't got such a big cargo aboard that you can afford to heave some of it over. I'm a goin' to foot it.'

'You'll ride,' said David, with determination. 'It will bring me good luck to do a good turn to a friend picked up on the road. Besides, I shall have sufficient. I shall sell this bicycle the moment I get to London. Then I shall be able to draw from the solicitor some of the allowance I am entitled to. But I mean to work; I'll not hang about depending on an allowance. I'll make a way for myself, if only to show my stepmother that I can do so.'

The breezy sailor brought a hand down on his shoulders with such force that David coughed and choked.

'That's you all the time,' he shouted. 'I could see when I first took a squint at you through my weather eye that you wasn't one of the soft kind. The kind fer instance that they turns out of a dry canteen, or a grocery store. Makin' a way for yerself is one of the finest things a man can have to do, only there's so few as realise it. But you'll do it; I'm tryin' the same. There's advancement for every one as shows he means to work. But here's a lot of stacks. Pipes out; dowse all lights. We won't risk firing property that doesn't belong to us.'

They searched for a suitable spot, and very soon were stretched on a mass of loose straw which had been piled beside one of the ricks. Pulling a heap of it over their bodies a delicious feeling of warmth soon came to them, and in a twinkling they were asleep. The sun streaming on his face wakened David on the following morning.

'Now,' he shouted, waking Andus, 'a wash and then on for breakfast. We'll walk together as far as the nearest station.'

Half an hour later David had the satisfaction of seeing Andus enter a railway train, and of shaking his hand heartily as the latter steamed out.

'Don't you wait a little bit,' called out the hearty sailor, waving his hand in farewell. 'Go right off to that solicitor. Stick to your guns, and you'll come through in the end.'

Far happier for the meeting with this wayfarer, and for the chat he had had with him, David mounted his bicycle again, and pedalled briskly along the main road for London. He no longer felt that doubt and uncertainty that had oppressed him on the previous day. He had made his plans, and a man of the world, an honest fellow gifted undoubtedly with common sense, had approved of his actions. Henceforth he would push on without a halt and without hesitation.

'I'll sell the bicycle, find rooms in which to live, and insert an advertisement for work,' he told himself. 'Then I'll see Mr. Jones.'

It was an hour later before the even course of his journey was disturbed. He was running gaily before a strong breeze, with a hot sun streaming down upon him when in the far distance he saw a vehicle trundling along the road. Rapidly overhauling it, he soon saw that it was a brougham, with a coachman seated on the box, though whether there were passengers in the vehicle he could not say; but within a few minutes he came alongside, and, as he passed, caught a glimpse of two ladies within. Then he swept on, pedalled past a traction-engine engaged in hauling stones, and was soon on a clear road again. Then a loud shout reached his ears, followed by others. He turned his head and looked over his shoulder, with the consequence that the machine wobbled. Indeed, so occupied was David with what was taking place in rear that he neglected to guide his steed. In a moment therefore he ran into the ditch at the side of the road, and was flung headlong into a hedge.

'That comes of staring over one's shoulder,' he said, picking himself up at once. 'But there seems to have been an accident behind there. I saw the horse in that brougham rear as it got opposite the traction-engine. Then it dashed forward, and—why, the coachman has jumped from the box! The coward! He's left those ladies to be dashed to pieces—the coward!'

The distance was so short that he was able to take in the whole situation, and it was clear that the coachman on the box of the vehicle had lost his head and his nerve. David had watched him holding to his reins as the horse plunged; but the instant it bolted down the road the man had leaped from his seat, and striking the road heavily had rolled over and over into the ditch. Left to itself, the horse was coming along the road at a mad gallop, the brougham swaying behind him in an alarming manner, and threatening to capsize at any moment.

'George! nearly over that time,' gasped David. 'The horse is scared out of its wits. It'll not stop till it has smashed the carriage and those in it. Don't that coachman deserve to be kicked.'

He darted into the centre of the road, and watched the maddened creature bearing down upon him. Behind, in the neighbourhood of the traction-engine, he could see men waving their arms, and running along the road, while a little nearer the coachman was sitting up in the ditch, holding on to a damaged elbow. A head appeared at one of the carriage windows for an instant, and David caught a glimpse of a very frightened face. A scream even reached his ears; then he leaped back from the road and seized his bicycle.

'I'll dodge that carriage,' he told himself. 'I'd never be able to keep up with it at the rate the horse is going unless on my bicycle; but on the machine I could do it. Anyway, I'll have a try.'

He swung himself into the saddle and pedalled gently along. By now he could hear the scrunch of fast-revolving wheels on the macadam, while more than one shriek came from the interior of the carriage. Then the horse seemed to make directly for him. David spurted forward, his head over his shoulder, and darted across to the far side of the road, just escaping the feet of the maddened animal. In a twinkling the carriage drew abreast of him, and for a while he raced along beside it, noticing that on many an occasion it was within an ace of capsizing. Then a brilliant manœuvre occurred to him.

'Couldn't possibly get aboard from the side or front,' he told himself. 'The pedal of the bicycle would catch something, and I should come a cropper beneath the wheels. I'll try the back; but it'll want doing. That brute is going all out.'

The runaway horse was indeed galloping as hard as he could, faster, in fact, than before, so that even had David wished to come alongside he found it impossible, for the carriage had now drawn slightly ahead. But with a desperate effort he lessened the distance, keeping directly behind the vehicle so as to escape the breeze, which at that pace was of his own making. Gradually he approached the rear of the carriage till he was almost between the wheels. Then, quick as a flash, he leaped from his saddle, abandoning his machine, and flung himself toward the back axle of the vehicle. His fingers fastened upon it, and an instant later he was jerked from his feet, and went dragging along the road. But he was not beaten. David was no weakling, and soon made an alteration in his position. With a jerk and a heave he regained his feet. A frantic spring took him on to the axle, and after that he felt that victory was before him.

'Over the top, on to the box, and then along the shafts,' he told himself. 'No use trying to clamber along the sides. This beastly thing is on the point of upsetting already, and with my weight added to one side would topple over. Here goes for the top.'

It was not an easy task he had set himself by any means, for the carriage wobbled dangerously, and there was no rail to cling to. But David made light of risks; he never even considered them. He stood on the axle now, and reaching up gripped the top. With a bound he was on it, and thereafter had all his work cut out to prevent being thrown off to either side. But slowly he won his way forward till near the box. Then a sudden swerve of the horse sent him sliding to the right, till legs and thighs left the roof of the vehicle. Even then he was not beaten. With a wriggle and a heave he flopped forward to the edge of the box seat, and as his body slid from the roof, he managed to grip the rail. One foot by good fortune met with a step, and thanks to that and his grip of the rail he was soon located where the driver had been. Once there David was in his element. He dragged the whip from its socket, stretched over the side of the box, and with a dexterous thrust of the stick managed to hook it under the reins, which were trailing along the road. In half a minute he had them in his hands. And then began a battle which would have delighted the heart of a horse-master; for David coaxed and endeavoured to control the maddened beast with both voice and rein.

'Whoa! steady boy!' he called, pulling firmly on the mouth. 'Whoa! gently boy, gently!'

However, finding that nothing resulted, he leaned back in his seat, braced his feet, and began to pull in earnest, sawing at the beast's mouth. Within a minute the pace had lessened. Promptly he began to call to the horse.

'Whoa! gently boy, gently.'

In less than five minutes he had brought him to a standstill, and dropping from the box had the animal by the head, and was patting and soothing him.

'Please get out and stand at one side,' he called to the ladies. 'The traction-engine startled him and caused him to bolt. He is still a little nervous, but in a few moments he will be calm again. It would be better, however, to get out. Please hurry.'

To tell the truth David was half expecting the animal to bolt again, for even as he spoke it reared up dragging him from his feet. But he had the huge advantage of understanding horses, and, as is so often the case, the frightened brute seemed to realise that. Sweating heavily and still trembling, it finally stood still, allowing him to pat its neck. Meanwhile a lady had descended, and had assisted another to follow her. David looked at them curiously. Both were very white after such a terrifying experience, but the elder of the two seemed to be more indignant than frightened. She walked across to David and inspected him critically.

'How did you manage to get on to the carriage?' she asked; and then, when he had told her, 'I consider you to have behaved nobly. You saved our lives, not to mention the carriage. It was a brave act, and I and my daughter are more than obliged to you. As for our coachman he is a coward. I shall dismiss him promptly.'

A flush of anger came to her cheeks, and a little later she turned to face the delinquent. 'You can drive back alone. I will walk,' she said severely, as the man came up with David's bicycle. 'You are not fit to be driving ladies. You deserted your post in the most disgraceful manner. Come, Charlotte, perhaps this gentleman will walk with us.'

'I will drive you if you wish,' declared David promptly. 'The coachman can ride my bicycle. Which way, please?'

He hopped briskly into the driving seat, and picked up his reins in a manner which gave confidence. Then, the ladies having entered the vehicle and directed him, he set off down the road. Within half an hour he pulled up in front of a country mansion, enclosed in fine grounds. At once a groom was called from the stables, and David was invited to enter the house.

'You will lunch with us of course,' said the elder lady. 'I am Mrs. Cartwell. This is my daughter, and—ah, Richard come here.'

She beckoned to a young fellow crossing the hall at that moment and introduced him as her son. Then in a few words she explained the situation.

'By Jove! That was a fine thing to do,' exclaimed the young fellow, whom David took to be about twenty years of age. 'A real plucky thing. How on earth did you manage to clamber on to the carriage when it was going at such a pace, while you were on a bike? But let me thank you a thousand times for your action. You have undoubtedly saved mother's life.'

Very cordially did he shake David's hand, and thereafter did his utmost to put our hero at his ease and make him feel at home. Then, after lunch, he pressed him to stay a day or so, for the two young fellows took instantly to one another.

'Come,' he said, 'you've nothing in particular to do. Off for a bicycle tour I suppose? Stay here a day or two and have a little fishing with me.'

'Can't, though many thanks all the same,' answered David, wishing that he could remain. 'I'm not on a bicycle tour. I'm going to London to find work. I've some important business to do there.'

In a little while his new friends became aware of the fact that our hero was launching himself on the world, and though he did not tell them his reasons for leaving home, they realised that he was justified.

'If you cannot stay, you can at least remember the address of this house,' said Mrs. Cartwell. 'We shall be glad to receive a visit from you at any time, and I shall expect you to write. And now we will no longer detain you.'

They sent him away with further words of thanks, while Dick Cartwell accompanied him some five miles on the journey.

'Mind,' he said, as they gripped hands for the last time, 'we shall expect to see you again, and hope you will write. I feel that we haven't half thanked you.'

David waved the words aside, and straddled his bicycle. 'I don't want thanks,' he said abruptly. 'But I'd like to come down. I'll write when I've found work and am getting on a little. For the present I have no time and no right to laze and enjoy myself.'

He went off down the road waving to Dick, never dreaming that the two of them would come together again under strange circumstances. Pedalling hard, he made up for lost time, and just as the shades of evening were falling, found his way into the great city of London.

'Please direct me to some little house where I can obtain a lodging,' he asked of a policeman who was walking on the pavement.

The constable, a fine, burly fellow, surveyed our hero from head to foot. Then he smiled at him, and brought a massive hand on to his shoulder.

'Come along with me,' he said. 'My missus wants a lodger. I was told this morning when I went off on duty that I was to try and hear of one. You'd do for a time. How'd you like to come?'

David smiled back at him promptly. 'Splendid!' he cried. 'I'd be glad to come. I shall be saved heaps of trouble hunting for a room.'

That night he slipped into a cosy bed between the cleanest sheets feeling that fortune had been really kind to him; for since he left home he had done nothing but make friends. There was Andus, the breezy sailor, Mrs. Cartwell, to say nothing of Dick, her jovial son. And now there was the constable; for a nicer fellow than Constable Hemming did not exist, while his wife took a motherly interest in David. It was a good start in life; but would the future be equally prosperous?

Chapter III
Wanted a Job

The rattle of wheels in the street outside, and the brilliant rays of the morning sun awakened David on his first morning in London. In a twinkling he was up and dressed.

'Suppose you've come up to start life, sir,' said Constable Hemming when his lodger put in an appearance. 'Breakfast's ready, and you can have it at the back in the parlour, or here in the kitchen along with the missus and me.'

'Then I'll stop with you,' declared David, smiling. 'Yes, constable, I'm here to start life. I shall have to look round for work; but first of all I must go into the city to see a firm of solicitors. I shall have to find my way there.'

'I'll guide you,' came the answer. 'House rent is that dear towards the city that I have to come out here. Every morning I take a 'bus to the central police station and there get my orders. I'm on special duty these days. We're hunting for a gang of foreign burglars that have come to London to bother us; but what are you going to do? Medical student, eh?'

David shook his head vigorously. 'Nothing so grand,' he said. 'I have to find work of some sort, and I don't care what it is at first, so long as I can earn something with which to pay my way while I look round.'

The constable's eyes opened wide with astonishment, and for a little while he regarded his lodger critically, while his wife busied herself with putting the breakfast on the table. He remembered the conversation which he had had with her on the previous night. They had agreed without the smallest hesitation that David was a young gentleman used to more or less fine surroundings. There was nothing secret or underhand about him; but they did not imagine that he had left home with the intention of making his way alone in the world. This information that he must find some sort of work showed at once that he was dependent solely on himself.

'Why,' declared Hemming, 'you look as if you ought to be in an office, or in the army as an officer. Want to find work? What about your parents?'

Probably his official training caused him to regard David again, and this time with some suspicion.

'I left home hurriedly after a row,' said our hero promptly. 'I was told I was not wanted. There was a quarrel about money; I came away determined to make my own way.'

'But,' began the constable, like Andus, the breezy sailor, feeling that he ought to give some good advice here, advice culled from his own age and somewhat wide experience. 'But, look here, sir. Ain't you made a great mistake? Wouldn't it be better to think things over and turn back? Most like your parents are advertising for you. I should have to give information.'

David stopped him with a pleasant smile, lifting his hand as he did so. Then in a few short words he told the constable and his wife what had happened, refraining, however, from telling them about the will.

'Now,' he said, looking from one to the other.

'I take it all back; no chap with a bit of pride could do otherwise,' declared Hemming, warmly. 'So you want work, any sort of work?'

David nodded. 'Anything to tide me over for the time being,' he said. 'Ultimately I mean to leave the country.'

'You wouldn't sniff if I was to mention the job of lift-boy?' asked Hemming, somewhat bashfully, as if he were almost ashamed to introduce such a job to David's notice.

'Where? When is it open? Could I work the lift?' asked our hero promptly. 'To-day I could hardly begin; to-morrow I shall be free.'

'Then you can come along with me to the city,' said the constable, laughing at his eagerness. 'It so happens that an old soldier, who belongs to the corps of commissionaires, told me a night or two back that his firm would be wanting a young chap. It's one of the big London stores; we'll see what we can do for you.'

David thanked him warmly, and then, remembering his bicycle, mentioned it.

'I want to sell it,' he said. 'I have some ready money on me; but the machine will be useless here, and the cash I could get for it useful.'

'Of course, and I could take you to a place where a fair price would be given; but if you'll take my advice you'll wait a little. Supposing this London firm is a good way from your lodgings, a bicycle would be handy to take you to work; the machine'll come to no harm for the moment, and will fetch it's price whenever you want to part with it. You keep it for a while. Now, sir, if you're ready we'll set out.'

In five minutes the two were in the street, the constable looking fine and burly in his uniform, while the gentlemanly appearance of the young fellow walking beside him caused the neighbours to remark. They clambered on to a motor-bus at the end of the street, and made their way into the city. Then they descended close to the Mansion House, and were soon in conversation with the commissionaire.

'You mentioned a firm as wanted a young fellow for the lift,' said the constable. 'Is that job still going?'

The commissionaire looked David up and down with an experienced eye, and noted his straight figure, his good looks, and his general air of superiority. Then he nodded his head several times in succession.

'That job's still going,' he said, 'and a young chap same as this is just what's wanted; but he don't want to have kid gloves on his hands all the while. This firm's looking for a lad as can appear smart when he's in the lift, and can strip his livery off next moment and clean and tidy things. Chaps as don't care to dirty their fingers ain't wanted.'

'Then I'm your man,' David blurted promptly. 'I'm not afraid of dirtying my fingers with clean work—honest work I mean. As to smartness, there I can't pretend to judge.'

Hemming winked slyly at his friend, who went by the name of Tiller, while the latter again surveyed David with a critical eye, till the latter flushed red under the scrutiny. Then Sergeant Tiller's head began to wag forward and backward again, in a manner evidently characteristic of him, while a smile broke out on his face.

'You'll do I should say,' he declared. 'Ready to work now?'

David thought for a moment. 'Ready to begin at this moment,' he said. 'But I must see some one in the city during business hours to-day. To-morrow I could take to work steadily.'

'Then you can leave him to me, Hemming,' said the sergeant, 'I'll take him right along, and the chances are he'll get the post. I used to work for the same firm, and seeing as they knew that I had the best idea of what sort of young chap they wanted, they left it to me to find a man. One moment, mister, I'll get leave to be off for a while; then we'll take a 'bus along to Oxford Street. The firm I'm talking about have a big fashionable store close to Bond Street.'

Within an hour David and his new friend were at their destination, waiting within the huge glass doors of an establishment, the size and rich decoration of which filled our hero with amazement; for trips to London had not often come his way. Mrs. Clayhill, his stepmother, had never troubled to take him with her.

'There's thousands of pounds worth of things here,' whispered the sergeant, as they waited for an interview with the manager, 'and, very naturally, the firm is careful as to whom it employs. There's the lift yonder. The man working it should really be at the door. From that I take it that the hand who was here has left. That'll make 'em extra anxious to get a substitute. Ah, come along.'

David's heart fluttered a trifle as he was ushered into the sanctum of the manager; for he felt that the interview meant much to him. To be truthful, he would rather have begun his life at some post more in accordance with his upbringing; but then, he reflected, beggars must not be choosers, and so long as the work was honest, it would tide him over a difficult time. Besides, there was his interview with the solicitors. It would be fine to be able to declare that he had already found a job, and was in need of nothing. A second later he was before a diminutive man, dressed very smartly, who regarded him with the same critical eye as in the case of the sergeant.

'Just the young fellow, sir,' said the latter, nodding towards our hero. 'Constable Hemming introduced him to me. He's fresh to London, and this will be his first job.'

'Know anything about lifts and machinery?' demanded the manager sharply.

'Yes, sir; I've worked in the shops at school, and meant to become an engineer.'

David blurted the words out thoughtlessly, and then could have bitten his tongue off the next instant. For if he had been candid with other people, and described how he had left home, here, where he might be employed to work, he wished his past history to remain unknown. But he forgot that his whole appearance, his speech, his carriage, all told the tale of his upbringing. He did not see the old sergeant wink at the manager. He watched him bend forward and whisper.

'Constable tells me he was driven away from home, sir,' said the sergeant, in the manager's ear. 'The lad's as honest as they make them. I'll back him to give satisfaction. Give him a trial. He's the kind of lad you could turn on to anything; he's a gentleman all over.'

David would have flushed red could he have heard the words, but he was watching the manager. The latter looked closely at him again, smiled suddenly, and then asked a question.

'What wages?' he asked.

'Fifteen shillings a week,' answered our hero.

'Nonsense! We start our men with a pound a week. We will give you a month's trial. Hours eight-thirty in the morning till six. When can you come?'

'To-morrow, sir. I'd like to have a trial now, but I must see some one in the city this afternoon.'

'Then go to the lift and have a lesson. To-morrow we shall expect you. Have you a dark suit?'

David nodded promptly.

'Then come in that: we have livery which ought to fit you. Good-bye.'

It was a much-excited David who emerged from the manager's office. The sudden succession to a post at a pound a week made him feel giddy, it was such good fortune. He hardly heard the old sergeant explaining his errand to the lift-man. Almost unconsciously he shook hands with the former and thanked him for his help. Then he entered the lift, and watched his instructor as he ran it up and down. Ten minutes later he was controlling the affair himself, and within half an hour was efficient. That morning, he ran the elevator for some two hours all alone, to the entire satisfaction of his employers, conveying a number of purchasers to other parts of the building.

'You'll do,' declared the manager, when mid-day arrived. 'You're steady and keep your head. Don't forget, it is a strict rule that all doors be closed before the lift is moved. Accidents so easily happen. Now take a word of advice. Every one can see what you are. Don't talk; keep yourself to yourself and you'll make no enemies. To-morrow morning at half-past eight.'

He dismissed him with a nod, and very soon David was out in the street once more.

'And now for Mr. Jones, the solicitor,' he told himself. 'I don't feel half so bad about the interview as I did yesterday. That job makes such a difference. I'll telephone down to his address, and ask when he can see me.'

He went at once to a call office, and promptly was able to arrange to see the solicitor at two o'clock. Then he journeyed down into the city, ate heartily at a cheap restaurant, and finally went to Mr. Jones's office. It was a very astonished solicitor who received him.

'Why, you of all people!' he declared, as our hero entered. 'Sit down there. You've got something to tell me; something is troubling you, that I can detect at once. What is it?'

David at once told him how he had left home, and the cause for such action.

'I made up my mind to fend for myself,' he said. 'I decided to find work in London, and to decline the post in an office which Mr. Clayhill offered.'

There was a serious air on Mr. Jones's face as he listened. 'That was a bold course to pursue,' he said. 'Work is hard to find in this huge city. There are so many applicants; but, of course, there is your allowance. It will enable you to live for the time being.'

David shook his head promptly. 'I've got work already at twenty shillings a week,' he said. 'I want you and the others to understand that I mean to stand alone and fight my own battle. I mean to be independent; I'll not call for that allowance till I actually need it.'

'Then, my lad, all the more honour to you,' declared Mr. Jones, gripping his hand. 'But, of course, the allowance is yours. I shall make arrangements to have it at my own disposal, not at that of your stepmother's. So there was a scene, David? You were told to go. But why? Money, I suppose.'

In a few words David recounted what had happened, and how he had been told that he had next to no interest in his father's possessions.

'I knew that father had written home,' he declared. 'He sent me a letter saying that he proposed to change his will, and he wrote to my stepmother intimating the same. She denies this fact; but there is my letter.'

He drew it from his pocket and waited, watching Mr. Jones while the latter perused it And slowly he saw the solicitor's expression become sterner and sterner.

'This is very serious, David,' he said at last, 'and though this letter proves without doubt that your father made a later will, and that your stepmother has deliberately obscured that fact, yet I fear that matters cannot be altered. This later will is not to be found. Evidence has come to hand which is so conclusive that the courts have presumed your father's death. Nothing can now prevent the execution of the will now in our possession.'

He looked thoughtfully at David for some few moments, and then pushed his spectacles back on to his furrowed forehead. 'Nothing can alter the matter now,' he added, 'unless this later will is found. That seems to me to be out of the question.'

'I think not. I intend to find it; I shall go to China.'

David's sudden and unexpected declaration took the breath from Mr. Jones. He pulled his spectacles from his forehead, wiped the glasses feverishly, and put them back on to his nose. He gripped the two arms of his chair before he replied.

'What!' he demanded. 'Go to China! But—'

'China is a vast country, yes,' agreed our hero, taking the words from his mouth; 'but I was in close correspondence with my father. I know precisely where he was staying, and the roads he travelled. That limits the part to be searched. How I shall go out there I do not know. It may take years to bring about; but go I will. Something tells me that I shall be fortunate.'

There was a long silence between them before Mr. Jones ventured to break it. At first he had been inclined to look upon David as a foolish young fellow; but he had some knowledge of the lad, and of his father before him, and knew our hero to be a steady-going individual. Moreover he had heard that he was practical, and extremely persistent. He conjured up in his mind's eye the figures of Mr. and Mrs. Ebenezer Clayhill, and turned from them with some amount of annoyance.

'The whole matter is very unfortunate,' he said at last, 'and were it not that I now feel that I have your interests to protect, I should be tempted to retire from the post of executor to which your father expressly appointed me. Of course, I shall have an interview with Mr. Ebenezer and Mrs. Clayhill, and, as I have said, I shall insist that I have the paying of your allowance. Further, I will consult one of my legal friends on your behalf. With this letter before him, it is possible he will advise you to apply to the courts to arrest the administration of the will by Mr. Ebenezer Clayhill and his wife, pending a further search. In that case you would have time to go to China, and traverse the ground covered by your father. But how you will manage to get there passes my comprehension.'

He looked across at David, and slowly his serious expression melted into a smile. He recollected some words which Mrs. Clayhill had let fall at an interview he had once had with her. Of David she had remarked, when Mr. Jones had asked after him, 'he is an obstinate boy. Once he has made up his mind to accomplish a thing, nothing will shake him. He is just like his father.' And there was David searching the solicitor's face, unconsciously wearing an expression of dogged resolution. The square chin, already at such a youthful age showing firmness of purpose, was set in bulldog fashion. The thin lips were closed in one strong line. The eyes never flinched nor wavered.

'George!' cried Mr. Jones, suddenly stirred out of his professional calm, 'I'll help you. I like your spirit immensely; and, unofficially of course, I believe that you are being victimised. If it's money, why—.'

David held up his hand promptly. 'No thank you, Mr. Jones,' he said, warmly. 'I am going to do this on my own. It's awfully kind of you to think of offering money; but I'll make what I want, and put it to my allowance if need be. If I can, I won't touch the latter. Those people at 'The Haven' shall see that I am equal to my word. But you are helping me enormously by discussing the matter. Consult with this friend of yours, and if he says that an application on my part, with this letter of my father's, can arrest the splitting up of all his possessions for the time being, then there is hope. I shall have some time. I may be able to find the will we know he made.'

Looking at the matter when left to himself, Mr. Jones could not but admit that there was something of the wild-goose chase about our hero's resolution to go to China. The finding of the will left by Mr. Edward Harbor, since murdered by Boxers, was so extremely improbable that the effort seemed but wasted energy, failure but a foregone conclusion.

'But, on the contrary, the boy might have luck,' he told himself. 'There is a Providence that watches over such young fellows when their own parents ill-treat them. Perhaps David will come across the document, perhaps he will not. In any case, travel to China will open his mind and help him in the future, and if that is so, the time will not be wasted. That he will go there I am absolutely certain.'

He had dismissed our hero with a warm and encouraging shake of the hand, and a promise to communicate with him; and less than a week had passed when David was in the solicitor's office again.

'I have consulted with my friend,' Mr. Jones told him, 'and he believes that an application to the courts would be successful. I shall have it made on your behalf, and, of course, I shall bear the expense. Some day you may be able to repay me. If not—.'

David stood up at once. 'I shall repay you without doubt,' he declared solemnly. 'I mean to get on in the world; some day I shall be able to spare the money.'

'And that "some day" will be soon enough. In the meanwhile I shall go to the courts. This letter of yours, which I shall take care of, will be put in as evidence, and the judge will be told that you are going to China. As a result he may very well order that the estate be left in the hands of trustees, the income to be given as in the will we have, while the estate itself will remain untouched for a certain period. In three weeks' time the case should come forward.'

During those days our hero worked very hard at the establishment where he had charge of the lift.

'We couldn't have obtained a smarter young fellow,' the manager had declared more than once, 'while nothing seems a trouble to him. He keeps his lift and his livery spotlessly clean, and is most careful with our clients. I shall raise his wages.'

And raise them he did, David receiving twenty-two shillings a week after he had been there a fortnight. Up and down he travelled all day long in his lift, announcing at each floor the various departments of the store to be found there. Sharp young fellow that he was, he soon knew the ins and outs of the establishment, and was a perfect mine of information. He looked up trains for the firm's clients, directed others to various parts of London, and always displayed willingness and politeness. It was not to be wondered at, therefore, that he gained the esteem and confidence of his employers. As to the other employees, he was on excellent terms with them, except in a very few cases, the latter being men who, like the rest, detected our hero's evident superiority, and being jealous endeavoured to make matters unpleasant for him.

'Call David Harbor,' sounded across the floor of the store one day, when the place was empty of customers, while our hero was engaged in cleaning his lift. Promptly he rolled down his sleeves, slipped on his livery jacket, and stepped briskly to the manager's office, wondering why he was wanted.

'Sit down,' said the latter, when he had entered and closed the door. 'Now, Harbor, I wish to be confidential. For six weeks past we have been missing a number of valuables.'

At the words David rose from his seat, flushing a furious red, while his eyes flashed at the manager.

'You don't mean to suggest that I— —'

'Tut, tut,' came the interruption instantly. 'Sit down, Harbor. I said that valuables had been disappearing for the past six weeks. You have been here one month exactly; things were going before you came. Your arrival here has made no difference.'

David pulled his handkerchief from his pocket and mopped his forehead; for the news, the sudden thought that he might be the suspected person, had thrown him into a violent heat. 'I'm glad you put it like that, sir,' he said. 'I began to feel uncomfortable.'

'And I endeavoured at once to show you that you were by no means the suspected person. I told you I wished to talk to you confidentially. Well now, there is some one engaged here, we believe, who is robbing the firm. Up till now our efforts to trace the miscreant have proved unavailing. We applied to the police. They advised us that some one, wholly trustworthy, Mr. Harbor, wholly trustworthy, and whose resolution and pluck we could count on, should be left here to watch. The directors asked me to suggest a name. I gave yours without hesitation.'

He sat back in his chair to watch the effect his news had on our hero, and smiled serenely when he saw the latter tuck his handkerchief away and assume his most business-like expression.

'Yes, sir,' said David promptly, awaiting further information.

'This is the plan. You and the police are to work together, and when every one has left this establishment, you will pass in again with the help of a key I shall hand you. You will patrol the various departments during the night, and slip out before the hands arrive in the morning. Your place at the lift will be taken by a substitute for the time being. It will be given out that you are ill. Of course, there might be some risk attached to the undertaking.'

'I'll chance that,' declared David at once. 'I should rather enjoy the experience, not that I am anxious to be a thief taker. Still, I am in your employ and will obey whatever orders are given me.'

'Then you consent?' asked the manager.

'Certainly: I shall obey your orders seeing that I am in your service.'

'But you could decline to take this risk if you wished. However, we have considered the matter. There will be a salary of a pound a night while you are watchman, and a liberal reward if the offender is apprehended. Now I want you to finish your work, and join me at the police station. Don't let other employees see you going there. We will make our final arrangements with the officials of the police.'

It may be imagined that David was somewhat excited after such an announcement. Not for one moment did he think of declining the task required of him; for he looked upon it as a duty. He obtained good wages, these people had been kind to him, and if he could serve them, all the better. Besides, it might lead to a better and more highly-paid post. He polished the brass of his lift, put aside his livery, and emerged from the building, leaving one of the officials to close the establishment. Then, taking a side street, he hurried to the police station. Once there the final arrangements were soon made. The manager already knew that David was lodging with a policeman, and to our hero's pleasure he learned that Constable Hemming was to take duty outside the store, being relieved by a friend. Both were to be provided with keys, while David was presented with a basket containing food and drink. An electric torch was handed to him, as well as a life preserver and a whistle. Thus equipped he drove back to the establishment at ten that night, and slipped cautiously into the store.

Just keep moving and doing things all the while,' Hemming advised him. 'Lights are always kept going on all the floors, so that you'll have no difficulty in seeing. But it's wonderful how sleepy a fellow gets, especially when he's done the job on more than one occasion. Keep moving is the thing. Always remember to walk softly. If you spot anything funny, keep quiet, and come along to warn me. The end of a stick pushed through the letter-box will tell me I'm wanted. Don't get scared. It's only fools and babies as fly from their own shadows.'

Nevertheless David found the ordeal of promenading the huge store all alone in the silent hours of the night something of an ordeal. For there were a hundred minor sounds and queer noises to arrest his attention and rouse his suspicions. However, he mastered his fears, and soon began really to like the work. Nor did he forget the constable's advice. During the whole time he was on duty he never once sat down, save to eat a meal. All the rest of the time he was walking through the place, making not a sound with his cotton-padded soles, and because of the movement easily managing to keep awake. Indeed, so well did he sleep during the day when he returned with the constable, that he found no wish to rest at night. The exercise he took kept him wakeful and brisk, ready for anything. But a week came and went, and till then nothing had happened. It was on a Saturday night, soon after midnight, that our hero suddenly realised that another strange mixture of sounds was coming to his ear and echoing dully through the store. Instantly he was on the *qui vive*.

'Some one moving down below,' he told himself. 'Yes, in the basement: I'll slip down in that direction.'

Gripping his life preserver, and with the electric torch in his other hand, he stole across to the stairway, and crouching there peered over the banisters. No one was to be seen, and now his ear could not detect a noise. Then, suddenly, a sound reached him. It was a man whispering. Instantly David clutched the banister and lowered himself head foremost till he was able to look into the basement, in the centre of which one single light glimmered. Click! There was the sound of a muffled footstep, and then a sudden gleam of light over on the far wall. As David looked he saw the door of a huge cupboard, in which employees were wont to hang their hats and coats, slide open, while the figure of a man appeared. There was an electric torch in his hand, and with this he lit the way behind him. Then another figure appeared, and following him two others. They stepped into the store, carrying a heavy burden with them.

'At last,' said our hero, struggling back into the stairway. 'Time I went to warn Constable Hemming.'

Chapter IV
A Responsible Position

There was the muffled sound of many feet in the basement as David slipped across to the doorway of the store, where was situated the letter-box through which he would be able to pass a signal to Constable Hemming; and for a while he stood still listening.

'Better make absolutely sure that they are coming up here,' he told himself, tip-toeing back towards the head of the basement stairs. 'And there's another thing to consider. If they have entered through that cupboard, they will escape that way, unless, of course—my word! that would alter matters very materially.'

For at first sight, and remembering what he had read about other burglaries, David had taken it for granted that the men he had seen stepping into the basement had gained access to the cupboard through a hole in the wall. Then, suddenly, the idea had flashed across his brain that probably they had merely secreted themselves there during the day, unseen by any save, perhaps, an accomplice in the store. In which case their retreat was cut off.

'Out of the question,' he told himself, bending over the basement banisters. 'There is that heavy parcel. They couldn't have brought that in. No, they have broken through the wall in some manner. Let me see.'

In his mind's eye he inspected the surroundings of the store, but obtained little help from his review of the dwellings. For though a mixed property lay adjacent to the store, and, indeed, was attached to its walls, the majority of the premises were divided into numerous offices and workrooms, while there was an enormous number of tenants. However, his reflections were suddenly cut short, for one of the four men below suddenly put in an appearance, and came hurrying up the stairs, his rubber soles making not a sound. Instantly David took to his heels and ran across to the manager's office, the latter affording a safe asylum near to the door through which he was to give his signal. He bolted through the open swing-doors of the office, and turning round peered through the glass screen which helped to form it. His heart began to beat furiously; for the men had all reached the ground floor by now, and were advancing direct for the manager's office.

'They'll see me at once, of course,' thought David, on the verge of panic 'I can't get out without their catching sight of me. Where am I to hide?'

The answer came to him within the second as he ran his eyes round the office, for all the world as if he were a hunted animal. 'Ah, behind the bookcase. That'll do for me.'

Quite close to him, with its back placed within a foot of one wall of the office was a big desk, with a leather top, on which ink, paper, and pens were scattered. And posted on it, right at the back, was a small bookcase, filled with directories and a heterogeneous mixture of books and papers, besides a bale of leather samples. It afforded the only hiding-place possible, and David slid towards it eagerly. The space behind was barely sufficient to accommodate him, for our hero was inclined to be somewhat bulky, and showed promise of one day possessing broad shoulders and big limbs. However, by pushing firmly, he was able to roll the desk a couple of inches outward on the parquet flooring, and that without so much as a sound. He was hardly ensconced in the space behind when one of the strangers entered.

'Bring it in here, bring it in here,' David heard him say, with a peculiarly nasal accent, while the words were slurred as if a foreigner had given vent to them. 'There, lay it down, we are not ready for it yet. Bah! why not a light here of all places? There are lamps going all over the store, and the police know them and take no further notice. But here, where we want them, none. *Peste!* How stupid of the owners!'

There came a snigger from the man directly behind him, while David could hear the deep breathing of the two who were carrying the long, strange object.

'It's heavy, at any rate,' he told himself. 'Let's take a squint at 'em. Jolly glad I am that there isn't a lamp going here. The light would come through between the books and show me nicely. My word! This is a fine peep show! There are a dozen niches through which I can get a view. That's an electric torch. Ain't the chap careful to keep the light on the floor too! Every one of them wearing gloves. This is interesting.'

He almost forgot to think of himself and the undoubted danger of his own position. For the four men in the manager's office, one of them not more than the desk's width from David, occupied the greater part of his thoughts. It was true that there was no light in this particular part of the store; but, then, elsewhere there were electric lamps, and the illumination of the whole place and of this office in particular, though not brilliant, was ample for our hero. His eyes were used to the dimness, and as he stared between the books on their dusty shelves, he was able first of all to detect the fact that all four burglars wore kid gloves on their hands and rubber shoes on their feet For the rest, three were undoubtedly of dark complexion and wore moustaches, while the fourth, the only one whose aspect was decidedly English, was clean-shaven. He leaned his back against the wall close to the bookcase, and breathed heavily while David surveyed his companions.

'Can't think why them cylinders are so heavy,' our hero heard him grumble. 'From the look of the things, with their rope coatings, you'd say as they was that light a child could play with 'em. But, my! they make a chap blow. Where's the safe?'

'S-s-sh, my friend. People will find us before we find the safe if you make such a bother,' declared the man who had led the way into the office, and who for a moment had used his electric torch. 'The safe is here, without doubt, seeing that it was here this morning, and such things are not moved as easily as are boxes. Behold the safe, my friend.'

Tucked away in his hiding-place David went hot all over, till beads of perspiration streamed from his forehead, and his clothing clung to him uncomfortably; for in the leader of the gang—for such the speaker seemed to be—he suddenly recognised an official of the store who had had some years of service with his employers, and who was an expert in the jewellery department.

'And is a burglar all the while,' thought David, common sense telling him that the man was an expert in this branch also; for otherwise, how could he wear such a business-like air? How could he appear so unconcerned, so used to midnight entries into closed premises? 'Queer,' thought our hero. 'It just shows his cunning. The articles which have been disappearing have not been stones or jewellery. Valuable furs have gone, and Henricksen has nothing to do with that department. So they're after the safe? I should laugh right out if it didn't happen to be distinctly dangerous; for our manager took care to empty it. There are useless books inside; nothing more.'

'Behold the safe, my friend,' said Henricksen again, triumphantly, his eyes flashing as he turned towards the clean-shaven man beside the bookcase, while his electric torch played on the huge mass of painted steel, wherein the most valuable jewels and the money of the store were wont to rest at night. 'You grumble at the weight of a couple of cylinders; let us see if you will grumble when we come to handle the gold. But we must be moving; there is big work before us, and it is now twenty minutes after midnight. Yes, precisely that time.'

His coolness was amazing. David saw him refer to a neat little watch strapped to his left wrist, and noted at the same moment that the gloves he wore were of reddish colour, while the left one was split up the back. Then his eyes went to the cylinders lying snugly on the floor, and from them to the other men.

'They might be any nationality,' he thought. 'To look at them now they don't appear to be ruffians, but there you are, old ideas are being exploded every day of the year. A criminal face does not always mean a murderer or a burglar. Some of the most cunning fellows known to the police of late have had quite a sanctimonious appearance. The well-groomed, gentlemanly criminal who is a clever hypocrite has a better chance to-day than the man with the face of a bull dog, the forehead of a Cree Indian, and the narrow, half-closed eyes of a Chinee. What are they up to now?'

He might well ask the question, for David was not used to burglarious enterprises. Up till this moment he had hardly dared to imagine how the men would endeavour to force the huge safe in the office. Then he remembered the cylinders, and remembering them, and drawing upon his slender engineering knowledge, he realised that modern methods are adopted not alone by scientists who mostly discover them, and by up-to-date manufacturers, but also by up-to-date malefactors. The oxy-acetylene flame, he knew, would eat its way into a mass of steel so tough that not even a finely-tempered drill would touch it. Also, that it would burn a path far sooner than the same could be formed by the aid of the best of tools. His past knowledge told him all that. But how would these men set about the task, and — —

'That's not the sort of thing I want to be interested in just now,' he suddenly told himself. 'I want to get out of this, and without their knowing; how's that to be done? A fine fool I shall look if I have to watch their operations and see them get away without summoning those posted outside. How's it to be done?'

He might ask himself the question a thousand times, but yet there was no answer. Puzzle his wits as he might, he could see no way out of the difficulty. He was trapped; he was virtually a prisoner. A movement on his part would be fatal; these men were armed perhaps.

'Armed — that's a shooter, a magazine pistol!' He almost said the words aloud of a sudden, for his danger was brought full face before him. The man, Henricksen, pulled something from his trouser pocket and deposited it on the desk behind which David was crouching. The thing glittered in the feeble rays. It flashed brightly as the electric torch happened to cast a beam in its direction. It was a Browning pistol without a shadow of doubt. It brought David Harbor to a full stop for the moment; even his heart seemed to arrest its palpitations.

'Unstrap the rugs,' he heard Henricksen say, as if he were a mile off, 'fix the props, and let us get going. When all is ready Spolikoff will get along and watch the door and windows, while Ovanovitch will mount the stairs and clear every jewel that he thinks worth having. The Admiral will lend me a hand. Got those glasses, Admiral?'

The individual alluded to, he with the clean-shaven face, searched in an inner pocket, and produced two long cases. He placed them on the desk, and then proceeded to help his companions. Nor could there now be a doubt in David's mind that the gang was experienced and well drilled. There was not a hitch, not a false move in the proceedings. They went about the work like men who had done the same before, and who in each case knew what was required of them. A huge, thick rug or mat—David could not tell which— was unwound from the outside of the two rope-covered cylinders, and was quickly supported on four wooden legs, so contrived as to telescope at the will of the owners. A second rug was slung at one side, making a species of tent, the roof being meant without doubt to arrest the glare of the flame about to be employed, and keep it from reflecting on the ceiling. While the side curtain would keep the rays from the shop windows and from the eyes of curious or suspicious passers.

'And now for the burner,' Henricksen said, seating himself on a chair beneath the tent, and donning a pair of dark-coloured spectacles. 'Put on your pair of glasses, Admiral. I've known a man pretty nigh blinded by the glare of the flame, and in any case, supposing there was trouble, you wouldn't be able to see when you wanted to hook it. Fix those rubber tubes. We'll have things going nicely in a second.'

David took in a long breath as he watched the scene, and once more his eyes surveyed each member of the gang. 'Two Russians,' he told himself, looking at the dark moustached men told off to leave the office. 'Spolikoff and Ovanovitch. The sort of alien not wanted in this country, and the Admiral is, I suppose, an ex-sailor—a bad hat, dismissed from the lower deck, a confirmed criminal. The only Englishman amongst them—what an artful fellow Henricksen must be! Who would have thought that the man employed in the jewellery store could be such a double-faced rascal! And there's his pistol.'

Yes, there it was, twinkling in the dim light, fascinating David, drawing his eyes in its direction every half minute, inviting him to inspect it further, rousing his envy, making his fingers itch to possess and handle it.

'Why not? With a long reach I could do it. Why not? It's a risk. I'll take it.'

It was typical of the lad that he should come to a sudden decision, and having so decided, should proceed to carry the task out with all his courage and determination. Was that not David's character? Had he not already shown courage and determination? What were Mrs. Clayhill's words on our hero? 'Stubborn and obstinate,' she had misrepresented him. 'Perseveres in a thing he has decided on; just like his father.'

At such times her none too pleasant features bore a somewhat ferocious aspect 'Ain't she just angry?' David used to say, as he went his way, deeming it best to absent himself for the moment. 'Just sparks flashing from her eyes. She doesn't seem as if she could be friendly. I must be an out and out obstinate fellow.'

And so he was. David was an obstinate fellow without a shadow of doubt, but with this saving clause—he was not selfish, and he was possessed of common sense; he could criticise his own actions and impulses. If he once, on maturer reflection, came to the conclusion that a certain decision was wrong, he had the sense to change it. His obstinacy was confined to matters wherein he felt that there could be no error. Witness his intention of fending for himself, of making his way alone in the world. David had that as a fixed and firm-rooted purpose before him now. His strong chin squared itself in the most emphatic manner whenever the matter crossed his mind, which was nearly always. But here was the pistol.

'I'll have it,' he told himself, his muscles tightening. 'One long stretch and there it is. Ah! they're turning their backs; I'll have a chance before very long.'

'Now the match; set the flame going,' he heard Henricksen say, and looking beneath the tent-like structure saw a sudden flash, and the profiles of this man and the 'Admiral.' The latter was holding a match towards the end of the long brass burner which Henricksen gripped in his hands. David noticed that two separate pipes converged towards the end into one, from which a small flame now spouted, while Henricksen controlled two taps, one for each of the tubes, with his fingers. Farther back a rubber tube went to each of those of metal leading to the burner, and ended at one of the cylinders, or rather, to put it in the correct order, began there, carrying the gas to the burner.

'You two get off,' said Henricksen, seeing that he had a flame. 'Spolikoff, keep moving up and down, and if you hear a latch click, sit down as tight as possible. The police look into the store every time they pass, and might see you. Admiral, pull that rug round a bit. The light will break too much round the corner.'

What a clever criminal he was! David marvelled that it could be the same sleek, suave man who waited in the jewellery department, and enticed customers to buy the things he offered. Then his eyes closed suddenly, for Henricksen's fingers manipulated the taps of his burner, and at once a fierce flame spurted out, casting about it a dazzling light. Peering round the corner of the rug which the 'Admiral' had drawn towards him, and shading his eyes behind an enormous directory, David caught a glimpse of the intensely hot jet of flame playing on the door of the safe in the neighbourhood of the lock. It seemed that he could actually see the paint peeling off, while, almost at once, the metal beneath became white hot. In less time than he could have believed it possible it seemed to be pitting, as if the flame were devouring portions of it. Then, very suddenly, the 'Admiral' pulled at the rug again, and the glare and the figures beneath the tent were obliterated. David gently removed one of the ponderous volumes, stretched his arm through the opening, and possessed himself of the Browning revolver.

'So far, so good!' he thought. 'Now to get out of the place. Wonder whether I could climb over the glass partition? No, wouldn't do; I should be seen by Henricksen at once.'

He forgot for the second that the ruffian who went by that name, and who in his everyday life was looked upon as a clever and capable salesman in the store, was at that moment wearing dark spectacles, through which he could see nothing but the glare of the acetylene flame. David failed to remember that, even armed with those glasses, the glare was such that a man manipulating the blow-pipe would require a few moments rest to accustom his eyes to lesser illumination. Then the thought occurred to him. He stretched his neck round the edge of the bookcase, and caught a glimpse of the flame. Its brilliance was intense. It caused his pupils to contract with painful suddenness, and turning his head away, he found that everything was a dark blank. For the moment his own eyes were useless. The experience emboldened him.

'I'll creep out and across the office behind the tent,' he said. 'Then I'll dodge the Russian Spolikoff. Ah! what's that?'

A motor horn sounded suddenly out in the street, and he heard the rattle of a passing automobile. The next instant there came a sharp click, which was easily heard above the gentle roar of the oxy-acetylene flame. Promptly the glare died down. Henricksen had manipulated the taps and had shut down the gas.

'Stay still,' David heard him whisper to the man known as the 'Admiral.' 'It's a policeman inspecting. He won't see the glare; he couldn't with this tent. What's he making all that noise about?'

It was Constable Hemming without a doubt, and if the truth had been guessed at, the honest fellow had suddenly become fearful for the safety of our hero. There was a second constable on duty with him, patrolling the outskirts of the store, and the latter had reported a sudden glare within. Hemming was sceptical; but he went at once to the letter-box, and opened the flap with a loud click. Yes, there did seem to be a glare over the manager's office, he thought, but it died away at once.

'He's been having a feed,' he suggested to his comrade. 'Switched on a light in the office for a while, and then turned it out again. He'll have heard the latch go, he'd have shouted if there was trouble.'

But the sound he had made had been sufficient to alarm Henricksen and his comrades. David saw the 'Admiral' suddenly crouch close to the floor and grope in his pocket. Henricksen tore his glasses from his eyes, and emerging from the tent, groped on the desk for the weapon he had left there. A growl escaped him as he failed to find it. His fingers ran over the leather surface, over the pens and ink bottle and paper, but still they were unsuccessful. Then he turned to his comrade.

'That fellow made a heap of noise,' he said. 'I thought he might be suspicious. Suppose he didn't see or hear Spolikoff; but where's my Browning? I could swear that I left it on the desk here.'

'I saw you,' came the answer. 'You put it down close to the ink bottle: ain't it there?'

'Not a sign of it. Can't very well see yet, for that glare is terrific in spite of smoked glasses. But I've run my fingers everywhere, and there's no shooter. Spolikoff's taken it perhaps.'

Meanwhile, David had crouched behind the bookcase again, and for the moment almost shivered. It was true that he was now armed; but would that help him against such miscreants, considering he was like a rat in a trap, hemmed in the closest quarters? He even thought wildly of making a dash for the outside of the manager's office, and was bracing his muscles for the effort, when a dusky figure came sliding in through the glass doorway, to be detected instantly by our hero, but not so by the others, for their backs were in that direction, while even if it had been otherwise their eyes were still hardly fit for such a task.

'S-s-shish!' said the man, whispering. 'It's Spolikoff. A policeman came to the opening and rattled. I dived down and sat still; then I managed to get to a place where I could see through a chink in the shutters. Two constables were talking outside. I saw them part and walk away along the pavement. It's all clear again.'

The 'Admiral' gave vent to a sigh of relief, and wiped the sweat from his forehead, while Henricksen turned round and stared hard at the man, still unable to see him.

'You get back to that peep hole right away,' he commanded gruffly, 'and watch out for the police. Give us a signal when they're coming. I'm afraid they may see the glare. Did you walk off with my shooter?'

Spolikoff denied the charge promptly. 'Here's my own,' he said. 'But perhaps Ovanovitch took it; he has a way of borrowing things! I will go and ask him.'

'You'll just get right off to that peep hole,' he was commanded. 'Ovanovitch can hand over the gun when he comes down. Should say he'll not be long; that place upstairs don't take long clearing. My! won't this be a haul! I've done the firm in for a thousand pounds already during the past six weeks. Monday's their day for banking, and I reckon we shall clear double the amount once we get this safe open. Get along, Spolikoff. Now, Admiral, put your back to it; we've a long job before us.'

David breathed more easily as Henricksen gave up for the moment his quest for the revolver. Then he watched the two men creep into the tent again, and drag the side curtain still more round them. He waited till the glare of the flame once more reached his eyes, and then began to slide along to the far side of the bookcase. Bang! crash! A volume which had been resting unbeknown to him on the very edge of the desk toppled over at the movement, and went to the floor with a thud. Henricksen and his comrade darted from beneath their covering as if they had been shot.

'What was it? What was it?' the former asked breathlessly, evidently scared by the noise. 'Something fell quite close to us. Look about.'

But that was just exactly what they found a difficulty in doing, for they had again donned their smoked spectacles, and had had their flame playing on the safe. However, the 'Admiral' dropped on to his knees and went groping about the floor close to the desk till his fingers came in contact with the fallen book. A low guffaw broke from him.

'Here's what's caused all the pother,' he laughed. 'In searching for that shooter you must have just balanced the book on the edge of the desk. Of course it went bang: it would do—just to scare us. Blessed if these glasses don't bother a fellow. Even now I can't see a thing; it's all feeling. But it's a book all right, no mistake about it.'

Another growl came from Henricksen: he hated such interruptions. True, he had had to put up with them before in the course of his criminal career, but he imagined that by now he was hardened. It angered him to find himself so easily scared. For the moment, too, he was almost suspicious; the strange disappearance of his revolver, coupled with the fallen book, tended to alarm him.

'I'm jumpy to-night,' he told himself, with an oath. 'Fact is, if I am ever to be taken I'd fifty times rather have it elsewhere, and not here where I'm at home as it were. Come along, let's get to at the job; it'll take a couple of hours to work round this lock.'

A couple of hours: then David had plenty of time before him. Should he stay where he was, and not risk further movement till matters had settled down a little?

To be absolutely candid regarding him, there was doubt in his mind on this occasion, doubt engendered by fear of what might happen. And who, remembering all the circumstances, could feel surprise? Where he was there was security. He had already had it proved to him that the back of the bookcase was an excellent hiding-place. Why not stay there in safety, then? Why not wait a little and see what turned up?

'Bah!'—he could have kicked himself—'Funking, are you?' he almost growled aloud. 'Putting your tail between your legs because you are afraid of these men—afraid when you've got a revolver! Gurr!'

He flicked beads of perspiration from the corners of his eyes, and once more squeezed stealthily along behind the case. Yet again he caught the glare of the oxy-acetylene flame, while the gentle buzz of the jet struck upon his ear. Another motor car passed in the street with a gurr and a blast from its horn; then there was silence. David reached the edge of the case, looked cunningly about him, and stole straightway to the door. He turned to watch the glare, and caught a glimpse of the 'Admiral's' leg as it showed beyond the curtain. Then he stared into the main portion of the store looking eagerly for Spolikoff, but without success.

'Got to dodge him,' he told himself. 'Got to reach the door and give the alarm. Supposing I do? What'll happen?'

He was now some fifteen paces from the office, and stood for a few seconds considering the question. What would the burglars do once the alarm was given, and Constable Hemming had placed his key in the lock and thrown the door open?

BURGLARS AT THE STORE

'It's as clear as daylight,' thought David. 'They'll run below right away. Perhaps they'll shoot as they go. In any case, they'll be out and away before the police can guess what they're doing. I've got to put a stop to that.'

He stole forward again in the direction of the door, wondering what course he ought to pursue; then, as if doubtful, he turned towards the entry to the stairway leading to the basement.

'Why not?' he asked himself. 'I'll go down there and—'

His hair almost stood on end; his heart seemed to stop abruptly and his muscles felt paralysed all in one brief second; for a figure was coming towards him, a dusky figure, sidling silently across the floor; and in a flash he recognised the man. It was Spolikoff, the Russian, sent by Henricksen to keep watch and ward.

Chapter V
London's Alien Criminals

If ever David Harbor had felt inclined to play the coward it was at the precise moment, on this adventurous night when he came so abruptly, and so unexpectedly, face to face with one of the men who were engaged in robbing his employers' store. Behind him, in the office, he had left Henricksen and the ruffian known as the 'Admiral' busily engaged with their oxy-acetylene flame, eating a hole into the safe which they hoped and imagined was well filled with gold. Upstairs was the man Ovanovitch, clearing the cases of all their portable valuables, while here, on the main floor, was Spolikoff, a Russian—a man given naturally to deeds of violence—placed there to watch for the very police whom it was our hero's object to summon. The very man from whom he wished to keep farthest away was stealing towards him in the semi-darkness.

David drew in a deep breath. His hand clutched the revolver he had managed to secure. With an effort he controlled his muscles.

'Run! Shout for help!' some one seemed to scream in his ear. 'Steady,' he told himself, summoning all his pluck. 'Steady, my boy; play the game. No use bolting; he'll be just as surprised as I am.'

But, as it turned out, there was no question of surprise. While David was prepared for anything—to shoot at the man, to knock him to the ground with his fist, to rush over towards the door and bang upon it—Spolikoff sidled up to him, and spoke in a whisper that almost cloaked his foreign accent.

'That you, Admiral?' he asked. 'They've passed again, those policemen; but I didn't signal. There's no need; no one can see the glare now. You've pulled the curtain round so well.'

David nodded. He was wondering whether he could trust himself to answer the fellow, for it was obvious that his own identity was not even suspected. Then, emboldened by that fact, he answered the man in a hoarse whisper.

'I came along out here to make sure. It's fine, ain't it? Them police couldn't suspect that we'd got a hot flame going against the safe. Look here, my boy, Henricksen wants you to go along up to Ovanovitch and give him a hand. When you've cleared the jewels, get away up to the next floor. He says some new furs came in yesterday, and you could carry away in your arms enough to keep you for a year. Get along quick.'

The Russian looked at him for a moment as if he suspected, though, as a matter of fact, he was merely puzzling to translate the meaning of the words, for as yet he was not an excellent English scholar.

'Get along up and help Ovanovitch, yes,' he repeated. 'Then—I did not follow—you said?'

'S-s-sh! The police!'

There came a sudden rattle at the letter-box, whereat both he and the Russian sank promptly to the ground, while David imagined that a faint light over by the office lessened. Then there was silence again. A heavy footfall was heard on the pavement, and after it, silence once more. Slowly he and the Russian rose to their feet.

'What was it?' asked the man. 'You said I was to help Ovanovitch.'

'Listen,' whispered David, speaking very plainly, 'help Ovanovitch with the jewels.'

'Yes, yes; I have that'

'Then take him to the floor up above.'

'Floor up above. Yes, yes; I have that too.'

'Where you will find some valuable furs brought in only yesterday.'

'Only yesterday, furs; valuable furs. Yes; go on.'

'You can carry enough away on your arm to make you rich for a year. Got it?'

Spolikoff nodded vigorously, and gave expression to some guttural words of approval.

'Now?' he asked. 'You watch here?'

'Yes,' said David, 'Go at once; no need to hurry back.'

His hand was shaking ever so little as he took the Russian by the sleeve and urged him towards the stairs; for the feeble light above the place had suddenly shown him another figure. The man was descending the stairs, and was almost at the bottom. David could see that a bundle was suspended over his back. It was Ovanovitch without doubt, descending now that his task was completed.

'Tell him; go up at once,' David managed to whisper, though his tongue almost stuck to the roof of his mouth. 'I am going back to Henricksen.'

He slid off at once, slipped behind a huge showcase, and then stared back through the glass at the two Russians. And as he did so the tight feeling about his chest and neck slowly lessened. He drew in the first comfortable breath he had taken for some minutes. A sigh almost escaped him; for Spolikoff had been absolutely deceived. It was clear that he was not in the smallest degree suspicious. He had taken our hero for the Admiral, and was obeying instructions in a manner almost child-like. He went at once to Ovanovitch, and for a few seconds they whispered on the stairs. Then they turned their backs to the ground floor and went up two steps at a time, as if eager to get to their destination.

'Got 'em,' David could have shouted, though he restrained himself, hugging his arms instead. 'Got 'em, I do believe. Now for the rest of the business.' His brain had been working hard in the last few minutes, and already he had mapped out a course of procedure. After all, that was exactly like the young fellow; his friends knew him to be exceedingly practical. Edward Harbor, his father, had endeavoured to train his boy to conduct matters of any moment with sense and discretion.

'Decide first of all what you're going to do,' he had often said. 'Don't start without a plan, all haphazard, and find when you are half way through that matters aren't promising. Stand away a bit, as it were, and have a clear view; then make your plans, and set to at the business.' Practical? Of course it was. Common sense management? Who can doubt it? A little advanced for one of David's age? Certainly, if you wish so to describe it. But that is worth remedying. Others can be trained as our hero had been, and the training has its undoubted advantages; for a practical young fellow is of infinitely greater value in these strenuous days than a lad always wool-gathering, who lacks energy and initiative, who begins a task only to fail, who succeeds only where a course of procedure has been already laid down, and when previous practice has made perfect. It is the uncertainties we want to train our lads to face, as well as the hum-drum certainties of this life.

'Got 'em,' David ejaculated again, in a deep whisper. 'Now to close the holes and divide the conspirators. First downstairs—that is the main burrow I have to see to.'

He had lost all his trepidation now. True, he was more than a little excited; but his hand no longer shook. He had seen already the possibilities of making a gigantic success of what had at first appeared to be an enormously difficult task. Straightway he stole across to the stairway leading to the basement, and tripped down three steps at a time. Then he ran across to the cupboard through which the four men had gained access to the store. Out came his electric torch, and a beam was flashed into the interior.

'As I thought: these fellows must have hired a house or a room in one of the buildings lying up against this place, and have knocked a hole clean through the wall. Then they cut through the back of the cupboard. No; no they didn't; they bored holes through the wood in a big circle, and so managed to remove a piece without making a sound. If they had employed a saw I should have heard them. Now, I shut the cupboard, and lock the door.'

It was not a flimsy affair, this cupboard, but a strongly built piece of furniture, firmly attached to the wall, and having doors which slid along in grooves. David gently moved the doors into place, found a key in the lock, and shot the bolt to. Then he tried to open the cupboard. It was closed and defied his efforts.

'Number one loop hole gone,' he said. 'Now for the warning and number two.'

He had planned out the whole course of movement, and came hopping up the stairs again, three at a time. A quick glance told him that the oxy-acetylene flame was still in use. A dull glow on the ceiling told its tale without shadow of error, while as he listened a gentle buzz came to his ear. From the upper floor there was not so much as a sound. At once he crossed to the door, and pulled the flap of the letter-box open. Click! Down went the glare over by the manager's office. Lying prone on the floor, and staring in that direction, David saw a man's head protruding from the opening. Then the fellow stepped out and stood listening. A whisper came to his ear, and at once the Admiral—for he it was without doubt—slid back into the manager's office to help in the task of forcing the safe. The reflection on the ceiling told its tale again promptly.

'Out with the life preserver, and then upstairs,' said David. 'No time to wait; those fellows will have found their furs by now.'

Very craftily he pushed the end of the life preserver through the flap, and left it wedged in position. Then he ran across the floor to the stairs and raced up them. Passing the first floor, he was soon at the entrance to the second. And as he reached it his eyes fell on the two figures of the Russians. They were staggering along the centre passage between the glass show cases, their arms piled with furs. They were thirty paces away, perhaps, whispering as they came.

Dare he do it? Dare he pull the door of this portion of the store to in their faces?

David closed his teeth with a firm click; his chin assumed that very bulldog squareness for which he was notorious. He stepped coolly into the opening, gripped the iron fire door, with which the entrance to every one of the departments of the store was furnished, and brought it to with a bang. The hand-operated latch went to its socket with a scrunch. The door was fast. Number two loop hole was closed. The burglars were inevitably separated.

'And now for the last move.'

Conscious that the noise he had made might well have reached Henricksen, and yet hopeful that it had not done so, David descended the stairs faster than ever before in his life. He reached the ground floor just as a sound came from the letter-box. He fancied he heard voices outside. He was sure that the oxy-acetylene flame was working, and at that second watched as its reflection seemed to be wiped away from the ceiling above the manager's office. Then he did a smart thing. He opened the outside doors of the lift with a bang, leaped in, and ran the elevator up till it was half way through the gap leading to the first floor. He brought it to a rest there with a sudden jerk, and throwing himself flat on its floor, levelled his weapon at the door of the manager's office. And by then there was a commotion in that direction. Two figures come helter-skelter from the opening, their hands held before them, their smoked glasses already torn from their faces. At the same instant there came the sound of a key in a lock, and then the main entrance of the store was burst open.

'Stop there, Henricksen and the Admiral!' David shouted. 'Stop where you are or I fire. Constable, hold the door, I have closed the other places.'

Ping! Bang! From some point up above our hero, there came a revolver shot, and he heard the missile thud against the roof of the elevator and tinkle on to the floor near him. Ping! A second came, and then he felt the elevator moving. It was ascending. Some one had put it into operation from above. At once he guessed what had happened. The two Russians, shut into the fur department, had heard the lift working. They had torn the doors open, and reaching through had gripped the rope by means of which it was operated. David at one sprang to his feet and gripped the handle which operated the rope. Instantly he brought the machine to a stop, and turning the handle again, brought the elevator back to its former position, a shot coming from above as he did so. Then he cast his eyes into the store, and at once took in the position, which had altered in the space of a few seconds. There were two constables at the door, Hemming and another, the latter of whom was at that moment lustily blowing his whistle. At the entrance to the stairs leading to the basement stood the Admiral, a revolver in his hands, while the other rascal was nowhere visible; but a minute later he came racing up the stairs, and burst into the department.

'Give me the shooter,' he cried, breathlessly. 'They've shut the cupboard below and boxed us in. Give it me. I'm not afraid to use it.'

He seized the weapon from his comrade's hand, and in an instant there was a flash. The constable blowing his whistle staggered into the doorway. David at once leaned forward, levelled his own weapon, and pulled on the trigger. And in the space of a second he had ejected three bullets in the direction of Henricksen; for his was an automatic pistol, the class of weapon that wants careful controlling, and which will fire seven shots in less number of seconds, automatically moving a fresh cartridge into position after each shot. Certainly the bullets astounded David, and Henricksen also. He swung round, and then our hero knew what it was to be under fire. Something hissed past his cheek. The hair on his head stirred restlessly. A red-hot brand appeared to have been of a sudden thrust right through his body. But he was game to the last. He leaned over a little, fixed his revolver sights as well as he was able, and pressed his trigger again.

An instant later Henricksen went staggering up against one of the glass show cases. He upset the whole affair, and came crashing to the floor with glass smashing and splintering all about him; then his comrade darted forward, and stooped to pick up the weapon which he had dropped.

'Stand away from that place,' David commanded hoarsely. 'I'll drop you, Admiral, as sure as you move a step. Now, hands up above your head.'

'Admiral, Admiral, what's that?' came from the doorway. 'Where are you, David Harbor?'

'In the lift, half way up,' our hero called out, wondering vaguely at the weakness of his own voice. 'Half way up, Hemming. The man who fired at you, and whom I have just sent down is Henricksen, one of the employees here. The fellow with his arms up is known as the Admiral.'

'Phew.' There came a shrill whistle from Hemming. 'The Admiral did you say? Wanted in a dozen capitals. Swindler, forger, burglar, everything.'

'And two Russians upstairs, whom I have trapped in the fur department. Now, Hemming, got those handcuffs?'

Feeling curiously shaky David touched the handle of the lift again, and brought it down to the floor level, unmindful of the shots which still came from above. And all the while he held his weapon directed at the man standing so close to Henricksen.

'Now, Hemming,' he called out. 'Shut the door, or he might try to bolt. Slip the handcuffs on him; but first of all, switch on the lights just inside the door.'

It was all done in a few moments. Constable Hemming was a sharp officer, and was not above taking advice or instructions from any one. He flooded the store with light with one movement of his finger. Then there came the metallic ring of steel. Something bright flashed under the electric lamps, while the officer strode across the floor, banging the door behind him. Click. One of the bracelets went over the wrist of the disconsolate Admiral.

'Come you along here,' commanded Hemming, dragging the man across to a radiator, bolted to the floor. 'Put that other hand there. Now, move if you can. You'll have to take the house with you.'

He passed the end of his chain through an interval in the radiator, and clicked the bracelet over the man's other wrist, leaving the Admiral firmly chained to the place.

'What now?' he demanded. 'Guess you've made a haul here. The Admiral! Gosh! The most wanted of 'em all! This is a doing!'

'Get to the door and open it. First, though, pick up that shooter,' said David. 'Don't forget that we have those Russian fellows upstairs.'

'Russians! Who? Where?' demanded Hemming, his face expressing unbounded surprise.

'Spolikoff and Ovanovitch, two men of about thirty years of age, dark complexioned, wearing black moustaches,' answered David, staggering out of the lift. 'They've done nothing but fire down on me. The top of the lift is like a sieve.'

He tripped as he stepped, and went staggering up against one of the show cases, to which his fingers clung. Meanwhile Hemming stood back exclaiming.

'Spolikoff! Ovanovitch! Russians. Men of about thirty. Dark. Dark moustaches—Mister Harbor, you've hit up against a fine crowd. The wonder is that they haven't made mincemeat of you. Spolikoff and Ovanovitch! Notorious anarchists; burglars who have been cracking cribs up and down this country.'

He wiped his forehead with a brilliantly red handkerchief which he withdrew from the inside of his helmet, and puffed cheeks and lips out. It was a staggerer to Constable Hemming, this capture which he and David were making. Then he walked across to the door as if he were in a dream, and opened it just as three constables arrived on the scene.

'We heard the whistle and came along,' explained one. 'Crispen lay on the mat. He's hit in the head; a bad scalp wound I should say. We've applied a first dressing. He's sitting with his back against the wall, feeling chippy. What's all this?'

'What's all this!' Constable Hemming could hardly contain himself. 'What's all this!' he gasped again. 'Why, just a fine capture! You know there's been a young fellow watching. Bless me, he's cornered the Admiral. I've got the bracelets on that gentleman and have chained him fast to the radiator. There's one of the fellows down, while upstairs, barred in, are two Russians, the two Russians we have been after this many a day—Spolikoff and Ovanovitch.'

There was no doubt that the news impressed his comrades, who came crowding into the store after Hemming.

'They'll shoot at sight,' said one of the constables, as they discussed the matter. 'How are we to nab them?'

'Let's ask Harbor. Harbor,' shouted Hemming, coming across the store, while a further reinforcement of half a dozen police officers poured in at the door. 'Where is he?'

They discovered David grovelling on his knees, looking particularly white about the gills.

'Felt a little upset,' he explained lamely. 'What's happened? Have you taken the Russians?'

There was little doubt but that he had actually lost consciousness while the officers were discussing matters, and now was puzzled to know what they had been doing. Hemming helped him to his feet and looked sharply at his lodger. He wondered what had caused David to fall to the floor, and never guessed the reason.

'Too much excitement, perhaps,' he thought 'Anyway, we'll give him a draft. Here, Sergeant, some sal volatile for this youngster.'

They mixed the stuff before his face, and David drained the glass at a gulp.

'Now,' he gasped. 'Those Russians?'

'They're upstairs right enough,' said the sergeant. 'I heard 'em a moment ago. How are they placed? Give us an idea as to how we can get at them? Suppose they're armed?'

The young fellow, looking so exceedingly pale still, took the officer by the sleeve and led him into the lift. Then he switched on the light and invited him to inspect the roof.

'Goodness! There are a dozen holes, bullet holes. And—blood on the floor. Whose? Yours?'

He swung round on David instantly, and like Hemming treated him to a very critical stare.

'A mere nothing,' said our hero, somewhat feebly, smiling all the same.

'Set men to watch all round the place.'

'Done already,' came the prompt answer. 'I placed the men as soon as we heard there was an alarm.'

'Put two at the entrance to the basement staircase, and send two more down to the large cupboard with its back to the wall—here's the key. Let them go through the hole these burglars entered by, at the back of the cupboard, and learn what happened there, whose premises they are, and all that.'

'He's like an officer,' cried the sergeant. 'Hole in the wall! You don't mean to say these fellows broke through from outside premises, and cloaked the entrance by means of a cupboard? That looks like an inside accomplice.'

'He's there,' said David promptly, jerking his finger at the form lying amid the debris of broken glass and the contents of the overturned case. 'Henricksen we knew him as; from the jewellery department. Sergeant, there's a steel flap on the outside of the fire doors I closed on those Russians. Second floor, don't forget. A man might see them through it. Then we might rush them through the door or get at them by the lift.'

It took but a few minutes to prepare their plans. The sergeant relieved David of his revolver, and himself went to the door upstairs, reporting that the Russians were to be seen at the far end of the store. Then Hemming joined him, while a constable was sent off to the nearest station to procure more arms. By the time he was back again there were fifty constables on the scene, the outside of the house as well as the inside being guarded. As for our hero, that he was wounded by Henricksen's shot he knew, and no doubt the shock and loss of blood had caused him to lose consciousness. But he had got over that now. The draught he had received had revived him wonderfully, and that and the desire to see the matter to its very end kept him bright and smiling. He took a revolver from one of the officers, and at a signal from the sergeant above, set the lift in motion. With him there was an inspector and four officers, all armed with revolvers.

'The sergeant and Hemming have orders to fire if the men do not halt at their order,' said the former. 'You can take us clear up, please. We're going to rush them.'

He had hardly spoken, the elevator had not reached the level of the first floor when there was a loud call from above. Dull reports were heard, and then two sharp explosions. David jerked the handle over and sent the lift shooting up. With another jerk he brought it to a stand still at the second floor, and threw the doors open. Instantly all the occupants burst out. But, fortunately for them, there was no need for fire-arms. The sergeant had managed the situation with wonderful skill. He had seen the two Russians running towards him, and waiting till they were near enough, had ordered them to stop. Shots at once answered him, the bullets crashing against the door. And then he had sent two in return. Only two, but with the desired effect. Spolikoff dropped his weapon and nursed his right arm. Ovanovitch plunged forward heavily and fell on his face. In two minutes they were securely in the hands of the police.

When Hemming and the inspector, together with the manager of the store, hastily summoned to the scene by the police, went in search of David, they found him huddled in a corner of the room, as white as a sheet, bleeding slowly from the mouth.

'Chest wound,' said the inspector, gripping the situation with an experienced eye. 'We have a surgeon below; I'll send for him.'

When our hero came to his senses he was lying in a beautifully comfortable bed, with bright rays from a warm fire playing on him. A nurse stood near at hand, and beside her, discussing some matter very seriously, was some man whose features seemed to be familiar. David puzzled wonderfully. He began to fret about the matter; then, fatigued by even such a little thing, he went off into a blissful slumber.

'The best of everything, please, nurse,' said the manager of the store, before he departed. 'Order anything you want. I will be responsible for all expenses. And please do send constant information to the porter at the lodge. I am arranging with him to 'phone to me constantly.'

'Wouldn't lose that lad for a whole heap,' he told Hemming, when the latter was ensconced in his office with the manager of the store. 'He did magnificently; splendid pluck and resource he showed; seemed to have worked his plans out like a general. I feel horrible about the matter; as if by offering such a bright young fellow such a job I was accountable for his wound. Certainly, I'll send you a wire every three hours, saying how he is progressing.'

Yes, David had made a stir in the London world. Mr. Ebenezer's none too handsome face went scarlet when he read the accounts, and saw the photograph of our hero in the papers. He blew his huge nose violently, then he sat down and stared moodily into the fire. David Harbor had already become an excessively big thorn in this gentleman's side.

Chapter VI
The Professor makes a Suggestion

'So you've been fighting again, have you?' quizzed Mr. Jones, when he came to visit David in the accident ward of the general hospital, to which he had been conveyed straight from the store. 'And this time there has been real bloodshed. Do you know that you have lain here precisely four weeks, two days short of a complete month?'

'And a precious long time it does begin to feel,' came the joking answer, for the patient so ill but a short while before was now well on the high road to recovery. 'I'm just longing to be out again. To-morrow I get up; in a week I am to be allowed out in the park. In two I shall be back at my lodgings.'

'Perhaps,' agreed Mr. Jones, drawling the word in a manner decidedly professional. 'If you are well enough. If not—well, no matter for the moment. But you are strong enough to sign your name; listen to what I read, and sign if you agree. Of course, I am not going to bother you with a number of details. You can rely upon me implicitly; I will manage things for you.'

He rapidly intimated certain matters to David in connection with the letter he had had from his father, and the will which Mr. Ebenezer Clayhill was so anxious to have settled. Then he obtained our hero's signature.

'The next thing you will hear about the matter will be from the papers,' said Mr. Jones, as he bade farewell. 'I hope we shall be successful.'

Imagine the interest of the public when it leaked out that the hero of the burglary near Bond Street was also the claimant through his solicitor to have the execution of a certain will delayed. The papers rapidly obtained the whole story; for Mr. Jones, though accustomed, as a rule, to professional taciturnness and silence, now opened his lips with a will, and told the whole story as he knew it.

'Not that the tale will affect the judgment of this matter,' he told his friends. 'British justice is too evenly balanced for such a thing; but it will gain more friends for the boy. It will put his case as it is, not as others might garble it, and will obtain the sympathy of all.'

And sympathy it did gain for our hero. Not only that; for information having been received he would be out of hospital very shortly, the case was put back for trial on a later date, no special reason being given.

'Unless, of course, the Judge and jury are anxious to see you,' laughed Mr. Jones, coming to see David again, and quizzing as was his wont. 'But I'm glad to hear you are doing so well. In a week you come home.'

'Home,' said David. 'Yes, to Constable Hemming's. He's been here to arrange.'

'Home with me,' interrupted Mr. Jones, placidly. 'You must understand that you are an invalid as yet. You require care and comfortable surroundings. Not that I assert that Constable Hemming would deny you those; but you will obtain them to greater degree where I live, in the country, outside London. Hemming knows of the suggestion and approves. By the way, he's Sergeant Hemming now — promoted for his share in the work of capturing those men. Now I'll see the House Surgeon and get his report.'

'Oh, David?' said the latter, cheerily, when accosted by the solicitor. 'Davie is going strong; we've had him examined under the Roentgen Rays. The bullet struck the fourth rib on the left side, and ought to have killed him outright. But he has luck; he was born to be lucky it seems. The bullet turned along the rib, left it half way back, and emerged. The trouble with him is that the rib was fractured, and one of the broken ends pierced the lung. Hence bleeding from the mouth and other nasty and troublesome symptoms; but he'll do now if he takes it easy for another month. When can he go out, Mr. Jones? Let us say in a week's time.'

Accordingly David was driven away from the hospital at the termination of that period, deeply grateful for all the care and kindness shown him, and leaving many a friend behind. A motor car conveyed him to Mr. Jones' house, and thereafter he came under the care of that gentleman's wife. Three weeks later he attended the inquest on Henricksen, and there for the first time gave a description of how he had seen the burglars come into the store, and of how he had been forced to hide himself. Then followed the trial of the Admiral and of Spolikoff and Ovanovitch, the latter two having by then recovered from their wounds. Needless to say both Judge and jury highly commended the behaviour of our hero.

'Of course, we don't expect that you will care to come back to us,' said the manager of the store, when the trial was finished, 'though if you wish to come, we shall be glad to have you. But you are so well off now that you can look for something better. To begin with, our directors have handed me a cheque for one hundred pounds, to be paid at once to you.'

David coughed at the intimation. It made him breathe so deeply that his already healed wound pained him. 'One hundred pounds,' he gasped. 'That's enough to take me to China.'

'Hardly, I think; but there is some more. Spolikoff and Ovanovitch were much wanted by the police for extradition to their own country. They are a dangerous class of criminal who have infested this country of late. In Russia they were Anarchists, and are known to have held up and robbed a train. Russia became too hot for them, and so they came to these hospitable shores to continue robbing. There was a reward offered for their apprehension. You, of course, obtain that. The sum is three hundred pounds.'

Little wonder that David gasped again. When he agreed to remain on watch at the store he was almost penniless. True, he had a few pounds by him, as well as a bicycle, while there was always the small allowance which was due to him; but the prospect of earning much was by no means brilliant. And here were four hundred pounds—four hundred shining sovereigns, to do with as he liked, to pay his passage to China if he wished it.

'Then off I go to China!' he cried, when he had recovered from his astonishment at such good fortune. 'I'll sail on the first opportunity.'

'Which means that you will go when I, as your appointed guardian, allow you to do so,' exclaimed Mr. Jones, severely, endeavouring to hide a smile; for David's eagerness and enthusiasm delighted this gentleman. Mr. Jones was the sort of man whom a stranger would imagine never even smiled, much less laughed outright. David had himself always considered him somewhat of a wet blanket; but he did not know him so well then. As a matter of fact the solicitor was the prince of good fellows, and kind-hearted to a degree. And it was true that he had constituted himself David's guardian.

'Till the court has put me in that position officially,' he said, 'and, of course, till you are fit again; for then I am well aware that you will kick over the traces, and put up with no interference. Now, David, hand over that money to me. I'll give you a formal receipt for it, and when you need money you can have it, and without a question. For the moment I'll take care of it. Golden sovereigns have a way of burning holes in the pockets of young people.'

When at length the case in which our hero was so interested came before the courts, he was perfectly restored to health; and his straightforward evidence, the narrative of how he had set out from home to make his own way in the world, and his adventures *en route* won for him the good-will of hosts of people. The whole case read like a romance, and proved wonderfully attractive, while Mr. Ebenezer, who was compelled to give evidence, as was also his wife, provided the villains to this all-absorbing drama. Then came the intimation that David had decided to go to China, there to make inquiries and search for his father's will.

'As a sensible man I suppose I ought to throw cold water on that scheme,' declared the judge, 'but, honestly, it has my sympathy. I like the pluck of the claimant.'

It appeared that others did also. For while Mr. and Mrs. Ebenezer Clayhill were thoroughly exposed, and held up to public execration, David became more of a hero, and the following day received a most important letter.

> 'Dear Sir'—it ran—'Having read the facts of your appeal to the courts, and being, moreover, an old friend of your father's, I have the pleasure to offer you a post on the staff I am collecting to take to China. We go to investigate old Mongolian Cities, the ruins of which have been long since located. I understand that your father was also interested in this work. We sail in rather less than a month, and should you accept this proposal, your passage will be paid, as also the return, while the question of salary can be arranged in the immediate future. Kindly write by return.'

David telegraphed. 'Coming. Delighted,' he sent, laconically, though he was not given as a rule to such abruptness, while the following morning found him at the address which headed the letter he had received. A short, stout, clean-shaven man rose from a seat as he was announced and advanced towards him with outstretched hand.

'David Harbor?' he asked, with a welcoming smile.

'Yes, sir. Come on the receipt of a letter from Professor Padmore. Is—er—are you—?'

The little gentleman laughed outright now, beaming on our hero, while his fleshy chin shook visibly. 'Am I the Professor?' he shouted, putting a hand on David's shoulder. 'You don't think I look like one, now do you? Admit to that. As a Professor I should be as bald as a coot, wear enormous goggles, stutter a trifle, and be somewhat deaf. Eh! isn't that it?'

David couldn't help laughing; the little man's good temper was strangely infectious. Nor did he attempt to deny what had been said; it was true enough. Professors were often enough the class of individual painted by this gentleman. 'You're so different, sir,' he blurted out. 'You're——'

'I'm Professor Padmore, a terrible person, I do assure you,' chuckled the little man, 'and I happen also to have been a friend of your father's. A fine man, David, a gallant fellow, but rash, a trifle rash. Trusted the Chinese too far. That was the cause of the whole trouble. Well now, sit down. Smoke?'

He held out a cigarette case, but David shook his head.

'Never mind then,' smiled the Professor. 'No harm if you don't. You may later on. You're plenty young enough yet—too young, in fact. Boys who smoke are fools, fools, sir, with a capital F to it. But I wrote you, yes, I saw the name in the paper, and was attracted by the case. It was so unusual, the majority of such disputes are so commonplace. All are sordid; this one had peculiar features. It so happened, too, that I was wanting a young fellow, a gentleman, you understand, to come out to China with me. Well then, there you were, openly stating your desire to go to China. You were just the man for my situation, while I was just the opportunity you were looking for. Good; I wrote. You are coming; there'll be danger and hardships innumerable.'

He had lit a cigarette by now, and turned on the hearth rug at his final words to stare hard at David. He found the latter laughing.

'Eh? What?' he asked pleasantly.

'Nothing, sir,' declared David, 'only everything is so jolly and so pleasant I was just thinking then that you were just the reverse of the usual Professor. You ought to be very severe and unbending to young fellows.'

'Whereas I am not. Exactly so; to tell the truth I feel young myself, as young as you do, and try hard to forget that the years are going along, and that I am getting stouter as they go. But I can be severe. David, there will be many dangers to be faced, and many hardships. I want you to know that I want you to be fully prepared. And though I am pleasant enough as a general rule, there is one thing to learn—without discipline, without one recognised leader, and one only, no expedition can be a success. This expedition must succeed. I have led several others, but this is more important than all. Absolute obedience to my orders must be the rule, and you must be prepared to give it.'

For a few brief seconds the character of the little man seemed to have entirely changed, while certainly his facial appearance had done so. For of a sudden he became stern. Lines wove themselves across his forehead, while the half-closed eyes regarded David in a manner which impressed him. He realised then, if he had not done so before, that Professor Padmore could be a very different gentleman to the jolly individual who had welcomed him a few minutes earlier, could be stern and dictatorial, and could lead men whenever needed, and however pressing the danger.

'I am prepared to give the same obedience I should give in the army,' said David, soberly. 'As for the dangers and hardships, they come in in the day's work. I do not look for ease and enjoyment out in China. My business is serious. I shall not succeed with it until I have travelled far and had many an adventure.'

'Then you will do for me. Sit down there; now for your salary.'

It took but a few moments to decide that item, and then the Professor proceeded to outline his project.

'There are these Mongolian cities,' he said. 'Well, I have already done some excavating, and have brought some rare objects home with me; but there are thousands still lying buried for every one we have unearthed. We go to find them. Our ship carries us to Hong-Kong. There we disembark and remain for a while till we have obtained the necessary servants, some of whom I have employed before. Then we take steamer for Shanghai, and finally travel to Pekin. When we leave the city for the north, our real work will begin. You still wish to come? You are not frightened?'

David laughed again. He could not help himself; for the Professor was once more the jovial, pleasant comrade, treating the young fellow as if he himself were one also. 'I will come, and only too happy to be one of the party, sir,' he said. 'How many do you take?'

'We shall be four sailing from England. When we march from Pekin there should be twenty of us all told. Labourers for the task of digging can be obtained at the various spots we visit. Now for an outfit I shall purchase that for you; I have a list by which I always go. Long experience has taught me what is wanted.'

It was no use for David to exclaim at such generosity, and to mention the fact that he had plenty of money. The Professor silenced him at once.

'Put it away, sir,' he said. 'Put it into a safe investment. Don't worry about it till you come home. By then it will have grown wonderfully. But come along now; we'll drive to the house which always provides my equipment.'

When David returned to Mr. Jones' roof that evening he had been measured for a couple of thick tweed suits, of a brownish, khaki colour. Likewise for two pairs of strong boots and gaiters.

'The shirts and things of that description we can get ready made,' the Professor said. 'In the hot weather you will wear cotton only, and that sort of thing is best obtained in China. In the very cold weather, and often at other times, we shall wear native costume. Now you will want a magazine pistol, of the same pattern as carried by us all, thus necessitating only one class of ammunition for that sort of weapon, a rifle, and a gun. Those, with a compass, will complete your equipment. Come here in a week's time, and we will see the clothes tried on.'

Those were busy days for our hero. There seemed a thousand and one things to be done, so much so that the hours flew. But at last the most exciting day of all arrived. He bade farewell to Mr. and Mrs. Jones, and went over the river to see Sergeant Hemming and his wife. Then he joined the Professor, and together they drove to the docks. It was not till the following morning, when they were well away at sea, that David was introduced to the two who were, besides the Professor, to be his travelling companions, and who went to complete the staff of the expedition going to China to investigate Mongolian ruins.

'David,' shouted the Professor, unceremoniously, as he leaned against the ship's rail talking with a passenger, 'come along and meet one of the band. Dick, this is David. David, Dick. Shake hands.'

'You! Why, this beats me altogether!'

The passenger who had been conversing with the Professor swung round, smiling, as the words were spoken, and stretched out his hand; but the instant his eyes fell on our hero he started back in amazement. The next second he had leaped forward, and was shaking David's hand as if he would never cease.

'You! David Harbor of all people! You and I to be travelling companions, on the staff of the same expedition. This is too good!'

It was Dick Cartwell, the young fellow to whom David had taken such a fancy on his eventful ride up to London, the son of the lady who had so narrowly escaped an accident in a runaway brougham.

'Ripping!' ejaculated David on his part, delighted beyond anything. 'I never asked the name of the other fellow. Just fancy it's being you! What a time we shall have together!'

'Perhaps,' said the Professor, smiling at the keenness and the friendship displayed by the two, and delighted beyond measure to find that they knew one another, 'perhaps you will have the goodness to explain. When Dick Cartwell came to me and begged of me to take him on this trip, I hesitated.'

He looked severely at the handsome young fellow, though there was a smile on his lips.

'I say!' exclaimed Dick, protesting.

'I hesitated,' went on the Professor, silencing Dick with uplifted finger. 'I said to myself, I want a man, a steady man, used to expeditions. Besides, I had just read about a certain David Harbor, quite a youngster, and I conceived that one young fellow would be ample trouble and to spare. But I gave way, and here I find you known to one another. Did David tell you to come to me, sir?'

Dick protested again, amid much laughter, and then turned abruptly on the Professor. 'It's just all chance, sir,' he said. 'But the happiest chance imaginable. David and I became acquainted only a little while ago. He made my mother's acquaintance on the high road to London. There was almost a nasty accident. He stepped in in the nick of time.'

'As he did in the case of the burglars. Tell me all about it,' asked the professor, in the peculiar jerky way he had. 'And so you saved those ladies, David,' he said, a little later, becoming serious. 'I'm glad; you have shown now on more than one occasion that you have a cool head on your shoulders, and that is just what is wanted out in China. I hope Dick will cultivate similar coolness, and joking apart, I'm delighted to have you both with me. Now to introduce you to the other member of our party. He has been with me once before, and is perfectly invaluable. Here he comes. Alphonse, *mon cher.*'

The jovial Professor had set his eyes on the quaintest figure of a man imaginable, and called to him as he promenaded the deck. And at his summons the passenger approached David and Dick and their employer in the most humorous manner. A little man, smaller in fact than the Professor, Alphonse was remarkably broad. His shoulders were extraordinary in their width, while one was struck by the fact that his head—a tiny, bullet-like head, covered with the shortest, bristly crop of hair, which stood upright everywhere—was sunk deep between the shoulders. For the rest, an extremely ample waistcoat expanse, short, thick legs, which nevertheless moved very swiftly, and a most engaging face made up the personality of Alphonse. From the long, pointed toes of his French boots, to the crown of his stubble-covered head, the passenger was an oddity, while voice and jesture added to his eccentricity.

'Monsieur, I have the honour to hear you call,' said the little man, advancing at the Professor's summons, with little prancing steps which might have been employed by a professor of dancing, while he bowed deeply, flourishing a cap with a mighty peak, again, like his boots and his whole person, entirely and convincingly French in origin. 'You called Alphonse.'

'To make him known to these two gentlemen. Alphonse, these are the two who accompany us. I trust that they may be as well pleased with you when our travels are over as I have been. Alphonse Pichart, David, Dick.'

The three shook hands eagerly, with vast enthusiasm in the case of the Frenchman. Indeed, David found himself unconsciously wondering at the little man, and marvelling whence came all his energy. And how the face of Alphonse attracted him. Beneath the stubbly, shock head of hair was a wide forehead, a pair of honest, sparkling, blue eyes, a good nose, and strong mouth and chin.

Not a hair was visible on this shining, healthy-looking countenance till one arrived at the chin, from which depended a peaky little beard, cut very narrow and curling forward at the tip.

'I shall have the honour and the pleasure to serve all three, then. Eh?' said Alphonse, backing and bowing once more, and replacing his hideous hat with a flourish. 'Monsieur can rely on me. I shall see to every one's comfort. And now, if Monsieur will permit, I go to the cabins to unpack.'

The Professor dismissed him with a nod and a smile.

'The best of fellows,' he exclaimed. 'Came last expedition as cook and valet.'

'Cook and valet!' exclaimed David, surprised that such individuals should be necessary, when the members of the expedition were obviously going to a part where they would have to rough it. 'I thought we should do our own cooking, or have a Chinaman for the job. As for a valet, why, clothes won't trouble us much I should think.'

'Perhaps not,' came the answer. 'But then, Alphonse is more cook than valet. I shall tell you something. An army, it is said, lives on its stomach. An exploring party does so, but in a different sense. The work is sometimes arduous, and all our attention will be required. Very well, one might have a good native cook. On the other hand one might very well have a villainous one. See the result—uncooked food, dyspepsia; you and I and Dick unfit for really good work. Lost time. Lost opportunities. Besides, Alphonse does more than cook or valet. He is shrewd, and has an abundance of courage. But you will see. He is the life and soul of the expedition. He keeps us and himself all going.'

Before the ship had been at sea a whole week, Dick and David found this to be very true; for Alphonse was always smiling, always humorous. And if there happened to be nothing in his actual words to make one laugh, his comical antics, his bows and flourishes always drew a smile, if not a roar of laughter, at which the little man beamed, for he was never angered.

No need to describe the voyage as far as Hong-Kong. It passed as other voyages do, with numerous deck games amongst the passengers, an occasional dance or concert, and one terrific gale, which swept the decks clear of all but the crew and confined the passengers to the saloon. Dick and David revelled in the movement of the ship. Not once did they shy from the saloon when the hours for meals arrived, nor feel squeamish.

'Just the lads for me,' the Professor told himself, rubbing his hands together, his face shining with enjoyment and good health. 'Nothing mamby pamby about them. They will prove excellent companions.'

At Hong-Kong the party transhipped to a coaster, and having reached Shanghai chartered a native boat.

'Our journeying may be said to begin here,' said the Professor, as he watched Alphonse arranging their belongings in the huge, roomy cabin aft. 'We run up the coast to a certain spot abutting on a portion of the Gulf of Pechili. Then we land and inspect certain ruins of which I have heard. From thence we can return to Shanghai, and take the train to Pekin, or we can journey overland. My lads, to-morrow we shall don our rougher clothing.'

That cruise up the Gulf of Pechili proved to be a most enjoyable experience, and David and his friend Dick made the most of every hour of it. They fell in with the four native hands whom the Professor had engaged at Hong-Kong, Chinese whom he had had in his service before, and helped the crew of the huge, wide-built boat haul at the ropes, and hoist extra canvas on her. Then, at the Professor's wish, they studied the language for three hours every day, sitting amongst the men, or more often with the four engaged with the expedition. And even a week, they found, saw some improvement in their knowledge.

'You have only to stick to it and you will become excellent linguists,' declared the Professor, 'and will find the power to converse most valuable. As for your instructors, a Chinaman when he takes an interest in anything is not to be beaten, and those servants of mine seem to have made up their minds that you shall both learn to speak in a record short time.'

Head and baffling winds delayed the progress of the boat immensely, so that ten days after leaving Shanghai, she was only half way toward her destination. Then there came a fair wind, lasting two whole days, which bore her a long way in the right direction. But towards evening it fell away altogether, leaving the huge native vessel wallowing in an oily yellow swell, and slowly drifting landward.

'Nothing to do but wait and hope for a change for the better,' said Alphonse. 'Monsieur the Professor can sleep; the other gentlemen can work at the language. Already they know more than I, who have been months and months in the country.'

But there were other things to attract the attention of our hero and his friend beside the Chinese language. Indeed, that very night there was an interruption. Awakening in the small hours David listened for a moment to the flop of the swell as it heaved against the side of the vessel. Then he heard a chain rattle, while, an instant later, a gentle hail came across the water. Throwing off the mosquito curtain, under which all now slept, he slid out of the deck cabin, and went to the rail. There was a figure already there dimly seen against the places where the swell broke at its summit and washed in white froth across the surface. 'Hist!' David heard, and a moment later realised that it was Alphonse.

'Ah, ha, that is Monsieur David? Good,' he heard the little Frenchman whisper. 'I can trust Monsieur David. He has been in danger before; he understands caution.'

'But—what is it? Why is there need for caution?' asked our hero, careful to keep his voice low, and wondering what the Frenchman could mean. 'I heard someone hail us; there must be another ship.'

At once Alphonse's arm swung out, he became as rigid as a board, while he pointed towards the bows of the vessel.

'See there, Monsieur. You are right; there is a boat. She has come alongside, and so silently that few of us have heard her. Does Monsieur know what she is here for?'

David could not even guess, but then he had never been in the Gulf of Pechili before. However, Alphonse knew the part, and had an idea of its dangers.

'Listen, Monsieur,' he whispered. 'I saw a boat three days ago, and thought I detected signals passing between us and her. She sailed right out of sight, but that night a lantern flashed right ahead of this vessel. To-night I detected the same, but knowing that there was a calm I felt sure that none could approach us without our hearing, for they would have to employ sweeps. *Bien!* I would not sleep. I crawled out on deck. I waited and watched. And presently a gentle breeze got up. Our men made no movement; they made no effort to put the vessel on her course, though they were moving about on the deck. Again I saw a lantern flash, and then, just a few minutes ago, I caught sight of a stranger approaching us. Monsieur, that is a Chinese pirate. She comes to take our weapons, and to loot those boxes the Professor carries with him.'

'Then the sooner he is warned the better,' said David, his voice hardly audible. 'This is serious.'

'Monsieur will perhaps go to the cabin and wake the two gentlemen,' suggested Alphonse, not a tremor in his words. 'I will remain and watch.'

'Listen to this,' whispered David, eagerly. 'I will warn the two in the cabin, and will then go to the four Chinese who form part of our staff. I will bring them back to our quarters as soon as possible. Meanwhile, if there is a movement in this direction, retire to the cabin yourself, and close the door firmly. It is the only means of entrance, except by way of a large port under the companion ladder leading to the roof of the cabin.'

'And that?' asked Alphonse, still as cool as ever, as if this were an everyday matter.

'Will do for me and the four men,' declared David. 'If the main door is shut we will slip in there. Warn the others about it.'

He was gone in a moment, and within the space of half a minute had awakened the Professor and Dick. In a few words he related what was happening.

'Stand by the door and admit Alphonse,' he said. 'I am going for the men we engaged at Hong-Kong; they are to be trusted.'

He took his magazine pistol from the rack in which all the weapons were housed, and slid out on to the deck again. Then, bending low, he ran towards the hatchway which led to the quarters occupied by the men attached to the expedition. He was just disappearing down it when his eyes fell upon some two dozen bent and dusky figures creeping along the deck. A moment later one of them gave a sharp order, and at once, with shouts and cries, the whole party dashed toward the stern of the vessel. The attack on the Professor's party was about to begin. David's retreat was entirely cut off by the enemy.

Chapter VII
At Sea on a Chinese Junk

'Steady!' David commanded himself, feeling for the moment as if he were about to give way to panic. 'Go below and get the four men, then make a rush. You couldn't get back to the cabin alone.'

He stood on the narrow steps, with his head just above the level of the hatch and watched for a moment; for the sudden view he had obtained of the attackers, and their unexpected rush aft had taken him unawares. As he stared into the gloom he could see the figures which had passed him at a rush moving about from side to side of the vessel, just outside the huge deck cabin that occupied the whole of the stern. He heard blows struck against the woodwork, and a loud, resounding bang, as the door was locked and bolted. Then the shouts died away. A man stood out prominently from his comrades, and gave a sharp order. A second later there was a blinding flash, a deafening roar rolled along the decks and over the sea, while the flame lit up the surroundings.

'Fired a blunderbuss or some other ancient weapon,' David told himself. 'Blew a hole clean through the door. I do hope that none of my friends were behind it. Ah! that is the answer.'

For one brief second he had obtained a clear view of the attackers. Some twenty-four in number, they crouched on the deck as the weapon was fired, so that the ruffian who pulled the trigger became all the more prominent. He was a tall, lanky Chinaman, dressed in loose cotton clothing, and with arms bared to the shoulder. David even caught a view of his swaying pigtail. Then darkness descended again, and blotted out the figure. A moment later startled voices came to his ear from below; at once he dropped to the bottom of the ladder.

'Gently, Ho Hung,' he whispered, calling to one of the four men who had joined the staff of the expedition, and who had been with the Profess on a previous occasion. Ho Hung, indeed, was well known to our hero, fc was he who made such valiant efforts every day to teach him the langu: 'Gently, Ho Hung,' he called again, speaking in Chinese as well as he co 'I am here, at the bottom of the ladder.'

Something touched his leg. Strong fingers closed about the ankle, and sent a thrill throughout David's frame. He clenched his teeth, and stooping, gripped the wrist of the man below, prepared to throw himself upon him.

'Speak,' he commanded, hoarsely. 'Who are you?'

'Ho Hung, Excellency. I heard you call; there is trouble on the deck?'

'Listen,' said David, breathing deeply, a huge sigh of relief escaping him. 'We are attacked. My friends are in the cabin; we must reach them, you and I and the other three. Where are they?'

Not a sound had he heard below, save Ho Hung's voice; but at his question three more figures rose up before him as if they were ghosts, though in the dense darkness of the 'tween decks he could not perceive them. But the men spoke huskily, their tones strangely different from the high-pitched notes they were wont to employ.

'Lo Fing, Excellency, here, ready.'

'And Hu Ty, at your orders.'

'With John Jong, Excellency, prepared to obey.'

The latter individual impressed his presence upon our hero by stretching out a long, thin hand in the darkness, and laying it upon his shoulder. But that was often this Chinaman's salutation in the case of David or Dick, though he would never have dared in the case of the Professor or in that of Alphonse. Still he was a merry, privileged rascal, and enjoyed the name of John, probably because of its similarity to his own of Jong, and also, perhaps, because he was the only one of the four who could understand and speak English.

'Allee lightee, Excellency David,' he said, using his queer pidgin-English. 'Allee four here. What then? Trouble above? Dat rascal captain up to some nicee little game?'

But David ignored the questions. Ho Hung was the leader of this little quartet, and by far the most reliable. He swung round upon the Chinaman, who still gripped his ankle, as if to assure him of his presence all the while, and spoke hastily, his knowledge of the language, small though it was, proving of the greatest service.

'You will stand by us then?' he asked.

'We swear it,' came solemnly from Ho Hung, while the other three gave guttural approval. 'And you are armed?'

From the neighbourhood of John Jong there came the sound made when a match is struck, and almost at once a flame illuminated the surroundings,

showing the four Chinamen, their eyes strangely big and prominent in the flare, and David at the foot of the ladder. Jong held the match forward, and each man in turn showed the weapon he possessed.

'See, Excellency, a staff,' said Ho Hung, displaying a massive staff, that would prove a formidable weapon.

'And knives here, and here, and here.' Jong pointed to the one he had in his own belt, while Lo Fing and Hu Ty held theirs forward, smiling grimly.

'Then wait while I see what is happening. We have to join the others, and I have arranged to make use of the port under the ladder leading to the top of the cabin. We shall have to make a rush—you understand that? You follow what I mean?'

The match had burned down to Jong's finger tips by now, and he let the end drop on to the boards, stamping the ash out with his feet; but the light given even by such a small incandescent piece of wood in the darkness was sufficient to show up the figures for a few seconds. David watched the men and nodded. There was no doubt that they had understood his laboured rendering of their own language.

'Then wait,' he said curtly. 'I will see what is happening. One of the crew fired a gun at the cabin door. I heard a shot in return, and believe the man fell; since then there has not been a sound. Wait; I'll be back in a moment.'

He stole softly up the ladder, for he had only a pair of soft bedroom slippers on his feet, and they were as good for the purpose as even the cotton-soled shoe worn by the Chinese themselves. In a twinkling his head was on a level with the hatch, and then he cautiously raised it.

'Men creeping about as if they were in search of something,' he told himself, seeing moving figures. 'One lying on the deck just where that fellow stood to fire his shot. Killed, I expect, by our own party. What on earth are the rascals up to?'

He was puzzling his brains as to what could be passing, for there seemed no object in the movement of the men on deck, while the attack on the cabin appeared to have been forgotten. Then a sharp exclamation reached his ears, and one of the attackers stood upright, lifting something from the deck. David could not be sure, but believed it was an axe, and again wondered what would be done with it.

'Break in the door, I suppose,' he told himself. 'That'll want doing; there are pistols there, my friend, as you will soon learn to your cost. Ah! Another seems to have discovered a similar weapon.'

It was not at all remarkable that such a search should be needed for these two axes—and axes they undoubtedly were—for the methods of the commander of the native boat were anything but excellent. Untidiness was noticeable everywhere; odds and ends of things, bales and boxes and coils of rope and tackle of every description littering the deck. And amidst the various items were the axes.

'Talking the matter over amongst themselves,' thought David, seeing the dusky figures come together at one side of the deck. 'That shows they counted on winning their way into the cabin at the first rush. They made sure that they would pounce upon us unawares, and never imagined that we should be ready for them. Now they'll decide upon some plan for forcing their way in. This would be our chance for rushing along to join our comrades.'

The thought had hardly crossed his mind when those long, firm fingers closed again round his ankle, a sure signal that Ho Hung wished to communicate with him. Instantly David slid down into the depths of the vessel.

'Well?' he asked, somewhat curtly, for he was anxious not to lose sight of the enemy. 'They have been searching the decks for axes and have discovered two. I think they are about to rush at the door and attempt to beat it in. That will be the moment for us to run. You have all that, Hung? Can't make it a bit clearer.'

A guttural response reassured him. 'We have understood. His Excellency speaks plainly, though he makes many mistakes. Hung wished only to tell of something which has been forgotten. There is no need to go out on deck and enter by the port, for there is a path to the cabin by this way. Does his Excellency forget that meals are brought to his friends through a hatchway leading up through the floor of the cabin?'

The position of that hatch flashed across David's brain instantly, and he could have struck himself for having forgotten it so readily. Of course, it was the only way by which to rejoin the party in the cabin, and offered a perfectly safe road.

'We will make along it at once, Hung,' he said. 'Let Jong run and warn our friends immediately. I will watch at the top of the ladder, while you and the other two search about for something with which to block the foot of the ladder leading up to that hatch. Quick with it! They may have remembered it too.'

Feeling sure that his orders would be carried out promptly, he swarmed up to the level of the deck again, and once more cautiously protruded his head. At the same moment a heavy thud reached his ears; there came the sound of splintering wood, then the sharp, distinctive snap of a magazine pistol. As on a former occasion, though to a lesser degree this time, the flash of the weapon gave our hero an instant's view of his surroundings. Thirty feet away was the wall of the cabin, with the dark lines of the doorposts in the centre, while the deck on either hand was occupied by crouching figures. One Chinaman alone was prominent, and he stood before the door, frantically struggling to drag the blade of the axe he had been wielding out of the woodwork. He staggered backwards with the weapon, as the darkness fell like a screen about him. Then the sound of splintering wood was repeated, a pistol snapped, and after it another, illuminating the scene for the space of a few seconds. David saw the Chinaman reel across the deck, and heard the axe fall heavily upon the boards, then his eye fell upon other figures. Half a dozen men were creeping towards the hatchway from which he was watching, and the leader of the band was within a few inches.

'One of the foreign devils,' he heard a man call. 'Hold him! Seize him! He has stolen out of the cabin.'

'I have him. Follow. Push your knives into his carcass.'

The leader so close to our hero recovered from his astonishment far sooner than did David, and hardly had his companion shouted when the man threw himself forward as if he were diving, and landing full upon the lad, who was standing on the steep steps that lead to the 'tween decks, gripped him round the neck in an embrace that was stifling. The result must have been as much of a surprise to him as it was to our hero; for the latter's feet slipped, his soft, felt soles failing to grip the rungs of the ladder, and at once both were precipitated to the bottom.

'Yield, foreign devil,' the man hissed in his ear. 'Yield, or I will thrust my knife through you.'

He made frantic efforts to get at the weapon, and releasing one hand groped at his belt. But the fall had shaken the weapon from its place, and had sent it tinkling on to the boards, while the movement gave David an opportunity he took the utmost advantage of. Naturally strong and active, and by this time fully restored to health, he was a good match for the Chinaman. Indeed, he was more; for, exerting all his strength, he thrust the man beneath him and held him there, wondering what next he should do with him. However, he was not to be spared time for such a purpose, for by now a second man was beside them. David felt his hand on his shoulder as the Chinaman sought in the darkness to assure himself which was friend and which foreign devil. In a moment he would know, for the clothing would tell its own story promptly, and if David were to escape a thrust from the long knife the rascal bore he must act on the instant. It may have been an inspiration—perhaps the whole thing was done unconsciously—in any case our hero braced his muscles as he had never done on a former occasion, and stretching out a hand gripped the pigtail of the man beneath him. Then he lifted the head sharply and sent it back against the deck with a sickening thud that stunned his antagonist instantly. A moment later something struck hard against his own shoulder, and, though he did not realise the fact then, the explanation came afterwards. The second Chinaman had thrust at him in the darkness, and missing his aim, had sent his blade within a couple of inches of his back, and far across it till his wrist came against the shoulder.

'Which shows he means business in any case,' thought David, recoiling before the blow. 'How's that?'

Kneeling up, with a swift motion, and realising that he had no time to get to his feet, he lunged forward sharply with his right fist, met something solid and sent it flying. Indeed, he heard the man stagger across the alley-way, and crash against a bulkhead two yards from him. Then, long before the fellow could pounce upon him, David was on his feet.

'Hist!' he heard at his elbow, then there was the scrape of a match against the roughened paper on the box. A flame suddenly illuminated the 'tween decks, showing our hero, dishevelled and somewhat breathless, close to the foot of the ladder, Ho Hung beside him, and the Chinaman advancing again with upraised weapon. More than that, it showed faces filling the dark square of the hatchway, and a man already half-way down the ladder.

**"A FLAME SUDDENLY ILLUMINATED
THE 'TWEEN DECKS**

'On to him,' shouted David. 'I'll see to the other.'

His hand dipped into his pocket swiftly, and reappeared with his magazine pistol. Before the flame had quite died out, or the Chinaman could reach him, he pressed the trigger, and caught a glimpse of the fellow as he doubled up like a rabbit, and crashed to the boards. A second later he was swept from his feet by Ho Hung and the Chinaman, who had by now reached the foot of the ladder.

If ever there were a time when David felt inclined to lose his head and act in an aimless manner, it was at this very moment, when he was swept from his feet by the fall of Hung and the villain who had grappled with him. Tumbled on the deck with a crash, he stretched out his hands to help himself to rise, and, instead of feeling his fingers fall upon the boards, realised at once that they had come in contact with a man. He pounced on the fellow, and after gripping his arms, he shifted his fingers to the neck. A growl of vexation escaped him.

'He's the other fellow. The chap I shot a moment ago. Call this acting steadily?' he asked himself fiercely. 'Where's Hung? What's he doing?'

It was useless to ask the question, for the sound of a violent scuffle at his feet, and the fact that he was again nearly felled to the deck provided sufficient answer to any but the most unintelligent. Obviously Hung was locked in the arms of one of the enemy, and in the darkness who could say who was the victor? Then that coolness which David had momentarily lost, and which was so essential under such circumstances, returned to him like a flash. He dropped his pistol into his pocket, extracted a box of matches and struck one.

'Now,' he thought, 'we shall see how matters are going. Ah! another of the fellows.'

The many faces of which he had caught a glimpse a little while before filling the dark square of the hatchway were blotted out by the figure of a Chinaman sliding down the ladder, while the light was reflected brightly from almost a yard of steel that was gripped between the newcomer's teeth. In a second or two he would be at the bottom of the ladder, and then, even if David wished to help Hung, he would be unable to. It was just one of those acute moments when instant decision is necessary, and immediate action, consequent on that decision, of vital importance. We have said that David Harbor was assailed but a minute earlier by one of those strange panics which come to the best of men, to the very bravest. Who knows? perhaps his meeting with the burglars in the store so close to Bond Street had in a measure unnerved him; or even, though his healthy colour and obvious robustness gave the lie direct to the suggestion, he was not yet entirely recovered from his injury sustained in that memorable conflict with Henricksen and his accomplices. Whatever the cause, David had without a shadow of doubt been on the verge of losing his head and his coolness entirely within a few seconds of Hung's arrival to help him. Perhaps the shame he felt immediately afterwards helped him now to behave in the coolest possible manner, and with a promptness that was commendable. Seeing the Chinaman just at the foot of the ladder, he tossed the match to the floor, and stepping forward seized the man round the waist. Then he lifted him from his feet as if he weighed a mere nothing, and using all his strength threw him across the alley-way. The crash had hardly died away when he had another match burning.

'Now we will run to the cabin, Excellency,' he heard Hung say, and turning towards him he saw the gallant fellow standing within a foot of him, a long knife in one hand, and the staff which he had carried at the foot of the ladder. Also the light showed the hatchway above, with its gallery of staring faces, and a huddled figure at Hung's feet. As for the man David had tackled, he lay in a heap against the bulkhead, stunned and helpless after such a rough experience.

'Lead the way,' commanded David, promptly. 'I'll bring the ladder with me. Stand aside, and let us have another match.'

He gripped the sides of the steep ladder leading from the hatchway, and, as Hung fumbled for a match, tore it from its flimsy fastenings. Then he pointed down the alley-way, and seeing Hung advance, slid along after him. Nor was their retreat undertaken a moment too soon. For as David stepped away from the hatchway a dozen more heads were suddenly shown there, standing out dimly against the starlight. Men shouted and bellowed, while one yellow ruffian slid a long, skinny arm downwards, took hasty aim, and pulled the trigger of a huge horse pistol. The concussion in the narrow alley-way deafened our hero, though the bullet did not touch him—for it was as big almost as a pigeon's egg—and crashing against the deck planks, it bored a hole clean through them. The smoke which belched from this antique weapon formed an excellent screen, behind which Hung and his companion were able to cloak their movements.

'You follow closely, Excellency,' David heard the Chinaman say. 'Not safe to strike more matches, for some of the men may have dropped through the hatchway and will fire at us. Follow closely, and bring the ladder. Our friends are within short distance of us.'

'And they have warned the others?' asked David. 'They have made some preparation to hold the enemy?'

'That I cannot say,' came the swift answer. 'But Jong is cunning, while the others will have obeyed his Excellency's orders. Ah! we have arrived. Hist! we are coming towards you.'

In the black darkness at the end of the alley-way a faint sound was heard, as if some one had sharply closed the lid of a metal match-box, though as a matter of fact it was the cocking of a pistol held in Dick's hands. Then the light from a lantern was thrown for one brief instant in David's direction, showing the walls of the alley-way, Hung's hurrying figure, and ahead of him a huge square mass, covered in sacking. Dick's cheery voice broke the silence immediately.

'Cheer oh! David!' he cried. 'What news? We were beginning to get the fidgets about you. Thought those fellows might have bagged you altogether. What's happened?'

'Heaps,' came the laconic answer. 'Just let me get past this bale and take a breather. I've never been so scared in all my life.'

There was a savage note in his voice, a note altogether foreign to David, and hearing it Dick realised that something altogether out of the common had happened.

'Come and sit down on the deck beside me,' he said. 'You can go up into the cabin later. I've sent word to say you were arriving. What's upset you?'

'Look here,' David blurted, turning upon him, 'would you feel yourself if you had been within an inch of proving a funk, of running away with your tail between your legs? Would you? Eh? That's the question.'

'Depends,' came the cautious answer. 'Perhaps there was reason for getting funked. I tell you I was at first when you woke me. Well? What's all the bother?'

'I'll tell you,' said our hero, feeling somewhat relieved and in better favour with himself, now that he heard Dick admit to the fact that he himself had been scared. 'I met our men at the bottom of the hatchway, and sent them on various errands. Then, as I watched from the top of the ladder a beggar threw himself on me, and we both went crash to the bottom. A second fellow followed, and then a third, whom Hung tackled. Well, I stunned my first man, and knocked the breath out of the second. I could feel Hung scuffling with his man in the darkness, and I tell you I nearly bolted. I got into a panic, and might very well have fired in all directions. Gurr! It makes a fellow ashamed of himself.'

Dick roared with laughter, till a sharp command from the cabin above stopped him. 'You do amuse me, David,' he said, dropping his voice to a whisper. 'Stun one man, knock the wind out of another, and then get scared. As if a fellow hadn't a right to be, after such an experience; but what happened then?'

'Pulled myself together, I suppose; did the only sensible thing under the circumstances. I struck a match, and only just in time. There was another beggar at the foot of the ladder, with a whole heap staring through the hatchway. I bet I shook that last rascal. I heaved him across the alley-way as if he were a box, and I should say that he's hardly fit to move yet awhile. Talk about collaring a chap out of the scrum, or getting a quick man extra well when coming all out down the field—that Chinaman don't need to fear a game of footer in the future. He'll never be collared or slung harder. Well, there you are: Hung had finished his man with the most murderous knife you ever saw, while I ended the matter for the moment by tearing the ladder away; but they won't be long in coming after us. What have you done?'

'Half-blocked the alley-way near the bottom of our hatchway with bales of cotton, leaving room for you to come through. Jong's been shoving others into position since. Beyond that I've done nothing; the Professor and Alphonse have been watching the door of the cabin.'

'Then supposing we show that lamp again,' said David. 'If all's clear I'll hop up and report progress, then I'll get leave to come down to you. There'll be a ruction in this neighbourhood before many minutes.'

Dick reached for the dark lantern from the corner in which he had placed it, and turned the slide swiftly, showing first the figures of Jong, of Hu Ty, and Lo Fing crouching behind the barrier erected in the alley-way. Then he flashed the light over the top of the bales of cotton, and illuminated the alley-way beyond. The rays fell upon a dozen eager faces, upon a mass of half-clad men hemmed in the narrow place, and was reflected from a number of brandished weapons. A deafening shout greeted the appearance of the lantern, and the bales it showed barring the progress of the attacking party. Then the same lean, skinny arm which had dropped from the other hatchway, and had fired a horse pistol, jerked itself into a horizontal position, a crashing report filled the alley-way, while a bullet roared between the heads of Dick and David, and thundered against the woodwork behind. Hidden by the eddying smoke the Chinese pirates struggled forward and threw themselves with fury upon the barrier behind which lay the Professor's slender party.

Chapter VIII
In a Tight Corner

'Excellency, we will see to those men for a time,' said Hung, as the mass of Chinese pirates crowding in the dark alley-way came charging forward. 'The bales of cotton will hold them in check, and a knife will be easier to use in such crowded quarters. But bring the lamp; hold it above our heads, so that the rays do not fall upon us, but upon the enemy.'

He gabbled the words at such a rate that David could scarcely follow his meaning, nor Dick either. But Jong came rapidly to the rescue, stopping for a while on his way to the barrier.

'Him tink you speakee and understandee ebelyting, Excellencies,' he said, smiling as if the fact amused him, and as if the affair in hand was a mere nothing. 'Hong say, supposee you comee along, leavee de fight altogeder to us Chinaboys. Yo hold de light high, so as to shine on de enemy only. Soon kill all dem men.'

He was wonderfully confident, and now went forward at a run. Meanwhile the other three Chinamen had reached the immediate neighbourhood of the barrier, which was placed some four yards along the alley-way, leaving, therefore, ample room for the defenders to stand at the foot of the ladder leading to the cabin above. At once Dick snatched up the lantern, while David dragged his magazine pistol from his pocket.

'Come along,' he shouted, for the din in this confined space was appalling. 'I think I know a trick that'll trouble them. Get along with the lantern, and hold it up at arm's length. I'll make use of the ladder I took from along there, and get well above our fellows; then I shall be able to shoot down into the enemy. Ain't they kicking up a row?'

'Enough to deafen any one; but be careful when you're roosting on that ladder. Don't forget the fellow with the pistol.'

David made a note of the warning promptly, and having reached the scene of the conflict, reared his ladder against one wall of the alley-way, leaving, however, ample room between its foot and the bales for Hong and his comrades to have free movement. Dick pushed his way right to the centre of the barrier, and finding a foothold on the edge of a low case, which formed the base of the obstruction, stepped on to it, and lifted the lantern at arm's length. At once he heard an exclamation of satisfaction come from their friends, for till that moment it was almost impossible for the defenders to take any action against the enemy. All they knew was that the latter were slashing and tearing at the far side of the bales, and with such exertion that the whole barrier threatened to topple over. However, the lamp flung its rays forward on to the struggling mass of men, leaving the part behind the barrier in dense darkness. At once a roar of anger went up from the pirates. One thin and exceedingly active man, whose eyes seemed actually to blaze in the lamp-light, pushed his comrades back forcibly, and with a howl of rage leaped at the top of the barrier. Clutching the sacking with his fingers, and digging his bare toes into any crevice he could find, he was on the summit in a wonderfully short space of time. Then his hand sought the long knife which, as seemed to be the custom with these marauders, he carried in his mouth. He was on the point of launching himself down upon the defenders, while David had already levelled his pistol at the man, when Hung gave a loud shout.

'Stand aside, let me deal with him,' he cried, and turning swiftly, as he dropped his pistol, David was able to catch a view of the gallant fellow as he prepared for the attack. His arms were thrown back over one shoulder, and the faint light reflected from the sides of the alley-way, and from the cotton clothes of the enemy, showed that he gripped in his hands the huge staff which he had showed some minutes before to our hero. It swished through the air as Hung swung forward, and meeting the Chinaman above as he leaped downward it felled him to the deck, striking him so hard that the man never even moved once he had fallen, but lay in a heap, his limbs curled up and contorted beneath him. Then, indeed, the turmoil and the din became so great that those defenders might have been forgiven had they suddenly lost heart, and, turning tail, had rushed to the ladder, there to struggle for the right to be the first to ascend to the security of the cabin above. But Hung was no chicken. To look at Jong he loved this class of thing, for he burst into a roar of laughter as the Chinaman was struck down, while Hu Ty and his comrade crouched behind the barricade, their sallow faces flushed, their eyes dancing, eager for more active effort. But let us remember that David and Dick never once flinched. The latter had been forced to step aside, else the man who had leaped upon the barricade would have jumped down on him, and also he would have been in Hung's way. But he was back in his place now, smiling, still holding the lamp above his head, cheering madly at this first success. As for David, all his old coolness had come back to him. Perched on the ladder well above the combatants, he felt as a general does who is posted on some commanding hill from which he is able to observe every movement in a battle, and give swift orders accordingly. He shouted encouragement to Hung, and then called suddenly to all his comrades to be cautious.

'Some more men have come into the alley-way,' he said, 'and there'll be a strong rush in a moment. Keep well down below the barricade; I can see that rascal reloading his pistol.'

He handled his own weapon, for through a break in the mass of men in front he had caught a view of the skinny individual, who was possessed, by the way, of a most malevolent and ugly countenance, busily ramming a fresh charge into his ancient pistol. Through the sudden silence, which followed the downfall of the man who had attempted to scale the barricade, there came the ring of a ramrod, and now as David watched he saw the rascal pushing his way forward.

'Lie low all of you,' he called again. 'That fellow's going to fire his pistol.'

Up went his own weapon, though he did not fire, for other men as yet covered the ruffian. Suddenly the man with the pistol appeared to have caught a glimpse of the figure perched above the level of the barricade. He shouted; the same skinny arm was thrown up, and before David could realise his danger he was staring into the expanded muzzle of as murderous a weapon as could be found anywhere. Yes, murderous; for it was but ten feet away, and carried a ball like a young cannon-shot. And how it roared as the rascal pulled the trigger! A wide stream of flame spurted from the muzzle, and then such a dense cloud of smoke that the alley-way, the men within it, even the barricade was swallowed up. Moreover, the bullet as near as possible put an end to this narrative, and to the quest of David Harbor; for it tore past his cheek, rattled and ricochetted along the stout wooden wall of the passage, and striking the runner of the ladder behind more than half severed it. In addition, it considerably startled our hero.

'Hit?' called out Dick, swinging his head round, for, of course, he like David had obtained a clear view of the man. 'There still, old chap?'

A growl was his only answer, and then a hasty order.

'You've swung the light off him, though the smoke is too thick to let one see just now. Get it shining down the passage. We must put a stop to that fellow's antics; his bullet as near as possible took my head off. Ah, steady! I can see.'

Yes, he could see. The lamp-light shining into the alley-way was directed upon the ruffian who had just fired; but it showed more than he. It showed a couple of dozen men pressing along behind him, the look on their faces telling plainly that they were determined to rush the barricade. Instantly David gave warning, and levelling his own weapon fired at the pirate who had so recently discharged the pistol; but he did not stop him. The bullet went astray, and striking a man just behind him brought him tumbling to the deck. However, the next proved more successful. The rascal howled with pain, then, as if driven frantic by it, he threw his pistol at the figure which he could only dimly discern above the barricade, and led his comrades forward. For ten whole minutes none of the defenders had so much as a breathing spell. Those four Chinamen at the back of the barricade fought as if they were possessed, and fought too, like Englishmen, in silence. Their knives rose and fell constantly. Now one of them would spring upward, and grabbing an attacker by the shoulder would haul him within reach; now Hung would give vent to a guttural exclamation, at which Dick and his comrades would unconsciously move aside. Then there came the thud of the huge club he wielded, a sickening, dull thud, followed by a heavy fall on the far side of the bales placed across the alley-way. A sudden fusillade from David's magazine pistol drove the assailants out of sight, and allowed the defenders to rest after their exhausting efforts.

'Put the lamp on the top of the bales,' said David at once. 'We must chance a fellow firing at it and smashing it altogether. Hung, post a man up here to watch. I'll go up and report progress, unless, of course, you'd like to, Dick.'

The latter shook his head vigorously, and was about to answer when another voice came from behind them in the alley-way. It was the Professor, jaunty and high-spirited as ever, a silent witness of the late conflict. He stepped from the foot of the ladder, and came towards them, turning the slide of a lantern he carried. And the light reflected from the narrow passage showed up everything distinctly—the dead Chinaman at the foot of the barricade; David on the ladder, and Dick and the other defenders at their posts. It even showed the huge splinter of wood half torn from the ladder by the bullet which had so nearly put an end to the existence of one of the party. And the Professor was as easily seen as any one. There was a bland smile on his clean-shaven face. His eyes sparkled; he laughed outright.

'Please don't move,' he said, coming closer. 'A more perfect picture I never beheld; but I do congratulate you all. You know I hate fighting, and always have done so; but when it's necessary, I can admire the men who show a good front. No need to report, David boy; my own eyes have shown me everything.'

Turning suddenly to the Chinamen, he spoke to them in their own language, which he knew as a native, praising them warmly, and sending the blood flying once more to their cheeks.

'A gallant fight, well organised and generalled,' he said, turning again to Dick. 'Whose idea was the ladder?'

'His,' came the curt answer. 'He fixed everything: David is a born leader.'

'I say!' came indignantly from our hero, who was still perched on his ladder.

'It's true,' came warmly from Dick, for the young fellow had formed a great opinion of David. Secretly he had admired the lad, partly for the courage which he knew he possessed, for had he not been instrumental in saving Dick's mother; and also there was the case of those burglars at Bond Street. But it was not pluck alone that roused his enthusiasm for our hero; it was his grit, his staunchness.

'Just fancy a fellow doing so much all on his own,' Dick had exclaimed more than once to the Professor. 'Many fellows of his age would have been browbeaten by that man who married his stepmother. Very few would have taken the post of lift-boy as he did. I've known young fellows sent up to London to make their way who would have turned up their noses at it, and because they could not get just the class of job that suited them would prefer to live with relatives and do nothing. That's out and out cadging. And here's David, still all alone, determined to go out to China to find a will which may never have existed.'

'I beg your pardon; it did exist,' the Professor corrected. 'I knew Edward Harbor. If he said he had made a new will, he had done so without doubt. He was most exact and painstaking in everything. He made that will in David's favour, but circumstances over which he had no control prevented his having it conveyed to a safe quarter. He perished; perhaps the will perished with him. Perhaps it was purloined along with his other belongings by some rascally mandarin, and is lying forgotten at the bottom of a heap of rubbish at this moment. But I interrupted.'

'I was saying he's so determined,' said Dick. 'He says he'll go to China when he has hardly a sixpence to bless himself with. But he takes the post of lift-boy, and in a twinkling he's made enough to take him round the world. It's grit that does it, sir. Sheer perseverance and doggedness.'

'And knowing that your cause is just; yes,' reflected the Professor.

But to return to our friends in the alley-way, the Professor again demanded who had led in the conflict which he had watched from the foot of the ladder.

'He did without a doubt,' declared Dick, pointing at David. 'Ask him about the ruction along there, sir, and then ask Hung and the others.'

Slowly the Professor dragged the details from David and from the Chinamen. Then he solemnly shook hands with every one present.

'I'm awfully glad I wrote that letter to you, David boy,' he said, when he came to the figure still perched on the ladder, 'and it was a lucky chance which sent Dick here along to trouble me. Together you've made a fine defence in this quarter. Alphonse will be delighted. But now let us go to the cabin; Hung and his friends will watch here and send us a warning if there is to be another attack. Meanwhile, there are other parts to be considered. I tell you plainly, those demons will not rest till they have taken every one of us and looted our belongings. I know the pirates of this gulf; they are a detestable set of cut-throats. But don't let that statement trouble you; we're a long way from being taken, or I'm much mistaken.'

The smile came back to his face, a cheery, confident smile. He spoke swiftly to the men present, and then skipped to the ladder.

'My word,' he cried, as he reached it, and his lamp fell upon the woodwork. 'That must have been done by the shot I heard. It was a big bullet that tore away this piece of the ladder.'

'And precious nigh took David with it,' laughed Dick. 'He got quite angry.'

That set them all laughing, for, somehow, what with the success they had already had, and the Professor's cheery presence, there seemed ample cause for merriment, merriment that was accentuated to no small degree when they reached the cabin; for Alphonse was there, in his shirt sleeves, and posted beside a huge rent torn through the doorway.

'Ah, ha!' he cried, coming towards them. 'You have made much noise below. There has been shooting. None are hurt I hope?'

'None but the fellows who attacked us,' answered Dick. 'How have things gone here?'

'Wonderful! I tell you, wonderful.'

The little man puffed out an enormous chest, and stretched his arms before him. He was pomposity itself, while the manner in which he swung the rifle, that he gripped with one hand, hardly gave one confidence. That and his peaky little beard, which seemed to project even more abruptly forward now, the huge check pattern of his shirt, and the long pointed-toe boots, which he still insisted on wearing, made one more inclined to smile at little Alphonse; and if not at his appearance, then at his gestures and his antics, for the lamp which the Professor carried played full upon him. But a moment or two later one gathered a different impression of the man.

'Ah!' he ejaculated suddenly, bending his head to one side as if he were a bird, and placing his hand behind the ear. 'Did I hear some one coming? Monsieur, Alphonse was never deaf, and he has trained his ears to catch the sound of bare feet. You do not believe it? *Bien,* then see.'

His eyebrows went up a little, as if he were unable to credit the fact that his listeners did not believe him, then calling on all for silence, he stole towards the door of the cabin, and almost at once his rifle went to his shoulder. He bent swiftly, then there came a sharp report. A crash on the deck outside, and a thunderous explosion told all within the cabin that Alphonse had accomplished something, and crowding at once to the gaping hole which the ringleader of the pirates had torn in the door with his muzzle-loader, they stared beyond at the deck. A man was crawling painfully along the boards, while immediately outside the door, as shown by the lantern, the blunder-bus the man had carried, that undoubtedly he had intended firing through the hole in the door, lay still smoking after its recent discharge.

'*Parbleu!* Did I not say so?' declared Alphonse with a flourish. 'I have ears to hear, monsieur. I caught the slither of a bare foot and I was warned. My shot caught him just at the right moment. But it might be well to hold a council. Eh? A council of war, monsieur.'

He dragged a seat close to the door, and sat down there with his head at the jagged opening. The Professor drew a cigar from his pocket, bit the end off with a snap, and lit the weed.

'A council, yes,' he said. 'I will state the facts. We chartered a ship at Shanghai captained by a rascal, and with a crew none the better. They had accomplices in the Gulf of Pechili, and the ruffians hoped to secure their booty without a struggle. Of course, we should have been cut to pieces and dropped overboard.'

Alphonse shivered, though every one could see that he was merely making pretence to be frightened. '*Dites donc,*' he cried pleadingly, 'but that is dreadful. It makes me feel faint. They would surely not be so harsh with us.'

The grimace he made set Dick roaring, while the Professor smiled grimly.

'Easy enough to make fun of it, Alphonse, but if it hadn't been for your watching we should be down below already. Other Europeans have suffered in the same way, have disappeared and never been heard of again.'

Unconsciously David's thoughts went to his father. He had been assailed more than once when in China; for even at this day, when Western influence is slowly beginning to gain ground in the Celestial Empire, Europeans are still foreign devils to the common mob, intruders, to be killed whenever possible. True, in some quarters the old animosity is beginning to disappear. Wealthy Chinese travel now-a-days, and return home imbued with the wish to give up old and useless institutions and habits, to substitute a modern education for one dating back to the days of Confucius, and to throw open the doors of their native land, so that the miles and miles of rich territory may be developed and bring forth its wealth. That is something. Thirty years ago there was hardly one single Chinaman amongst all the millions the Emperor boasted of who had been away from his native shores, and though an ambassador here and there may have returned with his eyes widely opened, with a desire to westernise his country, what was the value of his influence when all else were against him? It was death almost to suggest change. Arrogance was always a failing of the pig-tailed race, and only time and severe lessons could teach the people that there were other races on a higher footing. And lessons China has had. She has seen foreigners snatch corners of her territory. She has stood helplessly aside and watched Russia enter Manchuria and lay her railways to Port Arthur, and again has watched her neighbour, whom she formerly despised, throw herself upon the Russians and conquer them. And why? Because she had westernised her people. Because Japan had organised her navy and her army on modern lines, and armed them with modern guns. Then why should China not follow? Slowly but surely the desire to do so is filtering through the country, and slowly the change will come. As we have said, a European is still a 'foreign devil' to the bulk of the people to-day. To-morrow he may be as a brother.

'My father was killed during a sudden attack,' said David. 'He was up country, north of Pekin——'

'Where I shall hope to take you all,' interrupted the Professor. 'That is to say, if these rascals will allow us.'

'There was a missionary with him, one who knew the people well. But they were murdered for what they carried, and, as it afterwards appeared, on a sudden suggestion made to the people in the nearest village. There had been several cases of fever, and four persons had died. It was put down to the white men, and that was the excuse for their murder.'

'And that is nearly always the case ashore,' agreed the Professor. 'A missionary, for example, is the best of fellows. He helps the people, is great friends with them, and all goes well till some bigoted ruffian comes along. He wants the odds and ends the missionary possesses. He trumps up some paltry charge, works up his ignorant comrades into a fury, and sends them to murder the "foreign devil." The rascal himself generally disappears with all the white man's possessions. But here there is no working up. The pirates of the Gulf have existed for centuries; murder and pillage is their profession.'

'Hark! I heard something more; stay still if you please, messieurs.'

Alphonse again canted his head to one side like a bird, and one could see that he was listening. His peaky little beard seemed actually to bristle. He jerked his head. His blue eyes sparkled in the lamp-light, then he leaped to his feet.

'The lamp, monsieur,' he cried, 'put it out. They are above us; they have clambered on to the roof of the cabin.'

David could hardly believe it, and though the whole party stood absolutely silent for nearly five minutes, it was not till that time had elapsed that a sound came to their ears to confirm Alphonse's statement. There was a loud bang on the roof, followed by others.

'Pardon, monsieur,' said Alphonse quietly, taking the lantern from the Professor's hand. 'I go to see what is doing. Perhaps one of the messieurs will support me.'

He moved to the doorway promptly, and David sprang to follow. Dick and the Professor drew the bolts silently, though there was little fear of being heard, for the noise above was now very great, the sound of rending wood coming clearly to them. Then they pulled the door open, and Alphonse and David stepped out.

'Up the ladder, *mon cher*,' whispered the Frenchman. 'I will climb, and you after me. I will cast the light upon them, and at once descend. You can cover me with your pistol; but first to see if the deck is clear.'

They stood still for some seconds, staring into the gloom. But already the light was coming, so that they could see further than at the beginning of the attack. Without a doubt the deck was unoccupied, save by the bodies of those who had fallen. Alphonse nudged David at once, and slid across to the ladder that mounted to the roof of the cabin right at the side of the ship. In a minute both were high enough, then Alphonse coolly turned the slide and threw a broad beam on the enemy. The roof was packed with them. A dozen men, at least, armed with native adzes, were hacking at the deck in as many different places. The Frenchman, undismayed by the angry shouts which greeted his appearance, coolly cast the beam on either side, and only desisted when one of the enemy, a huge fellow with muscular limbs, leaped forward, swinging his adze.

'Monsieur, I think it rests with you,' he said quickly, sliding to one side to allow David to clamber a little higher. 'Monsieur shoots well. He has nerve, eh? That fine fellow will trouble us no longer.'

There was no trace of excitement about him, even when David with a well-directed shot brought the ruffian crashing to the deck. Alphonse merely chuckled, then squeezed himself still more to one side, politely making more room for our hero.

'We will return now if monsieur is ready,' he said. '*Merci*, I will follow.'

He came slowly down the ladder after David, and entered the cabin again as unconcerned as if he had merely been out to look at the weather. As for our hero, the recent exploit concerned him far less than did the report he brought to the Professor.

'Two dozen of them, working like demons to break through into the cabin,' he said. 'I can't see how we can prevent them. We can shoot through one or more of the gaps, but when there are so many we shall not be able to watch them.'

The Professor took a long pull at his cigar. David and Dick saw the end of the weed redden in the darkness, while the smoke he blew from his lips was visible in the reflected light. Then Alphonse opened just a crevice of the lamp, thus allowing them to see one another. Even now the features of the leader of the expedition were anything but mournful. The jaw was, if anything, a little squarer. The Professor wore the appearance of a man who is confident, but who at the same time has his back against a wall.

'Call Hung,' he commanded, and when that worthy appeared, 'Run along beyond the barricade,' he urged him. 'Take Hu Ty with you. Report if men are in the bows, and if so, how many. Do not appear on deck. Send the other two to me.'

They came clambering up from the dark alley-way a moment later, Jong still grinning, the more so when he listened to the racket taking place overhead, while Lo Fing kow-towed before his master.

'We are here, Excellency,' he said. 'Your orders?'

'Take everything you see that is of value. You know what the boxes contain; carry them down below at once. Quickly! There is no time to lose. Dick, David, Alphonse, put your backs into the work.'

'Going to make a stand down below,' thought our hero. 'The only move we can make. I wonder if we could get right forward.'

Like the others, he seized upon the boxes that contained all their possessions, and which the Professor, with a knowledge of Chinese cupidity and cunning, had insisted should be stacked in the cabin. Then, when after some three minutes every bale and box was below, he ventured to broach his ideas to the Professor.

'Thought of it myself,' came the short answer. 'Go along with Hung. He's been back to say that the coast is clear. Report as soon as possible if there is a place where we can make a stand. I don't care for this alley-way. Too much like rats in a trap. Quick with it, David.'

In that instant, if never before, David realised that here was indeed a leader; for the Professor was not in the smallest degree flurried. His cheroot still glimmered redly. He drew in the smoke and blew out huge billows. But all the while he was listening to the sounds above, calculating the chances of his party, thinking how best to act so as to secure their safety.

'Why not?' he suddenly exclaimed aloud. 'It's been done before. Why not again?'

'Pardon, monsieur,' ventured Alphonse, standing beside his master, as if to guard him. 'You spoke.'

'Of something that occurred to me. All in good time, my friend. What do you think of the situation?'

The Frenchman threw up his eyes and shrugged his shoulders in a manner sufficiently expressive. 'Monsieur knows better than I,' he said. 'I shall still live to cook and valet for monsieur.'

'Then you shall if I can contrive it. Ah, there is David. Well?' asked the leader of the party.

'Not a soul forward. It's lighter by a long way,' reported our hero. 'I sneaked on deck, and counted forty-three Chinese over our heads. They are hacking away like madmen.'

'Then we will leave them to it. In five minutes at least they will have broken through into the cabin. Get below and shoulder a box, David. We are following.'

The Professor marshalled his little force into the alley-way, and stepped coolly down the ladder after them. Not one word did he utter to hint what were his intentions. All that his supporters knew was that they were retreating from a position that was no longer tenable. But as to the future — well, Alphonse's shrug gave them little indication.

Chapter IX
A Game of Long Bowls

'Excellency, we have come to the end of the passage; we can go no further,' declared Hung, some two minutes after the Professor and his party had set out down the alley-way. 'A ladder leads to the deck above, while there are sleeping places for the crew on either side. Is it here that you will make a stand?'

'Halt! Put your loads on the floor and wait. Come with me, David.'

The leader of the expedition, still puffing heavily at his cigar, and showing an almost unruffled countenance in the lamp-light, stepped casually to the foot of the ladder and began to ascend to the deck of the native craft which he had chartered at Shanghai for the accommodation of his staff, and upon which such a treacherous and unforeseen attack had been made. But if he were the essence of coolness, and declined to hurry, he was by no means a fool, as he showed very plainly in the course of a minute. For while the Professor refused to be frightened and scared out of his wits, he declined at the same time to throw away the lives of his party for the want of necessary caution.

'Don't come higher,' he whispered to David. 'I'll beckon if I want you. Ah, it is still too dark for those ruffians to see us from the poop where they are at work. Come up, lad, and look about you.'

He tossed his cigar over the side, and David heard the hiss of the water as it met the burning weed. A moment later he was beside the Professor.

'Well?' demanded the latter, when some seconds had elapsed. 'What do you say to the situation? Critical I think, eh? Very critical. By the row those demons are making they have broken through into our cabin in more places than one. In a few minutes they will have a leader, and then there will be a rush. We certainly couldn't have stemmed it; they would have killed us with the greatest ease; but where shall the next stand be made?'

Where indeed? David cast his eyes in every direction, piercing the gloom as far as possible. The bare decks gave no promise of successful defence. To retreat to the wide cabin below, which served as the crew's quarters, was but to repeat a former experiment. There remained the rigging and the alley-way, and neither was very enticing. He shrugged his shoulders, as if he had caught the habit from Alphonse, and then turned to his employer.

'We can put up a fight anywhere almost,' he said. 'Out here we should soon be rushed and knocked down. In the alley-way we could hold them for hours. But it couldn't go on for ever; there are too many of them. My idea was calmly to board the other ship and push her off. That would give us a breathing spell. We could then discuss matters again and consider our plans from a different standpoint.'

The Professor chuckled loudly; unconsciously he reached in an inner pocket for his cigar case, and extracting a weed, bit the end off. David even heard the sharp snap of his teeth coming together. 'Boy,' suddenly exclaimed the leader, 'they say that great minds think alike; then yours and mine are great indeed, for the plan you have suggested is mine also. That is why we carried our baggage all along the alley-way. Summon the others on deck. We go aboard the stranger and merely change our quarters; but bid them be silent, for even now those fiends might hear something to rouse their suspicion.'

However, it was not a likely contingency, for as David went to the hatchway to call to those below fiendish yells rose from the poop of the vessel. Then some ponderous weapon was fired, the flame for a moment allowing the Professor to catch a sight of the crowd on the roof of the cabin. A second later they were swallowed up in the gloom, though their shrieks and shouts still told of their presence.

'All on deck, sir,' reported David in his most official manner.

'Then follow to the other ship. Not a sound, friends; not a sound. Once aboard David and Dick run to find a suitable place which we can defend; Hung and his comrades set their boxes down and prepare to stop a rush. Alphonse and I cut the hawsers which hold the two ships and push them apart. Forward!'

In one corner of his mouth the unlighted weed was held, and all unconscious of the fact that he had not set flame to it, the Professor sucked hard at the weed, exclaiming as he found it did not draw. Then, as if habit were too strong for him, or perhaps because he realised that none were likely to see him in that gloom, he stepped back to the hatchway, descended a few rungs of the ladder, and opening his lantern sucked at the flame. Then he followed the others, and was soon at the side of the vessel. Casting his eyes upward, he could see the rigging of the other ship against the stars, while a dull creaking, and an occasional bump showed that the two ships were riding close together.

'But with rope fenders between them,' he told himself, 'else in this swell they'd grind holes in one another. Ah, the rascals threw planks across from rail to rail, which was most thoughtful of them.'

With half his attention given to the enemy, and the other half to his own following, he helped to hand the various bales and boxes across the planks connecting the two ships. Then he crossed over himself, and searched for the ropes it was necessary to sever. Here a sudden difficulty presented itself. One of the connecting links was a stout chain, which the swell and the drift of the vessels had pulled so taught that there was no unloosening it.

'We shall have to cut it,' cried the Professor. 'Alphonse, an axe, quick, those rascals are dropping into our cabin.'

But to call for such an article when just arrived on a strange ship is one thing; to find it an altogether different matter. Neither Alphonse nor Hung, nor any of the Chinese could hit upon one. And while they searched the uproar made by the enemy, which had almost ceased for a time, became of a sudden even more deafening.

'Discovered our absence; awfully bothered,' ejaculated the Professor. 'But they won't be long in discovering our ruse. Can no one find an axe? David, the scheme fails if we do not hit upon one within the minute.'

Alphonse ground his teeth in a manner which would have made our hero squirm on any ordinary occasion. The Professor sucked hard at his cigar and muttered beneath his breath, while Hung threw himself upon the tantalising chain and tugged vainly at it. Then David recollected an incident he had watched at the beginning of the battle between themselves and the Chinese pirates.

'One moment, sir,' he said. 'An axe? Yes, I know where to find one.'

Without hint of his intentions, he cooly stepped on to the planks still uniting the two vessels, and leaped down upon the deck of the one which had proved such insecure shelter for them. Not a sound did his light shoes make, while his figure was swallowed up within a few seconds; for though it was already lighter, the dawn was not there yet, and gloom still hung over the water. Behind him he left a Professor not so unruffled as he had been. To speak the truth the leader of the party was dumfounded for the moment, and only awoke to the danger our hero was necessarily likely to encounter when the latter was already out of sight. He called to him loudly; he even leaped on to the planks himself. Then Alphonse stopped him with a grimace and a tug at the sleeve of his jacket.

'Pardon, monsieur,' he said, 'a leader stays with the bulk of his command. It is the young and brave who attempt such deeds. Monsieur David is no chicken; he will be back with us within the minute.'

'Or hacked to pieces by those villains; but you are right, I will stay. Still I wish that I had guessed his intentions. Dick there, and all the others, get ready, in case he is seen and pursued.'

Alphonse clicked the lock of his rifle promptly, while Dick ranged up at the end of the planks, his magazine revolver gripped in his hand. Then the ever-smiling Jong lisped an apology, pushed the Professor aside, and solemnly clambered on to the planks and crossed them. There was a huge knife in his hand, and his smile was but the cloak to a most sinister expression.

'Velly likely he no wantee helpee,' he lisped, as he dropped to the deck of the other vessel. 'But velly likely also he velly glad. Jong stay here unless he happen to see de Excellency; den p'laps he go towards him.'

The words had hardly left his lips, and his padded soles scarcely gained the deck when a figure was seen coming swiftly towards him. It was David. No, it was a Chinaman, a burly, thick-shouldered individual; then close on his heels another figure followed.

'David,' whispered Dick, scarcely able to breathe. 'George! that other chap is coming aboard.'

Certainly that was the man's intention. He was returning to his own ship to fetch a mighty muzzle-loader which he had previously forgotten. He reached the rail, placed a hand upon it, and was about to spring on to the plank bridge when Jong was upon him. And if any one had ever doubted the grinning Chinaman's courage before, his doubts would have been for ever silenced if he could have witnessed what followed. For this was not one of those sudden conquests, when an unsuspecting man is struck down without time for self-protection. The stranger saw Jong as the latter moved towards him, and faced round with the swiftness of a panther. Then his head went back, and such a shout went up that none could have failed to hear it. A moment later the two were locked in one another's arms, rolling this way and that on the deck, tearing madly at one another. And over them David stepped, with an axe across his shoulders.

'Grandly done! Bravely done!' cried the Professor, showing not a little excitement. 'David, stand by to cut that chain. Hung.'

But Ho Hung was not there to acknowledge the summons. He had flown across the bridge of planks the instant David gave room for passage, while Lo Fing chased close on his heels. How exactly they ended the contest between the two rolling figures none of their own party ever knew; but end it they did.

Meanwhile a lamp flared suddenly in the cabin which David and his friends had so recently vacated, while shouts resounded from various parts. Then the half shattered door of the cabin was burst open with a bang, and a crowd of men swarmed on to the deck. They were met by another group ascending from the hatch by which the Professor had brought his party, and then by a solitary man, who shouted and bellowed at them.

'They have fooled us; they have slipped across into the other vessel. While we have been cutting holes through the roof of the cabin they have been transferring themselves and their possessions.'

The greeting which the news received was such that Dick winced, and felt almost unnerved for the moment. But the Professor reassured him; a glance at the leader showed that he was still drawing heavily at his weed, while his features and his general pose were almost jaunty.

'Shout yourselves hoarse, my beauties,' Dick heard him say. 'I fancy we've fooled you finely. Now, lad, you can strike your hardest.'

And strike David did, careless of the shots which two of the enemy aimed at him. He brought the edge of his axe down with a thud on the chain, and severed it easily. Then he leaped from the plank bridge and helped to throw the boards over.

'Moving asunder already, sir,' he said. 'Might just as well get under cover.'

'Quite so; it will want an active man to leap that breach. Get beneath the rail all of you,' commanded the Professor. 'Don't trouble to return their fire, for they cannot damage us easily, while we have already read them a handsome lesson. Ah, they are more than vexed, I fear.'

Through the rising gloom it was seen that the rail of the ship which so lately borne David and his friends, and which had proved well nigh a death-trap, was lined with men. Some had clambered on to it, and held their places there with the aid of the rigging. All were shouting and gesticulating, all save the few possessed of fire-arms, and these rammed charges home with frantic haste, and poured their shot into the vessel slowly and steadily drifting away. If their defeat so far had enraged the piratical crews, their anger now was almost stifling. At the very beginning the feat of murdering the foreign devils, and of purloining all their possessions, was one not to be considered twice. Had the Professor been gifted with second sight, or had he had the help of some clever native detective, he would have learned that the rascally captain who had been so eager to charter his boat was already gloating over his gains when the ship set sail from Shanghai, while the leader of the pirates treated the whole affair as if already accomplished. There was to be a secret meeting, a sudden attack, and then cold-blooded murder. And see the result! Men here and there stark and dead on the deck or in the alley-way, others grovelling in the scuppers useless to their comrades, stricken hard by the knives of Hung and his fellows, or by the bullets of the foreign devils. Worse than all, the men whose death had been aimed at were drifting quietly away, not showing so much as a head, bearing with them all their possessions—yes, all their possessions. The pirate leader had already assured himself of that fact, exclaiming bitterly at it. David and his friends caught a glimpse of the man, a bull-necked, almost bald-headed Chinaman, with long, swinging pigtail, and possessed of most powerful arms and legs. They saw him standing on the rail, clinging to the rigging, brandishing a huge sword which, could it have come into close contact with them, would have done grave injury to more than one. The rascal seemed to be almost mad. The failure of a well-laid scheme, the loss of his own vessel on top of that, seemed to have combined to rob him of his wits. His eyes were staring. He frothed at the mouth, while the cruel lips curled back from a row of fangs as yellow as his own skin. And how he shrieked! Then he suddenly dropped back on to the deck, and they saw him beckoning to his comrades, rushing at those nearest him and dragging them along with him by main force. He drove them with threats from his weapon to the halyards, and shouted at them as they hauled at the rigging.

'Going to set sail on her,' said the Professor, raising his head now that a greater distance separated the two vessels, and the shot had ceased to hail upon the one on which he and his party had taken refuge. 'Well, two can play at that game. I'm not much of a sailor myself, but Alphonse knows something about other things besides cooking and valeting. Eh, *mon ami*?'

'*Parfaitement*; the Professor has a memory. Alphonse can certainly sail a boat, though he has never attempted much with one of these native craft. But the thing shall be done. Will monsieur be good enough to order the hands to come to the rigging?'

It was remarkable how swiftly the gloom lifted, now that the dawn was actually at hand. A second or so before it had seemed certain that the two vessels drifting slowly apart would soon be out of sight of one another. But though the distance sensibly increased David could still see men lining the rail of the enemy. He could still hear frantic shouts, while now and again a muzzle-loader belched forth its contents, the flame of the discharge showing less redly than on former occasions. Then the dawn arrived. The expanse of oily, yellow sea, hitherto invisible, widened on every hand, while a pinky redness towards the east told of an approaching sunrise. The Professor sucked with satisfaction at his weed and glanced aloft. Alphonse was swarming into the rigging, no doubt to inform himself of its arrangement. Then he came scuttling down, his frightful check shirt fluttering in the fresh morning breeze.

'It is easy, monsieur,' he said, with a bow, dropping on the deck at the Professor's feet. 'All is plain and straightforward. I shall set the sails with the help of our friends, and then I shall go below and see what can be done in the way of coffee and something to eat. *Parbleu!* but the inside needs attention after such a night There are things a man loves more even than fighting.'

He called loudly to the Chinese, and then, with David and Dick and the Professor to help him, soon got sail on the ship. A vast expanse of coarse canvas was soon stretched from the rigging, and catching the breeze caused the vessel to career nicely. She gathered way, and was soon tearing away with white foam washing about her stern post. Meanwhile the pirates had crowded every stitch of canvas they could find on to their own ship, and came heading up a little in rear and on a parallel course with the one the Professor had so cleverly taken from them. As for the latter, his jovial, fleshy face shone with good humour and *bonhomie* as he stood at the tiller. Now and again he took his cheroot from his lips and regarded it affectionately, then he put it back between his fine, white teeth with such relish that one could see that he was decidedly enjoying it. In fact, Professor Padmore was proving himself a leader in more than one respect. For after all, beyond the power to command, such an one has need to show other virtues. Of what use even the most astute leader, if he be not confident even in the midst of acute danger? For confidence is as catching as is a display of fear. Men will run from a fight with little reason if there be one suddenly to set the base example and arouse needless alarm. And on the other hand even those possessed of no extravagant share of courage will stand firm if they have a leader who laughs at danger, who scoffs at the enemy, who openly exposes himself to bullet and shot. But here there were no cravens. David and Dick had proved their fortitude, while the four Chinamen were to be trusted entirely. But the odds were vastly against them, so great indeed that even bold men might have been intimidated. However, the Professor smoked as if he had forgotten the existence of the enemy, though now and again he cast his eye over his shoulder.

'Holding them nicely, I think, David. They're not likely to come alongside before breakfast's ready, and that'll be a comfort, for I confess to being ravenous. Just fancy a professor being anything so vulgar. But there you are, I admit to the vulgarity; this morning breeze spurs a man's appetite.'

He felt in his waistcoat pocket, and drew out a metal case, somewhat bigger than a watch. With a movement of the finger he sprang the lid open, and exposed the face of a compass.

'H-hm! North-north-east,' he said. 'That's our course. Not for a moment will I allow those ruffians to set me off it.'

Perhaps a quarter of an hour elapsed from the time when sail had been set before Alphonse put in an appearance. He came clambering to the deck, his enormous hat set far back on his head, and showing the stubbly growth beneath it. In one hand he bore a smoking coffee pot, and with it beckoned to the Professor.

'I have the honour to announce breakfast!' he exclaimed, in his most pompous manner, and with his most portly bow. 'There is a cabin below decks, not big, monsieur, not very clean either; but serviceable, and possessed of a table. There I have laid the things.'

The whole thing seemed so impossible, that as they squatted before a table not more than a foot high, and ate rashers of bacon which were steaming hot, David could hardly believe that but an hour ago they had been fighting desperately. The change in their circumstances was so extraordinary. It was so entirely unexpected, and withal, so fortunate. And here they were, satisfying the inner man, for Alphonse was an excellent caterer. The boxes which the Professor had brought with him contained a multiplicity of things, including cameras and other instruments necessary for exploration. And amongst them was one fitted with all the implements to make a field kitchen. There was a charcoal stove, as well as one designed for the use of kerosene under air pressure, an instrument with which a good-sized kettle of water could be made to boil within a few minutes. Then there were pots and pans innumerable, while other boxes contained stores of groceries and tinned goods sufficient to keep every member of the expedition satisfied for a considerable period.

'Now to discuss the position,' said the Professor, when he had swallowed a third cup of coffee and had begun to smoke again. 'Hung has just sent a report to inform me that we still hold our place ahead of those men who so dearly long to draw level with us. We sail, as I have said already, on a course which suits us exactly. That being so, we shall continue till we reach some port, where we will run in and demand protection, or until we meet with some other vessel. There are gun-boats in these waters at times, and we might have the fortune to hit upon one belonging to Great Britain, or to France or Germany. I fancy those rascals would quickly beat a retreat if that were to happen.'

'Meanwhile, perhaps, sir,' began David, 'we might as well see if, supposing the worst were to happen, there are means aboard to make those fellows keep their distance.'

'Cannon?' asked the Professor.

David nodded. 'That was my idea, sir,' he said. 'This vessel belongs to pirates; the chances are that they have some sort of weapons.'

'And we might make good use of them. Good! we'll make a search. Alphonse, we leave you here for the moment.'

They clambered to the deck hurriedly, to find the ship careening well to a freshening breeze, and bowling along merrily through a sea that was sunlit in all directions. Some distance astern, and now on a dead line with them was the other craft, white foam at her fore foot. Even her white decks could be seen as she canted over, while with the naked eye one could distinguish figures moving about on it. Suddenly Dick gave a shout of satisfaction, and pointed to a canvas cover at the back of the steersman.

'A long tom, or I'm much mistaken!' he cried. 'Covered up to keep the weather from it, and used only to bring some stubborn captain to his senses. Couldn't we manage— —'

'I rather think so,' agreed the Professor, smiling gleefully. 'I rather fancy we might make use of that weapon, Dick. Strip the covering, and let us obtain a glimpse of it.'

It took but little effort to lift the cover which had attracted Dick's attention, and then, as they had suspected, there was a long, swivel gun cast in brass, and no doubt capable of throwing a shot some considerable distance.

'Then we'll put it in action,' decided the Professor. 'Not that I want to damage any more of those rascals; but there might be some accident to our rigging. Or, in a fresher breeze, which I fancy is coming, this vessel might prove slower than the other. We'll make the most of fairly smooth water and of our new possession; perhaps it will scare them.'

Once more the handy and invaluable Alphonse was in request. The natty little Frenchman seemed to have had a hand in almost everything. He could cook, as all knew, particularly his employer, while he was the tidiest of valets. Moreover, Alphonse could fight, and with a spirit that matched the Professor's. Now he showed his capacity as a gunner. He led the search for shot and powder, and then ranged himself behind the gun.

'Once I was a soldier, monsieur,' he said, 'and though I did not belong to the artillery, still I had to do with a gun; for I was in garrison where a mid-day gun was fired, and to me that duty fell. *Oui, vraiment,* we shall be able to manage. We must guess the charge of powder. Not too much at first, monsieur David; else there will perhaps be only pieces of us left for the pirates. We will watch where the ball strikes the water, and add more if necessary. You shall see; Alphonse will send those men a pill which will make them ill at ease and cause them to go elsewhere in search of a doctor. Ah, there is the powder; we have rammed it home. Now a piece of the sacking as a wad. Now the ball. Push with me on the rod and we will soon send it home.'

The practical little fellow slewed the muzzle of the gun round, and used the screw as he squinted along the sights. Already he had sprinkled powder on the touch hole, and presently announced that all was in readiness.

'I have laid it to be fired as we rise to the top of the swell,' he said. 'Now for a match with which to fire it.'

David had thoughtfully prepared a match, consisting of a candle end tied to a stick, and shaded by a paper hood which kept the wind from it. It was a makeshift affair, and the flame blew out twice in succession. Then the gun splashed out a stream of flame, followed by a dense volume of smoke, which, however, blew away instantly. Their ears were still tingling after the loud report when a jet of water was seen to rise a hundred yards in front of the pursuer. Instantly Alphonse tossed his hat into the air and shouted.

'*Bon! Bon!* The next time we will do it, yes,' he said. 'Now to sponge the gun clean, and then for a fresh charge.'

That second shot proved far more encouraging. The ball struck the surface just to one side of the vessel that was following them, and ricochetted some three or four times before it finally sank to the bottom. But the third shot plumped clear on to the deck of the enemy, causing considerable commotion.

'*Bien,* we have the charge at last, and with this long swivel the aim is easy,' cried the Frenchman. 'Let us try again.'

A roar of applause greeted the fifth shot, for though fired by amateurs it struck the mast of the pursuer, and as they watched, the Professor and his friends saw the rigging sway and come tottering over.

"A ROAR OF APPLAUSE GREETED THE FIFTH SHOT"

'Thus ends all our trouble,' he cried. 'We can shorten sail, and go on slowly.'

Late that evening Hung announced a ship in the offing, and before darkness had fallen a gun-boat ranged up beside them. In fact, she fired a shot across the bows of this suspicious-looking vessel, and then sent a boat's crew aboard her. A dapper little Chinese officer swarmed up on her deck, and even he, with all his native impassiveness, showed unusual surprise as his eyes fell upon the Professor and his party.

'English?' he asked pleasantly, bowing courteously, and then, when he had received an assuring answer, 'Then there is something to explain. We are in search of a notorious pirate.'

He spoke English with hardly an accent, and his face lit up wonderfully as the Professor answered. Then, as he listened to the tale the latter told him, a flush rose to his sallow cheeks.

'You will please to come aboard at once,' he commanded. 'This news is very important. My commander will require the fullest information.'

It appeared, in fact, that news of the pirate's presence in those waters had come to the Chinese navy officials, who had despatched a gun-boat.

'Some one gave information in Shanghai,' explained the dapper little officer. 'No doubt he did so for a reward. But we learned that some Europeans had set off in a native boat, and that there was a plot to seize them. We made sure when we sighted you that you were the pirate. Now, of course, we shall take them easily.'

Which actually happened, for four hours' steaming brought the gun-boat within easy range of the vessel that had so lately accommodated the Professor and his party. Then, such is the summary justice handed out by the celestial race, the ship was callously bombarded, and sent with all the villains aboard her to the bottom.

'For which one cannot really grieve, though it does seem a barbarous way of executing them,' said the Professor. 'And now to get ashore and pursue our search for ruins.'

Two days later saw them landed, and within a little while the expedition had left for the interior.

Chapter X
Ebenezer Clayhill's Inspiration

Mr. Ebenezer Clayhill was not the man to be thwarted without displaying some show of opposition, and though the course which David Harbor had taken, and the result of his action in the Courts had considerably perturbed the owner of 'The Haven,' the latter did not remain despondent for long.

'The young rascal!' he exclaimed to his wife one day, as they sat in the flat which they had rented in London, for longer residence in their own house was hardly possible, the publication of their doings having roused the ire of the countryside. Indeed, both Ebenezer and his wife had been hooted in the village, while, on rising the morning after their return from the trial of the case they had been astounded to discover a huge notice board in the garden, prominently displayed, with 'To Let' in large figures, a very obvious hint that their presence in those parts was no longer required.

'The young rascal!' he exclaimed again, blowing his huge nose with unusual violence. 'I suppose he thinks to have things all his own way.'

'And so far he has won all along the line,' came the brusque if not very encouraging answer from Mrs. Clayhill. 'I knew what it would be if you quarrelled with the boy. A more stubborn, strong-headed youth I never met. It was your sending him from home which upset matters.'

Mr. Ebenezer glared at his wife over the top of his handkerchief, and when he at length exposed the whole of his countenance it was flushed a deep red to match the wonted colour of his proboscis.

'We won't discuss that,' he said icily. 'The boy hasn't won, though he appears to have done so. Recollect that he has yet to find that will, and China is a big country.'

The reflection appeased Mrs. Clayhill for the moment. 'Yes, China is a big country,' she agreed, thoughtfully. Then she again recurred to David's stubbornness, as she was pleased to characterise his pluck and staunchness. Indeed, the reader will have been able to draw his own conclusions. If standing up for oneself, and fighting one's own battles when a most evident wrong was attempted was stubbornness, then David was undoubtedly of that persuasion, decidedly stubborn to say the least. 'China is a big country,' as Edward Harbor was never tired of telling me. But he'll do it. If that will exists, as I believe it does—for my late husband was most careful and particular—then David will discover it. Drat the boy!'

'Precisely! We will allow that he will hunt high and low,' said Mr. Ebenezer, assuming a soothing tone of voice. 'We will even assume that he will find the will, though of that I am extremely doubtful. But will he bring it back in safety? That is the question.'

At his words his wife looked up sharply. She was accustomed to Ebenezer now, and had found him to be a schemer. Not that that fact annoyed her. On the contrary, as has been already mentioned, this lady was not of the nicest disposition. Had the whole truth been known, she had schemed to marry Edward Harbor, knowing him to be a rich man, while she was almost penniless. She was, indeed, not altogether guiltless of scheming herself, and found in Ebenezer a man somewhat after her own heart. She looked up sharply, questioningly, and waited for him to continue.

'Well?' she demanded, after a while, finding he remained silent, save for the fact that he drew his handkerchief from his pocket again and applied it to his nose, trumpeting loudly, an old and disagreeable habit that was often annoying. 'Put that handkerchief away, Ebenezer, and tell me what you mean. What are you driving at? The boy may find the will, you say, but you doubt his bringing it back safely. Why shouldn't he be able to do so? If he actually finds this will, surely that is the most difficult part of the task. I don't understand you.'

'My dear,' came the answer, as Ebenezer pulled at his handkerchief again, and then, suddenly remembering that it annoyed his wife, tucked it away. Instead he rose and placed himself in his favourite position on the hearth-rug, expanded his chest, and put on an air of great importance. 'My dear,' he said, 'let us assume that he gets this document. He discovers it in China, in the part where his father carried out research work in connection with some old Mongolian city. I say, let us assume that he is so fortunate. Well, China is a country of disturbances. Foreign devils are not over loved, and—er—well, you see—er—sometimes there are robberies committed. Edward Harbor was murdered, probably for his small possessions, his guns and other things necessary to him on such an expedition. David might——'

'Be murdered! You don't mean that!' exclaimed Mrs. Clayhill, holding up her hands in horror, and sitting up sharply in her chair. For that was going too far. A scheme was a scheme, she told herself. She had gone so far already in her efforts to oust her stepson from all benefit in his father's possessions, that she would not hesitate to scheme further; but she drew the line sharply at personal violence. That was against her wishes altogether.

'Ebenezer,' she cried severely, 'I forbid you even to talk of such a thing. If we cannot enjoy this money without doing actual violence to David, then I will at once go to the solicitor, Mr. Jones, and show him that letter Edward wrote me. If I produced it, there is not a shadow of doubt but that a judge would advise a jury against the will we have put forward. The wording is so strong that there can be no doubt not only of my late husband's intentions, but also of the fact that he actually executed a will in David's favour. It would end the matter for good and all; we should be almost paupers.'

Mrs. Clayhill was quite agitated, to say the least, and was almost angry with her husband. In any case she was consistent; for while she was not averse to a scheme which would do no one personal or bodily harm, she would rather resign all interest in the possessions of her late husband than have David injured. And as might be expected, Ebenezer was not left altogether unruffled. The excitement was too much for his powers of self-control. He dragged his handkerchief from his pocket and trumpeted again, a shrilly, discordant note which seemed to match with Mrs. Clayhill's temper. Then he regained his coolness, and held his hands up in a soothing manner.

'My dear, my dear,' he cried, somewhat querulously, still hot and perturbed at the thought of the consequences of such an act as his wife had threatened, 'whoever said a word about violence? Not I; of that I am sure. I merely remarked that China was a disturbed country, and that Europeans are hated people, open to robbery and violence. I was about to proceed when ——'

'What then?' asked Mrs. Clayhill, abruptly, relieved to hear that no violence to David was premeditated, and eager at the same time to learn what her crafty husband could have thought of. 'What is the scheme, Ebenezer? You keep me in a whirl. The anxiety of this will is making me quite miserable. See what has happened already. The people in the village actually insulting, hooting us in the street; servants leaving us *en masse*, even the outside staff ceasing work and departing. Why, we shall have to let the house. We can never show our faces there again. And then think of what the papers said. It makes me hot and cold all over in turn as I remember the names they called us.'

It was all very true. Mr. Ebenezer and his scheming wife had imagined that everything would go very smoothly for them; for they had but a lad to deal with. Up to the time of David's being told that he must now work, and must leave home for London, there had not been even a question as to the succession to Edward Harbor's money. It had been a recognised fact that all his wealth was to descend, and at once too, to Mrs. Ebenezer Clayhill and her husband. Even the solicitor, Mr. Jones, with a natural liking for our hero, and, therefore, with every wish to see him done justice to, had been unable to demur. Unwillingly, it is true, but as a matter of ordinary business, he had carried through the proving of the will put forward by Mr. Ebenezer Clayhill and his wife, and had obtained judgment allowing him to presume Edward Harbor's death. Then, when everything should have gone smoothly, trouble had begun. David had for the first time shown an inclination to contest the will. He had mentioned the existence of a letter from his late father, evidently written at the same time as that sent to Mrs. Ebenezer, and intimating that he was to be the chief beneficiary under his father's will. That bomb-shell had caused consternation, even greater consternation than David's sudden determination to leave home. From that moment the two schemers had known little peace; their scheme was threatened. They began to wonder whether they would actually succeed to the money, and whether also by their action in suppressing that important communication from Edward Harbor they laid themselves open to punishment. David's sudden accession to popularity, the laudatory remarks made concerning him in the papers after the burglary at the store near Bond Street had served to increase their ire and vexation. Finally, they were forced to attend the courts to show reason why the will of the late Edward Harbor should not remain unexecuted, pending a search for a later one mentioned in the letter which David's advisers laid before the courts. Let the reader imagine their anger and mortification. Let him add to that the fact that Ebenezer and his wife were the talk of the country, universally condemned by all, and that their own home no longer afforded them an asylum; he will then readily agree that retribution was coming, that these two schemers were not finding their path of the smoothest. But they were not beaten. Ebenezer spread out his hands again, in an attitude meant to be most soothing, and addressed his wife once more.

'We are wandering from my point,' he said, as placidly as he could, though he found it hard to keep his temper. 'I mentioned no violence to the young cub whom you have the misfortune to own as a stepson. I merely said that he might find it difficult to bring the document home with him, even if he were so fortunate as to discover it.'

'Ebenezer, you have something to tell me,' came the sharp answer. 'What is it? You have been hatching some plan.'

His wife smiled encouragingly at him, and awaited his reply with obvious eagerness. For she had found in this new husband a crafty fellow, and even now had faith in his powers to bring this matter to a successful issue. 'Come,' she said, 'what have you done?'

'I have had a most distinct piece of good fortune. All this prominence which the papers have given us, and which has been so disagreeable, has been useful nevertheless. It has roused a vast amount of interest in the case. People have read every word the papers have written.'

'As we know to our cost,' sniffed Mrs. Ebenezer.

'Precisely. People have read every word, even foreigners, and as a result I received a few days ago a letter from a man living in the east end of London—from a Chinaman.'

Mrs. Ebenezer pricked up her ears; the plan was beginning in a promising manner. 'A Chinaman,' she ejaculated. 'Indeed!'

'A Chinaman engaged in the East End; a man recently come from his own country, where he had come in contact with Europeans. He had actually been with Edward Harbor on one occasion, and seems to have made himself invaluable, for he speaks English well, and can cook and do other things. He offered to help us.'

'For money, of course!' exclaimed Mrs. Ebenezer, satirically.

'Of course, my dear; for what else? He has no direct interest in us. But supposing he were to succeed in helping us, then his interest comes in. We could afford to reward him handsomely.'

The lady leaning back in her chair nodded sharply, and looked at her husband with a cunning gleam in her eyes. She was beginning to see daylight Here, perhaps, was a means to defeat David Harbor and without subjecting him to violence. She fanned herself with a newspaper, for the sudden hope which the tale brought made her feel oppressively hot. 'We could afford to reward him handsomely,' she declared, in the most unctuous manner. 'What did you offer?'

'I gave him a hundred pounds for his expenses, and promised a thousand if he were successful.'

Mrs. Ebenezer clapped her hands energetically. She was delighted, and thoroughly in agreement with her husband. What a shrewd fellow he was, to be sure, she thought. Why, a thousand pounds was well spent if only they could destroy that will, the existence of which paralysed their own schemes, and might make paupers of them. Then a sudden doubt came to her mind, for like every schemer and dishonest person this lady was quick to perceive where this plan might break down. She imagined herself in the place of the Chinaman who had come to her husband, and cogitated what she would do under similar circumstances.

'Why,' she suddenly declared, in no little alarm, 'a hundred pounds is riches to a Chinaman. Supposing this ruffian makes off with your money, and does not try to help you. Supposing he forgets all about us once he has left the country?'

'He has left the country already,' came the swift and somewhat disconcerting answer. 'I sent him off hurriedly; he will not fail us.'

'Why?' Mrs. Clayhill was insistent. More than that, she was more than usually artful. In fact, Edward Harbor, poor fellow, could not have come across a woman less suited to his tastes and feelings, while Ebenezer Clayhill found in the widow of the late Edward Harbor a woman cunning and clever, and to some extent unscrupulous. To some large extent one might say, for who could describe the action of this pair as other than unscrupulous? Alas! the attempt to deprive a near relative of possessions due to him is nothing new. The same sort of sordid scheme has been practised many a time with variations, and sometimes with success. Not every case has been associated with a lad of David Harbor's nature, nor with one possessed of his determination and courage. Still, if in this particular affair there were such a person, as these two schemers had found already to their chagrin and cost, on the other side our hero was opposed to a couple of crafty people, of whom Mrs. Clayhill was by no means the inferior.

'How do you know that this fellow will not fail us?' she demanded, rising from her seat and walking to the window, which she threw up, as if the room were too hot for her. 'How? I am suspicious.'

'You always are, my dear,' chuckled her husband. 'But it will be all right. This Chinaman is the very man we want. I told you it was a piece of extraordinary good fortune his writing to me, for there is more to tell you about him. He is a deposed mandarin.'

'I thought no such person existed,' said Mrs. Clayhill quickly. 'A mandarin at fault is a dead mandarin, so far as I have been able to gather.'

'Unless he escapes. Unless he escapes, my dear,' suggested Mr. Ebenezer.

'Then this man? — —'

'Escaped. Disguised himself, and made for Canton on a river boat. Then, thanks to his knowledge of English, he was able to ship aboard a vessel sailing for England. Once China was left behind he was safe, and the crafty fellow so contrived matters that it was assumed in his own country that he had become desperate, and had thrown himself into the river. That mandarin, to all intents and purposes, is dead. He can begin life again in China as an altogether different person, without incurring any suspicion. No one, not even the mandarin who had his trial in hand, and who had caused him to be arrested for an attack upon some Europeans would recognise him. Dao Chang is a name which none will associate with Hang Chiou, the mandarin who was to have been beheaded.'

'Attack on Europeans! This man a mandarin, and yet a servant to Europeans,' protested Mrs. Clayhill. 'I am bewildered. There is something missing in your description, Ebenezer.'

It was not at all remarkable that she was to some extent confused, for at the beginning of his tale of this Chinaman, the ruffian, who was the instigator of this attempt to rob David Harbor, had declared that the man had taken service with some Europeans, and could cook, as well as speak English. Then how could he be servant and mandarin at one and the same time? Surely there was an error in the narrative! But Ebenezer smiled cunningly as he noticed his wife's bewilderment, and again spread his hands out in a manner calculated to soothe her. Then he made a dive for his handkerchief, but remembering in time, rubbed both fat members together as if he were washing them. To speak with absolute impartiality the man looked, as he stood there in front of the fire, precisely and exactly what he was. He had the appearance of a mean, sneaking villain, capable of planning the most cunning plot from the security of his fireside, but sure to turn tail and decamp at the first sign of danger. But his wife was blind to his imperfections. Had she been as other women are, no doubt, she would have recoiled from this man. But Mrs. Clayhill was what she was, and guile and cunning pleased her. She went back to her chair, and sat down in the most placid manner, as if she were listening to the most ordinary tale.

'Go on, Ebenezer,' she lisped. 'You interest me vastly. Tell me more of this man who was mandarin and common servant.'

'And who was arrested for complicity in the murder of certain Europeans,' remarked her husband, promptly, and in the quietest tones, to which, however, he contrived to lend some subtle note that was easily detected. Swiftly his wife looked up, loosing all appearance of placidity.

'For complicity in the murder of certain Europeans,' repeated Ebenezer, watching his wife closely, and bringing into special prominence the last two words of his short sentence.

'Certain Europeans 'What do you mean? Ebenezer, I do declare, you bewilder me. Certain Europeans! Why, you can't mean that——'

There was a sleek smile on the man's face as she looked up at him. He appeared to be in that position where he hardly knew whether it would do, considering all the circumstances, to show pleasure here, though, knowing his wife as he did, he rather fancied she would not take umbrage if he were to show some trace of satisfaction. And he was right. Mrs. Clayhill smiled. After all, poor Edward Harbor was only a bitter memory to her.

'You can't mean that this man had to do with the murder of poor Edward,' she cried, attempting to assume horror, though there was no doubt at all that she was vastly interested. 'Tell me more,' she demanded eagerly. 'This man is a find indeed. I can't believe it possible. He implicated in that wretched affair! You will tell me next that he had something to do with this will which David has gone in search of.'

If Ebenezer ever allowed himself to laugh outright, he was as near as possible permitting himself that luxury on this occasion. His fat face reddened and beamed. His nose became peculiarly prominent on account of its heightened colour, and once more his hands washed oilily together. Ugh! He would have given an honest person a cold shiver.

'You are wonderfully far-seeing, my dear,' he laughed. 'And now you seem to have got to the depth of the story. This Hang Chiou, or to give him his modern name, Dao Chang, is as crafty as he is long-headed. It appears that Edward Harbor and his staff were working in his district, for Chang was only a minor official, and very poor at that. He saw that the expedition was possessed of certain riches, and moreover, he knew that they had discovered ancient bronzes which would bring money in one of the open ports. He decided to have that money. He gave out that he was going to Pekin on an official visit, and quietly disguised himself as a coolie. Then he took service with Edward Harbor and his partners. One day he led a band of coolies against them, and killed them all. Then he swore all the coolies to secrecy, and declared himself as the mandarin of the district. Of course, the bulk of the booty fell to him, and with it all Edward's papers. He had hardly returned home, however, making believe that he was from Pekin, when he was betrayed by a coolie, and at once arrested. You know the rest of the story.'

Truly it was a marvellous narrative; it was almost unbelievable—yet, why not? Unless the whole thing was a plot to obtain money. Mrs. Clayhill promptly voiced the doubts in her mind.

'He may have fooled you,' she declared. 'One hundred pounds would hardly tempt him to return to China. Most likely he is still here.'

But there was no doubt in the face of the man who had been speaking. Ebenezer looked confident. He chuckled as he thought of his own astuteness.

'My dear,' he proclaimed, with unusual emphasis, 'it requires a clever man to deceive me. Besides, I am very careful. I booked the man's passage. I saw him off. He was aboard when the ship was in mid-ocean. The wireless telegraph told me that with ease and certainty. No, let us have no doubts. Dao Chang does not require money alone to tempt him to China. He willingly risks his head to get even with the coolie who betrayed him, as also to work his revenge on the mandarin who was the actual cause of his downfall. Besides there is another reason. If he could earn the money I have promised, he could buy evidence to clear his name with the greatest certainty. He could even buy a position of some power, and of greater affluence. In fact, he could reinstate himself. There is his object.'

'But— —'

'You cannot see farther. Quite so,' said this soft-spoken ruffian. 'I will proceed at once. Chang sailed promptly so as to land in China before the party to which David is attached. He will enter himself as one of their servants. Then he will earn his reward from us by taking possession of the will should they happen to find it. If not, he himself will make search for it on his own account. Should that happen he will have done with your stepson and his friends, though I suspect that he will relieve them of any valuables. He will send us the document so that we may destroy it, and will then be free to carry out his own business. Our affair first, you understand, his own afterwards.'

It was a crafty piece of scheming when all things were considered, and looking at the matter from Ebenezer's point of view there was no reason at all why he should not be eminently satisfied. For fortune seemed to have played fairly with him. The very ruffian who had instigated the murder of Edward Harbor had offered his services; and it was this Chinaman's direct interest to find the will for which David was journeying to the country of the Celestials. It was not as if the man had been asked to discover a jewel of vast value. For then one might easily have suspected his honesty and good intentions. Here only a document was in question, a piece of parchment, perhaps, with a few written lines upon it, valueless to all but our hero and the two schemers who should have been father and mother to him. Valueless in any case to Chang, the ruffianly Chinaman, so useless, in fact, that he would be eager to change it for the thousand pounds so readily offered by Ebenezer. Undoubtedly, the man who had married David's stepmother was delighted, and by the time he had finished his narrative, so also was Mrs. Clayhill.

'It is all wonderful and most fortunate. I can sleep in peace,' she ventured, 'for I know that no violence will be offered.'

She departed from the room in high feather, while hardly had the door closed when her husband smiled broadly, and in a most suggestive manner.'

'Clever woman,' he told himself. 'Precious clever; but I have to remember that she is a woman, with natural distaste of murders and sudden attacks.

Glad I didn't tell her all that Chang hinted. What luck to be sure to have dropped on the fellow. You could have knocked me down with a hat pin when I received his letter.'

Perhaps it was as well that Ebenezer had not told his wife all the story; for there were parts of it to which that lady would most certainly have taken exception. As Ebenezer had remarked, Chang had hinted many things, and had, in fact, spoken openly.

'You leave it to me to stop this English boy, then?' he had asked, prior to his departure on the boat. 'If, for instance, I could send certain news that he was killed or drowned, or something of that sort, that would be sufficient?'

'I will pay a thousand pounds for that will with pleasure,' Ebenezer answered promptly. 'Of course, should this young fellow come by an accident, and his death be sworn to by a British Consul, then the money would be paid with equal pleasure.'

There was no need to say more. The two ruffians parted with the most perfect understanding, Chang to formulate schemes to bring about David's undoing. And very soon he had an opportunity to carry them out. He disembarked at Hong-Kong, and waited for the arrival of the steamer on which David and his friends had left England. Then he sneaked on board as a deck passenger, disembarking at Shanghai, where it will be remembered, the Professor and his party landed. And at once news reached Chang that a native boat was about to be chartered. It was an opportunity not to be missed. The Chinaman dived in amongst the ruck of men in the bazaar, and soon discovered others of equal villainy. It took little persuasion on his part to induce a man to offer his boat to the Professor, and but little work to organise a scheme of attack with a piratical vessel. Then Chang watched the departure with a grin on his ugly features.

'I think I shall be able to apply for that money very quickly,' he told himself. 'The scheme of attack is one which can hardly fail to be successful.'

Yet it failed, much to his fury. Thanks to Alphonse's watchfulness, and to the heroism of the whole party David and his friends escaped. It was the miscreants hired by Chang who suffered in the adventure, and indeed lost life and everything. Chang found himself at the beginning of his task again, and what was worse, was now far removed from the Professor and his party. However, that was a matter which could be remedied, and taking a boat along the coast it was not long before he landed at the port where the gun-boat commanded by the dapper little, English-speaking Chinese officer had set them.

'Foreign devils marched up country,' he was told, when he made cautious enquiries. 'Been gone some days, but you will easily catch them. They are making for the Ming To ruins.'

It was in that neighbourhood that the rascal Chang actually came up with the expedition, and thereafter set his wits to work to bring about the destruction of the party, and failing that, the death of David Harbor.

'I can crawl into the camp at night and slay him,' he told himself. 'Or I can fire at him while at work in the ruins. Yes, that is better. I shall certainly kill him.'

He crept off to a hovel where he had obtained a lodging, and throwing himself upon the kang, closed his eyes and gave himself up to deep contemplation. In Chang David had all unknowingly an enemy even more subtle and more dangerous than Ebenezer Clayhill.

Chapter XI
David goes on a Journey

'And now to investigate the secrets of the ruined city wherein dwelled Tsin the mighty, Tsin, the ruler of a tiny principality, who years and years ago set himself one of the biggest tasks man has ever undertaken.'

They were seated in their tent in the light shed by a candle lamp, and the Professor lolled back on the tiny camp-bed which was to be his own special property. Indeed, a glance round the camp showed clearly that the expedition was organised thoroughly, and promised by the equipment it carried to give comfort to every one. For first, there was the large tent for the use of the Professor, David, and Dick, with its three narrow beds, its collapsible table and chairs, and its waterproof flooring. Then, a little distance away was a smaller, bell tent, in which Alphonse was to repose, and beside it, within easy reach, a field kitchen, while further still was a third tent, similar to that occupied by Alphonse, for the accommodation of the four Chinese.

'Of course, those whom we employ to help us with the digging will have to find their own quarters,' said the Professor at the very beginning of their forming camp. 'There happens to be a village some two miles away, and no doubt the inn there will take them in. But there are also one or two old buildings still standing in this ruined place, and they will probably elect to settle there.'

That, in fact, was what the dozen coolies whom he had hired had decided on. Already they had secured the basement of what had been a two-storied house, though now the upper part had gone, while to effect an entrance into that below needed quite a lot of excavation. For the rest, the camp was pitched on a grassy knoll some hundred yards from the ruins and within three miles of the huge Chinese wall, which, not so perfect now-a-days as it was wont to be, is still a marvel of human ingenuity and perseverance, stretching as it does for fourteen hundred miles over hill and valley, cutting the northern provinces of China from the rest of the world.

'As I was saying,' began the Professor again, 'we are about to investigate the ruins of the city—quite a small place, I imagine—in which dwelt Tsin, the one-time ruler of a small province in this neighbourhood. You must understand that he was one of many kings controlling the numerous provinces into which China was divided some two thousand years ago, a somewhat different condition to that now ruling, for there are only some fifteen provinces now-a-days. Tsin, like all the rest of these little kings, was for ever squabbling with his neighbours, so that there were frequent little wars, and as a natural consequence many additions were made to, or territory taken from, the various lands belonging to these kings. However, Tsin seems to have been fortunate, for he made additions. In fact, he ate up his neighbours, and with more wealth and more men increased wonderfully in power. He ended by conquering every part of China, and becoming Emperor of the Celestial Empire.'

'And richly deserved his reward, no doubt,' ventured David. 'I should imagine that the people were all the happier for having one ruler only. Trade and other matters must have gone more smoothly.'

'I agree with you; things probably were more fortunate. But Tsin was not without his troubles; his kingdom was for ever being invaded by Mongolian nomads from the north, nomads who were as elusive as they were warlike. They devastated portions of his kingdom, and when armies were sent in pursuit they melted away, taken in ambush, or lost hopelessly in the desert. It was to check those nomads that Tsin started the Great Wall of China beside which we lie, and no doubt, once completed, it fulfilled its purpose. It will repay a visit one of these days.'

Dick and David had, as a matter of fact, already visited the huge wall, and had marvelled at its vastness. For this Great Wall of China is not merely an erection two bricks thick; it is a huge earth wall, faced with masonry, buttressed and supported everywhere, and freely supplied with fortified gates and quarters for its garrison. Fourteen hundred miles of it, stretching across the kingdom! Think of the enormous labour, think of the host required to guard its length. And to-day it is deserted, or almost so. The broad track on its summit, constructed of such a width that three carts could conveniently be driven side by side, is now no longer of service. Mongolia has ceased to send in her nomads. Perhaps the very presence of the wall has prevented them, or maybe they have become less warlike. There the wall lies, a work to rouse the admiration of modern-day people.

'And now to speak of these ruins. They are small, as I have said already,' the Professor told them, 'and since I do not expect to discover much of interest, I have decided to send you two lads forward. John Jong shall go with you, while the naval officer who spoke such excellent English has provided me with passports. It seems that his father is a mandarin, and commands the district a hundred and fifty miles north, where are located the Mongolian ruins I am so anxious to investigate. Will you go?'

Would they go? David and Dick were as eager as the Professor himself to dip into the past by investigating the ruins of the city in which Tsin had dwelled so many hundreds of years before. But a journey through China offered superior attractions; and besides, there was another city to be visited, or rather the ruins of one that had formerly existed.

'Go, sir? Of course!' declared David, with marked enthusiasm. 'Nothing I should like better.'

'Quite a little experience for us, sir,' declared Dick. 'Do we march or ride?'

'The latter. You will go in state; that is, you must create a good impression wherever you travel, for that will appeal to the natives. I don't think that there should be any difficulty, nor any danger. The passports I have and the letter you will carry to Twang Chun should command attention, for it seems that he is a very important official. More than that, like his son, he is westernised, speaks English and French, and longs for the day when his country will be less bigoted and cramped. Of course you will take arms with you, and since it is always as well to keep on the right side of the natives and attract little attention, you will travel in native costume. Jong will see to that part for you.'

There was jubilation in the faces of our hero and his friend. They glanced at one another as the Professor ceased speaking, and then grinned openly.

'Ripping!' exclaimed the latter. 'Swells we shall be. Jong will be too big after such a journey to speak to his countrymen. But how about putting up for the night, sir?'

'As far as possible you will avoid staying in a village, and in case it should happen that you find yourselves a long way from a town of any importance, you will camp in the open. I brought three *tentes d'abris* with me, and those will accommodate you very nicely. Of course you might go to the native rest-house or inn; but I don't advise it. There is, as a rule, only one guest-chamber, with one long *kang* or couch on which to lie, and since the Chinese are none too clean in their persons you would find such quarters most unpleasant, besides laying yourselves open to robbery. In the big towns you will at once ask for the residence of the mandarin, and this letter which I shall entrust to you will certainly obtain a lodging under a fine roof and with comfortable surroundings, unless, of course, the mandarin happens to be bigoted, and hates all foreign devils. There are few, I imagine, who will care to displease Twang Chun, the Governor of the province. Now, as practice in such matters is excellent for all people, I leave it to you two to organise your own expedition. Get out a list of the things you imagine you will want. You will each have a Tartar pony for riding purposes, and can take three more besides the one Jong will ride, making roughly a spare horse apiece for your baggage. Let me see the list when completed.'

It may be thought that such a task as was now given to the two young fellows would take but a little while to complete. But when they came to make the list of which the Professor had spoken they discovered that they were often in doubt. For instance, with regard to the question of ammunition.

'Twelve rounds apiece for magazine pistols, ditto for rifles,' said Dick, as if he had been at this sort of work a long while.

'More!' exclaimed David, with a knowing wag of his head. 'There might be a ruction; we might be attacked.'

'Pooh! Never did come across such a firebrand,' laughed Dick. 'Always imagining that we are going to run our heads up against some sort of trouble. Still, if you think so, we'll carry more. Say forty rounds each. How's that?'

'Right; far more sensible. Now for grub. My word, we mustn't run short of that!'

David was always a good man at his trencher. The open-air life they were now leading, the novelty of his surroundings, and the exercise he enjoyed had given him an appetite there was no denying.

'Of course we might shoot something,' he said, 'though we haven't seen much so far that would be worth the while. Besides, in this queer country one hardly knows what it would be proper to kill and what not. The Professor says one has to be careful not to touch other people's belongings, and the latter are often straying about. Vote we make our list of stores a handsome one.'

In the end they took sufficient tinned meats to last them for two weeks, having reckoned that the journey would not take longer than eight days. A small bottle of brandy was included in their stores, rice for Jong, a bag of biscuit, and a box of dried apples.

'Makes a splendid sweet,' declared David. 'Soak 'em over night in water, or milk if you can get it. Same with the rice you mean to use. Then put the two into a cloth, tie up the top and pop the whole into a kettle. Boil it, my boy, till the rice is done to a turn, and serve it with a sprinkling of sugar. That reminds me—tea's wanted, sugar too, and don't forget a kettle, a frying-pan, and a saucepan.'

'Besides tin mugs, a teapot, spoons, forks and knives.'

'And a filter to pass the water through. Can't be too careful,' said David. 'Water supplies in this country are not often too reliable, and though one can be quite secure by drinking boiled water, yet one hasn't always the time, nor the fuel, so we'll take a filter.'

Having completed their list to their entire satisfaction, they consulted Jong, and with his help packed their stores into three lots, which were so arranged as to be easily secured on the pack saddles which the Professor had purchased. Then they took their list to the latter and asked for his approval.

'Very complete,' he agreed. 'All that I can suggest now is cash. You will want an abundance of the small coins on which the Chinese coolie places such value. A little scattered now and again will gain friends for you. A handful will buy you a sack of rice when your store is exhausted; I shall hand over a sufficiency, while for funds on your arrival, should you need money, this letter will obtain the same from Twang Chun. And now, the sooner you get away the better; let us say to-morrow. You had best be up early so that Jong can complete your toilets. Don't forget that it is necessary that your appearance should be correct in every particular, just as if you were endeavouring to disguise yourselves.'

On the following morning, before the sun had risen, and while still a grey mist hung over the cold land, David and Dick turned out of the tent, took a dip in a lake close at hand, and then submitted themselves to Jong's attentions.

'Allee lightee,' he lisped, grinning as they came to him. 'Soon makee Excellencies same as one Chinaman. Allee same, so that mother not be able to knowee dem. Jong shavee de head now. Den put on de pigtail. Not eber wear him before, Misser Davie? Den you soon see. Fine, Misser Davie. You one great big swell, wid a tail reachin' lightee down to de middle ob you. Now boil de kettle, get de soap, sharpen de razor.'

He set about his work humming a Chinese refrain devoid of all tune, while Alphonse emerged from his tent in his shirt sleeves, and using a native bellows soon had his fire going. It made the lads laugh to watch him hopping quickly about, and to see the extraordinary costume which he still adhered to. For if David and his friends out there in China were still, in spite of their local surroundings, in spite of essentially Celestial environment, undoubtedly Englishmen, Alphonse was as decidedly a Frenchman. His peaky little beard, and the way he carried himself, as well as the quickness of his movements, told one that. It was not necessary to regard his extremely loud shirt, his appalling cap, nor the pointed boots which he found comfort in wearing.

'*Bien!* You depart to-day. *Bon voyage, messieurs,*' he said, as he brought them each a steaming cup of tea. 'Let Alphonse tell you that you will find native costume comfortable, as comfortable as is mine, for he has tried it. *Oui, messieurs,* he has tried it. He owed his life to the disguise once.'

David could not imagine how any disguise could cloak this very obvious Frenchman. He smiled a little dubiously.

'Ah, you do not believe. Then I will tell you. It was on our last journey, the Professor's and mine. The people were angry with us; we were foreign devils who had caused the rain to fall for a month in succession. They surrounded the house; guns were fired; there was a great commotion.'

'What happened then?' asked Dick, eagerly.

'They dragged us out, the Professor and myself. They put us into wooden cages and carried us in them to their mandarin. But he, though he did not love foreign devils, was afraid to harm us. He took us into his house, saying to the mob that he would hand us over in the morning. Then he dressed us like natives, and passed us out through a back door very secretly. *Bien, messieurs,* we strolled through the mob. They would have torn us to pieces had they known that we were the foreign devils they had captured. We passed through them and got right away. It was what you call a narrow shave.'

'And the mandarin, how did he explain your flight?' asked David, curious to hear how such a matter would be arranged in this country of surprises, of ignorance and bigotry.

'I will tell you. He barred the door and the window. He burned our clothes. In the morning he took the ringleaders of the mob to the room and announced that they were free to kill us. Then he feigned as great surprise as they. He pointed to the charred remains of our clothing, and suggested that we had vanished into the air, perhaps to stop the rain, for as luck would have it, the downpour ceased that very evening. I tell you, for us it was a close shave.'

He bustled off to his camp kitchen, leaving the lads wondering greatly. To them the tale seemed impossible. But then they did not know China very well. They had no idea of the crass ignorance and superstition which even to-day sways the mass of the people. Had they had more knowledge, they would instantly have realised that such a sequel was possible, and that in the Celestial Empire one can encounter hopeless ignorance on one hand, and a depth of cunning adjacent to it. But Jong had his pot of water boiling now, and had put a fine edge on to the wedge-shaped native razor which he intended to use. He quickly lathered the hair over the temples and round the crown of each lad's head, and rapidly removed those portions. Then he produced two wonderful pigtails, and having snipped the hair left on the crown as short as possible, he heated the base of the pigtails, thus melting the adhesive already there, and applied them. A touch with a stick of charcoal to their eyebrows made a vast effect, while a line drawn outside the eyes gave a distinctly Celestial expression. After that it took but little time to don the native costume, and before Alphonse announced breakfast both David and Dick were dressed for their journey.

'You look at least forty,' declared the latter, surveying his friend, and bursting into a merry peal of laughter, 'and as wise as any judge.'

'While you should be at least the governor of a province,' grinned David, delighted at his friend's appearance. 'Now for the Professor.'

'Excellent!' declared the latter, walking all round them. 'I can find no fault; Jong has turned you out wonderfully well. But you mustn't stride along like that, David—nor walk with such an elastic step, Dick, my lad. Recollect that a Chinese gentleman, as you are supposed to be, has little if any call to show energy. He is essentially a tranquil person. His face is as impassive as that of a Red Indian's, while he seldom smiles. And above all he is deeply imbued with his own dignity. So, however youthful and merry you may feel when by yourselves, remember to look austere when in the company of strangers. And now to discuss the route. I have a map here, and as I have been over the ground before I have been able to put down all the chief towns you will pass. Of course there are thousands of completely walled cities in China, particularly up in this direction, where Mongolian incursions are always likely. You will pass several, and will, no doubt, sleep the night in more than one. Now, I have looked over your list of stores, and have suddenly remembered drugs. Alphonse has packed a box containing useful tabloids and other medicines, besides a supply of bandages and dressings. Ah! breakfast's ready; come along.'

An hour later the little cavalcade was ready to set out, and once more the Professor inspected the lads and their mounts. To speak the truth, even a native of the country would easily have been deceived, for David and his friend looked exactly what they were meant to look, namely, two Chinese gentlemen of some importance travelling through the country with their servant.

'Of course you are not bent on commerce,' said the Professor. 'No Chinaman of any importance would soil his hands with trade. You are two officials going through to see Twang Chun. Good-bye! Look for me in a month's time.'

'Gee-up!' shouted Dick, shaking his reins. 'Good-bye, Professor!'

They headed at once for the road that stretched across the country adjacent to the camp, and which perhaps had even borne Tsin, the mighty ruler of the Celestial Empire in those far-off days. Then they settled down to their long journey, David and Dick alongside one another, chatting and laughing, and Jong behind, his bare toes in the stirrups,—for the cold weather was not yet on them,—his reins knotted on his pony's neck, and leads from the other three animals attached to the bow of his native saddle.

'I rather fancy it will be as well to have some sort of regulations for marching,' said David, when they had accomplished some ten miles, and the camp was only a memory to them. 'You see we are foreigners, though we don't look it, and something might turn up when we least expect it.'

Dick laughed loudly. David vastly amused him, and, if he had only made a clear confession, interested him also. For the lad displayed so many sides to his character. At one moment he was as dashing and plucky as one could wish. A regular fire-eater he had shown himself in the affair in the gulf of Pechili. And at other times he was as cautious as any old woman.

'You do make me smile,' declared Dick, searching for a handkerchief, a luxury which neither had yet abandoned, but for which, nevertheless, it was somewhat difficult to find a handy place in the strange garments they were wearing. "Pon my word, you make a chap roar. Always imagining danger's coming; always taking precautions; always getting ready; and then, no sooner does something spring up, all unforeseen, as it were, than you chuck all precautions, venture out into the open, and practically invite people to shoot you. Look at the ship—helped to get the party away from what was an ugly trap, and then, when all were safe, walked peacefully back in search of an axe. You do really take it.'

'Shut up!' growled David, crossly. 'I'm serious.'

'So am I.'

'Look here,' declared our hero, with some warmth, 'I'll not stand any more of—oh, I say, let's be serious,' he laughed, for who could be angry with Dick—Dick the merriest and most light-hearted of the party? For if ever contrasts were asked for, a better example could not be brought forward than David and his companion. The one, as Dick had said, a strange mixture of dash and daring, and of shrewd, almost nervous caution; and the other, Dick Cartwell, as jolly as the day was long, the most thoughtless individual breathing, an inconsequent, harmless sort of fellow, who made friends of all and sundry with an ease which was astonishing. Caution! Dick threw it to the winds.

'Don't get looking round for trouble till trouble troubles you, old boy,' he had said on more than one occasion when twitting David. Dick followed the proverb strictly. He made no effort to look into the future, to prepare for squabbles, even in a country not altogether friendly. Left in command of the Professor's party, he would have been soundly asleep when the pirates so stealthily slipped aboard the vessel and slid along the decks towards the cabin. But once the danger was present, once he was with his back against a wall, there was no better nor more reliable fellow. Dick fought with as light a heart as he possessed when eating his dinner. Light-heartedness was his one fault, in fact, if one could actually declare it a fault; for on the march and under everyday conditions it cheered his companions and helped wonderfully to keep every one going.

'Well, let's hear all about this matter,' he asked, smiling at our hero, and urging his steed beside him with a kick from his heel. 'You are anticipating trouble.'

'Nothing of the sort. I do declare you are an aggravating fellow. I say that we are in a country where foreign devils are not too popular, and though we don't appear to be foreigners, yet people might discover our nationality. In fact, they are sure to when we put up in the towns. Very well, then. We must take it turn and turn about to watch, Jong doing his share with us. Of course I'm speaking of the time when we are out on the road, or in camp, should we settle down outside a village or town. In the house of a mandarin we should be free from interference. Now, what do you say to the plan?'

'A beastly bother, but necessary perhaps. I agree. When do we start?'

'Right away; nothing like getting settled down to our duties. We'll have a chat with Jong.'

They pulled their ponies round and edged them up alongside the single store pony trotting at the Chinaman's left hand.

'We're going to take it in turns to watch when on the road,' said David. 'I'll start now, and continue till noon; then Dick till late in the afternoon; then you'll come on duty. We'll share the night out evenly when we're in the open.'

Jong took a few minutes to absorb his meaning. Not that the man was dense; it was simply because he had not a very abundant command of English.

'Allee lightee; savvey,' he exclaimed at last, with a curious little lisp which rather became him. 'Jong say dat allee lightee. Watch, den no easy to be cut to piecee. Neber know who or what comin' along. P'laps dere robbers. Dey make mincemeat of de lot of us before you have time to breathe. Jong watch like a dog. Him savvey!'

'Then I start right off; let's get back to our places.'

The two young fellows kicked their lazy little ponies into a canter, and pulled them in again when they were some fifty yards ahead of the Chinaman. And until the hour of noon David kept a careful eye all about him. Then they halted for a spell, Jong quickly getting a kettle over a fire and the water boiling. A cup of tea and a slice from a tin of meat put all in a good temper, and made them ready to proceed. That evening, as the shades were lengthening, they slid through the gates of a walled city. Dick's hours for duty were almost ended. In a little while they would be under a roof and, they hoped, in hospitable quarters. But neither Dick nor David nor the talkative Jong saw that figure trailing along behind them on the main road. Not one had observed a man creep from a ditch a mile from the gates of the city, and slink cunningly after the party. For it was Chang, and his object so far was to remain in the background, undiscovered till the hour for action had arrived.

Chapter XII
Chang announces his Errand

Never before had David or Dick been within a Chinese city, and from the moment of their arrival at Hatsu they were vastly interested with their surroundings.

'Lidee light through de gate, Misser Davie,' advised Jong. 'Not take no notice of de guards. Dey common fellows. Den Jong lead you to de house of de mandarin; you have fine food and lodgin' dere.'

But as it turned out, there was no easy admission to the city. A dozen quaintly dressed Tartar soldiers barred the way, bearing modern rifles across their shoulders.

'Who are you? Say where you come from!' demanded one, who seemed to be an under-officer. 'Do you come from the country where sickness rages?'

Jong at once came forward as interpreter.

'My masters come from the sea-coast,' he said, with an air of authority, which carried weight at once with the soldiers. 'There is no sickness in the parts where they have been. They bear important letters to Twang Chun, and passports for your governor.'

'Show them,' demanded the Tartar under-officer, who seemed to be bursting with his own importance. 'Perhaps you are telling lies. Show the letters.'

He stepped up to David and seized his pony by the head. Then he closely scrutinised our hero.

'Bring a lamp,' he ordered one of his men. 'It's too plaguey dark to see, particularly under this gateway. Bring a light; we shall then be able to look at these fellows.'

He jerked at the bit, causing the animal to rear, and the man himself to let go his hold. At once David put his heel to the pony's side, and sent him plunging in amongst the soldiers, upsetting the officer with a crash. At the same instant a lamp was brought, and the light showed the Tartar picking himself up, while already he had drawn his sword. Then, fuming with rage, he advanced again and seized the pony.

'Let us look closely at you, you who bear important letters,' he cried. And then he gave vent to a shout of astonishment. 'Mandarins of importance, did you say, rogue?' he shouted, turning on Jong. 'These are foreigners, white men, hated foreigners from the West.'

He gripped at David's clothing and would have torn it from him, had not the young fellow again set his mount plunging. Then Jong pressed his own animal forward; for whatever else he might be, however amusing and garrulous, Jong was not a laggard where blows were being given and received, nor did he hang in the background when there was need for instant action. He gripped the Tartar by the shoulder and shook him as a dog would shake a rat.

'Fool! he growled, angrily. 'Who said that my masters were indeed mandarins? They are people of importance, and bear important letters. Are you so anxious then to incur the anger of Twang Chun, the Excellency who commands the province, that you thus interfere with us? My masters will show the letters, but you shall not read them. Bring the lamp; if you are not careful we will take you with us to His Honour who commands in this city.'

At a sign from the faithful fellow David produced the pouch in which the letters were carried, and showed them to the man, looking askance as he did so at the soldiers, for it was evident that they were fully ready for mischief. Indeed, had he but known it, Hatsu bore none too enviable a reputation. It appeared, indeed, that only some few months before an attack had been made in this city upon some European missionaries, and had resulted in the death of one. As a consequence the commander of the place had been dismissed, while a number of the delinquents had been beheaded; and the common people still smarted under what they imagined was a grievance. However, the magic name of Twang Chun carried the day. The Tartar officer drew back grudgingly, eyeing Jong as if he would dearly have loved to kill him. Nor did he regard the disappearing figures of David and his merry companion with any better favour.

'Foreign devils in disguise!' he growled to his men. 'Why in disguise? Tell me that. Answer me that question. Why do foreign devils come to our city and demand entrance when the dusk has fallen? Why?'

He held the lamp up to each face in turn, and receiving no answer bade them enter the guard-house with him. He caused the doors to be closed, and then spoke with no little show of excitement.

'Why do foreign devils reach us when the evening has come, and attempt to pass us disguised as mandarins? I will tell you now. You who are ignorant and do not gather news have heard only as a rumour, perhaps, the fact that death stalks through the provinces of Manchuria—black death!'

They recoiled from him at the words. Lethargic and eminently fatalists as are the Celestials, their fatalism and their easy resignation to all that is inevitable are not proof against the terrible epidemics that sweep across the country at times. Even small-pox, which makes its ravages in different quarters practically the year through, and being, therefore, no new thing to the natives, scares them wonderfully when it makes its appearance in any particular locality. But small-pox is not to be compared with the black death, not to be mentioned in the same breath with that hideous pneumonic plague, which decimates cities in a week, attacks both young and old, and once it has seized a victim, rarely spares his life. Besides the Tartar officer was right. Pneumonic plague had appeared in Manchuria, and was stalking through the land. Cases had even been reported in the adjacent provinces of Russia, while the disease was spreading in the direction of Pekin. Everywhere in the neighbourhood of the infected area distracted creatures were fleeing, carrying the disease with them, and spreading it across the land. What more natural thing in a country of amazingly simple and ignorant people than that the onset of this black death should here and there be put down to some outside influence? The foreign devil was a target at which to throw all the blame. And this Tartar under-officer, no doubt as bigoted and ignorant as his fellows, found in the coming of David and Dick a subtle scheme to import the plague to Hatsu.

'We have heard that there is great sickness,' said one of his men. 'We have been told that plague assails the people. It has even been reported that soldiers have been called to positions north and east of Pekin to hold the frightened people back.'

'True, comrade, true, every word of these reports. Our commander has himself been called away to receive orders with regard to the placing of the soldiers. But see how the foreign devils manage these things. They come to us in disguise. They enter our city with letters of introduction to his Excellency Twang Chun. With forged letters, you may be certain.'

The gaping mouths of his audience showed how the news affected them. Give the Tartar soldier his due, he is one of the best soldiers China possesses, but he is as ignorant and as bigoted as any of the people. Moreover, he is just as ready to run from the cry of plague as he is ready to discover in a European the cause of his misfortune. Growls of anger came from the men, disturbed, however, a moment later by a loud challenge from the sentry. He was calling for men to help him to shut the gates—for the hour for closing the city had arrived—and as he did so espied a figure creeping in through the archway. He brought the man to a stop with his bayonet within an inch of his breast.

'Move not,' he commanded, 'else will I plunge the blade home and send you to converse with your ancestors. Son of a dog, what do you here at this time?'

Another shout brought the Tartar officer running out with his men, while one carried the native lantern, a huge affair of oiled paper. They held it up close to the stranger's face, while the officer approached closely.

'Who are you?' he asked suspiciously. 'A follower of those foreign devils?'

'In their service, no,' came the emphatic answer. 'Take this; let us talk.'

The man pulled a handful of money from a bag suspended to his girdle, and gave it to the under-officer. 'Let us talk,' he repeated. 'I follow these foreign devils it is true, but not as their servant. I come to bring a warning.'

'There! did I not say so?' declared the officer instantly, his sallow face flushing. 'I have but just told these comrades that Hatsu would be well without such visitors. I have warned them of the plague.'

Chang, for he it was—the rascal paid to proceed to China in search of David, paid by Mr. Ebenezer Clayhill—beamed on the soldiers, and followed them into the guard-house eagerly. To speak the truth, the artful scoundrel knew something of the history of Hatsu, and recollected that certain of her people had received punishment for an attack on Europeans. He had come to the city with the intention of stirring up popular hatred of the foreigners, if that were possible, and of setting the people on them. If not here, then elsewhere. And here, there was already a beginning with an excellent excuse for further action; for the faces of the Tartar guard showed that even the mention of foreign devils caused them to grunt with anger.

'Then you have been speaking to them, friend,' said Chang, when he was comfortably seated. 'Tell me their story.'

'There is little in it I was suspicious of them on the instant my eyes fell upon them, in spite of the dusk. Mark you, these foreign devils came in the gloaming, in disguise, and told of letters to Twang Chun, the Excellency who commands the province.'

Chang's crafty features twisted at the mention of the high official, for he recollected that it was he who would have executed him. But he told himself that absence and his change of name, to say nothing of the fact that it was supposed that he had been drowned, made him safe from detection. He laughed loudly at the story.

'And you believed all this?' he asked, feigning incredulity.

'I knew they lied. I was but just telling my comrades that they came to bring plague to us, no doubt to increase the punishment already suffered by our people for the justifiable attack made on others of the same race.'

'Then you told them the truth. The foreign devils will scatter the plague in this city of a certainty if they be not removed. Listen, friends. Who knows of their arrival, who but you?'

'None, none save the deputy-commander,' came the answer. 'They have gone to him to seek a lodging. Their letter to his Excellency Twang Chun will command attention. They will be handsomely lodged.'

'And this deputy-commander; tell me of him.'

Chang's eyes gleamed maliciously as he listened to the reply. He tucked his hands into his baggy sleeves and hugged himself with unrestrained delight. Already he began to feel the weight of that thousand pounds which his rascally employer had promised.

As for the Tartar officer, he at once allied himself with this stranger who had come so opportunely to warn the people of Hatsu. Not only because in his ignorance he was genuinely a believer in the fable that David and his friend, or any other Europeans for the matter of that, could at will bring a plague to the city. No, that was not the only reason for his instant decision to help this Chang. It was because he himself, this Tartar under-officer, had suffered for the death of that European attacked some while before. Cunning alone had saved him his head. He had been degraded and soundly thrashed, for in China punishments are by no means half-hearted. People are still put to the torture, wretched criminals still suffer penalties that have long since disappeared from the penal codes of other nations. The man had been degraded and soundly thrashed, and the indignity and the sting of the lash were still fresh with him.

'Listen,' he whispered hoarsely, his eyes glinting dangerously. 'This deputy-commandant is no lover of the foreign devil. It is well known, though it is denied, mark you, that he it was who led the soldiery in that affair when certain people of the west were attacked. He would have been governor here, but the suspicion that he was one of the attackers caused him to lose the high post. Of a surety he is with us.'

'And would dare to hang these wretches on the report we bring him?' asked Chang, his wicked face lit up with eagerness. 'He is bold enough for that?'

The cunning smile on the face of his listener told its own tale. What need had such a man as Chang to question further? For had he not arranged such little matters himself many a time? To a Chinaman was there any difficulty in such an affair, demanding cunning and intrigue? Let it be remembered that in all our dealings with the Celestial race craft has been always met with. In business circles amongst the large commercial firms of which China can now boast, it has come to be well understood and believed in that a Celestial's word is as good as his bond; that he does not depart dishonourably from an undertaking; but amongst the high officials such trust has not been gained. China's word has too often been broken. And here was this deputy-governor of Hatsu at that very moment receiving David and Dick with every sign of deference, though, to speak the truth, the man's ugly face was heavy with scowls when his guests were not observing. Would he dare to attack the foreigners who were about to eat his salt and partake of his hospitality?

'My brother,' declared the Tartar officer, becoming wonderfully friendly with the stranger, 'his Excellency Tsu-Hi will defend his guests if need be with his life. But— —'

'But, Yes— —'

'But he has other duties. He goes the rounds two hours after sundown, and repeats the visit once more before he goes to his repose. In his absence— —'

Chang grinned an expansive grin. This little Tartar was a man after his own heart, and was proving a wonderful ally. He sat as immovable as a statue for some few minutes, his eyes shut, reviewing every side of the situation.

'No one knows of their arrival save these guards here,' he told himself, 'and, of course, the servants employed by his Excellency. Now if a mob in the quarter of the city where his house is situated rises when he is absent on the walls, and captures these foreign devils, how can his Excellency be blamed? How can I be made to appear in the matter, when there is this lusty Tartar to do the work for me. It shall be done. I will proceed without delay.'

Meanwhile David and Dick had been received by the deputy-governor of the city, and had been shown to their rooms, which were plainly but beautifully furnished. Then, as the governor excused his immediate absence on the plea of duty, the two lads called upon Jong to supply them with refreshment 'Not like dis,' said the faithful fellow, as he came into David's room bearing a steaming dish with him. 'Dis not receiving guests as a mandarin or high officer should do. Not at all. Not light. Him should stay and give a feast dat takes much time eating. He should put allee de best dat he have before de foleigners. He should bow allee de time, and ask what next he can do. Not go off as if he hate de sight of white men.'

'Can't say I took a violent fancy to the fellow myself,' laughed Dick, who ate as if he were as hungry as a hunter. 'Can't say the beggar was over handsome either. Seemed to wear a scowl on his face most of the time, as if he particularly disliked foreign devils. But that don't make any difference to a fellow's appetite, do it? Pass along that dish again, David. My! Jong's a cook in a hundred.'

The Chinaman grinned appreciatively, while David scarcely seemed to have heard his friend. His brow was furrowed; he paused long and often between the mouthfuls.

'Bothering again. Letting trouble come along and trouble you before it's time to trouble?' laughed Dick. 'Here, David, I give you fair warning. This is my second go. If you're not pretty slippy the dish'll be empty. You'll be hungry when you go to your bed.'

'I shall sit up to-night.'

'What! sit up! Watch in the house of the governor of Hatsu? David, you're a bit mad I'm beginning to think,' cried Dick, still eating heartily and quizzing his comrade. 'But, seriously,' he went on, 'where's the need? The jolly old fellow didn't wear the most handsome of faces, as I've admitted; but then he's our host. Twang Chun—beg his pardon, his Excellency—seems to be the kind of boy it would be bad practice to fall foul of. Supposing this governor fellow, what's his name?— —'

'Tsu-Hi, deputy-governor, I understand.'

'Don't mind what sort o' governor he is any way,' laughed Dick, who was feeling wonderfully jolly and facetious. 'Let's call him Hi for short. This Hi, we'll suppose, hates foreign devils like poison; but there's always Twang Chun, ain't there? There's always this jolly old boy Twang, who, we're told, is ready to wring the neck of any fellow who doesn't offer us hospitality. *Bien!* as Alphonse says. There we are, safe as houses.'

'Just so,' agreed David, curtly. 'All the same, I shall watch to-night. I've got a kind of feeling that something may happen.'

'Indigestion!' cried Dick. 'Better let me dose you, my boy. One of those pills of the Professor's'll make you feel as right as a hay-stack—A1, in fact. A good sleep'll put you right by morning.'

But though David enjoyed his friend's chaff, and indeed laughed heartily at his last suggestion, he shook his head when invited to turn in. Why, he could not explain. But the fact remained, indigestion or no indigestion, the lad was filled with a sense of insecurity. Perhaps it was the roughness of the Tartar under-officer, perhaps it was the sounds of brawling which had come lately to his ear—who knows? It may have been a genuine premonition. He saw Dick plump himself on the narrow *kang* in his room, and bade him good-night. Then he lay down on his own, his eyes wide open and staring.

'Suppose it must be indigestion,' he said after a while, 'or is it the face of this Tsu-Hi? I didn't like him. I swear I caught him scowling and muttering.'

As is so often the case with those who lie awake in the silence, David's busy brain was occupied with a vast number of things—matters some of little moment, passed and done with, others of greater interest, his own aims and ambitions in this country of China. He wondered what his stepmother was doing, and sighed when he thought of how things might have been had she been a different woman. Then his mind branched off to the sturdy sergeant of police who had lodged him, to his pleasant little wife, and to Mr. Jones, staunchest of friends and solicitors. Then he gave his thoughts to the matter always uppermost in his mind, the finding of his father's papers; perhaps the discovery of some evidence which would prove or disprove his death. Perhaps even an agreeable surprise was awaiting him. Stranger things had occurred before. It might be even that Edward Harbor was still living. Ah! there was a noise of shouting out in the street. David rose and went to the window. Gently pushing back the wooden frame, with its oiled-paper covering in lieu of glass, he stood in the moonlight listening.

'Nothing,' he told himself. 'Some brawlers, perhaps. I suppose even in this country of placid people, there are men who return late to their houses, and who make a noise in doing so. I'll leave 'em to it.'

He lay down once more, his head on his hands, and gave himself again to thinking. It seemed but a minute later when he awoke with a start, for he had been sleeping. There were men in the room, though none of them uttered so much as a syllable. Four or more gripped his hands and feet, while another thrust something between his teeth with decided roughness. Then David pulled himself together; he strained every muscle to throw off his silent attackers. He struggled, kicking one man to the end of the room, and causing the *kang* to topple over; but, in spite of his strength and the rage which added to it, he was helpless. The men held him as if he were in a vice. In a trice he felt ropes being tied about his hands and feet, while one of the attackers secured the gag in its place with a strip of linen, thereby almost smothering our hero. A minute later he was being carried from the room, and before he could realise what was happening, was tossed like a bundle into what was evidently a basket. And then how he kicked! He made the basket roll on its side with his efforts, while he himself was pitched half out of it; but a moment later he was hustled into the depths again, while something pricked his chest, causing him a twinge of pain.

'Lie still, fool,' he heard in English, though the man who spoke was decidedly a foreigner. 'Lie still, else will I plunge the blade home here and now. A dog of an Englishman deserves no mercy.'

Bewildered and utterly confused by all that had happened, and not a little exhausted after his efforts, David lay still as he was ordered, and presently the silent band lifted the basket and bore it between them. A gust of cool air came through the wicker, while David fancied he could see stars overhead. Or was it the light of the moon? He could not be certain, for a length of cotton matting had been thrown over the basket. He found himself counting the almost noiseless footfalls of his bearers, then he eagerly strained his ears to catch the sound of rescuers; but none came. The street was silent, silent but for the slither of the padded soles of the attackers, silent save for that and the almost soundless tread of others following bearing a similar burden.

'That fellow Tsu-Hi is responsible for this, I suppose,' groaned David, breathing as deeply as he could. 'But what is his object, and how is it that they took us unawares?'

Bitterly did he blame himself for his carelessness in falling asleep; for he realised now with a pang of remorse that that was what had happened.

'Made a whole heap of fine resolutions,' he growled beneath his breath, 'and then was weak enough to break them. I deserve to be trapped. But why? What can be the meaning of this sudden attack?'

Well might he ask the question, for there must be some reason. David had no knowledge of that rascal Chang, hired with Mr. Ebenezer Clayhill's money. He had no idea that the sinister individual who had married his stepmother was even then awaiting news from the Chinaman he had engaged to do his bidding, and that, with a cunning which matched that of the Celestial, Ebenezer had arranged that anything might be done if only David Harbor could be silenced and finished—anything at all. Yet, when his wife broached the subject, as she did with great regularity, once at least every day, he would smile and answer her in a manner all his own. It was always his habit to take up a commanding position on the hearth-rug, and there, with a preliminary blast of his gigantic and exceedingly red nasal organ, to hold forth with a pomposity which suited him not at all.

'Violence, my dear! Violence to be offered! Why do you harp so constantly on such a matter? Of course there will be no violence. This man Chang goes in search of the will, not of the young pup you have the misfortune to own as a stepson. Don't be alarmed; no harm will come to him through Chang.'

But, once his wife's back was turned, the ruffian would tell himself with a chuckle that if anything did actually happen to David, why, it would be at the hands of some others hired by the rascal he had sent to China.

'She'll never, know,' he said. 'As for me, I'd rather hear he was dead than have the actual will sent to me; for that young pup is capable of mischief. I'll not be comfortable till he's dead.'

Seeing that David was ignorant of Chang's existence, what else could he put this sudden attack down to? Tsu-Hi's cunning and enmity? Why? Then to what? For in these days of slowly gathering enlightenment a European can travel in China with some degree of safety, particularly when armed with a letter to the powerful governor of a province. True, there are sudden fanatical attacks; but then, he reflected, in such cases there is always a cause. Where was there a cause here? where the smallest excuse for this violence?

However, no amount of wondering helped him. His indignation merely made his breath come faster, and seeing that breathing was already a matter of difficulty, he soon lay quiet at the bottom of the basket, listening dully to the footsteps of his bearers; and then he felt that he was being carried up some stairs. A chilly sensation came to him, while the faint light flickering in through the wicker was cut off entirely. More stairs were mounted, the basket being borne at an angle that sent David into a heap at the lower end. Then the bearers went through a doorway. Of that he was sure, for he heard the creak of the hinges and the rattle of bolts. An instant later the basket was tossed to the ground with as much ceremony, or lack of ceremony, as would have been devoted to a bale of clothes.

'Bring him out,' he heard in guttural Chinese. 'Now cut his bonds; fetch the light hither.'

David was rolled out of the basket, jerked to his feet, and then relieved of his bonds, while the gag was dragged from between his teeth. It was a welcome relief. He breathed easily for the first time for some minutes.

'Now,' said the same voice, but in broken English this time, 'you see me, no doubt. You are David Harbor.'

'Right,' nodded our hero.

'I am Chang; I helped to kill your father.'

'And will probably kill me,' answered David, somewhat bewildered, and inclined to look upon this fellow as a madman.

'You are right. To-morrow evening you will be beheaded. I myself shall carry out the sentence.'

'But why?' asked David, cringing slightly, for the ordeal was trying. Indeed, the man standing over him, with the lamp shining in his face, looked a most heartless villain.

'Why?' he repeated, mocking our hero. 'The answer is simple. David Harbor has become a nuisance. There is a man of the name of Ebenezer Clayhill; he does not love David Harbor.'

So there it was. Even in his lowest estimation of the man who had married his stepmother, David could not imagine such a depth of villainy. But this fellow Chang was in earnest. He was undoubtedly speaking the truth. What answer could our hero give to him? He merely bowed his head, while a shiver of apprehension passed through him. Then he pulled himself together and faced the ruffian.

'I hear you,' he said. 'What then?'

'For you, nothing; for me, reward.'

The Chinaman swung round on his heel, gave a swift order, and strode out of the place. Then one by one the bearers followed. The door was banged to, the bolts shot home, and David was left alone, alone in his prison, with the moon staring in at him through a window high up in a stone wall, staring in inquisitively as if to ask how this young fellow would face the coming ordeal.

'So it is like that? Ebenezer's hatred of me reaches even to Hatsu,' thought our hero. 'He has hired this rascal to kill me, and it looks as if the man would succeed. So he will if I don't move a little. But I'm not dead by a long way yet; I've still got a kick or two left in me.'

Chapter XIII
In a Chinese Prison

If Chang, the man who had so unexpectedly and suddenly led an attack upon the little party journeying via Hatsu to interview Twang Chun, the governor of the province, imagined that he had left David in a condition of terror at the thought of the execution he had threatened for the evening of the morrow, he was very much mistaken, and showed therefore that he knew his prisoner very little indeed; for David was not the one to be long down-hearted. It was not in his nature to give in without a serious struggle. No sooner had the door of his prison been banged and barred, than his spirits rose wonderfully, while he set about seeking for a remedy to enable him to beat his enemies. And the first thing that caused him joy was a discovery he made within a couple of minutes.

'The fools!' he whispered to himself, chuckling. 'The fools! They took me because I was idiot enough to fall asleep, but they forgot to search my pockets. Why, here is my magazine shooter, and here the letters I was carrying. George! Mr. Chang, I shall have something to say when the time for execution comes along; but I ain't going to wait for it if I can help; let's have a look at this cage they've put me in.'

It was a long, narrow cell, with walls formed of hewn blocks of hard stone, and lit by a range of narrow windows placed close to the ceiling. The openings themselves were innocent of glass, or of the Chinese equivalent, namely, oiled paper. Otherwise, the floor was of stone, the ceiling of a dusky white, while, save for himself and the basket in which he had been carried to the place, there was not another thing present. All was in darkness, except a wide stretch of floor on which the moonbeams played, as they crept up one of the walls till the bright patch of light ended at an abrupt edge, a faithful *silhouette* of the range of windows above placed on the outside wall of the prison.

'Door as safe as houses; heard the bolts shot home,' David told himself. 'Then I've got to reach those windows. Should say they're a good twelve feet from the floor; perhaps the height's even greater. Couldn't reach 'em I fancy, even with a big leap. However, I'll try; nothing like trying.'

There was nothing like keeping up his pluck either, which David did with a vengeance. He was even smiling as he stared up at the range of windows, with their edges so unnaturally abrupt as the moonbeams streamed past them, while one hand went every now and again to the depths of the secret pocket in which his magazine pistol was lying. Then he walked over to the wall and felt the surface with his fingers.

'One could get a grip with these cotton-padded soles, I should say. I'll try a running jump and see where it will land me.'

He went back to the opposite wall, and squeezed hard against it; then he sprang forward, and leaping at the far wall endeavoured to run up it. He succeeded in gaining a point within two feet of the windows, or perhaps it was less. Then he tried again and again till he was exhausted.

'No good; can't do it,' he told himself. 'I shall have to think of something else.'

He sat down on the basket and cudgelled his brains, but the more he thought and worried, the longer he stared at the range of windows, the more impossible the task seemed. Then he swung round swiftly. There was a clatter outside the door, the bolts were being pushed back from their sockets. A moment or two later the hinges creaked, while the door was thrown open. A coolie entered at once, while a second held a lamp behind him. There were half a dozen more just outside in a dimly lit passage, while in their midst stood none other than the Tartar under-officer. David rubbed his eyes, and wondered where he had seen the fellow before. Then hearing him speak, he remembered.

'Put the food and water down,' he commanded, 'and leave. It is time that we were all in our beds. Do not go near the foreign devil. There is never any saying when he and his may do injury to one of our people.'

He eyed his prisoner with none too friendly a glance, and hurried the coolie from the room. David heard the bolts shot to again, and the faint slither of departing feet. Then he rose to his feet with flushed face and a new hope in his heart. Not a second thought did he give to the food and water, for who could say that it was not poisoned? If Ebenezer Clayhill could hire a ruffian to come all that way to molest him anything might be expected. No, the food and drink did not attract him. Our hero was roused by the help which the lamp had brought him; for it had shone on the basket on which he was seated, and in a flash David realised that the affair was not merely a flimsy collection of wicker, but a well-made basket of considerable length, strengthened with pieces of bamboo, which, although light, kept the whole in shape, and gave it considerable power to resist weights placed within it. He picked it up with an effort, and running his fingers along it, came upon the holes left for the bamboo runners with which it was hoisted on the bearers' shoulders. Then, with the utmost care, and in deadly silence, he propped it up on end against the wall, at the summit of which ran the range of windows. Would it reach high enough? David stepped back, and cast an anxious eye upward.

'Might,' he said, with a doubtful shake of his head. 'Might not; anyway, I'm going to reach those windows.'

He gathered his somewhat ample allowance of Chinese garment about his knees so as to free his legs, and began to clamber upward; and presently he had reached the summit. To stand there and balance himself on the end was no easy matter, and as if to persuade him of that fact the basket suddenly canted, bringing itself and our hero with a crash to the ground. Instantly his hand went to his pistol, while he crouched over the fallen basket, endeavouring to regain his breath, for the jar of the fall had driven it out of his body. But there was not a sound from the passage; not a sound from outside his prison. Not a foot stirred; no alarm was given.

'Shows I'm in an out-of-the-way place, for that basket made no end of a clatter. When once beat, try again. Don't give up in a hurry.'

He propped up the basket again, but this time with greater care, and swarmed up it, finding little difficulty in that part of the task, for it was almost as easy as climbing a ladder, there being numerous gaps affording a foothold in the wicker. Then he steadily raised himself to his full height, and stretched his arms above his head. The window was within two feet of his fingers.

'And has to be reached. Can't get much of a spring here,' he thought, 'but it's worth trying. I'll chance the fall, for if I miss, there's a good chance of coming down standing.'

With a sharp kick he leaped at the window, and actually contrived to grip the edge with the fingers of one hand. But they slid off instantly, and within a second he was back on the floor of his prison, not so shaken or jarred on this occasion, but hot and desperate, exasperated at his want of good fortune. But as we have had occasion to remark before, David was nothing if not determined. It was that very characteristic in the lad which troubled his stepmother, and which had, no doubt, carried him safely and successfully through many an undertaking. He propped the basket into place again, ascending with all speed and caution, and drawing in a long breath, made a huge spring at the window. On this occasion the fingers of both hands obtained a grip of the edge, and retained it. He hung in mid-air, flattened against the wall of his prison, listening to the basket as it slid sideways, and finally came with a crash to the floor. Then he pulled himself up, flung one arm round a pillar dividing the window, and soon had himself hoisted higher. After that it was easy enough to squeeze his body through the narrow opening, and to lie there securely while he regained his breath.

'And what now?' he asked himself, when he was again ready for further exertion. 'Outside here there's nothing that's very promising. We came up stairs. That is to say, I recollect that my bearers carried me up a flight before entering the prison. That makes the drop below me pretty big, bigger than I'm anxious to tackle. But there's nothing else.'

It did appear as if there were no other alternative, for as he cast his eyes downwards David could detect nothing that offered a foothold below him. The smooth stone wall descended sheer to the street, which ran along under the bright moonbeams some thirty or more feet under the window. It was not an impossible drop. On the other hand, it was none too easy, and might very well result in a sprained ankle, or something equally hampering and disagreeable. Then David did the wisest thing under the circumstances. Bearing in mind the old motto, perhaps, 'look before you leap,' he cast his eyes in all directions, first in front and then behind him, without obtaining any encouragement, and then up over his head. Ah! He could have shouted: the roof was within a few inches of his hand, a roof composed of large, flat tiles, with a deep channel at each side, and sloping so gradually that to walk upon it should be easy. He reached up a hand, gripped the edge of the roof, and hoisted himself cautiously upon it. Then he lay down flat, and rolled himself slowly upward. For there was something to alarm him. A man was standing out in the moon-lit road, and was gesticulating violently.

'Seen me I'm afraid,' thought David. 'Wants to make sure before he kicks up a ruction; but they don't have me without a little trouble. Out here on this roof I ought to be able to put up a fight that'll make them careful. Bother that chap! He must have been hiding in the deep shadow over yonder, and have watched me as I clambered out of the window.'

'Misser Davie, Misser Davie.'

The words came to him as if in a nightmare. David could not believe that he had actually heard them. He put his fingers to his ears and rubbed them vigorously. But he had no sooner removed them than the words came again, 'Misser Davie, Misser Davie.'

'Awfully queer,' he thought, mopping his forehead with the tail end of a voluminous sleeve, 'I could have sworn that that——'

'Misser Davie, am dat youself, Misser Davie?'

It was undoubtedly some one calling him, and that some one was the man down below in the street. The figure gesticulated even more violently, while the voice was raised to a higher pitch.

'Am dat youself, Misser Davie? Dis Jong, John Jong, de China boy, what's you sarvint.'

It set David's heart beating like a sledge hammer. He slid at once to the very edge of the roof and stared over.

'Jong,' he called. 'That you? What's all this business about?'

'Not know't all, Misser. Me asleep, den hear a noise, and hide under de *kang*. Men come into de place and look for me. Den hear dem going away carryin' baskets.'

'Carrying me, Jong. I was a prisoner till a moment ago. I've just crept out of the cell in which they placed me.'

'Where Misser Dick, den?' asked Jong, promptly.

'Dick? Isn't he with you?'

David asked the question anxiously, for the safety of his friend had given him cause for great anxiety, even in spite of his own sad condition. He had not seen that second basket borne along behind him, and had no idea that his chum Dick was also a prisoner. 'Where is he?' he demanded eagerly.

'Not know; but Jong follow de fellers, and see dem carry you both in dere in de baskets. Den him wait here to see what happening. Not know what to do, Misser Davie. If me go back to de palace, den Tsu-Hi take me.'

David whistled in a low key. This was indeed a facer, though, to tell the truth, the presence of Jong in the street below was a wonderful fillip to both courage and spirits. But Dick; what was he to do about his friend?

'Can't leave him all alone, that's certain,' he told himself without the least hesitation. 'Supposing I go on a tour of inspection, for it seems to me that there is no one watching or listening. Look here, Jong,' he called out gently, 'stay where you are and watch. I'm going to find Mr. Dick, if it's possible.'

Promptly he crept away over the roof, his feet making not so much as a sound as he went, for his native shoes were as soft as bedroom slippers. Then he came to a sudden halt. David's old characteristic asserted itself. His desire to be practical, to have a plan always where such was possible, came to the fore, and he lay flat again cogitating, trying to decide how to proceed.

'No use ranging round and round aimlessly,' he told himself. 'Where's Dick most likely to be kept a prisoner? That's the question. Where's he been put? If only I can find the cell I'll manage somehow to get at him.'

A couple of minutes later he was sidling slowly again to the very edge of the roof, for higher up there was no opening. The slight slope of the big tiles led to a wall some five feet in height, rising abruptly at the highest edge of the roof, and capped itself by a second roof of huge, artistic tiles, which overhung their support far more than was the case down below. This second part went steeply upward to the summit, where the ridge was capped with a number of ludicrous and marvellously wrought dragons. It was a dead end as it were, not only to the building in that part, but also to David's hopes in that direction. Obviously there was nothing to be done there, and equally obviously the wall below him, through which he had contrived to squeeze by way of the window offered something far more likely. For was it not in the bounds of possibility that the range of windows was continued, and, if so, why should Dick not be held a prisoner in a cell into which one of the openings gave light and air?

'Hist! Jong! are you still there?'

The figure of the Chinaman steeped out into the white road, silhouetted blackly against it, and fore-shortened from the aspect from which our hero observed him.

'Misser Davie, here John Jong.'

'I may want a rope; got one?'

'Find him easy; I go now to look. Be back and hide along here till you want me.'

The dark figure slid again into the dense shadow in the far edge of the road, and though David stared and stared into it, not a movement could he discern, not a sound did he catch. Not a sound? Then what was that? Surely voices? Yes, without shadow of doubt. He kneeled up to listen, and then, as if he had forgotten all thought of the windows, one of which, if they did indeed exist, might give access to Dick, he went crawling off up the slope to the erection above it. And arrived there he hastened along the wall till he came to the edge, when he slipped round the corner. About ten feet away there was a large gap in this other side of the building, and a soft light was streaming from it. Voices were also issuing into the night air. David crawled forward without a moment's hesitation, halted when close to the gap, which was, as a matter of fact, another large window, and craned his neck round the edge. Down below him, twenty feet perhaps, there were a number of Chinese, and amongst them the rascally Tartar under-officer who had admitted them to the city. The men were stretched lazily on a long *kang*, which did service as bed for all of them, and were discussing matters idly. David listened for a while, then, creeping past the opening, hastened to a second of equal size, and from which also a ray of light issued. A glance into the place caused him suddenly to duck his head and retreat a little.

'Chang, Chang, of all people, eating his supper, and writing as he does so. If only I dared.'

If only he had none others to think of, save himself, David could have shot the man where he sat, though such an act would have gone hard against his conscience and his ideas of what was proper and fair play. But there was Dick to be considered, and Dick was somewhere in the building.

'Mustn't wait,' he told himself, 'no good to be obtained by staring down at that fellow. Chang was the name he gave himself. I shall remember, and one of these days I shall hope to meet him under different circumstances. Now for those other windows.'

He slipped back to his old position, crawled to the edge of the roof on to which he had at first climbed, and hung his head over it. Yes, there was a long row of windows, all in darkness, any of which might give access to the cell in which his comrade was a prisoner.

'Can't remember which I came from myself,' he groaned. 'But I'll try the lot of them. First thing is to get down, then I'll make my way from one to the other.'

To an active lad the task was nothing out of the ordinary, and in a little while David was seated on the edge of one at the far corner of the building. He peered at once into the interior, and, with the aid of the moon's rays, was able to make out the opposite wall and the actual dimensions of the place. It appeared to be empty, but the dark shadow directly beneath him might contain someone. He called Dick's name gently, repeating it till he was sure that he could not be there.

'Even if he were asleep he'd hear that,' he told himself. 'But even Dick, the happy-go-lucky Dick, wouldn't be asleep now. This business would be far too upsetting for any man. I'll get along to the next. Ah! not there. That's the crib from which I so lately scrambled.'

There was no doubt on the last question, for the moonbeams played on the platter of food and the jar of water which had been brought to him, and he realised that this was indeed the cell he had so lately vacated, for the two objects were in precisely the same position in which he had seen them placed. More than that, the edge of the huge basket which had contained his own perspiring and wriggling body was peeping out of the shadow. At once he went crawling on again, peeping into four other cells, only to find each one tenantless. Then a gentle hail from below attracted his attention.

'Masser Davie, I'se got a rope; what den?'

Jong's strange figure stood outlined on the white road again, his face as clearly seen as in broad daylight, so powerfully did the moon play upon it.

'I found de rope along de road here, and borrowed him for a little. You found de oder one? You found Masser Dick?'

There was a note of anxiety in the faithful celestial's voice, and a responding note in that of David's. For his lack of success was making him feel desperate. Supposing he could not find his chum? Could he leave the place and desert him entirely? Never.

'I'm game to do something desperate,' he breathed. 'If I don't find him in this place I'll slip along to the palace where we were given quarters, and tackle Tsu-Hi. The rascal must have been an accomplice in this attack, and with him under my pistol I could do a great deal, a very great deal I imagine.'

He sat still for a little while, running the plan over in his head. And desperate as it undoubtedly was, he decided then and there that if he failed in his quest for Dick he would carry the idea out. It should be neck or nothing. It should be Tsu-Hi's life or Dick's. Then another inspiration floated across his mind.

'Chang, why not?' he asked himself. 'If he has the power to manage a thing like this, he will have further power. With a pistol to his head he would undo what he has already managed to bring about. But it wouldn't be quite as good as the deputy-governor. What's that, Jong?'

'You sit still dere while I throw up de rope. Now, catch him.'

A coil left the Chinaman's hand, and thrown with dexterity whizzed just in front of David. He caught it with ease, and at once slipped it about his shoulders.

'Remain there,' he said. 'I'm going on looking for Mr. Dick.'

'Den you take heap of care. Dere's a light a little farder along de wall.'

Jong's arms slid out and his finger pointed.

Craning his neck and stretching out from the wall as far as possible David thought he could detect a beam of light coming from a window a little farther along. But he was not sure, for the moon was so strong and clear that it stifled every other ray of light, just as the sun's rays quench a fire. However, Jong could see, and guided by him he scrambled to the roof again, crawled along it, and then leaned over.

'A light sure enough. Better investigate—here goes.'

He was over the edge in a twinkling, and since greater caution was needful here, he dropped the toes of his padded shoes very gently on the framing of the window. Then getting a grip of the upper edge he stooped and peeped into the interior. A paper lantern hung from the ceiling and showed him a bare room, with the same stone walls. But in the far corner there was a narrow *kang* on which a man was seated. He raised his head as David looked in, appearing to have heard a sound. And the brief glimpse our hero obtained told him that this was the Tartar under-officer, the officious individual with whom he had already come in contact.

'Evidently got tired of the others and come to bed. Hallo! here comes another of them.'

Right opposite him was the doorway, the door being half open, and through this stepped the same man who had brought the jar of water and the platter of food. A bunch of keys jangled at his girdle, while the man yawned widely.

'Prisoners safe,' he said. 'I shall now go to my rest.'

'One moment. You have fed them? Our friend who came to the city to warn us gave strict orders to that effect.'

The gaoler nodded sleepily. 'They are fed,' he answered surlily. 'The one nearly an hour ago, the second who is placed next to you this very minute. Now I go to take food and drink to the principal apartment. The stranger of whom you speak, and who indeed seems to be of the greatest importance, tells me that his Excellency comes to talk with him.'

'S-s-she! not a word more. Forget that, friend,' said the Tartar, eagerly, his voice hardly raised above a whisper. 'Remember that his highness Tsu-Hi is ignorant as yet of these matters. He goes the rounds on the walls. When he returns to the palace and discovers that his guests are gone he will raise an uproar. He will make good his face for the enquiries which must certainly follow. Mention not the name of the deputy-governor in this affair if you wish to live longer. There, go; I too am sleepy. But wait. You said his Excellency—er—this guest comes now to speak with our friend?'

'He comes now; he is expected any moment.'

'Then I will have a word with him. He must know that I too have had a share in this business. Perhaps it will fall out that I shall regain the post which I lost but lately. Ah! foreign devils were the cause of my undoing. Willingly will I slay all with whom I come in contact.'

'The ruffian! That's the sort of fellow I've got to deal with, is it?' muttered David, who had listened eagerly, and, thanks to his own quickness and keenness to learn the language, had managed to pick up the gist of the conversation. 'So Chang and the deputy-governor are hand in glove in this affair, and the deputy seeks to throw dust in the eyes of the authorities, in other words to make his face good, as is the saying in this queer country.

Why! If this isn't my opportunity! Supposing I find Dick and hoist him out, we are still in a walled city. We've still to get clear away, and very little chance of doing that as matters are. If this isn't the very thing I've been wanting.'

He shrank back as the gaoler left the room, lurching sleepily, and watched the Tartar as he too stepped towards the door. A moment later the man was gone, leaving the room empty.

'My turn now. Here goes to clear up the whole business.'

With reckless courage, and yet without neglecting his usual caution, David first peered into every corner of the room. Then he rapidly made fast his rope to the centre pillar of the window, waved to Jong in the deep shadow beyond, and at once slipped inside the building. A second later he was sliding down to the floor of the place in which the Tartar had been sitting.

Chapter XIV
Tsu-Hi is Astonished

For perhaps one whole minute David Harbor stood perfectly still, once he had slid down the rope from the window above and had gained the floor of the room in which he had seen the Tartar under-officer. He leaned forward, still gripping the cord, listening intently for any sounds there might be, and fancied as he did so that he could hear the soft-footed slither of some one in the passage.

'That fellow going along to interview Chang and the deputy-governor. Going to put in a word for himself,' muttered David. 'In that case he should be absent sufficiently long to let me take a look round. Let me see. Dick was in the next cell. Right! I'll make straight away for him.'

He crept across the stone-flagged floor, making direct for the doorway, and thrust his head round the edge so as to obtain a good view of the passage. It was empty as far as he could see. Almost directly overhead a huge paper lantern swung in the breeze, emitting a soft light, and casting its rays on either side. It was possible, in fact, to see as far as the end of the passage in one direction, where it evidently turned abruptly to the left and swept round the other side of the building. In the opposite direction shadow and gloom obscured the passage, but it made little difference to our hero.

'Runs along past all the cells into which I have already looked,' he told himself. 'I don't need to take any notice of it. Now for the one in which Dick is imprisoned. It ought to be just here on my right. No harm in searching for him at once. There doesn't seem to be a soul about this part of the building.'

He stepped into the passage promptly, and crept cautiously towards the bend where it turned along the other face of the prison. At the very corner there was a door, and the sight set his heart fluttering. But he did not venture to touch the bolts before taking the precaution to look along the gallery after it had turned. He craned his head round the corner, caught a view of a second elaborately painted lantern swaying like the first, for if this building lacked many comforts it was at least well-ventilated. The winds of heaven had free access to the interior by way of the unglazed windows, and gusts came sweeping down the gallery, beautifully cooling gusts which set the lanterns swinging slowly, twisting them upon the plaited ropes by which they were suspended, till they twirled this way and that, presenting a most picturesque appearance. But there were other things to remark on. This second lamp was hung some twenty paces along the gallery, at the foot of a flight of stone steps, by which, no doubt, the gaoler and the Tartar soldier had disappeared. David even noticed that the centre of each step was badly worn, probably with the coming and going of many people, proving either that the prison was of ancient construction, as was extremely probable, or that the stone was of a soft nature and readily worn. But here again was food only for passing interest. A man situated as he was does not find time for delaying, when his life and that of his friend are in the balance. The door just behind him had far more attractions for David, and at once he turned to it, casting his eye over the strong bolts with which it was secured.

'Done!' he groaned. 'The gaoler has the keys. How on earth am I to effect an entry?'

Then he suddenly bethought him of the window by which he had made good his own escape. Why should he not climb outside again, and creeping along the roof gain entrance to Dick's cell by way of the window? He turned to retrace his steps, and then stepping swiftly to the door he examined the lock. A second's inspection proved to him that the bolt was not shot. It was easy to make sure of that matter, for the huge, clumsy affair, the work of centuries before perhaps, was placed so far from the catch into which it should glide that one could see at once that it was not in order.

'Good! Then there are only the bolts shot by hand. This lock seems to be out of order.'

Up went his hand to the topmost bolt, and very slowly he drew it out of its socket, shivering lest the grating which was inevitable with such a rusty affair should be heard along the passage. Then he suddenly leaped round the corner of the gallery, for his ears had detected a sound. It was the slip, slip, slip of a native footstep, the slither of a cotton-padded sole coming down the flight of stone steps. The perspiration started to David's forehead, his heart beat against his ribs as if it were a sledge hammer, while the blows dinned into his ears till he felt deafened. And his eyes almost bulged from their sockets as he stared in the direction from which the sounds were coming. For though only the legs of the oncomer were as yet visible, they were sufficiently distinctive. The high boots, with their thick, white soles, could belong only to the Tartar under-officer. The colour of the garment coming into view was the same as that worn by the soldier, while, as the man's girdle came within David's vision, he saw the hilt of his sabre, heard the rattle of the scabbard as it dragged on the steps, and then caught a glimpse of the revolver which the ruffian carried. Yes, of the revolver, for if China to-day still lags behind western nations in much which appertains to learning and commerce and a host of other matters, there have been outside influences at work giving her subtle advice, and urging her to arm her soldiery not as before, with swords and lances and useless bows and arrows, but with modern rifles, with revolvers, and with the latest cannon. In that particular at least the efforts of some western nation have been successful. Careless of those of her own colour who in days to come, days perhaps very close at hand, may find themselves arrayed against the celestial nation, they have forced a market here for the surplus output of their arsenals, and have gathered Chinese gold for modern weapons which may well be employed to slay their own people. But here was only a single illustration. David had remarked when entering this walled city of Hatsu upon the modern rifles of the Tartar-guard. His sharp eyes had detected the weapon carried by their under-officer. And here it was again, proof positive that the man who was descending the last few steps was this very individual, than whom he would have rather encountered any one. What was he to do? Rush back into the cell and clamber up the dangling rope?

'No,' he told himself promptly, though he retraced his steps at once and darted into the cell. 'There's no time for that. He'd catch me half-way up, and besides, even if he didn't I couldn't get the rope hauled out of sight before he entered. I might slip along the passage, but I should be no better off, for still he would see the rope. I'll chance a meeting.'

As if it were the old days at school, and he were about to engage in a tussle with the gloves on, he gripped at the baggy sleeves which were such a constant nuisance to him, and folded them up near his shoulders, leaving his arms exposed. Then he stood stiffly upright behind the half-closed door to listen, holding his breath, trying vainly to still the beating of his heart. Suddenly as the Tartar's steps were heard outside the cell, David became as calm as he had ever been in his life before; for after all, he was by no means different from many men of the same temperament as himself. To worry before trouble came along, as Dick was so fond of saying, was only natural to our hero. He was by instinct cautious and careful, and as is the case with many of similar disposition, there was always a tendency to fluster and unusual excitement prior to a struggle. David had been all of a tremble before now, although he had acquitted himself right well when blows were actually falling. And the same thing had happened here. Like the man who enters an action with his knees knocking, and who readily admits that he is nervous, David had prepared for this inevitable meeting with a fast-beating heart, with trembling limbs, and with a forehead from which the moisture was dripping. One who did not know him might almost have accused him of cowardice. But now that the struggle was about to begin he was a different individual. His eyes were bright, his mouth fast closed, and his muscles braced and ready. Not the smallest sound escaped his attention. He heard the Tartar enter the cell, then saw his fingers close on the door and caught the creak of the rusting hinges. Then he stepped forward.

'Silence!' he commanded sternly, placing his back against the door and pushing it to with a bang. 'Not a word, or I will kill you.'

Utter astonishment was written on the man's face; the soft rays of the swaying lantern falling on his features showed that he was entirely taken aback. The corners of his mouth drooped suddenly, his eyes started forward, while his fingers clutched at his clothing. But it was only for a moment. An apparently unarmed man stood before him, the youth whom he had so lately helped to capture. Promptly his hand sought his revolver.

'Dog! It is you, then? You are my prisoner.'

The revolver was more than half out of the girdle by now, and in another second would be at David's head; but the latter was watching the Tartar like a cat. His sharp eyes caught every movement, and at once, with a swift movement, he was on the man. His right arm went back quickly, and then jerked out like a flash, the fist striking the Tartar hard and full between the eyes. The result of this telling blow, so far as the Chinese rascal was concerned, was disastrous. He was knocked clear from his feet, for the youth who had struck was no chicken. David had weight and strength behind his arm, and, moreover, a desperate man finds added strength on such occasions. The blow, in fact, tossed the Tartar backward, causing him to perform a half sommersault, and to come to the ground with an alarming crash, his head being the first portion of his anatomy to come in contact with the stone flagging. And in a second David was on him, gripping him by the neck.

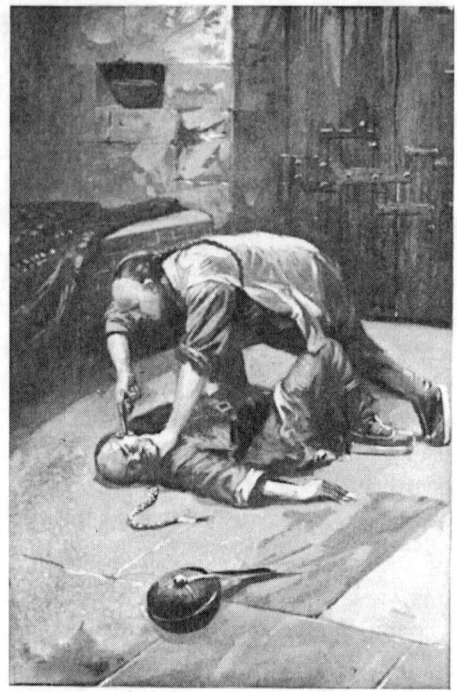

"IN A SECOND DAVID WAS ON HIM"

'Silence! Not a word,' he repeated, while his hand went to the man's revolver and drew it from his girdle. But the Tartar did not wince when the cold muzzle was thrust in his ear. He lay inert, his eyes closed, as listless as a sleeping baby.

'Stunned! Knocked out of time. Not used to an Englishman's fist,' gasped David. 'Let's make quite sure that he isn't foxing.'

He leaned over the man, and placed his ear close to his mouth. Yes, he was breathing—breathing loudly. In fact there was considerable stertor. David lifted a limp arm, and when he released it it fell back with a hollow thud to the ground. He tilted back the eyelids, and though he had but little knowledge of such matters, he could not help but remark that the pupils were equally dilated. There was little doubt, in fact, that the unfortunate but scheming and pugnacious Tartar was stunned by the terrific blow which he had received. It was altogether a revelation to the young fellow crouching beside him. He kneeled close by the man, staring into his face and wondering. He could hardly believe that a moment before he had been face to face with extreme danger and difficulty, and that one sudden movement on his part, one strong blow, had set aside the trouble.

'But has it? There are other people in the prison who will have to be dealt with. There is Chang; there is Tsu-Hi, the dishonest deputy-governor who has so far forgotten himself, and the honour to which all decent-minded Chinamen cling in their belief that, come what may, hospitality to a guest should never be abused. Yes, there is Tsu-Hi, who has shown the utmost treachery.'

David told himself sternly that they must be dealt with. He stood up, still with his eyes on the fallen Tartar. But he was not thinking of his late enemy; he was thinking of the arch-schemer hired by the man in England who should have been as a father to our hero. He was thinking also of the difficulties still before him, of the opposition still to be set aside before he and Dick and Jong could set foot outside the city. Then his face became sterner than ever; the eyes were half-closed as he stared at the Tartar. The scheme which he had first happened on when clambering along the ledge of the windows came back to his mind with redoubled force.

'Yes,' he said, 'they must be dealt with, those two men. First to release Dick, and then we'll talk to them.'

But even now he did not venture out of the cell. He pulled the door open quietly and peeped round into the passage, to find it deserted. There was not so much as a sound, save the gentle rattle of the stiffened paper streamers attached to the lantern swaying overhead.

'No one about. Goaler gone to bed, and the rest of them upstairs where I saw them with the Tartar fellow who is lying stunned in here. But supposing some one were to come along, I should be spotted in a minute. I must have some disguise, I——'

His eyes swung round to the figure stretched on the floor, and for a little while he stared at the fallen under-officer. A keen light came into his eyes, and once more he closed the door of the compartment. Then, swiftly and full of his purpose, he stripped the man of his clothing.

'Just about my size,' he told himself. 'Anyway, I've got to get into his things, whatever happens. Wish there was a glass here; but, as there isn't, I must make the most of it. Ah, boots fit to a T. Cap ditto. This big cloak fits only where it touches, so that don't matter. Now for the gentleman himself. Won't he have a headache in the morning!'

Quickly he pulled off his own garments, coiled his pigtail up on top of his head, and jammed the Tartar's cap on top of it. Then, having donned all his garments, which were voluminous, to say the least of them, he tied the frayed, silken girdle round his middle, attached the clanking sabre, and pushed the revolver home. When he stood up he was by no means a bad copy of the truculent individual who had first greeted him at the entrance of the city.

'And now to get rid of him and my own clothes. Ah! I know. Into the bed with him. Shy the clothing out of the window.'

He was not the one to waste time when the minutes were flying swiftly, and when there might be an interruption at any moment. David bundled the unconscious Tartar on to the *kang*, covered him with a faded quilt, and tied his own discarded clothing into a bundle. A dexterous heave sent it through the window, and if only he had known it, caused the faithful Jong the greatest consternation.

'What dat?' he asked, standing back in the dense shadow which hid him. 'Something come plump from de window. Not likee de look of him at allee, not at allee. Heart go plippee-plappee when ting like dat happen. Suppose I go over and have a look.'

He was in the very act of stepping out on to the white highway, which gleamed in the pure rays of the moon, when his sharp ears caught a sound. Some one was treading the narrow path which ran beside the road; some one was approaching. Jong lay flat in the shadow, hugging the wall, and stared out into the open. Presently a man's figure hove in sight—a man dressed in elaborate military costume, his flowing robes blowing about his feet, the flat cap on his head surmounted by a wide button. Nor did it want two glances at the stranger to disclose the fact that this was Tsu-Hi, the deputy-governor of the walled city of Hatsu, an official with absolute powers for the moment of life and death; one who, discovering Jong where he lay, could, with one single nod, condemn him to instant execution. No wonder, therefore, that the Chinaman shivered, and squeezed his body still further into the shadow, wishing that the ground might rise in a friendly manner and cover him. He scarcely dared to breathe, while, so terrified was he, that his teeth almost chattered together. Then, quite by accident, his hand touched the hilt of the knife he carried in his belt. The sudden contact seemed to bring him courage. Jong gripped the weapon and drew it, his eyes fixed all the while on the figure of Tsu-Hi.

'He is alone; he is the cause of all this trouble,' he whispered. 'Let him show that he has seen me and I will send him to join his ancestors; yes, to join them with treachery in his heart.'

But the official made no sign. He came stepping down the path slowly, as if deeply engaged with his thoughts. His hands were tucked into the baggy sleeves he wore, while his eyes were dropped on to the roadway.

He passed the spot where Jong was secreted, advanced slowly to the steps which led to the door of the prison, and lifted a hand to summon those within. Jong heard the clang of a gong somewhere in the distance. And David heard it. He was at that very moment about to slide back the last of the two bolts that secured the door of the cell in which he imagined Dick to be when the deep, musical note of the gong sounded down the passage, coming from a spot somewhere above, at the top of the flight of steps down which he had watched the Tartar descending. And then he heard a sharp rapping in the opposite direction.

'A visitor; perhaps Tsu-Hi,' he thought. 'What's to be done now? Who'll admit him?'

For one instant the mad idea occurred to him that he himself would go to the door and let the deputy-governor in.

'I could overawe him at once, and bring him in here,' he told himself. Then he shook his head emphatically. 'Might spoil everything. I want help before I move any further; I must have Dick beside me.'

Clang! The gong sounded again, the note ringing down the passage, and then there was silence. No one answered the summons; there was not so much as a step to be heard. David reflected that the gaoler was in bed, and fast asleep in all probability.

'While the fellow outside will be getting impatient, he'll make more and more noise, and we shall be having some of the Tartar soldiers. That won't suit my plans. There! he's hammering. I'll do it; I'll chance the whole thing. In for a penny in for a pound, isn't a bad motto on some occasions.'

He made up his mind in an instant, and pulled the door open. Listening for a few seconds, and hearing no sound from the interior of the prison, he hurried along to the left, where he guessed the door must be. And at the far end of the gallery, where the shadows lurked, he came upon it, and stood for a while listening to the rat-a-tat-tat of the impatient official outside.

'Open!' he heard the man call, angrily. 'Open for Tsu-Hi. Do not keep me waiting out here where folks may see me.'

David pulled the bolts back swiftly, and tugging at the door dragged it open, keeping himself well within the passage.

'Dog! Why do you keep me so? Sleeping, eh? Sleeping when you should be on duty? Have a care. Though the governor is away from the city on important business, there are yet powers in the hands of his deputy which may make a servant sorrow. A head has been chopped for an offence even less than this.'

If he had expected an answer Tsu-Hi was disappointed, for David still held himself in the background, kow-towing as he judged the gaoler would do, and saying not a word.

'Mustn't open my mouth or he'll see that I'm not a Chinaman, nor even the Tartar officer. If he don't move in precious quick I'll take him by the neck and drag him into the passage.'

Our hero's teeth were set fast together, while he was fully ready for any emergency. Now that matters had gone so far favourably for him, he was determined that this treacherous deputy-governor should not overthrow all his plans. That it was Tsu-Hi a swift glance had told him without error. His hands itched to get a grip of the ruffian, and silence him, but still he bent low, kow-towing humbly; and perhaps it was his silence and his apparent humility which appeased the governor. He stepped into the passage and waited there, his hands tucked out of sight again, while David pushed the door, and shot the bolts home.

'Now lead me to the room occupied by this Chang, who came so unexpectedly to the city.'

To say that David was in a serious dilemma was hardly to describe the situation correctly. He was desperate, for he judged that Tsu-Hi must have some knowledge of the prison, and was it likely that he would expect to discover Chang, a man considered already to be of some importance, in a cell abutting on this dreary passage? Surely there must be guest chambers, guest apartments for the few who came to such a place as a prison for any other reason than to fill the cells?

'Can't help it if there are,' muttered David. 'He's got to come with me, and if he thinks that the place in which I found the Tartar fellow is not good enough, well I can't help it. I'll give him a crack that'll knock the wind out of his body.'

He lifted the scabbard of his sabre, fearful that its clanking might arouse the suspicion of his visitor, and then stepped in front of him down the passage. At the open door of the room he had just vacated he came to a halt, kow-towing in that direction.

'In here! Why, fool, this is not a guest chamber.'

'In here, Excellency,' David murmured. 'He wished to be near his prisoners.'

Would the governor detect the broken accent? Did he already suspect that his companion was other than he imagined? For Tsu-Hi stood still regarding the man who had admitted him. Something about the accent undoubtedly attracted his attention. But he was thinking more of Chang than of anything or any one else, Chang and the foreign devils whom they, between them, had so cleverly captured. Then he put back his head and laughed, an almost silent laugh, in which there was a ring of triumph.

'He, he, he! So as to be near his prisoners,' he gurgled, opening a wide mouth between the thin lips of which an uneven and irregular row of yellow fangs were displayed. 'To be near his prisoners, as if he would take a tender farewell of them and see as much of their faces as possible before their hour comes. He, he, he! This Chang is a witty fellow.'

'What an old ruffian!' thought David, still, however, kow-towing. 'Little tenderness we may expect from him, or from Chang either. In a moment I'll make him laugh on the other side of his ugly mouth. Here, Excellency,' he murmured once more, pushing the door a little wider open. 'Enter.'

The gorgeously dressed official was still shaking with suppressed amusement as he passed under the doorway. His hands were buried in his sleeves, and he was actually hugging himself.

'A right merry fellow, this Chang! Who is he? Whence does he come with such a timely warning? He will be an excellent fellow with whom to chat and pass a few hours while others are sleeping. And then, when this thing is finished, he will go. The Government will send urgent orders for his arrest, while I shall have already despatched men to search for him, men who are led by a blind officer unable to find the right track.'

It made him hug himself the harder when he considered how cunning he was, and how he would hoodwink every one; for the deputy-governor was a cunning rascal. Still smarting under the severe reproof he had had administered on a former occasion when Europeans were molested in this walled city of Hatsu, and by the loss of dignity which had resulted, the man, like thousands more of his countrymen, bore a lasting grudge against foreign devils. He was one of the many jacks-in-office who still help to sway the affairs of the celestial empire, clinging tenaciously and with great stubbornness to old methods, for a Chinaman is nothing if not conservative. The views his ancestors held are good enough for him, their education fills his needs, while the ancient system whereby a few live in luxury, and the vast majority in grinding poverty is a model of all that is required. Some there are, and their numbers are steadily increasing, who have gained much by contact with the outside world, for whom travel has relieved them of much arrogance. But the knowledge they possess of the superiority of western nations in many things is lost in the sea of ignorance, of bigotry, which is prevalent throughout the kingdom. One swallow does not make a summer. One enlightened mandarin does not result in the rising of a mighty nation, in the break-up of all its cherished customs, in its advancement in the paths followed by others privileged to live under wiser government.

'To-morrow this Chang shall go. I myself will direct him, and also those who shall set out in pursuit in the opposite direction. Greeting, my friend.'

Tsu-Hi stalked majestically into the room and stood beneath the swaying lantern, his eyes blinking in the light as he searched for the man he had come to visit. He had half-expected him to be there before him, kow-towing to the ground, for this jack-in-office loved humility in those who served him. Then he caught sight of the figure huddled beneath the patched and stained quilt spread over the *kang*, and chuckled loudly.

'He sleeps, worn out with his efforts to warn us, but he will welcome the deputy-governor. I will rouse him.'

He stepped across to the kang, and touched the figure lying there. He pulled the quilt back with a sharp jerk, disclosing the face of the Tartar under-officer. But even then he did not realise that this was not Chang, the man whom the Tartar had brought so secretly to him that evening. It was only when, hearing the door bang, and turning slowly he discovered the figure of the Tartar who had admitted him advancing swiftly that Tsu-Hi became alarmed.

'Insolence!' he cried. 'What is this? Who bade you follow in here? Begone at once, else — —'

Even then he had not penetrated the disguise of the youth before him, though his alarm increased seeing that David did not halt, but came on towards him. But, of a sudden, he grasped the real truth, for a revolver already grinned within two feet of him. He started backward against the kang and fell upon it A second later he was up again, and running towards the door like a startled rabbit, but David stopped him in a manner to which this very important official must have been a stranger since his earliest boyhood. He gripped Tsu-Hi by the shoulder, and with a heave tossed him heavily into the corner. Then he dragged him to his feet again, and pressed the muzzle of his weapon hard against his head.

'Silence! Make a sound and you are a dead man. Strip off your garments.'

How Jong would have giggled had he been able to see what was passing, for he would have enjoyed to the full the terror of this mandarin. Tsu-Hi's eyes indeed threatened to start from his head, while he shook so violently that his limbs would hardly support him. But the revolver gave him some sort of strength, that and the threatening looks of this hated foreign devil. Rapidly, as if he longed to be rid of them, he dragged off his gorgeous garment.

'Boots, too,' commanded David fiercely. 'Now lie down on that *kang*. You can push the man farther over. Not a sound, mind, or I'll rid this city of a deputy-governor.'

Little more than ten minutes later David emerged from the cell, leaving Tsu-Hi trussed like a fowl, bound hand and foot with strips torn from the quilt, and nicely muzzled with a ball of the same wedged between his teeth and secured in position. He pulled the door to, shot the bolts home, and strode along the passage.

Chapter XV
Dick and David Turn the Tables

'Dick, it's time we were moving. Come along out of this hole, and give me a hand to get us out of the city.'

David had thrown back the bolts of the cell next to the one into which he had so boldly descended, and stood in the doorway holding a huge paper lantern before him. He had taken it but a minute before from the roof of the passage, the operation being easy for the simple reason that there was a pulley and tackle, whereby the man who saw to the replenishing of the lanterns could gain access to them. Now he was staring into the cell, his eyes fixed on the figure of his old comrade.

'Come along, lad,' he called again softly, seeing that Dick did not move from his position on the basket, where he sat somewhat disconsolately. 'Time we were moving.'

It made him laugh to see the prisoner rise slowly to his feet and rub his eyes as if he could not believe what they were telling him. Then he had occasion to speak sharply. For it appeared that Dick had fallen asleep while seated, and imagining that he had heard David's voice in a dream, and not when possessed of all his senses, he took it for granted that the figure at the door was actually that of the Tartar. He dashed forward swiftly, evidently with the intention of attacking.

'Stop!' cried David sharply. 'Don't be a fool. Shake yourself, and then you'll see who I really am. Quick! We've no time to waste. We've heaps of work before us.'

'Well, I never! You take my breath away. What next will you appear as?' gasped Dick, recovering his senses, and stepping forward to wring David's hand. 'What next? A Tartar under-officer now, and I suppose you had to steal to get the clothing. To-morrow you'll be stalking about as the deputy-governor.'

'No, I shall not; but you will.'

'I! Disguised as the deputy-governor! Look here, David, are you silly, or have I gone clean staring mad? I as Tsu-Hi, indeed! The rascal's safely tucked in bed at this moment.'

'He is; agreed,' admitted David curtly, a grin on his lips.

'As safe as houses in his gilded palace,' said Dick bitterly.

'Wrong! He's not in his gilded palace. He's tucked safely in bed along with that pompous Tartar under-officer. He's tied up as if he were a dangerous hyena.'

Dick scratched his head energetically, and rubbed his eyes again. He was seriously anxious about his old friend, who had so suddenly come to visit him. The stubborn look on his face, his evident determination, and the curtness of his answer roused an awful suspicion in his mind. Was David mad, driven out of his mind by this sudden trouble? Then he shook his head.

'It's I who am a fool,' he whispered. 'Here he is in Tartar uniform. That shows he's been moving. But this business of Tsu-Hi beats me altogether; it knocks the stuffing entirely out of yours truly.'

'It'll knock the stuffing out of someone else I know of.'

David blurted out the words gruffly, while a frown crossed his forehead.

'Sit down for a moment,' he said shortly. 'I'll tell you what's been passing. Don't ask a heap of questions. We're still in a beastly hole, and unless everything is in readiness we shall be too late to slip out of the city. Sit down; for goodness sake don't interrupt.'

He sate himself down beside his friend, and told him as swiftly as possible of Chang's visit, of his own escape, and of what had followed.

'And now you're going to be Tsu-Hi,' he said abruptly. 'No use in my changing these clothes. You can do the work as well as I can. Let's get along into the other room, and then you can strip off your things and dress in Tsu-Hi's gorgeous raiment.'

'And then?' asked Dick, beginning to grin and bubble over, for the adventure amused him vastly. 'And then, my noble sir, what do I do? Go to the palace and command the foreign devils to be brought before me. Sign their death warrants, and see them executed. Oh, Lor'! I see it all. Here's a splendid ending. We put this Tartar beggar into your clothes, and Tsu-Hi into mine, and let Chang behead 'em as if they were actually foreign devils.'

He would have roared with laughing, had not David stopped him angrily.

'Utter rot you do talk, Dick,' he said severely, though he was bound to smile at the reckless jollity of his comrade. 'You become the deputy-governor, and in due course you will go to the palace, and I with you. For the moment, you've got to dress. Come along—no more jawing.'

They crept along the passage to the cell in which Tsu-Hi and the Tartar lay together, where Dick quickly arrayed himself in the finery of the fallen governor.

'How do I look, old chap?' he asked, posing beneath the lantern, and before the eyes of the man he was representing. 'A bit of a sport, I think. What? Ain't I handsome?'

'You're an idiot!' declared David crossly, though he was bound to laugh. 'Tsu-Hi looks as if beheading wouldn't be enough for you. But let's get to business. Tie your own clothing into a bundle. Now, let me have it.'

Gripping the rope which dangled from the window-frame, and holding the bundle between his teeth, David swarmed up till he was able to get a grip of the edge above. He straddled it at once, and then whistled softly. At once Jong's figure shot from the shadow. The Chinaman crept into the centre of the road.

'Catch!' called David, tossing the bundle; 'and pick up the one I threw before. 'Listen to this, Jong. Mr. Dick and I have captured Tsu-Hi. We'll be coming out in a moment, when we shall go direct to the palace. Once there, you'll have to bring out the ponies without delay, and get our goods packed on them. I shall want a cart also.'

He waved to the man, and slid into the room again, slipping down the rope as if he were a sailor.

'Where'd it come from?' asked Dick, nodding to the dangling cord. 'Who fixed it?'

'I did. Jong is outside; he threw it up to me.'

'Then you could have slipped down then and there, and got clear away? Ain't that it?'

'I suppose so,' admitted David grudgingly.

'My uncle! Then why didn't you?'

Dick turned sharply upon him, his face serious, a flush on his cheeks.

'Why didn't you?' he demanded fiercely.

'Because—oh, look here,' said David lamely, 'we're wasting time. What's the good of jawing?'

'Why didn't you?' demanded Dick again, his manner resolute, ignoring his comrade's efforts to change the conversation; then, finding that David did not answer, he clapped a hand on his shoulder.

'All right,' he said, with a curtness which matched that of the lad who had released him. 'I know well enough. It's one up for you, anyway. Could have escaped, but wouldn't, simply because there was a wretched beggar owning to the name of Dick still left in the building. Right, my boy, I'm not going to forget it. Now, what orders?'

'Glad you've returned to business,' exclaimed David. 'What orders?'

'Yes. You give 'em. This is your own little affair. What are they? Call up the garrison, march to Chang's quarters, and then set fire to the city? Eh? What are they?'

The merry fellow was bubbling over again at the thought of his own impertinence. He smacked his thigh loudly, as he considered what a reversal of fortune the night had shown to the various parties. It made him giggle hugely to see Tsu-Hi, trussed indeed, glaring from over the top of the greasy bandage with which David had had the temerity to secure the gag that silenced him. In fact, Dick was ready for any piece of mischief that David cared to invent, and, if he were backward, this young fellow was ready himself to supply the want, and urge a plan which for recklessness would easily have matched that of his comrade. But then he was a merry, light-hearted youngster. He wanted the depth and stability that David enjoyed. The latter put a stop to his chatter with a sudden movement.

'Don't imagine we're out of the wood yet,' he said. 'I've got my plans, but whether we can carry them out is another matter. First and foremost, we have to collar Chang. I've seen him already in a room on a higher level than this, located on the other side of the building. You're game, I suppose?'

Dick led the way to the door, his eyes flashing. 'Game for anything,' he cried. 'But I'll be silent and cautious. You can trust me.'

'Then come along; bring the lantern with you. If we meet any one don't utter a word. Pass them in silence. Recollect that you are deputy-governor, the chief official of the city, to whom all will give obedience. And one thing more. This Chang is expecting a call from you. When we reach the room pass in boldly. I shall make a jump at him.'

Picking up the lantern Dick fell in beside David, and the two passed into the passage, having first, however, inspected their prisoners. The Tartar under-officer was breathing stertorously, and was still evidently unconscious. As for Tsu-Hi, he was as helpless as a baby. All he could do was to glare at the foreign devils; for his eyes were the only parts that the unfortunate governor could completely control. They pulled the door shut after them, and shot the bolts. Then they hastened past the cell in which Dick had been imprisoned, closing the door as they did so, and proceeded up the flight of stone steps which led from the far end of the passage. Nor had they much difficulty in calculating where Chang was in residence. For

David had a fair bump of locality, and his meanderings on the roof of the prison had given him invaluable information. He came to a halt opposite a narrow door, and motioned to Dick to move along farther. Then he slid to the floor, and applied his eye to the crevice which existed beneath the woodwork. A moment later he was on his feet, his face beaming.

'There's a light in there,' he whispered, 'and I'm sure I saw his legs. Half a minute while I make another inspection.'

This second time he was sure that he could see the feet of some individual, though whether it were Chang or some one else there was no saying. It was a man. That was sufficient.

'I'll give a knock,' he whispered. 'When he calls I'll push the door open and announce Tsu-Hi. Enter at once without hesitation. But first, pull that cap well down over your eyes. That'll do. Walk straight across the room. He's nearly certain to follow. Then I'll jump on his back. Got it?'

Dick grinned. He had got the plan securely. The effort he was about to make was just the one to delight him. It appealed to his merry mind, for the idea was so bold that there was huge excitement in the attempt to carry it out. How he longed to bring about the discomfiture of this rascal, for David had told him enough to allow him to gather what had happened, though it was hard to believe that the man who had married his friend's stepmother could from England, so far away, control the action of an accomplice in China. Chang was an out and out ruffian, he told himself, but nothing in comparison with Ebenezer Clayhill.

'Righto!' he smiled. 'I'm ready. You bet, I'll be his haughtiness himself.'

'Enter,' came a sharp summons from inside, as David knocked. 'Enter, and welcome.'

'I don't think,' muttered Dick, with a grin. 'Open it, David, my boy.'

It would have done the Professor's jovial heart a world of good could he have seen how the young fellow carried himself. It seemed that Dick was a born actor. He waited tranquilly for David to push the door open, and then, with hands tucked well within his sleeves, and his magazine pistol secured within one of them, he advanced pompously and slowly, casting a single glance at the individual who had summoned him to enter. It was Chang without a doubt. He had risen from the table pen in hand—for he had been writing—and stood aside to allow free passage to his Excellency, kow-towing deeply.

'His Excellency, Tsu-Hi,' announced David, mimicking as well as he was able the voice of the Tartar he represented.

'Enter, and welcome to His Highness.'

Chang kow-towed even more deeply, turning as Dick passed him. A second later he was sprawling on the floor, for David had leaped upon him, gripping him by the neck with both hands and capsizing him completely. As for Dick, he turned instantly, raced to the door and closed it, and then very coolly presented his weapon at the head of the individual to whom he had made a visit.

'Just one word,' he whispered, in execrable Chinese, 'and there won't be a Chang left to worry us. Just one little word, my friend.'

'Get up!' commanded David, for Chang had become of a sudden but a limp heap of terrified humanity. 'Don't worry him with your Chinese, dear boy. He understands and speaks English as well almost as we do. But listen to this, you rascal. If you stir an inch or make a sound you'll be shot without mercy. Now, stand there. No humbug, mind you.'

Leaving Dick still with his weapon at Chang's head David went to the door and completely closed it, having first of all peeped out into the passage. Then he returned, and sat himself down in the seat which the rascal had but lately vacated. There was an ornamental ink-pot within reach, while the pen which Chang had been using lay on the floor where he had dropped it. And just in front of David was a sheet of Chinese paper, on which the rascal had been writing. It is not the sort of thing that a decent Englishman does to read correspondence meant for other people. But here there was more than sufficient excuse. Chang might have been putting down some orders respecting his prisoners. David picked up the paper and held it closer. Then he started violently; for the Chinaman was using English, and the letter was addressed to Ebenezer Clayhill.

> 'Sir—This is to inform you that David Harbor, he of whom you spoke to me, has come by a misfortune at Hatsu, a walled city in northern China. He was accused with another of bringing plague to the people, and though the Governor attempted to protect him, the mob seized him during his Excellency's absence. He was beheaded this morning. Such news entitles your servant to the payment of one thousand pounds. Be so good as to mail it to the firm of Kung Kow, at Shanghai. Within I send you an official notice of the death vouched for by the British Consul.
>
> CHANG.'

David gasped. The words made him tingle all over. He glared at the prisoner as if he could eat him. And then he laughed. He rocked to and fro on the low Chinese stool, stifling his merriment as well as he was able.

'Of all the bits of cheek that I ever met, this really beats everything,' he declared. 'Here, read it, Dick; I'll put my pistol to this rascal's head willingly.'

He rose from his seat, and with the practice he had already had with the Governor of Hatsu, contrived to apply his revolver in a manner which made the trembling Chang squirm. Indeed, utter ruffian as Chang had proved himself to be, not alone by his recent interview with our hero, but by reason of the words which he had written, it was not surprising that such an one should turn out to be a coward of the worst description. Cruelty and courage do not often go together. The man who loves to browbeat others, and thrust his fellows into unpleasant places, likes least of all retaliation. Chang squirmed beneath the touch of the cold muzzle. He whined for mercy, and then sank in a dead faint on the floor. Meanwhile Dick had slowly read the letter, and from what his friend had already told him was quick to gather its meaning. One might have expected the merry fellow to roar as David had done, to see the funny point in this amazing writing; but there were some things which Dick resented, and this cold-blooded announcement of David's death, before that ceremony had taken place, rendered him furious.

'Of all the cold-blooded diabolical plots I ever heard or read of this is the worst,' he said. 'David, you will pocket that letter.'

'Why?'

'So as to prove the guilt of this Ebenezer Clayhill.'

'No, thank you,' declared our hero, slowly, 'There's been enough stirring of mud in our family. I don't want the world to know that I've such a connection.'

'Perhaps not. There's no need; the possession of this will make that ruffian retire from the position he has taken up with regard to you. He will no longer contend that his wife comes in for Edward Harbor's possessions. Anyway, I'll pocket the letter. We can discuss the matter later on. Now? What next. We kill this fellow.'

He was as cool as possible as he made the request. There was an angry iciness about Dick to which David was entirely a stranger. But he realised some of the thoughts passing through his friend's mind, and appreciated his attitude.

'Kill him,' he answered. 'Certainly not. For the moment it is necessary that he and I should change places.'

'What! More disguises? Why?'

'Because Chang, the friend of Tsu-Hi, your own noble self, is a far more important being than is the humble individual I at present represent.

Let's take him along to the place where we've left our prisoners. I'll do the changing there. By the way, bring some paper and that pot of ink. Now, blow the light out. I'll see to this ruffian.'

'He went out of the door, dragging the senseless body of Chang after him, and with Dick to help him soon arrived at the cell where Tsu-Hi lay glaring. Then David clambered to the window, and looking out, called to Jong. The faithful fellow popped out of the shadow instantly.

'Come over to the door. I want to speak to you,' called David, and promptly slid back into the prison. 'Now,' he said, when at last Jong was before him, just within the passage. 'We've captured a man called Chang, who was the cause of this attack, and also Tsu-Hi, the deputy-governor. Our aim and object is to get securely outside the city. Are you afraid to return to the palace with an order written by the governor himself? It needs courage, but the scheme should not fail. This is what his Excellency will write:—

"Hand over to the bearer of this letter the six ponies and the possessions of the foreign devils. Send also a cart with a strong animal between the shafts, and three men to help with the loading. Despatch a man to the northern gate of the city, and warn the guard that his Excellency comes with two in his service. There must be no challenge. He must be passed through in silence, for he bears important prisoners." Now, Jong, are you afraid?'

The Chinaman giggled. Perhaps he had caught some of David's own enthusiasm, or some of Dick's reckless jollity.

'Likee dat,' he said. 'Me go sure. Not know Jong 't 'all at de palace. Wait here for the letter?'

'Yes. Then go quickly. Make no noise when you return, but wait outside till I fetch you. Then do as I order. I will be with you in a few minutes.'

The lad's busy brain had been exceedingly active, while he had mapped out a course of action likely enough to stagger the placid folks of Hatsu city, and one, moreover, which would probably defeat the deputy-governor and the rascal who had aided and, indeed, instigated the attack made upon our hero and his comrades. David slipped back to join Dick, only to find Chang still semi-conscious. As for the others, the Tartar snored stertorously, not having yet shaken off the effects of the blow he had received, while the deputy-governor, wriggling in his bonds, looked the quintessence of rascality.

'Prop him up,' commanded David. 'Now show him your pistol.'

Dick did it with a vengeance. He demonstrated his power to the exceeding discomfort of Tsu-Hi, not to mention the damaging of his dignity.

'Now loose his hands, and put the pen and ink and paper before him. That's right; I'm going to stir Chang into sensibility.'

There was a jar of water in the cell, and David liberally sprinkled the countenance of Chang with it. In a little while he had the fellow seated on the edge of the kang.

'Listen to this,' he commanded sternly; 'you will tell the Governor what to write, and will see that he puts down what I dictate. If there is a mistake, if there is a secret warning in his letter, then— —'

Dick jerked his head on one side in an expressive manner. 'You've pretty well guessed what'll happen,' he laughed drily. 'Just you don't be foxy.'

Nor did Chang attempt such boldness. The man was in the depths of terror, and thinking perhaps to lighten his own punishment, eagerly dictated David's words to the Governor. As for the latter, the revolver tickling the nape of his neck was such strong persuasion that he wrote with a swiftness there was no gainsaying.

'Tie him up again,' commanded our hero, when the note was finished. 'Now, Dick, shoot this beggar if he dares to move while I'm absent. I am merely going to the door. Let him get ready to make an exchange of clothing.'

He went at once into the passage, and handed the note to Jong, who scanned it eagerly. 'Me lead samee as you, misser Davie,' he said. 'Dis allee lightee. No one tink dat dat not come from Tsu-Hi. Ebely one leady to obey.'

He went off at a run down the moon-lit street, careless if he were observed, now that he had that important letter. David watched him depart, and then strolled back to the cell. He began to feel that the worst part of their troubles were over, as if safety lay before them. The lines left his forehead as he thought of the success which had already attended their efforts, while he smiled a meaning smile as he began to pull off his clothing.

'Strip yours,' he commanded Chang. 'Quick with it.'

'And am I to dress in those of the Tartar, Excellency?' asked the wretch.

'Just as you like. In any case I'm going to provide you with another covering. I don't fancy there'll be any chance of your getting cold.'

'But, Excellency— —' whined the man.

'You be slippy and don't waste time talking,' cried Dick, beginning to fathom his chum's meaning. 'Going to provide him with another covering, eh?' he grinned. 'You don't mean that you're— —'

'Here, help me with these boots. I thought I should never be able to get into them. Now I'm a bit doubtful that I'll be successful in pulling them off.

Ah, thanks. Chang, your shoes are far more comfortable. Don't you trouble to put these boots on. You won't want 'em. You ain't going to walk.'

'Because, you see,' added Dick, enjoying the discomfiture of the rascal immensely, 'you'll be carried—carried, Chang. Got it?'

It was evident that the wretch had, for he shivered and whined as he sat on the edge of the *kang*. But David took no more notice of him for the moment. He coolly dressed himself in the clothes this secret enemy had been wearing, and then walked out of the cell. A quarter of an hour later, when Jong arrived on the scene, and the scrunch of wheels was heard outside on the road, two men stood ready to accompany the party.

'Carry out the baskets,' whispered one, who seemed to be none other than the man who had come to warn the inhabitants of Hatsu of the foreign devils. 'You will give all orders till we are out of the city.'

It took but five minutes to load those two heavy baskets on the cart, and then the party set forward, Chang, and to all who peeped at him, the noble deputy-governor following closely. David, as he stepped along the white, moon-lit road in the garments lately worn by Chang, could hardly believe that the fortunes of his little party had been so utterly changed. It was hard to credit the fact that the pompous individual beside him, at whose nod men cringed, was indeed, and in fact none other than, his chum Dick, while it brought a broad smile to a face, which he struggled hard to keep impassive, when he thought of the contents of the baskets. Could it actually be that those long, creaking shapes hid in their depths the mighty Tsu-Hi, deputy-governor of the walled city of Hatsu, and Chang, conspirator, villain, the hired ruffian of Ebenezer Clayhill?

But the gates of the city were yet before them. A challenge there, a shriek from the burdens the cart carried, the smallest untoward event would change their fortunes, and might yet land himself and Dick back in the prison, there to await the execution which had been promised.

Chapter XVI
Freedom Again

The gates of the walled city of Hatsu were not calculated to inspire a person eager to pass without them with a feeling of the greatest enthusiasm, for they stood black and forbidding against the moon-lit background, the battlemented wall on either side, the flanking towers and bastions sharply outlined. Beneath the towers yawned a huge cavern, so dark that no one could see beneath it, carrying the white road to the huge double doors which, if they were shut, could bar the egress or the entry of an army.

'Beastly looking place,' whispered Dick, as the little party came near to it. 'Hope there won't be any parleying. Ah! here's Jong, come to ask instructions.'

'Masser Davie,' whispered the man, 'what now? What do wid dese China boys I bring wid me to help carry out de baskets?'

'Dismiss them here. Wait till they have gone out of sight, and then go on. You have that note?'

'Yes, sar; him here. But not sure dat dey open de door for him. Suppose not? What den?'

'You can expect to be busy, Dick,' whispered David, as Jong went ahead again; 'if there's trouble here we've a way left out of it. You know which basket contains his Excellency?'

'One on the left, the heaviest. Being a governor gives a fellow a chance to put on flesh. He leads a life of ease and luxury.'

'You could manage, perhaps, to open it at the head, and pull the gag from the noble fellow's mouth?'

'In a twinkling,' came the ready answer.

'Then, if I call, do so. I'll cover the guard while you get the fine gentleman into a position for talking. If we're held up, he'll have to give definite orders to the soldiers to open to us. If not— —'

'If not?' echoed Dick, 'you'll shoot him.'

'Without hesitation, as if he were a dog, which indeed he is. Now, those men have gone. Jong's moving forward. It does look a beastly hole to go into.'

'Look, a gate is open,' whispered Dick quickly. 'That's promising. A man has come into the archway with a lantern. Hope he won't hold it up so as to inspect our faces.'

The same fear had evidently come to Jong, who was by no means a dullard, and without doubt the intention of the guard who had so suddenly stepped into the dark gateway was to take stock of those who passed with the aid of his dangling paper lantern.

'Beware at whom you look,' cried Jong suddenly. 'Has not an order come bidding you pass a party without noise and without inspection? Go then, else his Excellency will not be best pleased with you. Does he desire that any fool should see him passing, and be able to talk. Away with the lamp quickly.'

They were already beneath the huge gateway, and glancing upward David was able to distinguish the roof, which was blackened with the smoke of ages, for in the cold months the guards were accustomed to place braziers on the roadway so as to make watching possible. A second later, however, the swaying lantern disappeared, the man who carried it diving out of sight into a gallery leading from the gateway. On went the party, Jong leading the ponies, while David had taken the rein of the animal drawing the cart. He heard the wicker of the baskets creaking, and guessed that his prisoners were struggling with might and main. But there seemed no one near enough to hear the noise, while the strong native cart did not feel the movement of the ruffians it carried. Just at the very exit from the gates there stood one solitary sentry, and he, as if bearing in mind the caution which Jong had given his fellow, turned his face away. It was not well, perhaps, he thought, to look too closely upon the doings of such a high personage as the deputy-governor.

'Else it might happen that I should be called in evidence,' he told himself, 'when, had I, indeed, seen his honour, it would be hard to find a reason for denying the fact. A deputy-governor is a mighty person. He may come and go as he likes.'

After all, the incident in such a country as China, where conspiracy is common enough, was not so very remarkable. 'Saving face' is an expression thoroughly well known, and many and many an exalted person has been under the need of cloaking his movements, so that when an accusation of complicity in some conspiracy was levelled at him, he could bring evidence to prove that he had never been seen in that locality, and that, on the contrary, he was at home with his servants. And, no doubt, here was some similar movement. His Excellency was, without fear of contradiction, asleep in his palace. His servants could swear that on the morrow. It was not the business of the guard at the gate to inspect too closely, when he had received a direct message ordering him to pass the governor secretly. Besides, there were the foreign-devils, of whom the rumour had reached him that they had been attacked. Doubtless the baskets he heard creaking in the cart held them securely, though for his part, the guard was not going to be too curious.

'Pass! All's well,' he whispered, as the cart issued from the gate and crossed the drawbridge, with Dick in close attendance. 'Pass to your business.'

The revolving gate scrunched on its runners. The huge hinges creaked. The mass of wood, with its heavy bronze bolts and locks, swung into position with a bang. Then the dull reverberation beneath the drawbridge died away, while the wheels of the cart began to rattle on the hard roadway. David wiped the perspiration from his forehead, while Dick let go a gentle whistle. But not one dared to alter his position. There might be, and probably were, many pairs of eyes watching them from the narrow slits on the outer face of the towers and bastions, the slits from which, even now-a-days, should there be a siege, Chinese soldiers would discharge arrows, using precisely the same weapons as did their forefathers, and that in spite of the fact that many of their comrades were armed with modern rifles. Yes, no doubt, many an inquisitive glance was cast after the party, and it was still necessary to preserve caution. And so they continued, showing black and easily distinguishable on the white roadway, till the latter curled out of sight of the city in a stretch of forest. It was only then that David dared to bring the animal hauling the cart to an abrupt halt, while a whistle caused Jong to draw rein promptly.

'I think,' began Dick, struggling to keep his impassiveness, and yet almost bursting in consequence, 'I think things begin to look a little more healthy. A fellow begins to actually believe that he may be wanting another breakfast. In fact, one may go so far as to say that it's a case of all right.'

Then he went off into a fit of the most hilarious laughter, which doubled him up, till he looked anything but the noble Governor of the city they had just quitted.

'What a tale for the Professor!' he shouted. 'Won't he enjoy the whole thing, and roar when he hears how you've turned the tables.'

'I! We, you mean,' came sharply from David, who was enjoying his friend's remarks immensely. 'We, you should have said.'

'You're wrong. I said you, and I meant you. It's you all the time. There's no one else in it,' declared Dick warmly.

'But, you— —'

'Oh, yes, we know all about that,' interrupted the fine young fellow impersonating Tsu-Hi. 'I did a terrible lot. I started the business, of course. It was I who managed to clamber out of my cell, and was then such a good comrade that instead of getting clear away, as sensible fellows would have done— —'

'Sensible fellows! Oh, come now,' cried David hotly.

'Yes. Just what I said. Sensible fellows, just as sensible fellows would have done. I repeat, instead of clearing off as I had a right to do, of course it is well known that I went back again at the risk of my skin, knocked the sense out of the gentle Tartar soldier, took his place for a few moments, nobbled the Governor of the city, and then, when things were getting ship-shape, called in the help of my friend to cure the wounds of the wretches I had been operating on. Look here, David, here's my hand. I'm not going to chip in with heaps of thanks. But I know how it is that I am alive and capable of thinking of a breakfast.'

Out there, beneath the shade of the trees, they gripped hands firmly, and thereafter never a word did Dick say with regard to his gratitude. But he knew who was his benefactor. David had stalked inches higher in his estimation.

'What'll you do with the baggage?' he asked after a while. 'Drop it into the river, upset it at the side of the road? What?'

'Take those villains on another fifteen miles,' answered David. 'Then fish out Tsu-Hi and send him back. Guess he'll have a deal of difficulty in explaining his absence. As for the other, this Chang, I shall keep him till I can hand him over to the authorities. It seems to me that if I fail in that he may very well attempt some other game and perhaps actually earn the money Ebenezer promised him. But now for breakfast, then we'll put our best leg forward.'

That afternoon they dragged the discomfited and almost suffocated deputy-governor from the basket in which he had been reposing, and having handed him his clothing; for both lads had by now donned their own, they sent him back to the city of Hatsu a sorry and unhappy figure. Then they pushed on again, arriving in the hours of dusk at Chi-Luang, another walled city of great age, where their request to see the governor brought them at once a polite invitation written in purest English. Judge of their delight in discovering that Twang Chun himself, the enlightened governor of the province, was the writer, and that he was in those parts on a tour of inspection. He greeted them warmly, sent their prisoner to the cells, and at once arranged for comfortable quarters to be given to David and his following. And that night, after having joined them at dinner, which, by the way, was a feast of the utmost attraction, being of purely Chinese origin, and therefore most interesting to our heroes as well as appetising, Twang Chun called on the lads to give their story.

'I'm glad I had the good fortune to be in this direction,' he said, when Dick had finished; for no persuasion would induce David to tell of his own exploits in the prison. 'Very glad indeed, for had the question been left to the city's governor he would have found it difficult to decide how best to act. To be candid, foreign devils are still foreign devils to the majority of my countrymen, and more so at a time such as this is, when plague is stalking through Manchuria, and threatening to reach Pekin. I assure you that the people are driven frantic, and that I am here and am patrolling the province, solely with a view to making arrangements to stop all travellers who may come from infected areas, and to arrest, if possible, the course of the disease. But, as I said, Europeans are not much loved. The Chinese do not understand them, and in a case such as this, with such an exalted personage as Tsu-Hi implicated, the governor here could only hold him in prison till orders came from Pekin; that might take months. I have known years to elapse, so that the course of justice does not run either smoothly or for the benefit of the people. However, I am here, and will sift the matter. An example must be made of these wretches.'

Let the reader imagine the terror of Chang on the following morning when he was brought into the presence of Twang Chun, the governor who had once before condemned him. Little by little the whole story leaked out, so that David learned that this heartless rascal had been engaged in the murder of his father. In any case, there was no doubt of his guilt on this occasion. He had been taken red-handed, while the letter which he had had the boldness to write to Ebenezer Clayhill condemned him. Justice might be slow and lagging when the authorities at Pekin controlled it; but here it was swift—terribly swift—for the wrong-doer. Chang was beheaded that very morning, and thus Ebenezer Clayhill's rascally scheme came to an ending.

'To-night I shall be in the city of Hatsu,' said Twang Chun, when the sentence on Chang had been carried out. 'Perhaps you will accompany me.'

David and his friend agreed with the greatest pleasure, for seeing that they had now met the governor of the province, the very individual to whom the Professor had sent them, and had delivered their letter, it appeared hardly necessary to proceed.

'Might just as well return to our camp, and then come up with the whole party,' said David. 'Besides, I fancy his Excellency would be glad to have our evidence at Hatsu.'

This was, in fact, the case, and arriving at that city after nightfall, the party, who were accompanied by a strong escort of mounted soldiers, rested there for two whole days, two days of abject misery for Tsu-Hi, the rascally deputy who had so readily fallen in with the plans which Chang had formed. Indeed it was hardly likely that such an act as he had been guilty of could go unpunished, and, like his comrade-in-guilt, he too was beheaded.

'Do not think that I love these executions,' said Twang Chun, when seated with the lads. 'Had I my way, matters would be conducted as in your country. But we must always remember that we are in China, and that I am dealing with my own countrymen, who do not understand the meaning of leniency. In a case such as this the sternest example must be read, and were I to behead the Tartar under-officer alone, and merely admonish Tsu-Hi, the people of the city would see in such leniency an encouragement to attack Europeans again. And see what follows. The tale is spread abroad. Your people, Americans, all the white race having dealings with us will distrust us absolutely. That feeling of amity between the white and the yellow race, for which I and men like me aim at, will be farther away than ever. Incalculable harm will, in fact, be done, and the advancement of this nation retarded to some extent. Therefore, to deter others who should set a good example, and who, above all things, should never descend to a depth where guests beneath their roof are abused and injured, I have had Tsu-Hi beheaded, and with him the Tartar under-officer. Only by such severity will the lesson be learned.'

'And now, Mr. David, tell me more about yourself. I know the name of Harbor.'

'My father,' exclaimed our hero promptly. 'He came out here to investigate ruins, just as the Professor has done before. He was killed. Chang had a hand in his assassination.'

When they came to discuss the matter Twang Chun quickly learned that David was the son of the very man in whose interests Chang had once before been arrested. He listened with the greatest attention as the question of the will was propounded, and lifted a hand to arrest David's conversation.

'You have come out here on a hopeless errand, I fear,' he said. 'But that your father made this will I am positive, since I myself witnessed the signature, though I was not aware of all of the contents. As to the fate of the document itself, it was doubtless burned, for the camp in which the party of excavators was located caught fire. It is strange to think that you are going to the very same spot; for the letter which your friend the Professor has sent me asks permission to investigate the relics of an ancient Mongolian city situated outside the Great Wall, the same city which engaged the attention of your parent. Whether you will reach that spot is a matter of doubt at the moment.'

Dick's eyebrows went up questioningly. With this important personage he dared not be so free and easy in his remarks as with the Professor.

'But tell us why, your Excellency,' he asked, politely. 'What will prevent us, supposing you give your consent?'

'The plague may prevent your going,' came the answer. 'You have no idea of the nature or of the importance of this pest. Manchuria to-day is in the last stage of disorder. Thousands die every twenty-four hours, while there is no time and not enough men to conduct the burials. The victims are being burned. From Manchuria to Pekin is not such a far cry, while the neighbourhood of these ruins you seek is even closer to the infected area. You must understand me, I do not say that your own fear of contagion will hold you back. That is not the position at all. What I do suggest is that it may be prudent of your leader to remain in these parts, rather than go farther afield. For disaster does not come of its own accord in the eyes of my countrymen. You have seen for yourself how their thoughts run. The poor ignorant fellows believe that a pest is brought, is settled upon them by way of punishment, and should you and your friends be away in some savage part, all alone, you might very well be set upon as the cause of the disaster. In this city of Hatsu, thanks to the scheming of that rascal Chang, you were accused of this crime, and his ignorant tools snapped at the chance of killing you. In the neighbourhood of those Mongolian ruins the natives are, I fear, likely to be even more ignorant and stupid. However, we will see what can be done; I might be able to send an escort. And now I propose travelling farther with you. I myself shall visit the camp where your friends are situated, so that I may formally welcome them to my province.'

Imagine the Professor's astonishment at the return of David and Dick. He emerged from a deep excavation, which the coolies had been engaged in beneath the debris covering the ruined city wherein Tsin had dwelt once on a time, and advanced with something approaching consternation on his face.

'Returned already,' he cried. 'Why? And with an escort, and a mandarin too if my eyes don't cheat me. Not got into trouble, I do hope.'

'Heaps,' laughed Dick, enjoying the position. 'The exalted official following comes to greet you. He's already chopped off three heads while in our company.'

'It's Twang Chun himself, the governor of the province,' explained David, laughing at his chum's fun. 'We happened to meet him. The chopping off of heads is a long story. But his Excellency comes to welcome you to the province, and to discuss the question of your journey to the Mongolian city. He thinks there may be difficulties.'

'I trust not, indeed. This expedition of ours would be shorn of half its profit if we were unable to go to Chi-Seang, for, if report speaks true, there are relics to be discovered of the very greatest interest. But I will speak with his Excellency; bring him to the tent. I will get washed, and put on clean clothing.'

The meeting between the two gentlemen was most cordial, and as may well be imagined, every one belonging to the Professor's staff worked hard so as to prepare entertainment for his Excellency, since Twang Chun was, indeed, an exalted official, and as became one of his high rank and importance, travelled with an escort and retinue to match. In a very short space of time his camp had been pitched, when David had an opportunity of seeing how such things could be done in this country of the Dragon. A most gorgeous silken tent was erected, boasting of an inner lining of painted silk which made of the place a veritable palace. And in rear were placed tents for his retinue, less imposing perhaps, but grand in their magnificence when compared with those to be seen in this country.

'Him wonerful man,' lisped Jong, who was something of a hero now that he had returned to his comrades, and whose busy tongue was already wagging freely. Indeed, long before the Professor or Alphonse gathered the full details of David's exploit, and of Dick's assistance, all else within the camp were familiar with them. There was even violent movement amongst the stolid Chinese. Ho Hung leaped wildly into the air, and gave free vent to his enthusiasm, while the more placid Fing chuckled hugely. As for Jong himself, he vowed that he would never stop giggling, for the reversal of the fortunes of attackers and attacked was so amusing. It tickled the faithful Chinaman immensely, when he recollected how he and his masters had hoodwinked every one, and how they had conveyed the deputy-governor of Hatsu from the city and right under the noses of the soldiery. Next to David and Dick, perhaps the wise and strong Twang Chun claimed his admiration.

'Velly velly fine, Excellency,' he lisped again. 'Him knowee so velly well how to manage little tings like dat which happen to us. Him oh so nicee and gentle. Kuttee off de heads of de rascal nicee. Jong tink him fit almost to be de Empelor.'

It was queer to see even this somewhat Westernised native of the Celestial Kingdom cover his face and kowtow deeply when he mentioned the name of the Emperor of China, or when he even referred to that august personage. For while we in Europe give due observance and respect to rulers, and while the King of Great Britain and Ireland, and of the huge Empire we possess beyond the seas, is at once the king and the first gentleman in all our vast territories, yet one may speak of him without sign of fear, and without grovelling. But in China, the home of much that is extremely ancient and mysterious, the Son of Heaven, as the Emperor is known to his millions of people, is as far removed from the masses as is the sun from the earth. He is never seen save by the palace attendants. He lives for the most part in majestic seclusion. And should he venture abroad, borne in a palanquin of the utmost gorgeousness, it is not that he may be seen by those who bow to his rule; for in China it is death to look upon the Son of Heaven. All who happen to be abroad when the Emperor sets out in procession must fly to their houses, there to hide their faces, and if that is not possible, they must retire from the streets through which his cavalcade will pass, and turn towards the wall.

But if Jong were interested in Twang Chun, the governor of the province, so also was Alphonse.

'*Parbleu!*' he cried, when David accosted him, 'this is a man to cater for, this Excellency. I tell you he has travelled, he has dined on the best that Paris can provide, and where else, Monsieur David, in all this wide world is there entertainment to be found to equal that in Paris. Ah! You think in London. That is not so. I, Alphonse, tell you so. It is true that we send some of our finest gentlemen to London, some of the grandest chefs that we have ever produced. *Bien!* what then? There is the Parisian atmosphere. How can even the king of chefs turn out even so simple a thing as an omelet to perfection in your city of fogs and blizzards?'

The pompous little fellow bustled about his camp kitchen, still clad in those curious clothes, so altogether incongruous with such surroundings. The perspiration stood on his forehead, his peaky little beard was thrust if anything a little more abruptly forward, while the hideous hat he insisted on retaining was perched somewhat jauntily on the side of his head, where his energetic movements had jerked it.

'*Nom du Roi*, but he shall have a dinner to-night that even *Monsieur le Président* would not sniff at, this Excellency,' he cried, as he shifted pot and pan swiftly. 'Ah, you shall see, Monsieur David. Here, in the wilds, I will serve up a dainty feast that shall make the eyes to open. Yes, I tell you. *Hors-d'œuvres* to commence with. Soup, ah, you will wonder from what it is produced. An *entrée a la Reine d'Angleterre* that will make the Excellency clap his hands. *Légumes!* Pah! such a country as this is for their provision. I tell you not one *haricot vert* is there to be obtained between this and the south of China. But, there, it is not finished, the telling of this dinner. You shall see. You will applaud. His Excellency will be delighted, and when *Monsieur le Professeur* has complimented me, I, Alphonse, shall retire to bed as proud as any Emperor of China.'

That dinner was, indeed, a feather in the cap of the voluble and clever Frenchman. He surpassed all previous attempts in his culinary art, and delighted Twang Chun and all who sat at the table.

'My friend, this is indeed a surprise,' said the governor, when course followed course without cessation. 'And I speak not of the variety which you so liberally place before me. It is the cooking that delights my heart. Not that we in China do not produce chefs who study their profession, or art, whichever you style it; we do. But then the dishes are peculiar to the country. And there, believe me, is one of the charms of travel, even to the man who is not a gourmand. There is pleasure to be obtained by tasting food as foreigners eat it, and always there is charm in partaking of a dainty meal, such as this one, originating, as one may fairly claim, in Paris, and brought to a triumphant issue in the wilds of China. Ah! it brings one back to Western civilization.'

That night there was no happier nor prouder man in all the world than Alphonse. The statement is a bold and wide-sweeping one, we imagine, but still we repeat it. Alphonse was undoubtedly in the seventh heaven of enjoyment. The praise he received spurred him to greater effort, so that had Twang Chun been but a luke-warm friend on his arrival, he left the camp a firm and undoubted adherent of the party.

Then tents were packed, ponies laden, and the Professor and his staff set off for that Mongolian city.

'We shall have to chance trouble,' he said. 'I cannot afford not to see the place and undertake excavations. We must hope for the best, and if there is need, make good use of the escort the governor has promised.'

Two weeks later they arrived in the neighbourhood of the ruins, nor was it long before the Professor had reason to congratulate himself that Twang Chun had proved so friendly.

Chapter XVII
A Chapter of Adventures

Snowflakes were whirling through the air on the morning after the arrival of the Professor's party in the neighbourhood of the half-buried Mongolian ruins which they had come to inspect. When David emerged from the tent and looked into the open, an icy blast made him shiver, while he smiled at seeing Alphonse, still in his shirt sleeves, dancing about to warm his toes, and snapping his fingers to bring the circulation to them.

'*Parbleu!* but we may expect cold weather now, Monsieur David,' he called out. 'The winter is on us, and I say that it will be well for us all when the excavations have been begun.'

'And why? How will that help us?'

'How! Ah, it is clear that you have not been on such an expedition before, monsieur, nor experienced a Chinese winter. It can freeze here almost as it does in the Arctic regions, while the winds come sweeping across these plains unbroken, and with a bite that searches every joint, and finds every crevice in the dwellings. Who knows? It may even be that the brave fellows who lodged amongst these ruins years ago were driven thence by the cold and exposure. But I was saying——'

'You were going to tell me why it will be a good thing for the party when excavations are begun, Alphonse.'

'*Vraiment!* Then this is why. A rabbit loves to burrow below ground, where he can defy the weather. Just so, we can also smile at the worst winds and the most violent snow-storms, once we have dug a hollow. You follow, monsieur? We shall have a shelter which nothing can break down, whereas a tent, what is it? What protection does it offer?'

There was no doubt that the Professor with all his experience was also of the same opinion; for no sooner was the camp completely pitched—as they had arrived late on the previous evening they had not been able to complete the matter—than he set Ho Hung and his comrades to work.

'I imagine we must be very adjacent to the site chosen by your father, David,' he said. 'The prevailing wind is from the north-east, as one can tell at once by inspecting the cant of the few trees there are. Also, all the sand-dunes, of which there are so many, are heaped with their steep sides to leeward, and present a smooth, evenly-rounded surface to the prevailing wind. As you can see for yourself, we have the ruins between us and the wind, and so have shelter. Also, there is a stream near at hand. But this snow is not to be ignored. Ho Hung and his fellows will dig us a chamber somewhere in the ruins, where we can hide away and be warm. Once it is finished and furnished, and all other matters are seen to, we will set about getting helpers, for even small excavations demand a large amount of labour.'

That day and the three which followed were, indeed, very busy ones, so much so that few of the party wore their coats, strenuous effort being necessary, and even in that cold blast a coat was a hindrance. David and Dick themselves went in search of fire-wood, and with the help of axes cut down a number of fair-sized trees. These were lopped of their branches, placed side by side with the branches on them, and faggots on top all, then the whole was hauled close to the ruins by a team of ponies harnessed to ropes. That done, the trunks and branches were sawn in shorter lengths, and the big pieces split with wedges and a big mallet.

'We shall want every log you can cut,' said the Professor, looking his approval, 'and it is essential to make the most of the open weather. You have seen for yourselves that snow has been threatening. We shall get it any time now, and then there will be little moving around.'

Meanwhile, Ho Hung and his comrades had delved deeply. They had hit upon a spot where close investigation proved that others had been at work, though the fierce winds, which had blown since, had covered up almost all traces. Yet it was certain that a considerable amount of debris had been removed; and thanks to that fact the base of the actual ruins were soon reached.

'Might have been your father who had his men working at this spot,' said the Professor thoughtfully. 'On the other hand, it may have been a band of nomads wintering here. It is a wild district, very sparsely inhabited, and droves of men do ride here and there, not always with the best intentions I fear. However, with the half-dozen soldiers Twang Chun was good enough to lend us, we should be secure, for he has seen that the men are really trained, and I think we can rely upon their courage.'

David never knew whether to admire the huge expanse of ruins, to which they had come, more when a wintry sun poured down upon them, or when the moon's cold beams swept softly over them. In any case, there was something fascinating and awe-inspiring about this lonely place. Standing on a huge sand-dune a few hundred yards from the edge of what had once been a big city, he would allow his mind free play at times, trying to imagine the place as it was when tenanted, when its broad streets hummed with human activity, when its battlemented walls frowned down upon all would-be intruders, and when its dwellings sheltered thousands of families long since gone and forgotten. And always his eyes would wander to the relics of a tower, once a stately edifice no doubt, which even now, thousands of years after the chimneys of the city had grown cold and the streets had reverberated for the last time to the tread of inhabitants, was decidedly impressive. It seemed to beckon to him, to attract him strangely, as perhaps it had done his father. Once, since his arrival there, he had found his way across the ruins to that tower; for the feat was not impossible. Clambering up what appeared to be a breach in the rotting outer walls of the city—and who could say, since no history existed to tell of the doings in this part so long ago, that very breach might have been the undoing of the city? It may have given entry to a besieging army, and have resulted in the sacking and desolation of the place. David clambered over the sand swept into the breach and toiled over a sandy waste now piled into high pinnacles, and then drooping suddenly in a long line, where, no doubt, a street ran. Finding a way across this and others he at length arrived at a point within hailing distance of the tower. But to approach closer was impossible. A deep ditch surrounded it, with steeply sloping walls of soft sand, while on the far side a battlemented wall arose, tottering in parts, but strong and defiant in other directions.

'Just the place I should go for,' he declared when discussing the matter with the Professor. 'Should think it was the palace, and if it was, then one would imagine relics to be more abundant in such a place.'

'Precisely! And it is for that tower that I shall aim,' answered the leader of the party. 'But observe, the approach from any point outside is most difficult. To dig our way there, is almost out of the question, seeing that we have only a few months to spare in the effort. So that we must win our way by other methods, which you will see and understand when we begin to work seriously. And now, David, I have a task for you. Take two of the soldiers and Jong, and investigate the country north of us. I wish you to locate the nearest village, and make arrangements for a supply of labourers, also to discover the nearest point at which we can buy supplies, for that is more necessary even than to arrange for labour. If you take a couple of tents with you and two spare ponies you should be able to fare comfortably, and I needn't say that the sooner you are back with us the better.'

David seized upon the opportunity of a private expedition with avidity, for he had found something particularly attractive about a journey in this wild country. Carefully selecting sufficient stores and weapons, since one never knew what might happen, he set out with Jong and two of the Chinese soldiers, each of whom led a pony laden with a tent and abundance of warm coverings. Hastily swallowing his breakfast he was away almost before the sun was up, and at once rode off in a northerly direction.

'We'll do as we did before, Jong,' he said, speaking in Chinese, for it was good practice; besides he was becoming daily more proficient, so much so that he could now make himself understood with ease, while to do him justice, his rendering of the language was almost as good as Jong's mastery of English. By common consent, therefore, he spoke the native language, while the faithful servant with him adhered to English, probably with a view to showing himself superior to his two countrymen.

'We'll take turn and turn about to watch, both day and night. Every two hours the man on duty will be relieved, so that we shall have six hours free between our watches.'

'Dat good, mister Davie,' said Jong, with emphasis. 'Me not knowee dis part, but de soldiers been near before. Chu-li—de big man wid de tick lip and showing teeth—him say dere sometimes danger. Huan Hu—de fellow who look as if him sick and solly allee de while—him tell me dat him hab row once wid brigand. So Jong say watchee alee de while. Not sleepee too much, elsee perhaps sleep for good, and not want dat yet. No, Jong velly velly comfolable, tank you, sar.'

Plodding along at a slow walk—for the ground was too soft for a faster pace to be set—evening was approaching before the first sign of a habitation was discovered. It proved to be a small village, where David was received, if not with a friendly greeting, at least with civility. The sight of the two soldiers wearing the governor's own uniform, which was distinctive, and a letter from that august official obtaining quarters for the little party and an offer of fresh provisions. On the following morning our hero called the chief man to him and discussed the question of labourers.

'We will gladly come,' said the man, 'for here in the winter months there is little to do and still less to be earned. If, as you say, the required work is merely the digging away of sand which has covered the ruins, we can undertake that, though why any man with wisdom in his mind should desire to see what is hidden passes my comprehension. We will willingly engage, though had you asked us to excavate where our ancestors lie, we should have refused.'

An hour or more was then spent in haggling over terms, for the Chinamen of the north,—the natives in this part, who were of Mongolian aspect and descent,—were no different from the wily individuals who labour in the south of China. The head man of the village asked what was to him a fabulous wage. David promptly offered a quarter, and after expostulations on the part of the head man, and a heated statement to the effect that such a wage meant starvation, the cunning fellow at length acquiesced to one-half of what he had demanded, smiling affably as David agreed.

'And no doubt they will be coining money,' thought our hero, 'for though I don't know a great deal about this country, yet I do know that wages are miserably small. However, that's arranged. There are thirty in the village, and they will pack up and march to the ruins in a couple of days, taking their women and children with them. Now for supplies.'

Having completed a portion of his task in a most satisfactory manner, he rode on with his little party, intent on visiting a colony of nomads living some twenty miles farther north, and since the whole distance could not be accomplished that afternoon, they halted and camped under a sand dune as the light was fading.

'Shouldn't like to be lost in a bleak country such as this is,' thought David, as he surveyed his surroundings. 'One part is so much like another that one would soon lose all bearings, and if one were short of provisions or water it would mean disaster. Going to snow I think.'

Flakes were blowing about when he rose on the following morning, and continued to do so as they progressed.

'Tink we have a lot, Misser Davie,' said Jong, looking, for the first time since our hero had known him, a little anxious. 'Not like it to snow when we out here. Cold bitee oh so velly muchee. Not like de snow. Look as if wind comee wid him.'

They had just finished a mid-day meal when a gust of cold wind swept past them, causing David to look up. The sky was black in one direction, while the sand all around was distinctly disturbed. The flakes of snow were also more frequent, so that Jong's prophecy of more was likely to come about.

'Tink we better get along quick, sar,' he said, nervously. 'Not do to be caughtee out here in de open. Dat bad for us and de animals.'

By the time they had packed the few odds and ends that they had taken from their saddle-bags for the meal, it was snowing heavily, while the gusts of wind had increased in frequency and violence. Sand was whirling everywhere, while the falling snow had drawn a species of curtain across the landscape, blotting out all surroundings.

'We're in for a scrape, I fear,' cried David, as he jumped into his saddle. 'I don't like things at all, and as we must have shelter I shall make over there to the left where I caught sight of some hilly ground. In this open part a tent would never stand, and consequently we should soon be frozen.'

In less than ten minutes the threatening storm had burst, and David, with his experience of England, could hardly believe that snow could fall so heavily. It came whirling everywhere in thick flakes, that soon powdered the ground white, and then began to pile in ridges. He and his comrades were smothered in less time than it takes to record that fact, while the force of the wind was so great that the ponies could not face it. It was fortunate, therefore, that the hilly ground which David had located was in the opposite direction.

'Tell the men to ride in close to us, Jong,' he ordered. 'The snow is so thick that though they are only a few paces to one side I can scarcely see them. A man might easily stray away without himself or his comrades being the wiser.'

For a quarter of an hour the party plodded along, their heads down, and collars drawn up close to their caps. By then they could not see more than a dozen feet before them, and for all they knew might have been travelling in a circle.

'Wouldn't be difficult to do that,' thought David. 'But the wind helps; when we face it one can scarcely breathe. If we keep it astern all the while we must be going in the right direction.'

He was already deadly cold and frozen almost to the marrow before a shout from Chu-Li announced that he had made a discovery. He pointed to the front, and peering between the snowflakes David saw a mass of white barring their progress.

'Must be the hilly ground,' he shouted, for the wind was now so fierce and the noise so great that the ordinary voice was drowned. 'Swing to the left; we have evidently got a little out of our course and have struck the place beyond the end.'

A biting wind swept them, as they turned to force their way along the foot of the hilly ground. So keen was it that David found himself gasping for breath, and knew that unless he and his comrades could discover some sheltered spot swiftly, they would be overcome by cold and exposure. Pressing to the front he led the small party, encouraging his sturdy little pony at every stride. He gave a shout of joy when the white wall on his left suddenly fell away, and was lost in the obscurity of the falling snow. And what a relief it was to be able to swing again, and turn his back to the wind! None who have not experienced such an icy blast can judge of its fierceness. But even with their backs turned the danger was great, and to halt there was to court disaster. Stiffened in every limb as he was, David urged on his following, shouting to encourage them while he spurred his pony to still further effort. At last they had some reward. They rounded the tail end of the hilly ground and gained the sheltered side, where the full force of the wind could not play upon them. But even here shelter was absolutely necessary.

'Keep a sharp look-out for a gap in the rocks,' he called out. 'If we don't find a place soon we never shall, for we shall be dead men. What's that, Jong?'

'Tink I see a hole ober dere, sar. Not sure, but tink.'

His voice was almost completely muffled behind the mass of material he had wound round his neck, but the hand he held forward stiffly was sufficient. David halted the party.

'Wait here while I go and see!' he shouted. 'Call out now and again so that I can find you again. Don't move from where you are.'

He spurred his pony towards the face of the hill, and uttered a cry of delight when he discovered that Jong had made no error. At once he called the men.

'There's what looks like a cave here,' he said. 'Dismount and bring the ponies right in. Then we'll get a lamp alight, and take a look round.'

The lamp showed that they had gained the shelter of a large hollow, the opening to which was so large that, had the wind been in the opposite direction, snow would certainly long since have filled the place. As it was, it was already drifting in, carried by back eddies. The floor was covered with fine sand, blackened in one part where a fire had once been lit, while drift wood, blown from the outside plateau, filled all corners and crannies. David surveyed the whole place closely, then gave his orders without hesitation.

'Pitch the two tents at the entrance,' he said. 'They'll fill the gap and keep the snow out. Then we'll get a fire going, and with that and the heat from our ponies we ought soon to become a little less frozen. Lucky thing we happened upon this hole.'

It was, indeed, a fortunate thing for all concerned, for as they dropped from their saddles not one of the party could walk easily. Their limbs were stiffened, while even the ponies moved slowly, their heads down, their shaggy necks stretched out. However, movement would help the process of unfreezing, and at once David set the men an example. He helped to unpack the tents, and with the aid of the others soon had them erected in the very entrance of the cave. By then, too, Jong had a fine fire blazing, so that when the party had finished their labours, there was an air of comfort about the place.

'May just as well get something cooking,' said David, for the small experience he had had of travelling in the wilds had taught him that when men are in difficulties, and the position is still uncertain, a hearty meal, with warmth and comfort attached, go a great way to ease their minds, and make them look at possible danger lightly. 'Get a kettle on, Jong, and let us have a brew of tea. I'm beginning to unfreeze already, though a good hot drink would help matters wonderfully.'

The grinning Jong, who shivered violently between his grins, soon had a kettle unstrapped from one of the ponies, and a dash outside provided him with sufficient snow with which to fill it. In half an hour the water was boiling merrily, causing the kettle to sing a tuneful air, that attracted the eyes of all. Moreover, the Chinese soldiers proved most jovial comrades. Chu-Li, he with the prominent teeth and big lips, as Jong had made free to describe him, was a bit of a wag in his own way, and his remarks kept all smiling. In fact, the quartet settled down round the fire like boon companions, due respect, however, being paid to his Excellency, the young white leader of the party. Huge enamelled mugs held the steaming tea that Jong provided, while he had hardly poured it out when there was a mess of rice for the men, for they habitually steeped their rations for the following day over night, and sometimes half-boiled them, so that no great length of time was required to make the food fit for consumption. For the carniverous David there was one of those tins of delicious ready-cooked ration, consisting of beef and potatoes, with carrots and other vegetables, a regular Irish stew, in fact, for the preparation of which all that was required was to open the tin, and plunge it into a pannikin containing boiling water. Within a quarter of an hour there arose a savoury odour that set David's mouth watering.

'And now we may as well settle down for the night,' he said, when he had been to the entrance, only to find that the snow was falling as heavily as ever. 'I will take the first watch, and you others can arrange your turns. We'd better melt some snow in a couple of kettles and wash out the mouths of our ponies. That will put them on till morning, when we ought to be able to get away and find water. Fortunately we have feeds with us, so they won't go hungry.'

Before the night had fallen things inside the hollow wore a ship-shape appearance. Packs were stored not far from the opening, while a huge pile of brushwood was banked near the fire, so that it might be easily replenished. Then the Chinamen threw themselves down on the floor, and wrapped in their blankets were soon snoring.

'Where I shall not be sorry to be,' thought David, as he watched their figures near the fire. 'I could never believe that a snowstorm could be such a severe affair. That wind absolutely wearied me, so that I feel downright tired. However, a good sleep will make me fresh and fit again. Wonder how things are going outside.'

He went to the opening, and pushed back the edge of one of the tents. Flakes were still falling, but the wind seemed to have dropped with as much suddenness as it had arisen. More than that, the sky was clear, and was filled with thousands of bright, twinkling stars.

'Promising well for to-morrow,' he thought, 'though it won't be very easy travelling with this heavy fall on the ground. Perhaps we shall have to wait a little.'

As it turned out, the snow continued to sprinkle the ground all that night, and well on towards the following evening, so that David's little party remained in their snug quarters all day, save for a short excursion when they took the ponies out by couples and walked them up and down, allowing them to thrust their noses through the soft snow, and so obtain a few blades of grass.

'Fleezing hard now, sar,' said Jong, as the dusk fell. 'Dat be good for us, 'cos it harden de snow and let us get along easy. Not able to walkee much when de snow soft. It stick to de feet, and makee balls at de bottom of the ponies' hoofs. Fleeze to-night, den get away easy to-mollow.'

As it turned out, however, the movements of the party were not to be so straightforward a matter as Jong anticipated; for though it froze very hard that evening, as it can freeze in the north of China, the night brought more than intense cold with it. David's was the middle watch, and he was standing near the fire, struggling to keep himself fully awake, when of a sudden a distant sound fell on his ear. He listened intently, and then went to the opening. At once a faint whimpering sound came from a point some little way distant. He fancied he heard something remarkably like a loud snarling, while as he watched he was almost sure that he caught sight of several sneaking forms passing to and fro outside, like black shadows crossing the snow.

'Come and look out into the open,' he asked of Jong, whose turn it was to take the next watch. 'There is something there, but what I am not sure. Come and listen.'

They pushed the flaps of the tent back cautiously and stared out. Jong instantly gave vent to an expression of astonishment, not unmixed with alarm, and darting into the hollow waked the two soldiers.

'Come out and tell us what you hear and see,' he demanded anxiously. 'His Excellency heard sounds, and is sure he saw figures passing across the snow. The news is disquieting.'

There was a decided expression of fear written on Chu-Li's not too handsome features as he withdrew into the hollow.

'Excellency,' he said gravely, 'those are wolves who prowl about outside. In Mongolia they can be very dangerous, though I hardly expected to find them here, or would have warned you. But there is forest land to the north, and it may happen that the cold has been very severe there for a little while, causing these beasts to travel for their food. If they are hungry, then they become very dangerous. Their ferocity is extraordinary.'

David learned the news with a distinct qualm. He had fought against human beings already, and had displayed a fair amount of courage; but against savage beasts was an altogether different matter.

'Why,' he exclaimed, taken aback at the announcement, 'I had no idea that such beasts were to be found in these parts. And you think they may be dangerous, Chu-Li? What has attracted them?'

'The ponies, Excellency; they would smell the animals a long way off, and if there were none they would scent us. Their powers of detecting food are extraordinary.'

There could be no doubt, in fact, that the presence of David's little party had been the attracting cause that had brought the wolves in their direction, while all doubt as to the animals themselves was cleared up within a few minutes. Standing at the exit of the hollow or cave in which he and his men had taken refuge from the storm, our hero soon saw the wolves distinctly. They crept hither and thither past the hollow, their eyes always directed on it. Sometimes there was a whimper from one of the brutes, but for the most part they went to and fro silently like ghosts, making those within the hollow almost shiver.

'I suppose they are waiting till they can screw their pluck up for a rush,' thought David, surveying the new-arrivals with disgust. 'From the fact that they haven't attacked yet I should imagine that they are not over hungry.'

But Chu-Li shook his head promptly and with emphasis. 'Not good to think that, Excellency. They are hungry, else they would not have travelled to these parts. They merely await a leader. When one can rouse his courage to gallop forward, or when they are sure that the time for attack has come they will dash at us. It would be well to make preparations. Let us put more on the fire, and place stakes with their points to the centre. A blazing brand is a fine weapon I have heard. To shoot when they are running, and hit the brutes, is no easy matter.'

Ten minutes later it was evident to all that they would have to defend themselves against the wolves, of whom there must have been at least a hundred. Had David's party but known it, it was the flapping canvas walls at the entrance which scared the animals, and which so far had been sufficient to keep them from attacking. But hardly had the fire been built up, and brands laid in it, while all their packs were hastily bundled, so as to form a wall across the entrance, when a long, stealthy form crept beneath one of the tents, and suddenly became visible to all. For a moment or two it stood, its tongue depending from its mouth, its wicked eyes shining in the fire light. Then, as the frightened ponies neighed and stamped, the brute leapt the barrier with a bound and sprang full at David.

Chapter XVIII
Terrors of the Mongolian Desert

Never in all his existence had David had need for such rapid movement as on the occasion when the wolf suddenly sprang over the barrier at him, for the brute's flight was like that of lightning, giving but little time for preparation. And if the matter had, in fact, been left entirely to our hero, he would most certainly have been badly mauled. As it was, he drew his magazine pistol swiftly, and fired almost the moment it had left his belt. But the ball did not stop the animal, though it pierced his body. Nothing could arrest his attack, save death, and that Chu-Li brought to him swiftly. As the beast struck David on the chest his fangs closed on his coat sleeve, fortunately missing the arm, and clung there for a minute. By then Chu-Li had drawn his knife, and with a quick stab he ended the struggle.

'Did I not say that they can be dangerous, Excellency?' he said. 'When they are hungry they are as mad people, knowing no fear. Let us all take the brands in our hands. I will cast this animal out to his fellows. Perhaps that will appease them for a while.'

He stooped over the beast, and lifting him with an effort—for he was very large—cast him out at the side of the tent flap. And at once there arose such a snarling that all of the party within the hollow held their breath.

'It would be like that were we to be taken,' said Chu-Li grimly. 'Perhaps it is as well for us to know; for then we shall fight the more fiercely. I say that there are many who imagine, never having seen a wolf, that such beasts cannot be so very dangerous. One has to meet them to understand. Now, we will take the brands and stand ready.'

Giving a kick to the fire so that it burned more brightly the four men stood behind their barricade, flaming brands gripped in their hands. Nor was it long before they had need for them; for the wolves had by now devoured their dead comrade, and still scenting food within the hollow, and having as it were got their courage and their blood up, came squeezing in twos and threes beneath the tents. Their ferocity was extraordinary. Time and again David shot one of the brutes through the body with no apparent result, for it still came forward, leaping at the barrier and endeavouring to get at those behind it. The brands, however, were far and away the best weapon. When one was dashed into the face of a wolf it turned tail promptly and retreated; but it was back again within a minute, back with its comrades till the crush beneath the tents threatened to level them, and till the defenders were hard set to it to preserve their lives.

'This kind of thing can't last much longer,' declared David at last, when the wolves drew off after some fifteen minutes. 'They are getting bolder and bolder, and I am inclined to think that the tents help them. They sneak beneath them till quite close, when it is an easy matter to spring upon us. I am for firing the tents, and so having a clear view.'

'And I agree, Excellency,' said Chu-Li readily. 'Let us destroy the tents, when we shall be able to see the brutes coming. Moreover, we can fire at them in the open, and reserve the brands till they are close at hand.'

There was a quick nod of acquiescence from Jong and the other Chinaman, showing that they were in agreement. Jong, in fact, stepped forward to apply his brand to the canvas. But David stopped him quickly.

'Not yet,' he said. 'Wait till they come on again; perhaps having a blazing roof over them will give them such a scare that they will clear off. Besides, it occurs to me that once our tents are destroyed we shall find ourselves in sad need of them. Let us contrive to save one at least. Wait while I see what the pack is doing.'

His appearance at the opening was the signal for a chorus of howls and cries from the wolves, for all the world as if they were human beings. David watched them for a minute as they sat for the most part collected about the hollow in a wide circle, watching the place with sharp eyes which never strayed from it. Once one of the brutes, seeing him in the open, made a rush forward, but a quick shot caused it to halt and slink back amongst its fellows. Then our hero unhitched the rope outside from the peg to which it was attached, and signalled to those within to pull the canvas towards them.

'I'll watch the beasts while you do it,' he called. 'Pile it up on the barricade so as to make it higher. Hurry up. They've all got on to their legs and are moving.'

They had barely time to drag the tent within the cave when the pack of hungry and maddened beasts outside dashed forward, snarling and yelping, causing David to retreat at once to the shelter of the barricade.

'Wait till they are well in the opening before you fire the second tent,' he called to Jong, 'and take care that they don't catch sight of you. Once down there would be an end to any one.'

For a few anxious moments the defenders of the cave wondered whether they had been right in clearing the entrance, for now that there was ample room the wolves swarmed in in a mass, crushing one another, yelping and snapping viciously, madly struggling to come at those behind the barricade. Bullets made not the smallest impression. Even the red-hot brands failed to stop them. It looked, indeed, as if they would flood the place and kill the whole party. Then Jong set his brand to the second tent, and almost at once a sheet of flame flared across the opening. The result was wonderful. The pack of wolves struggled and fought to get away, and, finally freeing themselves, bolted into the open, where they sat themselves down again in a ring, their eyes reflecting the glare of the flames cast by the blazing tent. And there they continued to squat when the canvas was consumed, their tongues lolling from their mouths, their cruel white teeth showing.

'I think we might as well begin to fire at them,' said David. 'We have ample ammunition, but may as well carry out the work methodically, so that no two men will fire at the same animal. I will take those to the left. Chu-Li, you fire at those seated on the right. Jong and his friend will take the left and right of the centre of the circles. Aim carefully, and make every shot count.'

There was a huge commotion amongst the brutes seated outside as a volley burst from the cave. They started to their feet and dashed here and there yelping loudly. Then, led by one huge animal, they headed straight for the hollow, as if determined to gain an entrance.

'Fire quickly,' shouted David. 'Empty your magazines into them and then take up the brands.'

It was a fortunate thing for the party that the Chinese soldiers were armed with modern weapons, and trained to use them, and also that Jong had been provided with a magazine pistol. Otherwise the rush of the pack of wolves could not have been stopped. But as it was the storm of bullets pelting into their ranks, as well perhaps as the flashes of flame from the dark opening, caused the line to halt. Then those who had not been hit fell with terrible ferocity on their wounded comrades, tearing them to pieces.

'It's not a nice thing to look at,' said David, as he re-loaded, 'and I rather think a fellow will be inclined to dream the whole thing over one of these nights and have the jumps in consequence. But it will help us wonderfully by easing their hunger. Now, we will fire again. The more we knock over the better.'

Little by little the wolves drew away from the hollow as the bullets swished amongst them. At first they had contented themselves with changing their respective positions. But finding that their comrades were still falling, the bulk at length crept away till they were hidden in the darkness. But they were still within easy distance for a rush. Occasionally a slinking form crept into view against the white background, only to slide away into the shadow. And then, after hours and hours of toilsome and anxious waiting, the dawn came, causing the whole pack to turn tail and seek cover in the distance.

'May we never see or hear them again is what I fervently hope,' declared David, seating himself for the first time since the animals had put in an appearance. 'I fancy we have had as narrow an escape as is possible, and am devoutly thankful. Now, Jong, food and drink, and then we'll get away from the hollow.'

'And ride direct for the nearest village, Excellency,' advised Chu-Li. 'For one cannot say that the wolves have gone far. There may be a forest close at hand, and were they in hiding there, and to catch us in the open, then indeed all our struggling would have been in vain. With no hollow to help us we should quickly be torn to pieces.'

'Then before we go far we had better have a good look round. I shall climb to the top of the hill now. It is quite clear, and the sun looks as if it would appear. No doubt I shall be able to see a long way, and if there is a wood anywhere near I shall catch sight of it.'

David left Jong squatted over the fire, preparing a much-needed morning meal, and issued from the cave. The snow outside was a couple of feet deep, while here and there, where the wind had swept it into drifts, it was as much as twenty feet from top to base. Everywhere adjacent to the cave were the foot-marks of the wolves, with a distinctly outlined circle where they had squatted between their attacks. As for the beasts themselves, there was not a living one in sight. Only numerous half-knawed bones could be seen, for the ravenous beasts who had escaped the bullets of the defenders had eaten everything else.

'I couldn't have believed it possible unless I had actually seen such a result with my own eyes,' said David to himself. 'People in Old England would probably smile incredulously if I told them the yarn how a pack had simply devoured twenty or more of their fellows when knocked over by our weapons. But here's the evidence, as clear as one can wish it. Now for the hill top.'

It was hard work scrambling up, and many a time he slid down many yards on the surface of the hard-frozen snow. But by sticking to the task he at length reached the top. It presented in ordinary times, no doubt, a sharp ridge, that was now smoothly rounded by the snow, and which ran north and south for some four hundred yards. It was the only high ground to be seen, so that David and his little party were peculiarly lucky to have come upon it. And its elevation gave one a wonderful view over the snow-clad landscape, that glistened and shone now under a wintery sun. As far as the eye could see the white expanse was unbroken, save in one direction where there was a smear of black across it, from the neighbourhood of which smoke was rising.

'A village,' he thought. 'Not a sign of a forest, so I presume that those beasts have quitted this part of the country, only they must have gone precious quickly, for there is not one to be seen anywhere. I think we can safely set out.'

An hour later, after a hearty breakfast, the ponies were loaded with the stores accompanying the party, and David and his men set out. Though the going was not as easy as it had been when there was no snow, it was not particularly difficult; for there had been a severe frost, and the hoofs of the animals sank only a little way below the surface.

'I think we'd better keep well together, and have the pack ponies between us,' said David, once they were clear of the hill. 'To tell you the truth, now that we are in the open I'm beginning to wonder whether I can have made a mistake about those brutes. If they have gone right off, then they must have got away at their fastest pace, else I should have seen them. It makes me a little anxious.'

'It is one of those matters which one cannot well help, Excellency,' Chu-Li reassured him. 'It may be that the brutes have found some hollow which was not visible from the top of the hill, and have taken shelter in it. I mean some dip in the ground. There is this to be said in our favour. The animals have had a fine feed during the night, and will therefore not be so ravenous, while it is well-known that wolves do not attack so fiercely during the day time. But I have known of a party being torn to pieces, and for that reason we had best hasten.'

They urged their willing animals forward after that, and were soon more than half-way to the village, which could now be distinctly seen. It was then that Jong announced that there was something following the party, causing David to call a halt. At once he, too, caught sight of a slinking object, while Chu-Li declared that he had seen several.

'They are wolves without doubt, Excellency,' he said, 'and keep themselves as low down on the snow as possible, so as to come near without being seen. I had rather fight twenty men than the same number of those fierce brutes.'

'And I too,' agreed David. 'However, we have got to face the matter out. Jong, do you go on, leading the pack-ponies as fast as possible. Hu-Ty can take my mount as well as Chu-Li's, while we two will walk, firing at the wolves whenever we see them. A few good shots should make them keep their distance. If not, we will mount and ride as fast as the beasts will take us. In less than an hour at any rate we shall be at the village.'

Slipping out of his saddle he handed the reins to Hu-Ty, and took his rifle from him, together with a handful of ammunition. Chu-Li at once joined him, while Jong took the leads of the other animals and sent them towards the village at a smart rate. Indeed, the ponies were only too willing. For though they may not have seen the prowling enemy in rear, they shivered visibly and fretted greatly, showing that they had probably scented the wolves.

'Now, we will take it in turns, Chu,' said David. 'One good shot is better than twenty misses, and besides, if we knock one wolf over, he provides food for his comrades.'

Catching a clear view of a slinking form at that moment he dropped on to one knee, levelled his rifle and took careful aim. The snap of the weapon was followed by a distant howl, while the animal he had fired at leaped into the air and fell backward into the snow.

'Showing that a bullet at a fair range is more deadly than one fired point blank,' he remarked, remembering that when in the cave many of the wolves though perforated had still dashed forward.

'It was a fine shot, Excellency,' exclaimed Chu, with enthusiasm. 'As to a bullet being more deadly, I am sure of it. I have seen men dash forward with mad impetuosity. Nothing could stop them, unless the bullet struck them in the head or heart. Such fanatics seemed to feel nothing till they had given a blow, and then many a man fell never to move again. I know, for I was one of the few who helped my masters, the English, when the legations at Pekin were besieged during the revolt of the Boxers. Those were fierce times, Excellency.'

He drew himself up proudly, while David looked at the soldier in a new light. It was clear that Chu was something like his leader, the astute and travelled Twang Chun, Governor of the province. He at least was not one of the masses who saw in a European a foreign devil meant only to be killed.

'You have much to be proud of, Chu,' he said warmly. 'That must have been a fine experience.'

'It was, Excellency; we fought against huge odds, and the attackers were even as fierce as these beasts. But see: the others have fallen upon the one you shot. I will send a bullet amongst them.'

It was an easy shot, and the Chinaman laid a second wolf low. Then he and David leaped into their saddles, while the whole party went on at as great a pace as the ponies could accomplish, leaving the wolves, of whom there seemed to be a great number, huddled around their fallen comrades. It gave David and his men a breathing space, and for ten minutes they were able to press on without halting. Then the wolves, having devoured the two which had been shot, came after them again, slinking over the snow, and showing themselves as little as possible.

'We'll do as we did before,' cried David, looking over his shoulder, 'only this time, as there seem to be so many, we had better kill four at least if possible. Come along, Chu. No need to stop Jong and the pack ponies. We shall easily catch them up.'

Two minutes later when they were again in their saddles and had drawn level with Jong, the latter reported that he had seen some of the dark, slinking forms to his left, while within a few minutes Chu announced that others were coming up on the right. It was a very serious position, and though David discussed the matter quickly, no one could devise any other plan than that of hurrying forward.

'We've given those in rear reason to halt for a while at any rate,' he told his men. 'We must wait and see what these others are going to do, and if they look as if they were coming close in we shall have to halt and fire at them. I admit I don't like the business at all. How long will it take us to get to the village at this rate, Chu?'

'Half an hour, Excellency. By then if the wolves mean to attack, there will be little left of us.'

There was a deep line across the soldier's brow, while his eyes were drawn and anxious; but of his pluck there could be no two opinions. Chu-Li was a fine soldier and feared nothing, nothing perhaps that was human. But wolves were different altogether. However, the situation was one that had to be faced, and for that reason the party went on as fast as possible, taking no notice of the brutes which were attempting to outflank them. But at length the latter had drawn in perceptibly, while half-a-dozen were in front of the party between them and the village.

'Then there's nothing for it but to dismount and fire as we go,' said David, as he set an example by dropping from his saddle. 'Hu-Ty must help. The ponies are not likely to stray with these beasts so near them, and will more likely huddle closely together. Come, let us do our utmost to drive the wolves off.'

Walking rapidly beside their ponies David and the two Chinamen stopped every few seconds to fire at the wolves, knocking several over. But as fast as one fell, others seemed to leap into his place, as if they came from the snow itself. And a bad sign for the fortunes of the party,—the beasts were now ignoring their fallen comrades.

'Looks as if they preferred humans,' thought David, grimly. 'I begin to see that we shall have to halt and make a stand. Chu,' he called loudly. 'They look as if they were about to make a rush. They have come in a lot closer and are all round us now. If they run in make a dash for the ponies, and take up your posts in the very centre. It's hard luck for our mounts, but we must put them between us and our enemies. Ah! they're moving. That big one out there seems to be a leader.'

Up went his rifle, and the beast he aimed at howled as he pulled the trigger. But he did not fall as had the others. Glaring at David's party for a moment, he suddenly sank his head, and with his limbs bent beneath him came dashing forward over the snow. And as he came his mates followed, howling and yapping.

'Into the centre!' shouted David. 'Put the ponies outside. Begin to fire at once.'

Bunched in a little group, the forlorn little party made the utmost of the situation. The four stood close together with the ponies immediately outside them. And the poor animals seemed to have guessed that they were to act as a bulwark, for they cowered, shivering and stamping their hoofs, and pressing in upon the men who were to defend them. It was just before a volley belched from the rifles of his party that David heard a distant gong, and then a loud report. Looking round in the direction of the village he was overjoyed to see a number of men running towards him, many of whom carried flaming brands, while the weapons they bore were as many and as various as the garments of the strangers.

'Fire as hard as you can!' he shouted. 'The villagers are running out to help us, so that if we can keep the wolves at bay for a couple of minutes we shall be safe.'

Those two minutes were perhaps the most strenuous he had ever spent in all his life. Even Chu-Li admitted that the defence of the legations at Pekin was hardly equal to that last attack. For the wolves had heard the gong and the shout of the villagers, and as if determined that their prey should not escape them, they dashed in madly, their eyes flaming, their teeth parted in a snarl. More than one managed to leap on to the backs of the ponies, only to be at once shot or struck down by the knives the Chinese carried. One even fixed its fangs in the neck of a pony, till the poor beast, driven frantic with pain and fear, dashed away from the circle. Twenty wolves were on it immediately, and would have had it down and torn to pieces in little time had not a crumb of sense returned to the pony. It kicked madly in all directions, and then galloped back to its comrades, where Chu and Jong slashed at the wolves still holding to it. By then the villagers were close at hand, running forward in a compact body, and at once, with many a snarl of rage, the wolves took themselves off.

'Who are you?' demanded one of the strangers, who was muffled to the eyes, and dressed in padded clothing which made him of enormous size. 'You come from the north or the south? Answer immediately. If from the north, then in spite of the wolves you must go on your journey.'

'We come from the south. This Excellency is a friend of Twang Chun, the noble Governor of this province,' answered Chu, putting himself forward as spokesman. 'The Excellency bears letters to all whom it may concern. He is a noble Englishman.'

'Then follow; a friend of the noble Twang Chun is our friend. You will be welcome.'

David bowed as the Chinese headman kow-towed before him, looking as if he found it hard to bend, so many garments had he on him. Then our hero thanked him warmly, and asked why, if he had come from the north, he would not be welcome.

'Because, Excellency, there is plague there, and in spite of the cold weather people are flying from it. Mobs have passed us, but we have kept them at a distance. Elsewhere the frantic people have burst into defenceless villages, and have murdered every one so as to take their food supplies. We had rather welcome wolves than these maddened individuals. But tell me about the beasts who attacked you. You have had a very narrow escape without doubt. I myself have never seen the brutes attack so fiercely, and I am accustomed to them.'

Nowhere else had our hero been made so welcome as in the village to which they had now come, and he and his party spent three days there, resting after their adventures, and waiting till the snow had cleared. For a thaw had set in, and the wet made the ground almost impossible for horses. But on the fourth day they were able to start, and set out from the village, having made arrangements that supplies of rice and of chickens should be forwarded to the ruins weekly.

'Unless, of course, something occurs to prevent our despatching the food, 'said the headman.' We have abundance here, and shall be glad to sell it. But this trouble in Manchuria is very pressing, and it may be that we shall not be able to spare men to go to you. Everywhere reports say that mobs are parading the country, and when a Chinaman is homeless and hungry no law is sufficient to stop his thieving and killing. A fine journey, Excellency. It has been a pleasure to meet you.'

Three days later David reached the ruins where his comrades were working, and was hailed with delight by the Professor.

'I began to get really nervous about you,' he declared, 'especially when the snowstorm broke over the country. Come and tell me all that has happened to you.'

'And now let me hear something about the work here, Professor,' asked David when he had told him about the discovery of the hollow during the snowstorm, and the attack of the wolves. 'How are you progressing?'

'Splendidly; couldn't be better,' exclaimed the Professor, rubbing his hands together with energy. 'We seem to have dropped upon the very part which your poor father excavated. Of course, he did not go very far; that we know, for Chang and his ruffians so soon interrupted him. However, he removed a mass of debris, which has made our work all the lighter. We have already made discoveries. We have opened up some wonderful inscriptions, and Dick hit upon a buried bronze bowl which is unique I should say, and will find a place in the British Museum. The only contretemps we have experienced was two days after the snowstorm. A band of most villainous-looking fellows came this way and demanded provisions. They were from Manchuria, from the plague-infested area, and, of course, my workers would have nothing to do with them. They moved off soon afterwards, though there is little doubt that had they been in greater strength they would hardly have let us off so lightly. Come in, and see what we have been doing.'

For three weeks David worked with the excavators, finding the task of the greatest interest. For the diggers had come upon a covered way, built in stone, and absolutely perfect, and from this, as the debris was cleared away, it was possible to enter houses, the roofs of which were just visible above the all-pervading sand, while the interiors were often almost free of that material. And in them was found abundance of food for reflection — domestic articles in great numbers left by those ancient residents, tiled ways which could not be improved upon by the later Romans; and bronze vases and receptacles of every shape and design, some so elegant, in fact, that the Professor, who was a connoisseur in such matters, declared that the form was similar to that found in ancient Grecian vases, and that this old Mongolian civilization had undoubtedly sent its artistic wares broadcast, till they reached the far west, and were copied by a race less ancient than these Mongolians, but ancient for all that.

'Believe it or not as you will,' he said, impressively, 'but there is reason in my statement. Here are vases similar to those made by the ancient Greeks. But Greece was probably only rising in power and to the summit of her artistic attainments when this city had ceased to exist, for the civilisation of these parts is extremely ancient. Yet the work of the two nations has a decided similarity. What more natural than to conclude that here in China was laid down the model for future designers in bronze? One sees the same elsewhere. Japan, famed for long now for her art in bronze, is merely a copyist. Her designers took their curves and angles from the modellers of the Celestial Empire.'

It was all extremely fascinating, and David threw his heart into the work. Often and often, too, he wondered whether some day he and the diggers would come upon a part where there could be no doubt that his father had worked. And then, why should he not discover the will for which he had come to the country?

'It's not the money,' he said, many and many a time, when discussing the matter with the Professor. 'I don't really care a pin about it just now, though I daresay it will prove very useful. But I said I would come out to China to search for it. Here I am. I mean to discover it, if the will is actually in existence.'

'All of which proves you to be what your respected stepmother proclaimed,' smiled the Professor. 'David, I'm afraid you are an exceedingly stubborn customer.'

Stubborn or not, the lad had set his heart on the undertaking, and the further the excavations progressed the more eagerly did he move about the ruins. Then the course of his search was interrupted, for peace and tranquility are never to be long expected in such a country as China.

Chapter XIX
A Fight to a Finish

'Monsieur, I see men coming across the plain, and they are hurrying,' said Alphonse, one early morning, bursting unceremoniously into the huge apartment which the diggers had discovered in the ruins, and which for nearly a month now had served as quarters for the Professor's party. Indeed, thanks no doubt to the preservative nature of the material which for ages now had covered up the ancient Mongolian city, there had been no difficulty in finding room for all engaged in the work of excavating.

'*Monsieur le Professeur*, it would be well to come above with me and see who it is who comes,' cried Alphonse again, striding across to the little cot occupied by his employer. 'I declare to you, I was above lighting the fire so as to boil the water for a cup of tea when, in the far distance, I saw figures. There were many of them. They were hastening hither as if they were pursued.'

It took the Professor and his two young comrades less than two minutes, perhaps, to jump into their clothing, when all hastened out of the apartment, and passing along the ancient covered way, clambered up the steep, log-paved steps which led to the surface. It was a glorious morning, with a cold, wintery sun flooding the dreary landscape, and shining upon the uneven surface of sand where it lay over the ruins, and on the tower, tottering near the centre, the same which had attracted David so often.

'See!' cried Alphonse, dancing to the top of the steps as if he were standing on hot bricks. 'See, there are thirty of the figures at least, and now they are running.'

The Professor instantly threw up his field-glasses and fixed them upon the advancing strangers. There was a look of anxiety on his face when he lowered them again.

'Call Chu-Li and the other soldiers,' he commanded abruptly. 'Issue arms to Ho-Hung and our other servants, and tell the diggers we may need their help. David, those are the people who once helped you and your comrades when you were attacked by wolves in the open. They are running here as if they were pursued. I fear we are in for trouble, and had better make our preparations now.'

At a sign from the Professor, David doubled out from the ruins, so as to meet the men who were running towards them, and was soon in conversation with the headman, who panted so hard that he could hardly explain himself. But halting for a few moments he managed to tell his tale.

'It is as I have feared,' he said breathlessly. 'The country to the east of us is in a turmoil. Scarcely a day passes that stray parties fleeing from the plague scourge do not demand food from us, often with threats, while one village has to my knowledge been burned, and every soul within it murdered. The night before last we received news that a thousand men were marching south and west, and had turned in our direction from the more direct course, as soldiers had been sent to intercept them. They passed the night in a village ten miles from us, and ruthlessly robbed every one. Those who opposed them were killed. It was clear that they would serve us in the same manner, and for that reason we left hastily, bringing what possessions we could, as well as a supply of provisions. This morning the invading army was within sight of us, for they carry nothing but their clothes.'

'And are now near at hand?' demanded David eagerly, for common-sense and scraps of news which had reached him told him that the danger was real. The people of Manchuria, and portions of Mongolia, had in fact gone stark staring mad in the past few weeks. Black plague was upon them, and was decimating whole villages, while those not attacked were fleeing towards Pekin regardless of the consequences, and without having made provision for such a journey. And as a natural sequence they were soon on the borders of starvation.

'There's not a doubt that we have come to China at a most unfortunate time,' the Professor had declared. 'If I had heard of the plague in this district before we sailed, I should have delayed my departure. But it is always the same with severe epidemics. There is a case here, and another there at first; then, suddenly, the disease blazes out in all directions, spreads like wild-fire, and creates pandemonium and terror everywhere. China is a country less prepared for such an event almost than any other, for the people are so intensely ignorant. You see they think to escape by rushing away from the infected areas, forgetting that in every case they carry the infection with them.'

'There was news from a place forty miles to the east that a band had taken up its quarters in a town of small proportions, and were terrorising the inhabitants,' David reminded himself. 'Tell me,' he asked of the headman, who had now almost recovered his breath, 'what is there to fear from these fellows? A thousand strong you place them?'

'There is that number at least, Excellency. As to their intentions, I tell you they will eat up all before them. Already they have emptied every sack and bin in our village. That was two nights ago, or almost so. By now they are starving once more, and will seize the first provisions which come their way. They will know at once that men have been camping here. They will investigate, and will gather the fact that it is a European expedition, and therefore rich. That will be enough for this army of frightened people, for though the thought of plague terrifies them, they fear nothing else. Hunger makes them terribly savage. They will murder us all if we do nothing to prevent them.'

'If that's the case I shall certainly object, and pretty strongly,' said David, with a decision which seemed to put heart into the headman. 'Bring your men along. We will see at once what can be done.'

They found on their return to the entrance of the stairway that the Professor and his helpers had been wonderfully busy. Every article of value had been carried down from the surface, while even the ponies had been transported bodily and placed in a position of safety.

'We've done all that's possible, I imagine,' said the leader. 'Now we have only to wait and see what happens. I trust these people will pass without giving us a call. Perhaps they will miss us altogether.'

'I hardly think so,' ventured David. 'The headman tells me that they are wonderfully well informed, and that they have come round this way so as to avoid soldiers sent to arrest their progress, and who are situated at this moment about forty miles to the east. Wouldn't it be as well to send a message across to their commanding officer?'

The Professor jumped at the suggestion. He hastily scrawled a message in Chinese, explaining the situation, and then, having caused two of the ponies to be carried to the surface again, he despatched one of the soldiers with the note.

'Ride fast,' he ordered. 'If these men attack us we shall have need of all the help that can be sent.'

No one who caught a glimpse of the fleeing army from Manchuria could doubt that statement, for a more tattered and desperate set David had never set his eyes on. They reached the excavation works in a straggling mass of hollow-eyed people, many of whom were almost too weak to drag one foot after the other. But there were strong men amongst them, in spite of their sunken cheeks, men whose blazing eyes and hungry looks showed that nothing but superior force would prevent their carrying out whatever they aimed at. Nor did they leave the Professor and his party long in doubt as to their intentions. A couple of ragged but huge men came down the stairway, their pigtails swaying from side to side, and called hoarsely to any one who might be in hearing. The Professor at once showed himself at the door of the apartment which he and his friends were occupying.

'What do you wish?' he asked.

'Food; give us food,' cried one of the men, not as if he were asking for a favour, but as if for something that he would as soon take by force.

'I will give you three bags of rice; that is all we can spare,' answered the Professor steadily.

'Hear him! Three bags of rice, when we know he has a pile. Hear the foreign devil, brother,' shouted one of the men, the one who had not previously spoken. 'Listen, foreign devil,' he bellowed, as if he wished to terrorise the Professor by the force of his voice, 'we will be satisfied with fifty.'

'Three is the allowance I will make; take it or leave it,' came the curt answer.

'And you refuse more?'

The Professor nodded coolly. 'We refuse more; we have to provide for our own needs.'

'Then we will take every sack you have, and strip you of all your possessions. You have had fair warning.'

Without the smallest indication of what he intended doing the rascal levelled a pistol, and fired point blank at the Professor, sending a bullet crashing against the ancient doorpost. Then the two men turned and swaggered up the stairs, calling loudly to their comrades. Nor was it long before the latter put in an appearance.

'They will attack us without fail,' said the headman, when appealed to by the Professor. 'In fact, you may say that they are bound to do so, for the next place where they can possibly obtain food is more than a day's march from here. Also, no doubt, they have learned that you have a goodly store, and fancying you to be an easy prey they will fight to take everything from you, thereby supplying the needs of all in the band till they arrive in the neighbourhood of Pekin.'

'What arms do they carry?' asked David, suddenly.

'A few have pistols and guns, but the majority carry knives or swords, and a few pikes. But it is their numbers which make them formidable.'

There was little doubt that that was the true aspect of the affair, for this army of people flying from Manchuria, and rendered desperate by their hunger were dangerous even if unarmed. Their huge numbers told wonderfully in their favour, while the ease with which they had wiped out other parties had given them confidence. The situation was, in fact, one of extreme danger.

'Hadn't we better block up every sort of place through which they could fire?' asked David. 'We can easily leave port-holes for ourselves, and if we place them properly we shall be able to command the stairway. I rather think, too, that it would be as well to set our diggers at work to discover a way out of this apartment. We may be so hard pressed that flight will be necessary.'

The suggestion was one which the Professor eagerly accepted, and as promptly adopted. Calling Ho-Hung he set him to work to organise some of the diggers, and requested David to supervise the work they were to do until the enemy appeared in sight. Then every available man was pressed into the task of blocking up the wide doorway leading to this ancient house, and in filling the only window. But in spite of the many helpers the task was only half completed when there was a commotion above. The two ragamuffins who had descended and so haughtily demanded food appeared in sight, leading a huge following to the stairway. Those who led bore with them the trunk of a tree felled a week before to serve as fire-wood, but now intended to be used as a species of ram.

'Silence!' called the Professor. 'Let every man go on with his work quietly and take advantage of every second we have. Use anything you can lay your hands on to help the barricades so long as it be not provisions. Ah, they are coming in their hundreds.'

The wide stairway which the men employed by the Professor had made as they proceeded with their work, and which they had paved with stout tree branches, was now crammed with men who presented a terrible spectacle. For, whereas in former attacks David had noticed that the Chinese advanced with loud shouts, these people crowded down the stairway in a stony silence that was remarkable. Not one but wore a haggard appearance. Their faces were pinched without exception, while in every pair of eyes there was a desperate look, something altogether savage that reminded him of the eyes of the wolves which had so recently surrounded himself and his three comrades.

'One can see that it is not a question of bearing us ill will,' he whispered in the Professor's ear. 'It is a case of sheer necessity. Either they must secure what we have, or they will starve.'

'It is they or us, David,' answered the Professor solemnly. 'If I had food in abundance, willingly would I give it. But were I to dole out all we have, there would hardly be enough to go the round of this multitude, and even so we ourselves would starve. Tell me, what are the diggers doing?'

'Cutting a hole through the wall at the back, Sir. We thought it sounded hollow, and have an idea that there may be another covered way there. They will make only a hole large enough to let us get through with the ponies, so that we can easily fill it again. What are you going to do with these fellows?'

'Warn them that we shall defend our goods. Then leave it to them to clear off or to make the first attack. I hate firing at poor wretches such as these are, but, candidly, I look upon them as infinitely more dangerous than a well-fed mob.'

Rearing his head over the top of the barricade with which the doorway was now almost completely blocked, the Professor called loudly to the mob, and at once they came to a halt. Perhaps three hundred pair of hungry eyes were directed on his face.

'Good people,' he called, 'I beg of you to retire and be satisfied with what I have already said. If I feed you all, my stores will but allow for one meal at most, while I and my men must starve. Go, therefore, for if you persist I warn you I will defend this place till I and all are killed.'

A loud chorus of shouts greeted his words. Men shook their fists at him and brandished a hundred different weapons, while the very mention of food seemed to madden the desperate individuals. Then the rascal who had fired at the Professor, and who was leading the band, once more lifted his weapon and sent a second bullet thudding against the doorpost.

'Listen to him, comrades,' he bellowed. 'He admits that he has food there sufficient for all of us. Are then we who own the country to starve while foreign devils live on the fat of the land? Forward! We have cleared more than one roost now with more bantams in it to stand in our way.'

At once there was a rush outside. The covered way, which no doubt had sheltered many a thousand Mongolian in the old days, was soon crammed to overflowing, while still more of the mob thronged the stairs. Then with shouts the leaders cleared a patch for the men carrying the tree trunk.

'Rush at the barricade with it,' called the rascally leader. 'Smash it and then fetch out the food which is ours by right. You will know how to deal with the foreign devil and his supporters, my comrades.'

There was a growl from the mob, and then a roar, as the men bearing the tree trunk rushed forward. As for the defenders, they sprang to the loopholes which had been left and awaited the Professor's signal. It came in a moment, for the battering-ram almost levelled the barrier at the first effort.

'Fire on them!' shouted the Professor. 'Pick off every man who attempts to lift the tree. That is where our real danger lies. Once this barrier is down they will be on us; nothing can resist such numbers.'

David and Dick, with Ho-Hung and his comrades, as well as Chu-Li and his four fellow-soldiers, had before now each chosen an aperture for his weapon, and at once a hot fire was opened on the enemy. Meanwhile every available article was thrown on the barricade to strengthen it, for there were numbers of willing hands amongst the Professor's party. As for the mob outside, half a dozen fell at the first discharge, all of whom bore the ram, while every time a man leaned over to pick it up again he was fired at instantly. In three minutes a round dozen were biting the sand.

'Then let us tear it down with our hands, comrades,' shouted the burly ringleader. 'They can hit one man as he leans to pick this thing up, but they cannot kill us all. Better to eat than to live on starving.'

The words drew a howl from the mob. Those on the stairway were now so pressed and packed together that they could not turn, while the space below was filled to overflowing. With an angry roar the latter leaped forward close on the heels of their leader, and struggled desperately with one another to come at the barricade. Those who could reach it tore madly at the sawn logs, striving to pull them out of the way.

STORMING THE BARRICADE

'Steady, lads!' called out the Professor, by whose side stood Alphonse, his hat awry, his keen eyes shining. 'If they break through we must make a sortie. I shall lead the way.'

'With Alphonse beside you, monsieur,' cried the Frenchman. 'But I am thinking Ho-Hung can wield a stake, and Jong also. Those two perched on our barricade could deal hard blows to these ruffians, while we at the loopholes could shoot down those who have fire-arms. What says monsieur?'

'That the plan is excellent. Hung! Jong!' He shouted, and at once gave them their instructions. The movement did indeed help the defenders wonderfully, for few of the attackers had fire-arms, and those who had could use them with difficulty only owing to the press. With swinging blows the two Chinamen beat back the mob tearing at the barricade, while the more dangerous of the latter were shot down from the loopholes. Then the Professor again stood before them.

'Good people,' he shouted, so that all could hear, 'I beg of you to retire. You see for yourselves that we are able to oppose you, and already numbers of your brothers have fallen. Let that suffice. Go now before worse happens.'

For one whole minute, perhaps, there was silence outside, while not a man moved. No doubt the opposition had taken the mob by surprise, for elsewhere they had been able to rob and murder without danger or difficulty. The sight of wounded and fallen men unnerved a few, and made them wish that the stairway were not so crammed and that retreat were possible. But deep embedded in the hearts of the majority was the knowledge that they were hungry, and that failure here meant starvation. It needed, therefore, but a tiny spark to kindle their courage once more. The rascally fellow who had so nearly hit the Professor on two occasions was still at hand, and he it was who quickly had them once more racing for the barrier.

'It is a dodge,' he shouted. 'Believe not the foreign devil. Pull the barricade aside and you have every bag of food that belongs to these people. Hesitate now, and go on your way. What will happen? You will starve. You will leave your bones by the road. The dogs and the wolves will come and feed off your carcases. Forward, then. There is food, and plenty of it behind that barricade.'

He led a silent host at once against the defenders, a host frantic with its woes, rendered as fierce as any pack of wolves by its privations. And in a trice it seemed that it must succeed. Even the lusty blows of the two Chinamen and the shots of those at the loopholes failed to keep it back. Already a foot or more of the barricade had toppled over, while a dozen of the men outside had again seized the battering-ram. And then, so fickle and so changing is fortune in such matters, a small affair turned the scale in favour of the defenders. The excitement of those who were unable, because of their position on the stairway, to join in the contest was so intense that they struggled and pushed their way downward in spite of all difficulties till the covered way was crammed. But still they came till even those struck by the bullets from the loopholes could not fall on account of the press. Then someone above bellowed a warning.

'I see men coming!' he shouted. 'I see soldiers—they are galloping this way; they will cut us to pieces.'

Instantly there was a rush for the stairway. Two hundred and more frantic people fought to be the first away. They tore at one another with as much ferocity as they had displayed when attacking the barricade, and those who were strongest, or who had taken up the most commanding positions, prevailed. Men were dragged down and trodden underfoot, an eddy as it were on the stairway caused the mass thronging every step to heave backward, and at once numbers lost their balance and fell, helped to their death by those who were nearest. Knives flashed here and there. Men snarled at one another. Altogether it was a horrible and terrifying spectacle. And the movement itself proved to be as unnecessary as it was horrible in its results, for the same man appeared above once more.

'It was a false alarm,' he shouted. 'Stop, comrades, there is nothing to fear. They were not soldiers; they were men like ourselves who had stolen ponies doubtless from the last village. Stop or you will all be crushed and killed.'

Deep and bitter were the voices of those who had survived. They turned again, and slowly descended where a moment before they had struggled to mount And catching sight of David standing at the barricade they set up a howl which showed something more than mere desperation induced by the pangs of hunger. There was hate in their tones. The matter had now become a personal one as between them and the defenders.

'We warn you people down below that we will kill you all,' shouted the same leader. 'We will kill you slowly, making you suffer for what you have done. Stop, my comrades. I have a plan to propose. Let some rest here and watch for us; we will be back ere many minutes have passed.'

He raced up the stairway accompanied by a mob, leaving the Professor and his party to wonder what movement would now be attempted.

'Perhaps another battering-ram,' suggested the Professor.

'Or these rascals will supply themselves with hooks with which they will the easier be able to reach the logs on our barricade,' chimed in Alphonse.

'Or perhaps it's worse,' said David slowly. 'I wish we had shot that rascal, for he is capable of the worst mischief. Ah! see them! I guessed what they were up to. They are going to smoke us out.'

There could be little doubt as to the intentions of the mob. They had seized bundles of fodder kept on the level sand above for the use of the ponies, and a couple of dozen of the men were bearing these down the stairway, while the same mass followed on their heels, shouting excitedly, and shaking their fists in the direction of the defenders.

'Put them down against the barricade in a heap,' called their leader. 'Be not afraid of the foreign devils, for harm will not come to you. When the bundles are placed I will fire them.'

'*Parbleu*, I think not,' exclaimed Alphonse, smiling grimly, for he had understood. 'Monsieur, with your permission I will shoot this man.'

Shoot him the Frenchman did. His bullet caused the rascally leader to sway from side to side and to grip at the air. Then with a shriek he came bounding forward, and, clambering the outside of the barricade, attempted to enter. There was a flash as Dick Cartwell ended the matter.

'Look out! There's a fellow coming along with a torch,' called out the Professor. 'Shoot every man who attempts to light those bales.'

But in spite of every effort a cunning fellow armed with flint and steel managed to set fire to a bunch of straw which he picked from the ground and held behind his fellows. Then with a quick jerk he threw it forward, causing it to fall at the edge of the piled-up bales of fodder. Next second a sheet of flame was sweeping up to the ancient roof of the covered way, while, owing to dampness in the bales, a dense smoke was given off, and began to penetrate the apartment occupied by the defenders. Indeed, in a few seconds they were coughing loudly, while every member of the party was forced to retire as far as possible from the flames. Death from suffocation, if not from burning, stared them in the face. David and his friends were in a horrible dilemma.

Chapter XX
The Secret of the Ruins

Blank despair was written on the faces of the Professor and his party as columns of suffocating smoke were swept into their quarters; for all realised that in a very short space of time they would be smothered. More than that, the flames had now got such a hold of the bales of straw and fodder that the heat was terrible, driving every member of the party into the farthest corner, and even causing the enemy outside hastily to retreat up the stairway. And there, at the summit, looking down into the excavations which exposed this small portion of the ancient ruins they gloated over the foreign devils and their helpers, shrieking in their mad delight, and bawling every insult that their degraded minds could think of.

'I fear it looks like a case with us,' gasped the Professor, tying a handkerchief about his mouth and nose, an example which the others were swift to follow. 'We're in a horrible trap, with no way out of it, I fear.'

'Unless, monsieur, we could dash at the barrier and kick all the bales aside,' said Alphonse, coughing violently, for the exceeding pungency of the smoke made breathing difficult and speech next door to impossible. 'I am ready to make the attempt. It is better than being scorched here in this corner.'

At once he started forward, and with him Dick Cartwell, both eager to do something. But who could face such dense smoke, or the hot flames which poured in over the top of the barrier? Not Alphonse, even with all his dash and pluck. Nor Dick, with his reckless disregard of the consequences.

'It is sad but inevitable then,' declared Alphonse, with a resigned shrug of his shoulders. 'Monsieur, I have the honour to bid you farewell. I lose a good and generous master.'

'And I a brave and willing servant. But, Alphonse, where is Monsieur David? I have not seen him since we retired from the barrier, and the smoke is so thick now over there that one can see nothing. Where is the lad? I begin to feel anxious.'

It was like the Professor to think of his comrades at such a time. But the question brought a shout from Dick.

'He's over here, sir,' he called out 'As soon as they fired the bales I saw him dart back into the room, and couldn't imagine why. Running away from the thick of an attack isn't like him. David, where are you?'

'Here,' came the crisp and half-stifled answer, while the figure of our hero loomed darkly before them, his face muffled in the half of a garment which he had secured from somewhere. 'Come along this wall of the room with me. I realised when they fired that heap of stuff that our position would be untenable, and went to the men who have been working. They have managed to break a hole through the wall, and one has just slipped to the other side. Of course, if the place is filled with sand we can do nothing. I have hopes, though, that it will be clear, for how else could he have been able to pass through.'

Choking and coughing the party crept along the wall, keeping close to the base; for the smoke rose to the ceiling, and the latter being of great height gave it space in which to distribute itself. But in spite of that, the supply of air down below was small, to say the least of it. They had hardly proceeded more than ten feet when there came a cry of triumph from a point just in front of them, while the click of a metal instrument was heard.

'Come quickly. Come, Excellencies,' called the voice of the head man who controlled the excavators. 'Our comrade reports that the far side is quite clear. Some one has been at work there before us. Let us pass through at once, else we shall be suffocated.'

The words brought them rushing forward, and a gust of wind happening at that moment to sweep the smoke and flames away from the room, all saw that a hole had been cut through the wall, which being massively built, had resisted the efforts of a number of men armed with crow-bars for some time, but once the first stones were removed the rest was easy. The Professor took in the situation at a glance.

'I believe this will save the situation,' he cried, snapping his fingers, and then coughing so violently that his remarks came to a sudden ending. However, in a few moments he had regained his breath. 'See for yourselves,' he shouted, showing greater excitement than David had ever seen him display before. 'The draught enters by this hole, and is already sweeping the smoke from our quarters. It is driving the flames out into the covered way. Now, let the men pass through as quickly as possible. I shall stay here and attempt to save our goods and chattels.'

'And I too,' declared David, overjoyed that his men had been so successful. 'There are also the ponies; the poor beasts are up there in the far corner and must be almost stifled. Still, as we have lived through it, so also may they.'

'Monsieur, I also shall remain,' announced Alphonse. 'You will need helpers. I will go to the ponies.'

And go he did, with Dick creeping through the smoke after him. As for David, he seized a crow-bar, and with the help of others attacked the wall furiously. Meanwhile every one of the men who had joined them in such great haste that morning, and who to do them but justice, had shown a brave front, and had done their utmost to help in the defence, crept through the gap in the wall, each man carrying something with him. Jong and his friends too, made the most of the time at their disposal. Now that the smoke was clearing, and the heat decidedly less, they bustled about, gathering the belongings of the party, and were soon passing them through to their comrades on the far side.

'You can take it more easily now, David, lad,' sang out the Professor. 'This gap has checkmated the attempts of those fellows. There's a perfect gale coming through, and one can see nicely now, and feel quite comfortable in this atmosphere. It'll be an eye-opener to the enemy to discover us gone when the flames die down. Ah, here's Alphonse and Dick.'

One by one the latter led the ponies towards the gap, many of the poor beasts being almost exhausted. But they were able to use their legs, and were soon forced through to the far side. Then Dick and Alphonse followed David, and lastly, the Professor crept through the gap.

'Now pile all the stones into the hole again,' said our hero, superintending the job. 'As soon as the place is cool enough those gentlemen will return, and we shall want another barrier. Quick with it. Those bales are nearly burned out now, and a starving mob don't wait for much. A little heat under foot will be nothing if they can only appease their hunger. Poor beggars! I'm sorry for them. But then, what would you have? This is a case of saving one's self.'

Less than ten minutes later a man descended the stairway, and peeped over the barrier. His shout of amazement brought a crew of cut-throats racing after him; then such yells of anger and disappointment arose as they discovered the chamber empty that the men who had joined the Professor that morning were terrified. There was a determined rush for the gap, now more than half-filled, a rush which Chu-Li and two of his comrades checked instantly. Indeed, the enemy bolted at once from the chamber.

'Pick off every man you can see,' said David, staring over the barrier of stones. 'Don't let any one enter the room. This is a much easier place to defend than the other. Ah! They're moving. What new game are they up to?'

The whole party listened to the shouts of the enemy, and were amazed to see them bolting from the covered way. Chu-Li slid through the gap like an eel, and ran to the door. Then he waved his arms frantically, and rushed back to his comrades.

'They are bolting, Excellencies!' he shouted. 'They are completely gone. I heard firing above, and caught sight of several soldiers. I believe a relief party has arrived.'

Five minutes later there was no doubt of the fact, for when the Professor and his staff clambered up the stairway there was a troop of Chinese cavalry drawn up. Not a troop of men armed with ancient bows and arrows, but soldiers that China is training now-a-days, armed with modern weapons, equipped to the last button, able to manœuvre with the best. A dapper little officer spurred forward, saluted in German style, and at once addressed the Professor in the purest English.

'I have the honour to speak with the Professor who undertakes excavations, is it not so?' he demanded. 'Then let me explain. Five thousand troops were sent into these parts by His Excellency, Twang Chun, to arrest the movement of people from the plague-stricken country, and to break up the gangs of half-starved and dangerous men prowling about. I heard yesterday that a mob had passed west with the intention of evading me. I rode this way before sunrise, and met your messenger. I have the pleasure to find that I am in time.'

Near at hand the remainder of the gang which had attacked the party at the ruins were huddled together in a forlorn group, surrounded by soldiers, while the plain was dotted with the bodies of those who had shown fight, and had fallen. It was clear, in fact, that the danger had passed altogether.

'I give you the thanks of every one here,' said the Professor, gripping the little officer's hand. 'You came in time and have done us a great service. Step down below and see what happened.'

'Truly, you put up a fine defence,' declared the commander of the troop of horsemen, as he inspected the chamber below. 'That gap undoubtedly saved the situation, and not my arrival. Still, those desperate men would have fought on till you or they were conquered. I am vastly interested in this work which you have undertaken. How strange that you should have hit upon another part from which all debris had been cleared?'

It was more than strange; it was almost beyond belief. For when the matter came to be thoroughly investigated the Professor declared that they had stumbled upon the path by which Edward Harbor had gained entrance to the interior parts of the ruins.

'The whole thing is perfectly clear,' he said. 'He excavated a few yards to our right, and gained a spot at the back of the chamber in which we took refuge. Some of his diggers also worked on our side, but ceased, perhaps because the prospect was more promising elsewhere. To-morrow we will pursue the search more thoroughly.'

Let the reader imagine what a condition of excitement David was thrown into when it became established without shadow of doubt that he was actually treading in the steps his father had followed. For three days after the attack made by the band of Chinese he worked with the excavators, removing debris from parts which had evidently been cleared not so long ago, but to which the wind had again swept masses of sand. It was remarked, also, that on this side no objects of art or of any value were come upon.

'Been removed by those before us, proving we are in their works,' said the Professor. 'This is indeed most interesting. It must have been here that your father made that will, David, and here also, alas, that he lost his life. Chang fell upon him in the ruins, I am told, and even secreted his gains in these parts. Be patient, lad. Something may yet come of this quest of yours, though one can hardly hope that it is possible.'

On the morning of the fourth day the excavators came to a wall which had been broken through, and on passing to the far side discovered another covered way, as dark as pitch, but altogether free of sand and debris. David led them eagerly till they came to a part where the ruins had fallen in entirely, and where sand blocked their path. But three hours' work cleared it, and allowed them to proceed, there being still evidence of the fact that others had been before them. It was with a sudden fluttering of the heart that he realised that they were passing somewhere near to that tower which had so often attracted his notice. And then he gave vent to a shout of amazement; for undoubtedly excavators had been before them. The covered way led beneath the walls surrounding the tower into a wide, open space, from which the height of the surrounding walls had kept more than a little sand blowing. There was a wide doorway at the foot of the tower, the posts of which were tottering, while, now that he was so close, he observed that the original crown of the tower had gone, and one wall, the far one, crumbled away entirely. But the fallen stones helped to form a chamber, and that was piled with objects of every description.

'Here, undoubtedly, were stored all the bronzes which your father unearthed,' said the Professor, surveying the scene and inspecting the objects. 'This is a find, though it makes one feel sad, remembering what misfortune befell him. Ah! As I live, that is baggage.'

There was not a doubt about it. The sandy surroundings had preserved things wonderfully, and in one corner, covered with dust, was undoubtedly a pile of baggage, while there were cases galore, a box of cash for the payment of the workers, arms, and a hundred other things.

'Here you see the items for which that scoundrel Chang committed the foul murder,' declared the Professor. 'David, Dick, we will see into that baggage.'

More than one of the trio trembled as the locks were broken. For the first time for many a day David wore a pasty complexion. There was a subdued air of excitement about the lad which his comrades felt rather than saw. Then there came a sharp exclamation from the Professor as the last of the cases was opened, the others having been found to contain clothing only. There was a tin despatch-box nestling in one corner. He dragged it out and presented it to our hero.

'It belonged to your father; it is yours,' he said kindly. 'Open, lad. We will leave you if you wish it.'

'Stay, please,' came the answer. 'If I am to enjoy success I shall want your congratulations. If not, perhaps you will condole with me. In any case I have done what I decided was the right thing under the circumstances. I have come to this spot to set at rest a dispute which has been a good deal more than bitter.'

Cool and calm now that he was faced with the despatch-box, David broke the lock by inserting the edge of a spade beneath the lid. Then he slowly withdrew the contents.

'Five pounds in English coin, two notes of the value of fifty pounds, and a draft on a bank at Hong-Kong,' he said, his tones not in the least ruffled. 'A packet of letters tied with string. One to my stepmother. I shall hope to deliver it. One to myself. I am glad. Perhaps you will excuse my opening it at the moment. And one to Mr. Jones, his solicitor. Nothing else, Professor.'

'Open the last of the letters then, lad. Open! Open!' cried the leader of the party eagerly. 'If that does not contain the will, then look into your own. Quick, boy! The suspense makes me nervous.'

He wiped his face with his handkerchief and then fixed his eyes on the letters. David opened the one addressed to Mr. Jones, the friend who had helped him so much in England, and smoothing out the sheet read the contents slowly. 'It is a business letter purely,' he explained. 'This is what my father says: "Dear Mr. Jones, I have to-day sent away under separate cover the last will and testament I shall ever make, and you will find that it is duly signed and attested. I need merely mention the contents briefly, so that you may draft out something similar for my inspection and signature on my return to England, for posts in this country are precarious. I leave an annuity of five hundred pounds to my wife. The rest in trust for my son, David, till he is twenty-five years of age, when he will have it absolutely.

Trusting this may find you well, as it leaves me. Yours truly, Edward Harbor.'''

Dick looked positively glum as he listened. 'Bad luck!' he exclaimed. So the will's gone. Lost somewhere between this and Pekin.'

But the Professor chuckled loudly. 'That document is as good as any other,' he cried. 'Put alongside with the letter which was before the courts in England, it clearly shows Edward Harbor's wishes. See, it is clearly dated. David, you are to be heartily congratulated.'

No need to say that our hero was delighted. It pleased him wonderfully to know that in spite of many difficulties he had carried out his intentions. He smiled even when he considered what his stepmother would have to say, not a satirical smile, nor one of triumph, merely one expressive of pleasure.

'She'll put it down to my obstinacy and to good luck,' he thought. 'She won't know anything about the dangers and difficulties the Professor and all of us have gone through. Heigho! I'm glad it has turned out like this.'

Three months later he received a note from Mr. Jones in reply to the one he had sent. There were hearty congratulations and an assurance of the writer's good feeling. Then came an announcement of the utmost moment.

'You have done well, David,' ran the letter, 'but when you ask me of what value is the document you sent me, I say none, for circumstances have arisen which alter everything. Mr. Ebenezer Clayhill died soon after you quitted the country, while I regret to say that your stepmother followed him swiftly.'

'Then, after all, the journey wasn't necessary,' cried our hero. 'I'm awfully sorry to hear about the step-mater and Mr. Ebenezer. But—no, I'm not a bit sorry I came to China. I've enjoyed nearly every moment of this trip, and excavating is a job which suits me admirably.'

A year later he returned to England with his comrades, and by then had imbibed such a fondness for investigating ruins and ancient places that he decided to follow in the footsteps of his father and the Professor. David made a handsome allowance from his income to a home for the sick and needy; for those scenes he had witnessed had made a lasting impression on him. Then he went again to China. He is there at this moment, prying into the secrets left by the ancients.